GRIFFIN HAYES

PRIMAL SHIFT
Volume 2

Trebor Books

TREBOR BOOKS

Copyright © 2014 Griffin Hayes

ISBN: 978-0-9918881-6-0
eISBN: 978-0-9918881-7-7

Cover design by Keri Knutson
Edited by Jason Whited

Also by Griffin Hayes

A special thank you to Craig McGray, Jason Whited, and above all, to you, loyal reader, for joining me on this journey.

On July 4, 2017, as the country prepared to celebrate its independence, the skies were shattered by strange shimmering lights that sent most of humanity into madness. In an instant, law and order crumbled, plunging the planet into anarchy.

For those who survived The Shift, Rainbowland was supposed to be a safe haven from the chaos and barbarity around them, but sometimes appearances can be deceiving. Someone in the colony has turned to murder; killings connected to an old prophecy about two saviors with the power to rebuild a shattered world, or utterly destroy it.

In Volume 1 of *Primal Shift* ...

After surviving the devastation caused by The Shift, Finn, Dana Hatfield, Carole Cartright, and Larry Nowak struggled to find food and shelter.

Lured by a mysterious radio transmission, each of them began the long and dangerous journey for Utah and the salvation they hoped to find there.

But awaiting them in Uintah was no FEMA camp as they'd hoped, nor the last remnants of a fragile government. What they discovered instead was Rainbowland: a pacifist New Age cult hiding its own dark secrets.

Obsessed with a past he can't recall, Finn learns that a company called Tevatron may have been behind The Shift. A clue that leads him back to the desert of Nevada and the facility where he first awoke. There he discovers his own criminal past and treachery at the hands of Bud, a fellow Tevatron test subject.

Always the opportunist, Larry Nowak slowly gained the cult's trust after befriending a highly placed member. With more and more survivors trickling in every day and dangerous Wipers at their doorstep, Rainbowland's lack of security became the excuse for a coup Larry needed. When the cult leader, All Father, died suddenly, Larry was quick to take the reins of power.

After arriving in Rainbowland, Dana Hatfield struggled to find her place after a life spent following a strict chain of command. Shortly before his death, All Father offered her the role of sheriff; Dana jumped at the chance. But when the power shifted into Larry's hands, Dana was tasked with retrieving dangerous explosives meant for defending Rainbowland that had been stolen by Bud.

Following The Shift, Carole made it her objective to keep what was left of her family safe. But with her son, Aiden, lost at the Salt Lake City International Airport and her daughter, Nikki, kidnapped by Wipers, it seemed as though she failed on every level. A foolhardy mission to enter Alvarez' lair at the Grand America Hotel and trade her life for Nikki's ends when her truck is ambushed by Wipers, forcing her to flee into a nearby building.

And now begins the final chapters of *Primal Shift* ...

PRIMAL SHIFT 6: METAMORPHOSIS

Dana Hatfield

Pulling up to what looked like a solar plant out in the middle of the Nevada desert, Dana kept hearing Larry's frantic voice ringing in her ears. Bud had gone and taken the C4 right out of his Escalade, and Larry wanted it back. Least that's about all Dana could make out from the man's obscenity-filled tirade. It wasn't a secret where Finn, Johnson, and Bud were going, only why and what exactly they'd hoped to find once they got there.

Dana spotted Finn's Land Rover parked up ahead and drew her own car alongside it. She stepped out into the baking noon day sun. The ticking sound coming from Finn's SUV told her they hadn't been here long. Removing the SIG from the holster that hugged her right leg, Dana pulled back the slide and chambered a round. Whatever Bud and the others were planning on doing with Larry's C4, she couldn't imagine they'd be anxious to hand it over. She wasn't exactly ready to use deadly force, especially not against Finn, not that any of them needed to know that.

Dusty tracks led from Finn's car toward a set of double doors, and that's where Dana headed. Inside to the right was a desk with a row of flickering computer monitors – "This place has power?" she thought, amazed – and beyond that a pair of elevator doors, which had been pried apart.

The sound of a hand scrambling for purchase on the dirty floor at the foot of the elevator shaft made her heart jump wildly in her chest. Another hand appeared, this one holding a Beretta 9 mm, which it set down and slid a foot to the right so it wouldn't be in the way as the person climbed up. But here was the important part: Whoever this was, they didn't know she was there.

Dana reached the pistol at about the same time she saw Bud's bleeding and battered face emerge from the darkened shaft below. Swooping down, she scooped the Beretta up and slid it under the back waistband of her pants for safekeeping. Bud was up a second later, brushing himself off and wearing the panicked expression of a man who was about to miss a train.

Dana took a step back, positioning herself between him and the door and laid a hand on the grip of her SIG.

"What're you doing here?" he asked, not even trying to hide his surprise.

1

"That's far enough," Dana told him, watching a bloody tear roll down his cheek. "You know full well why I came, so let's cut the foreplay, shall we? You took something that doesn't belong to you, but judging by the way your face is busted up, I see now I caught you in the middle of something else entirely."

"I fell," Bud said, wiping the blood away with the arm of his shirt. "But if Larry sent his guard dog for those explosives they're in the car."

Dana could tell by the way Bud's eyes dropped to the floor as he spoke that he was lying, but by the time it registered he was already charging at her. Out came the SIG, and she nearly got it into a decent firing positing before he chopped it out of her hand with a hard strike to her wrist. A straight punch to her face was coming next, and Dana saw the windup coming a mile away. Bud either didn't know or didn't care that she'd once been in the Coast Guard and had gone through basic combat training. Her forearm deflected that one and gave her the opening to plow her right elbow into the side of his face. Bud reeled back, stunned he'd just been hit by a girl.

Plenty more where that came from, Asshole!

She was about to pull the Beretta out from her waist when Bud rushed, tackling her to the floor. From here, he'd be able to use his weight to keep her pinned down and beat her into unconsciousness. With desperate speed, she brought her knee up against the back of his buttocks, but it wasn't his ass she was aiming for. It was the back side of his balls, and the sudden grimace on his face told her right away the move had worked. She rolled him over, pulling the Beretta at the same time. Dana knew she could take care of herself, but someone had already worked Bud over before her.

"Finn and Johnson?" she barked, cocking the hammer with her thumb. "Where are they?"

"There isn't any time," Bud told her. "In case you haven't figured it out already, this entire place is about to blow."

"You already set the C4. But why?"

"For my family."

Dana pushed the barrel against his forehead. "You don't look like the mujahedeen type to me, Dipshit. Defuse it."

"Are you crazy?"

She moved the gun less than three inches and fired. The bullet skimmed Bud's skull, tearing out a flap of hair as it went. Up went his hand to cover the wound, blood running between his fingers. Looked like he had his answer.

2

Bud was about to start climbing down the ladder again, Dana's SIG trained on his every move, when she stopped him and pressed the button to call the elevator.

"How long do we have?"

Bud grit his teeth. "I'm telling you we're not gonna make it."

The two of them waited an agonizing minute, listening to the cables straining to pull the elevator up to their level. The building had clearly taken some damage during the quake that accompanied The Shift, but the facility seemed to have been built to withstand a decent amount of abuse. The elevator arrived a moment later, and Bud was the first one on, and almost at once he was mashing the button for basement level 2. Dana could feel her heart hammering up in her neck with anxiety. But to run away and leave Finn and Johnson to die when there was something she could do? No, she wouldn't have been able to live with herself. They passed the first basement floor, and in the distance Dana caught what looked like a pair of legs sticking out into the hallway.

"You killed them, didn't you?"

Bud didn't bother answering that one. A moment later, they reached basement level 2, and Dana followed him out, her SIG aimed squarely at his back as he hurried along a corridor littered with wires and piping from places where the ceiling had fallen in. They arrived at a door marked *Power and Maintenance* and headed inside. There, sitting on the floor, was an open silver briefcase with two bricks of C4, one on top of another. Taped to the sides were two detonators. On top was a cell phone counting down.

20 … 19 … 18 …

"You better do something quick," she said. Dana knew enough about C4 to know it would be rendered completely safe once those detonators were removed. She'd even heard stories of soldiers in Vietnam lighting the Plasticine-like putty to cook meals and keep warm. Seemed hard to believe, but right now, all she really cared about was Bud doing what he needed to do or she'd rightly shoot him in the head before both of them lit up.

17 … 16 … 15 …

Bud was tearing at the electrical tape to release the detonators. "I hadn't exactly planned to deactivate this thing. You have a knife on you?"

She didn't.

14 … 13 … 12 …

And she could feel the panic welling up within her.

These are the last minutes of my life, and I'm spending them with the prick who murdered me.

Bud was using his teeth now because he'd really taped those bastards on tight.

11 ... 10 ... 9 ...

Dana ran into the hall.

"Where the hell you going?" Bud shouted after her.

Across from where she was standing was the window into a laboratory filled with metal tables and fancy instruments, but it wasn't the room's contents she was interested in. Bud was counting down as she raised her pistol to the window. Shielding her eyes, she fired three rounds. The sound of shattering glass pierced her ears. She snatched one of the shards and tossed it to him.

"Use this, for God's sake." And that's when she saw the timer. It was down to five seconds. Bud started sawing through the electrical tape in short spastic motions, sweat pouring down his face. An almost overwhelming urge to run gripped Dana when the timer hit two seconds, but it wouldn't have mattered anyway. In a single motion, Bud yanked the detonators free and threw them across the room as the digital read out went to *0.*

Dana pressed her back against the wall, suddenly aware her body was covered in perspiration. "You stupid son of a bitch," was all she could say.

•••

They headed back to basement level 1. Dana was carrying the briefcase and the gun. Ahead of her was Bud, his hands tied behind his back with a length of wire she'd scavenged from the maintenance room downstairs. That same pair of legs she'd seen before were still poking into the hallway, and it wasn't long before she recognized the blue coverall pants they were wearing.

"They better still be alive," she told Bud. "For your sake."

And when they reached them, Finn and Johnson looked dead. Perhaps Johnson more so since her mouth was open, along with her eyes, which were staring off into the distance. The ghostly moaning sound frightened her. But the noise wasn't coming from Johnson. Finn's eyes peeled open, barely slits, and Dana could see by the paleness of his face he'd lost a lot of blood. She felt for a pulse on Johnson's neck and finding none, pulled off the black woman's shirt. Desecrating a dead

4

friend felt horribly sacrilegious, but Dana needed something to stem Finn's blood loss.

"What took you so long?" he whispered.

She smiled, not about to tell him the real reason she'd been sent. She undid the buttons on his coveralls and found two holes. One in the abdomen and the other near the ribcage. Sliding the sleeves of Johnson's shirt around him, she tightened it over the wound as a makeshift tourniquet.

Now Finn had his hand in the air, his index finger pointing across the corridor and into the next room. From here, Dana could see inside although she couldn't be sure what her eyes were seeing. It almost looked like a cryo-chamber straight out of a sci-fi movie. A glass porthole centered near the top and right below that a plate marked with a name:

J. BLACKWOOD.

Finn

Seated in a leather chair, reclined ever so slightly, Finn glanced around, sure he'd been here before. He was in a sterile white room somewhere deep within Tevatron, and some guy with a tattoo gun was carving Finn's convict number into his wrist. Johnny was his name, and under that lab coat he was wearing, nearly every square inch of his flesh was covered in ink. Only the letters along the knuckles of his right hand *H A R D* followed by *A S S* on the left offered the slightest hint he wasn't like the other Poindexters Finn had seen running around this underground laboratory.

You're dreaming, a tiny voice somewhere in the back of his mind called out, but Finn didn't care.

"So, this guy comes into the shop last week," Johnny says. "Musta been 6'5", 6'6". A real stretch with pasty-white skin like he hasn't left his house in months. Tells me he's never had a tat before, so I ask him, 'You got something in mind?' Guy says, 'Sure do. I want my girlfriend's name on my dick,' and then the crazy sonbitch drops his pants. 'Her name's Elizabeth,' he says, standing there with nothing bigger than a pinky finger poking out between his legs, and I say, 'Buddy, I don't think Elizabeth's gonna fit. How does Liz sound?'"

Tears were streaming down Finn's cheeks. "Ah shit, that's messed up."

"Hey, a job's a job," Johnny said, stopping briefly to wipe the blood from Finn's wrist.

Finn was still drying the tears when the door opened and in walked Harry Thomson. Hair as white as ash, cheeks sunken and ringed with prominent, almost spooky-looking cheekbones. The dark suit he was wearing made him look like some kind of undertaker. Johnny was back working on the tattoo, Thomson standing over him, watching the curve of the number five begin to take shape and for a moment the only sound in the room was the mechanical whir of the tattoo gun.

"I trust your accommodations are acceptable?" Thomson asked, staring at the tattoo as though it were a topless woman.

Finn scratched an itch on the tip of his nose with his free hand. "Sure beats the shit out of Ely State. But I got a question for you. You think this is gonna work?"

Thomson looked up from the tattoo, puzzled.

"You think it'll make me forget?"

"Your crimes? Is that what you're asking me? Will the procedure make you forget your crimes?"

"No," Finn replied emphatically. "I'm talking about those women who were killed."

"The ones you murdered," Thomson shot back. "Isn't that what you're really trying to say?"

"It doesn't matter one bit to you if I'm guilty or not, does it?"

Thomson seemed to contemplate this. "The memory erosion process is designed to wipe your slate clean, so to speak. A reprieve from traumatic memories, that's what we're after. Rehabilitation. Guilt or innocence has nothing to do with it."

"So then, answer my question. That horrible look on their faces," Finn said. "All I want is to stop seeing them every time I close my eyes."

Thomson laid a clammy hand on Finn's shoulder, and the touch made his stomach turn. "You will, soon enough."

•••

Finn came awake and threw up at once. He was in a tent stuffed with dead, still air, the heat stifling. The pillow his head rested on was soaked through, and even with so little to go on, he could tell the moisture wasn't from his stomach spilling out its contents.

A girl hovered over him.

Nikki.

She slid a bucket next to the cot he was lying on.

"How long was I asleep?" Finn asked, still wondering if this were a dream. The fingers of his right hand went to his face and found a thick tangle of beard where his cleanly shaven cheeks used to be.

"A long time," Nikki said. Her eyes fell to the bandages covering his chest and abdomen. "We weren't sure you were gonna make it. Count yourself lucky Kim was here."

"Kim? She a doctor?"

"Sort of," Nikki said, dabbing his forehead. "More of a veterinarian, but she was able to get the bullets out."

Nikki wasn't telling him something.

"How long have I been out?"

The young girl's eyes didn't waver. Her hair was tied back in a ponytail, and the sleeves of her shirt were rolled up at the elbows. "A while."

"How long?" Finn asked again, his voice rising this time.

"A month. Maybe more."

7

Finn fell back onto his pillow. "You're kidding me. What about Johnson? Did she make it?"

"I'm sorry."

Suddenly, Bud's face was all Finn could see. That and his fingers closing around Bud's throat.

"A lot's happened since you've been out," Nikki told him.

"What'd you mean a lot's happened?" Nikki stood and grabbed a pair of crutches resting at the foot of his cot. "Better that you see for yourself."

With Nikki's help, Finn rose on a pair of wobbly legs, a sensation strangely reminiscent of climbing to his feet after being ejected from that vat of goo. But he hadn't been unconscious the entire time, had he? There were snippets of memory in there. Dark figures wiping the sweat from his brow, peeling away his bandages to check on the state of his wounds. All things he had assumed were dreams. The way he'd dreamed of Thomson and the tattoo artist, Johnny. The way he'd dreamed of those dead women's faces staring back at him ... That last part really made him uneasy. It had been those very images that the old Finn had been trying to expel from his memory. And mixed in there somewhere was the suggestion that maybe he didn't do the horrible things he'd been accused of. But then again, didn't convicts always claim innocence?

Finn was on the crutches now, Nikki helping him past the tent flap and into a Rainbowland that was vastly different from the one he'd left. Spanning the length of the bridge, a mishmash of steel siding had been shaped into an imposing gate. Sturdy for sure, but ugly as hell. Although it made perfect sense to Finn. When the whole world was out to kill you, practicality trumped beauty every time.

But that wasn't the only thing that had changed. A palisade 15 to 20 feet high ringed nearly the entire compound. Every 30 yards stood a guard tower. It must have been a gargantuan job, and it still wasn't complete.

There had to be dozens of people working on one project or another. Seemed like nearly everyone in Rainbowland was doing something. Gangs of men and women dragged in logs stripped of their branches. Others sharpened the ends into deadly points. Even a makeshift pulley system had been set up to move the timbers into place. Perhaps the biggest shock of all for Finn was seeing the men who were manning those watch towers. Their hair was pulled back in long pony tails, and they were dressed in army fatigues, but it was what they were carrying that startled him the most.

"A cult member with a rifle in his hands?"

"I told you, a lot has changed. Probably in more ways than you think. And one more thing: It isn't called Rainbowland anymore. Larry changed the name to New Jamestown."

Finn let out a dry, sardonic little laugh. "I guess Larryland didn't have quite the same ring to it."

They stood quietly for a moment as Finn tried to soak in the different world he'd awoken to. After a while, he turned to Nikki. "I want you to know we didn't just run off to that facility in the desert without searching for your mother first."

"I know."

"When you see her," Finn said. "Will you send her over to say hi?"

Nikki's face crumpled with sadness. "She never came back."

An invisible fist took hold of Finn's guts and squeezed. Anguish for sure, but also guilt that he hadn't stayed to search longer. His need to unravel the mystery of his own past had been too strong to deny, and it was beginning to look like the price he'd paid had been a heavy one indeed.

Carole Cartright

Navigating through the maze of boilers and water pipes underneath the Grand America Hotel had taken some getting used to for Carole. Her trial by fire had come that first day when Russell – a thickset man with thinning hair and a grumpy disposition – had saved her from a group of rather determined Wipers. She'd seen him squeeze through a hole in the concrete wall and followed suit, the Wipers tearing through the store. One of them reaching in to snatch her when Russell released a lever and dropped 50 pounds of steel door on the Wiper's hand from above, severing it at the elbow. The sight of the arm on the ground beneath her, the index finger twitching, was a sight she couldn't erase from memory even though it had occurred more than a month before. Since that time, she'd lived mostly underground with Russell and a dozen others he managed to save, perhaps in ways not unlike how he'd saved Carole. It wasn't that she wanted to go back. Returning to Rainbowland without Nikki wasn't an option, but Carole didn't survive this long by allowing her emotions to make the most important decisions. Right now, a trip back to Rainbowland was simply too dangerous. Without the proper weapons and transportation, it would be little more than a suicide mission. In large part because the Wipers were all over the city. Some on foot, others in trucks. Russell had built himself quite a network here underneath the city, which included a number of spy holes they could use to assess the danger level outside. And these Wipers didn't appear to be hunting victims. They were collecting food. Canned goods as well as anything that hadn't already gone bad. All day and sometimes even at night the trucks roared overhead, emptying stores and houses of anything salvageable. And with every passing day, the Wipers were becoming more organized. It wasn't until Russell told Carole about a man named Alvarez – or was it Gomez? – that she began to understand that someone was leading them. But more than that. She learned there was something different about this man. The way the Wipers feared and obeyed him. The way he'd rallied the memoriless from miles around to his banner. Like Celtic warriors, Wipers followed their own archaic sets of rules. Each was an individual, and they weren't great at taking orders. Heck, most of them didn't speak English. Although according to Russell, once this Alvarez had showed up, all that had started to change. Which explained in part the heavy traffic outside that was keeping them hidden underground like a den of mole rats.

Shortly after her own salvation, Holly and Tamara had showed up. Plucked topside by Russell and brought down into the guts of this new city with ceilings and walls lined with pipes and water mains.

Holly was a young mother with dirty-blonde hair, when it was clean, and a pretty face with deep-blue eyes. Her 12-year-old daughter, Tamara, a brunette, shared her mother's sparkling eyes. The biggest difference between them was Tamara never spoke, not anymore, not after seeing her father killed before her, slaughtered by Wipers in the opening hours of the hell on Earth that was now their new reality. Not that staying behind was any safer. Not in the long run. That was why people had banded together in groups. Communities hiding behind strong walls were surely popping up all over the country as survivors returned to lessons learned in ages past. As for Tamara, since her own traumatic event, she communicated by writing on a tiny chalk board, holding up a powdery white message whenever she had something to say.

In the days that followed, Carole had quickly become something of a friend to Holly and a surrogate mother to Tamara. She saw something of herself in the woman. Husbandless and thrust out into a savage world, shackled not only with her own survival, but that of her daughter. Of course, Tamara and Nikki weren't the same age. Nikki was going to be sixteen soon, but each of them had folded in on themselves after The Shift, as though the pain of facing this new world was too great.

Regardless, a single truth remained, one Carole knew full well. If it weren't for Russell, none of them would be alive. He was a mechanical room engineer for the Grand America Hotel. A man doused in steam and sweat who'd spent close to 16 years maintaining the comfort of thousands of guests who never even knew he existed. Spending that much time in the basement had a funny way of eroding a man's manners, and Russell was no exception. He swore like a sailor and never hesitated to give you a firm piece of his mind, but somehow you always knew that deep down, under all that crusty exterior was a soft, gooey marshmallow of a man. The way he told the story, The Shift and the resulting earthquake had knocked things around plenty down here. His inability to raise anyone over the walkie-talkie had sent him topside to find out what the hell had happened. Opening the door, he said, was like looking into hell itself. People screaming, attacking one another. One of them even charging his way with a lust for blood Russell said he'd never seen before. He slammed the door to the boiler room and kept it barricaded until he was able to bring his welding torch up to make sure it wouldn't ever be opened again. Wasn't long before Russell realized the people on top, crazy as they were, had an edge over him.

They had access to food.

Russell didn't have more than his lunch pale and a thermos full of cold milk. What he had going for him was knowledge. He knew every corner of this basement about as well as he knew the deep lines along the back of his hands. Knew that nestled up against the far wall, past all the heavy machinery, was a row of stores. The wall there wasn't nearly as thick at that end, and if he could carve out a hole, he'd be able to move about right under their noses. Using improvised tools to hack away at the concrete, the work had been gruelling, but eventually he made it into a Victoria's Secret. From there, the gyprock wall that led into the convenience store was like cutting through butter. Although Russell hadn't said butter when he recounted the story. He'd said it was like margarine, since that's what he preferred and part of what he was after on the day he broke through into the 7-Eleven.

The booby traps had come next, and each of the holes Russell dug needed to be outfitted with one in case Wipers managed to find a way inside. Spring-loaded metal plates that would drop down and seal the tiny entrance with the pull of a string. Carole had seen what those plates were capable of, recalling with stark horror the way that Wiper's arm had been lopped off as he tried to grab a hold of her.

There were 12 of them hiding underground now, including Russell, Holly, and Tamara. Twelve lives saved from almost certain death. Most important, they would be leaving this place for good as soon as they could. Once, that was, the Wipers were done hoarding all the food they could get their grimy hands on. Carole hoped the streets would be quieter then, safer.

Every day, they would go topside in groups of twos and threes, peeking out from narrow slits in the walls that looked out onto the street. And that was exactly what Carole was getting ready to do now. Russell and Holly would come with her this time. A part of her enjoyed these reconnaissance missions, maybe even needed them. Apart from providing a much needed change of scenery, they'd become a secret opportunity to search for Nikki. Although it wasn't long after Carole had arrived that Russell had cleared the silly notion from her head that trading her life for her daughter's was a good idea.

"They'll just rape and then kill the both of you," he told her, shadows cutting deep grooves into his already weathered features. "Or worse."

Slowly, quietly, the three made their way from the boiler room and into the basement storehouse of the Victoria's Secret. From there, they headed up a flight of creaky steps and into the main storefront. Tables with dusty clothes. Some of them folded, although much of it was a shambles. Rows of sexy, half-dressed mannequins. One of them was missing an arm. Carole never breathed a word of it to anyone, but she'd found one of those mannequins in a storage closet downstairs once. The thing was dressed in a silk negligee, and Carole knew straightaway this was the girlfriend Russell was always on about.

But plastic girlfriends aside, the Victoria's Secret was also where they came to get the padding for their beds and clothes to keep them warm. It wasn't all just sexy underwear anymore, and Carole couldn't be more thankful. The storefront itself had been closed on the day the of The Shift, so there hadn't been a need to do much more than wrap a steel cable around the handles in case someone tried to kick their way inside. The point wasn't to stop intruders altogether as much as it was designed to buy the survivors time to retreat behind Russell's steel traps. They were living like rats in a hole, Carole thought, catching sight of herself in a full-length mirror and hardly recognizing the person looking back. She'd lost a lot of weight, and her face was covered over by a layer of dirt.

She, Russell, and Holly squeezed through an opening at the back of dressing room 3 and into the 7-Eleven stockroom. Once inside, the standard procedure was for two of them to gather supplies, while the third monitored the traffic outside. Most of the shelves were pretty bare by now. The majority of the convenience store's food was already safely underground, but even those reserves were quickly dwindling, and they were reduced to eating from jars of peanut butter and bags of stale potato chips.

Thankfully, Russell had the foresight early on to grab the perishables first. Once the power went off rendering the fridges and freezers inoperable, much of the food being kept cold would have started to decay at once. Eat what you can and throw the rest before it goes bad. If he'd started in on the canned goods first, the 7-Eleven woulda been swarming with insects. In short, their salvation would have become their undoing.

Carole was peering out the front window, while Russell and Holly picked over what little remained on the shelves. She glanced up to catch sight of the sun, that warm glowing ball of fire she rarely laid eyes on anymore. After a minute, she realized it was directly overhead and out of sight, which meant it was around noon. Right now, the streets were empty of cars and more importantly, devoid of Wipers. She was about to give the all clear when the rumbling came. A large pickup roared into view and slammed on the brakes. A group of men in the back dismounted in a hurry. They were heading for the 7-Eleven.

Carole pulled away from the door. "Wipers," she called out, finding cover behind a nearby shelf with jars of honey and chocolate spread. Russell and Holly retreated toward the stockroom. Russell was waving Carole over, and she was about to make a break for it when the door shook violently. Someone was trying to get inside, and when she peeked around the containers of chocolate spread, she saw their faces pressed up against the glass, searching inside.

The long scar down the side of the man's face removed any doubt they were Wipers.

He backed away and kicked the door. It rattled loudly. Another kick brought the sound of crashing glass. Just to her right was the Slurpee dispenser and below that, a cupboard where the store owner kept the Big Gulps. She swung the cupboard open, scooped out the remaining plastic cups and flung them away from her in the hopes it wouldn't be obvious that someone was hiding inside. She was barely able to squeeze herself in when the door shattered completely and swung open. In they came, crunching over the broken glass, speaking to one another in a strange guttural language that sounded like pig Latin.

Where they speaking English? she wondered. Or at least some strange perversion they'd taught themselves.

It was Carole's legs that were preventing the door from closing completely. She could see them clearly now through the slit in the cupboard door. The one with the scar on his face opened a bottle of honey and began pouring it down his throat. He stopped and motioned for one of his men to come to him. More crunching glass. When a young Wiper arrived, Scarface held the jar of honey out to him, moving it emphatically when the other didn't take it right away. Finally, the young Wiper relented, and when he turned to pour the warm sticky liquid down his throat, Carole saw at once she'd been completely wrong about this one. Not only was he not a man, he wasn't a wiper at all. Sure, his face was dirty and the hand holding the honey jar nicked with a half dozen scrapes, his fingernails caked in dirt. But through all of that, she recognized him immediately, and as she did her heart leapt. She'd found Aiden.

14

Larry Nowak

The office where Larry and All Father had squared off – where Larry had flung mud in the old man's face, promising it would stick – now belonged to him. The desk was all he'd kept. The day following All Father's death and Larry's decision to accept Timothy's offer to run Rainbowland, his first order of business had been to have the office whitewashed. Gone were the pastel colors and the outline of meditating monks. Gone too, was the book case filled with volumes of New Age psychobabble. Soon, even the name Rainbowland became little more than a memory.

A knock at the door.

"Enter," Larry said. He was scanning a list of the compound's remaining food reserves.

A cult member entered, his hair tied back in a tail and an AR-15 slung over his shoulder. The drab-blue pants and gray shirts had also been replaced by green camo. If All Father were still around, the sight would surely have horrified him. But knowing how Larry had pulled it off woulda done a lot more. The trick itself had been simple enough. He'd given a long speech in the gymnasium and read out what he said were All Father's dying wishes. "Do whatever it takes to protect the colony," Larry told them that solemn day. "That's what All Father whispered into my ear." Didn't matter in the least that Peter was already dead when Larry arrived. These people were grieving the loss of their beloved leader. They were directionless and vulnerable, and Larry gave them exactly what they needed. Reassurance. Sure, things would change, but only for the better and more importantly, in a way that woulda made All Father proud.

A cult member named Charlie Smith saluted. "Brother Timothy's here to see you."

"Very well, let him in."

Cult members acting like Marines wasn't the only change at the compound. Over the last few weeks, so too, had Timothy's face. The pudgy cheeks that spoke of his love of rich foods had largely melted away. The Timothy before him looked much younger, if not a tad bit sickly.

"I take it you know why I'm here, Larry."

Larry waved his hand, and the guard stepped outside, closing the door behind him.

"So, you can tell me for the umpteenth time that we're low on food."

"We aren't low, the pantry shelves are practically bare. You've spent too much manpower building these walls and foraging for weapons and ammunition. What good'll they be if we starve to death?"

Larry looked up at him without feeling an ounce of shame. "Foraging teams have been sent out, looking for anything they can get their hands on."

"Yes, I'm very well aware of that," Timothy replied. "But it isn't canned goods they're finding anymore. For some reason, those have been vanishing, which means either there's another colony of survivors that's sprung up close by who're stealing what's ours, or it's the Wipers. Security isn't only about high walls and big guns, let me remind you."

Larry was shuffling through the inventory lists when he stopped. "I don't need you to remind me of anything. If it weren't for my walls and guns, this place woulda been overrun long ago."

Timothy crossed his arms. "Peter's own son, Simon, was part of the latest foraging group. Do you know what they came back with?"

Larry waved a hand dismissively. It was beginning to feel like those final depressing days when Herbalife was collapsing in all around him.

"Rats and dogs," Timothy said. "Is that what we've been reduced to?"

"It's food, isn't it? Now that the world is empty of people, those four-legged bastards are scampering all over the place. They've become a real danger, you know. Spreading disease, forming into packs just like those ... "

"Wipers," Timothy finished. "Yes, I know. Just keep in mind, Brother Larry, I stepped aside so you could make things safe here. That was your mandate."

"One more thing I don't need to be reminded of." Above him, Larry could hear the groan of the windmill. The kind of project he'd been championing since that early conversation with Simon. Sure, it mighta been Dana who came up with the details, but it didn't take a genius to realize they needed a way to pump water up from the river and power the compound. Assembling the battery bank they'd salvaged from the innumerable cars littering the roads was the easy part. The wiring wasn't a big deal either. Was mostly a question of ripping what they needed from the homes nearby.

Finding an inverter. That was the real bitch.

They were also lucky to have two electricians. Well, one really. The other was mostly a jack-of-all-trades. Funny how in this new reality, all those fancy university degrees weren't good for more than wiping your ass with. Soon, it would be the tradesmen who would rule the world.

16

Timothy was still standing over him, like he was waiting for an answer. Didn't seem to matter that he'd turned this struggling little backwater into probably the best functioning survivor's colony in the whole country ... at least what was left of it.

From his breast pocket, Timothy produced a piece of paper and laid it on the table in front of Larry.

The page contained a list of vegetables. Cabbage, lettuce, beets, turnips ...

"What's this? Planning on hitting a grocery store?"

"Very funny. No, it's plans for a fall harvest. If we can find the seeds and get planting right away – "

"Plant them where? There isn't enough room within the walls for that sorta thing, and don't tell me we can plant outside the walls 'cause all that'll do is attract scavengers."

"We grow them inside the enclosure," Timothy replied. "But it'll mean tearing down some parts of the wall at the back and wrapping it around the field."

Larry stood up. "You're shitting me!"

"Do you have another solution? Because I'd love to hear it."

"We could take down those tents and start moving people into the gymnasium."

Timothy was shaking his head. "You put that many people in an enclosed space and you're just begging for an epidemic. Each of those tents can be outfitted with wood burning stoves."

Tearing down part of the wall when they were so close to completing it was a disaster. Already, he'd commissioned all hands on deck and practically driven the colonists into the ground to get this far. But Larry was beginning to see he would be screwed either way. Maybe Timothy had a point, even if he hadn't stated it in quite these terms. Even now, the world was always an empty belly away from revolution.

"There's one last thing I'd like to bring to your attention," Timothy added. There was a smug look on Timothy's face, one Larry didn't like one bit.

"With you there's always one more thing. What is it?"

"The oath you took when you first became leader."

Larry tried to play dumb. "Oath?"

"To step down once the colony was safe. For the most part, you've done a great job, Brother Larry, as I knew you would, but I want you to know that that time is fast approaching."

17

Dana

Lou poked his head into the trailer that was Dana's new sheriff's office.

"We got ourselves another problem with you-know-who," he said, sporting that characteristic Southern drawl that had won Dana over the first time they met. She brought the heavy tread of her boots off the desk, opened the drawer, and removed her SIG. She checked to see if the pistol was loaded and slid it into the holster that hugged her leg.

In spite of Romeo's impressive record on *Call of Duty*, to say his skills as a deputy were poor was a serious understatement. Wasn't long before she approached the people she thought would be perfect for the job. She needed three men who were honest, loyal, and more important, people who knew their way around firearms – real firearms, not their electronic counterparts maneuvered with joysticks and buttons. Lou, his son Ethan, and the Wyoming farm boy, Tanner, had come to mind right away, and it hadn't taken more than five seconds for each of them to say yes. Problem was Larry didn't want her to get rid of Romeo. Said maybe the boy needed a little more time. Eventually, she settled on a workaround. Keep the kid on as a part-time deputy. That way, she wouldn't be left completely high and dry if, God forbid, anything happened to Lou or the other two.

'Course, the conversation with the kid hadn't gone over particularly well. Mostly 'cause being downgraded to part-time deputy meant he would now be on work detail, just like everyone else. Seemed like Romeo and hard work really didn't get along. And that was at the heart of why Lou had come to fetch her. Chances were better than even that Romeo had been caught skipping work detail again. There was lots to build, and New Jamestown needed every able-bodied person they could find.

The draconian punishments Larry had instituted for shirking work detail was the part of the job she'd really come to despise. A single strike resulted in the loss of daily rations. A second strike meant the perpetrator was handcuffed to the pole of shame with a sign reading: *Slacker*, strung around their neck. Romeo had already gone through both of those and was in the final stages of having his part-time deputy status removed completely. You couldn't very well command respect from the community after you've ridden the pole of shame. But it was the punishment for committing a third strike which was, for many, the most frightening of all: banishment. With nothing more than a few stale biscuits, you were sent beyond the wall and toward certain death. The

Wipers were out there, drawing closer and closer everyday. Nor were they the same mindless brutes who stormed in here with Jeffereys more than a month ago. Guards in the towers were usually the ones to spot them, spying on the compound from the tree line. Watching for now, but surely taking mental notes and reporting back. But it wasn't just the spying that made it clear they were evolving. It was the way their comrades would retrieve the dead and wounded, sometimes under fire.

The defenses Larry had championed were perhaps the only thing keeping them alive, no doubt about that. But being tasked with punishing those who didn't work, some of them simply suffering from exhaustion, was just plain cruel. Wasn't a week ago that a man with a broken arm named Alistair was found resting in his tent. Larry had personally asked Dana to issue a first strike.

"But he's got a broken arm," She'd protested.

"Yes," Larry replied. "But the other one works just fine. Now strike him."

And she'd carried the weight of that one for the rest of the day. Now, it was Romeo's turn. Except he didn't have the luxury of a broken arm. His vice was sheer laziness.

As Dana arrived at the worksite along the rear of the compound, she found Lou there, hands on his hips. Facing him, Romeo stood, arms crossed over his chest defiantly, and Dana only caught the tail end of what the kid was saying, but it was enough to know he was lying. For Romeo, she'd come to understand, if his lips were moving, lies were coming out.

" ... been here the whole time, I swear," Romeo pleaded.

A cult member named Brother Tristan was shaking his head no. "He missed his entire morning shift, that's all I know."

"That's bullshit, I was here."

Dana could tell he was lying, the way she could tell Alvarez was lying when he swore up and down he hadn't killed Keiths. But the rules had to be obeyed. An able-bodied mouth to feed that didn't pull his own weight put everyone's life at risk. The power of life or death was in Dana's hands. In this case, it was Romeo's life. The kid was annoying, sure, and a slacker, perhaps from a long line of slackers. In the Old World, maybe he could have sailed through life eating Cheezies and playing video games. But that world was gone, and so, too, was the luxury of riding off of society's coattails.

"Cuff him," she told Lou.

Tears started rolling down Romeo's cheeks. "You're banishing me? Lemme talk to Larry."

Lou was patting Romeo down, searching through his pockets, when he came out with two thin pieces of metal. He held them up for Dana to see.

"What're you doing with a lock pick Romeo?" she asked.

"That's not mine," he tried to tell her.

Lou handed them to Dana who examined them. "Take him to the trailer," she told Lou, but as they headed out, it was clear Romeo wasn't done.

Romeo started to resist before Lou quickly overpowered him. "You tell Larry that if he doesn't want his dirty laundry laid out for everyone to see," Romeo shouted, "then he better do something about this."

A group of workers stripping the bark off a log had come to see what was causing the commotion.

They could still hear him ranting and raving as Lou dragged him to the trailer. She would have to fill out a report and inform Larry that Romeo would soon be sent beyond the wall. That last thing Romeo kept shouting, about airing Larry's dirty laundry. Dana couldn't help wondering if those were simply the desperate pleas of a terrified kid. Or an indication that New Jamestown was already becoming corrupted.

Lou was hauling off a crazed teenage boy when Finn arrived. The kid was shouting for Larry, that he needed to talk to him, that Lou and Dana were trying to kill him.

"What was all that about?" Finn asked.

She was still staring at them as they shrank in the distance. "Oh, nothing, just someone skipping work detail." Dana glanced over and did a double take. "You're awake."

"Alive and well and mostly in one piece." Finn glanced down at his crutches. "Legs are still a big stiff from lying down for so long, but I can already feel my strength returning."

"You look thin," she said.

"Yeah, so do you." Finn's eyes dropped to the gun on her hip. "A lot's changed since I've been out."

The workers who had gathered were beginning to disperse, and Dana nodded to them as they left.

"It has," she said. "And much of it for the better."

"I never thought I'd see cult members carrying rifles, had to scratch my eyes when I saw that one."

She smiled, and deep lines formed at the sides of her mouth. The thought occurred to him then that there probably wasn't much time for fun and games for Dana now that she'd become sheriff.

"I guess that's part of Larry's magic. He's a salesman born and bred."

There was something heavy on her mind, and Finn couldn't tell what it was. "Listen, I wanna thank you for what you did."

For a moment, Dana almost looked embarrassed. "It was nothing …"

"Don't be modest, if it wasn't for you I'd have been splattered against those facility walls."

Her thumbs dug into the loop of her belt. "What I meant was that it wasn't something I'd planned. It just happened. I didn't go there intending to be a hero; I went there to get Larry's C4 back. Catching Bud in the middle of a double homicide was what you might call a combination of luck and … "

"Combat experience. Nikki told me what happened, said the whole compound was talking about it for days."

"Basic training kicked in, I guess," Dana said with a touch of self-deprecation, and Finn could tell she was trying hard to be modest.

"Where is he now?"

"Who, Bud?"

Finn nodded.

"Locked away, somewhere safe."

"Lemme guess," Finn laughed. "He's at an undisclosed location. Shouldn't I get a chance to have a few words with him? After all, he did try and kill me."

She didn't answer him right away. Not before he could ask a question he might already know the answer to. "I know Johnson's dead."

Dana's fists clenched her belt. "By the time I got to you … there was nothing I could do. Looked like one of the bullets severed her spine. I think that even if she'd made it, rolling around in a wheelchair is no kind of life in a world like this." Her hand came out from her belt just long enough to make a wide arc, and Finn wasn't sure if she was referring to the world outside or the wall that hemmed them in.

"So, what about that chat with Bud?"

"I gotta run it by Larry first."

"Geez, he's really got this place by the nuts."

Dana nodded, and the way her gaze suddenly shifted, Finn wasn't sure if he'd said something wrong. Maybe speaking your mind was no longer allowed here in New Jamestown. "I hope I didn't offend you."

"No, it's not that. It's just that Larry's done a lot for us."

"He has, no doubt about that. But it's sorta like asking a fox to guard the hens, don't you think? It's great for the fox, but not so good for the hens."

A voice from behind: "What's not so good for the hens?" Finn turned to find Timothy standing behind him, a beaming cult smile plastered on his face. Their strict adherence to nonviolence might have been thrown out the window, but it appeared at least some things hadn't changed.

Dana nodded and excused herself and Finn watched her leave, wondering about that burden he noticed weighing her down.

Timothy's hand was on Finn's shoulder, and even the man's fingers looked thinner. "I trust you're feeling better."

"Nothing a monthlong coma can't fix, right," and the two men laughed, but even as they did, something about the tone of Timothy's voice reminded him of a dream. The one he'd had as his body struggled to heal itself. An image that was now etched in stark detail. The head of Tevatron's research wing, Thomson, not doing much to hide his certainty that Finn was a cold-blooded murderer.

"Everything OK?" Timothy asked.

Finn blinked hard. "I guess when you're out that long, the mind can't help dredging up the past."

"A memory?" Timothy asked. Someone must have told him that most of Finn's past was a foggy wasteland.

"Yes. Some new bits, but nothing Nikki hadn't already mentioned."

Timothy furrowed his brow. Clearly, no one had filled him in on the girl's abilities.

"Nikki can see things," Finn said.

"Are you referring to psychic phenomena?"

"Nah, nothing like that. She can't see the future, only the past. But she isn't plucking it out of midair like those psychic hotlines I saw billboards for in Vegas. She can see lost memories."

Timothy's face was a mask of shock and surprise. But it looked like more than a touch of understandable skepticism. It looked like something he'd been waiting for.

Alvarez

Anita peered into the pit, the grin on her face so wide even Alvarez couldn't help but smile. Down below, men, his men, were swinging large rock mallets to flatten the floor of what would soon become his new arena. A sizeable lawn next to the hotel parking lot proved the ideal site, and no sooner had the idea popped into his head than he had commissioned Jeffereys to find someone to lay the plans and begin construction. Protected by a fence so the combatants couldn't suffer a change of heart and attempt to escape, the arena also featured tunnels on opposite ends from which the fighters would emerge, both leading to holding areas where they'd be prepped and outfitted. All of this was dug underground and supported from collapse by 6-inch support beams. Projects such as this were only one of many luxuries Jeffereys and his nose for finding survivors had allowed. This particular enabler was an engineer named John Snow. He and his family had been found hiding in the basement of his rather palatial home. A fortuitous swim in their indoor pool at the time of The Shift had shielded him and much of his family from the effects. The research Alvarez had done over at Tevatron, back when he went by the name of Thomson, had taught them that even a thin layer of liquid surrounding the skin was enough to shield against at least some of the magnetic forces. After their capture, convincing John to draw the plans for the arena hadn't been harder than reminding him how much he loved his two lovely daughters and his sickly wife, suffering as she was from Type 2 diabetes. He wanted all of them kept safe and sound, didn't he? 'Course he did. And so John had done as he was told, and before long here they were, Anita glaring through the arena's chain-link fence and down into the depths with pure delight. Now that he had his gladiator pit, all that was missing were the gladiators. Alvarez was still admiring Anita's beauty when a thought popped in. This will sure beat the hell out of watching television.

But John wouldn't get all the credit. No, sir. None of this would have been possible if his brutes hadn't been there to do the back-breaking work. Those drones were the real unsung heroes. Then there were the slaves Jeffereys had captured from Rainbowland. This last month, they'd been hard at work, helping his men relearn many of the basics they'd forgotten. First, language and sanitation. Then, weapons and driving. And the progress had been spectacular. Soon, he began sending them throughout the city to scavenge all the canned goods they could get their hands on.

The plan was simple enough. Without adequate food stores, tensions in Rainbowland – and anywhere else survivors had gathered – would mount, revealing divisions, which he could easily exploit. In the end, his job would become that much easier. They began storing the bulk of the food in the ballroom, but before long, even that gigantic space proved insufficient.

Then there was that messy business with Bud, whose failure to return could only mean he'd failed at the job he was given. A pity since Alvarez had planned on killing him anyway. Whether Bud realized it or not, he was the enemy, to be used and manipulated, sure, but he could never be trusted. Not the way his brutes could be trusted.

Alvarez' mind returned to his new arena when a group of his men in a pickup arrived. A red triangle was painted on the side; an order Alvarez had given so his men could tell friend from foe.

With men crammed into the bed and hanging off the sides, it was a sight more at home on the streets of Syria. They were mostly dressed in leather now, a move that made sense since it cut the wind and offered a certain amount of protection. There was a boy with them, too. Not an unheard of sight, fact some of his most cunning soldiers were young boys. What they lacked in raw power, they compensated for with wit. But this young man was different. Although he was dressed like the others, the features of his face obscured with grime just how young he really was. As they approached, Alvarez saw he was barely a teenager. But there was something about the kid's eyes that struck Alvarez, and it wasn't only the red rings that circled them, a clear sign he'd been crying or wanted to very badly. Deep beneath the surface, he detected knowledge. Lots of it. And the closer the boy drew, the more Alvarez began to realize there was something special about this young man. No, not special, more than that. There was some something downright incredible.

Alvarez, Anita, and their bodyguards were still by the pits when he waved the group over. Each of these small raiding parties had a leader, and it was this person Alvarez normally gave the orders to. The head of this particular group was thin and wiry. The helmet he wore had two letters stencilled on each side: *AA* for American Airlines, which told him this particular group had likely formed from the pockets of survivors who had fought for supremacy over the airport.

The leader began to approach when Alvarez stopped him.

"Not you," he said and pointed past the man to the boy behind him. "I meant him."

With great reluctance, the boy approached.

"What's your name?" Alvarez asked him. "Do you remember?"

25

The boy hesitated when he saw Anita come forward, her hand outstretched to touch him. Al gave the leash she wore a little yank. Her head jerked back, and she cowered behind him. "Darling, not so fast, you're going to scare our new friend." He turned back to the boy, smiling now. "Oh, it's quite all right. There's no need to be afraid, young man. I don't bite."

"Aiden. My name's Aiden Cartright."

"That's a good strong name, Aiden. You're a very special young man, do you know that?"

Alvarez waved the rest of the airport crew away, except the leader didn't budge. The boy's uncertain gaze ping-ponged between the two of them. Alvarez waved the man away again, as though he were little more than a pesky fly. The leader's eyes dropped to the boy before returning to Alvarez. There was hatred there, and Al knew why. The loyalty in these tiny groups was unusually strong, a bond even Al was reluctant to break, but this time he would have to make an exception.

Slowly, the man turned and walked away.

Alvarez, Anita, and the boy began heading back to the hotel, his retinue of bodyguards close behind.

"I'm special 'cause I'm still alive, is that what you meant?"

Alvarez laughed. "Well, in part, I suppose. Do you remember anything from that day when everything changed? Something unusual happening inside of you?"

"Don't think so."

"What about inside your mind? Thoughts that weren't there before?"

"I don't understand."

"Did you know, Aiden, that humans only use a tiny percentage of their brains at any given time? There's enough space in there to fit the collective knowledge from every library in the world, many times over."

"I learned that in school."

"Smart boy." Al wanted to ruffle his hair, but didn't want to risk singeing it. "Are you thirsty? I'm thirsty. How about a Coke?" Al snapped his fingers, and two shirtless men approached, carrying a cooler. They opened the lid. It was filled with nothing but cans of Coke. He took one for himself and handed another to Aiden. "A bad habit of mine," he said, pulling the tab to that almost iconic sound. Aiden did the same, and both of them took a drink.

Aiden's eyes were watering, but this time it wasn't out of fear or sadness. It was from the bubbles tickling his throat. "Mom never let me have Coke, but Nikki drank it all the time. Was so unfair."

One of Alvarez' eyebrows perked up. "You have a sister?"

Aiden nodded and took another sip.

"Do you two look very much alike?"

"Uh, not really. She's almost 16 and has long dark hair."

"Is she a little taller than you with pale skin?"

The Coke fell from his lips. "Yeah, you know her? Is she here?"

Alvarez could tell the boy was trying not to sound too hopeful.

"I only met her once and very briefly, but she's a very special girl, Aiden. More special than I realized … before I met you, that is."

"She's not that special."

Alvarez' mouth split into a smile exposing a mouthful of yellow teeth.

"Do you like boxing, Aiden?"

"Hmm, it's OK, but I prefer UFC."

Alvarez clapped his hands. "Perfect! Then you'll love what I've got planned for tonight."

Carole

It was hours later when they were back underground in the boiler room that Carole finally told Russell she had seen Aiden.

"Are you sure?"

"A mother knows her own children. Yes, I'm sure." In the corner was a pile of leather clothing scavenged from dead Wipers as well as other pieces Russell had collected over the weeks. It was supposed to be part of their bug-out gear for when they left this place for good. The clothes would protect them from the elements and act as camo should they be intercepted by Wipers. Simple math showed there wasn't enough for everyone. Not yet. But Carole wasn't thinking of escape so much as infiltration. She shrugged one of the leather jackets on. There was dried blood on the collar.

"What are you doing?" Russell asked her.

"I'm going to get Aiden and Nikki."

"Are you insane?"

Now, Holly and the others were being drawn by Russell's bellowing voice.

"I'll sneak in and out through the ventilation system and grab them before anyone knows I was there. I'm not asking anyone else to go with me. If there's a chance I can find either of my children, it's a risk I'm willing to take."

"You won't just be killed," Rus said, driving home the point with a sharp, penetrating stare. "Killing's the thing they do when they've grown bored of making you suffer."

"I've lived through worse," Carole said. Josh moved next to her. In his hands was a can of tuna. He held it up. "This represents the last of our protein. After that, we're down to sucking on ketchup packets. Won't be another week after that before we're too weak to find any food at all."

Holly stuck a finger in the air, pointing to the hotel and the Wipers above them. "You know sure as hell those animals up there are sitting on a mountain of food. We see those trucks everyday, coming and going."

The room descended into deathly silence after that. Finally, Russell spoke.

"Quickly in and quickly out. Don't get greedy."

He turned to Carole. "If you wanna search for your kids, that's fine with me, but as soon as our bags are filled, we're gonna hightail it back and close those air ducts behind us, with or without you."

Carole tried to swallow, but her mouth had gone bone dry.

•••

A picnic bench in an alcove just past the giant boiler had become a war room. A set of building plans for the Grand America were laid out and kept weighted down on each corner with copper plumbing brackets. Russell pointed to a pair of blue parallel lines. Carole, Josh and myself will enter through here and make our way up this gradient toward the first floor."

"How do you know the food isn't being kept on another floor?" Josh asked.

"Without the use of working elevators, that would be foolish."

Russell then pointed to Holly, Tamara, and a teenage girl named Jessica.

"The three of you will climb in after us and wait inside. You'll be spread out, say, here, here, and here. Your jobs will be to get the food back underground as quickly as possible."

Holly, Tamara, and Jessica all nodded, although each of them looked scared out of their wits.

"One last thing," Josh said. "If this goes pear-shaped, and it doesn't look like we'll make it back, then you girls need to seal that vent."

•••

Less than an hour later, the raiding party members were inside the air duct's narrow confines. They entered through a maintenance flap accessed by a folding ladder positioned on the floor beneath it. Ahead of Carole were Josh and Russell. Behind her were Holly, Jessica, and Tamara. The heat inside was making the air thick and heavy. Carole's breaths were becoming deeper. Panic swelling up within her. Up ahead, Russell could hear her frantic gulps for air and tried to calm her down.

Just remember why you're doing this. Keep your mind on your kids, Carole!

She did exactly that, and an image of Aiden dressed in black leather settled before her eyes. He might not be killed if she walked away, not right away at least, but what sort of monster would they force him to become?

As they went along, they made sure to spread out to reduce the load on any particular section of the air duct. It was making a ton of squeaking noises, no doubt about it, but they were moving up from below instead of hanging from the ceiling, which meant they were less likely to be heard sneaking about. A divide up ahead split right and left. The left rose up toward the second floor. The right went along the lobby before snaking up to the ceiling.

It wasn't long before they reached a floor-level vent. Russell spent several minutes peering through the grate before he popped it out. Carole was struck at once by how easily he had done so, until she realized this wasn't the first time he'd snuck inside the hotel. 'Course, he'd mentioned using the ventilation shafts in the past to spy on the Wipers, but not that he'd actually made it into the hotel proper.

Josh and Russell squeezed out, and the thought of what they were about to do sent an electric current pulsing through her body. When it was Carole's turn to exit, she was struck immediately the by a stench that reminded her of the streets of New York City at the height of summer. Body odor and sewage was what it smelled like. They'd stepped out into a hobo convention, except if these hobos discovered who they really were, the outcome would be worse than a case of liquor halitosis. They were in the hotel's main entrance, a hallway that stretched in either direction. Large candles had been set up at intervals, casting an orange haze along the walls. But the deep shadows would help them from drawing unwanted attention.

The three of them were standing now. The hallway was empty of Wipers, and the sound of cheering Carole heard rumbling in the distance probably explained why. Russell was listening, trying to make sense of what he was hearing.

"What do you think's going on?" Josh asked.

Russell shrugged. "Doesn't matter, as long as it keeps them busy."

The two men set off with the bags, and Carole felt an almost overwhelming urge to follow them. Or she could hop back in the vent. She glanced behind her. Holly was pulling the grate back in place.

Even though she was dressed like a Wiper, Carol's heart was still pounding. All she had to do was act like one of them and maybe everything would be OK. Her face was caked with dirt and surely she didn't smell like roses, both things she hoped would help her blend in. Earlier in the day, seeing Aiden with that group of Wipers left her with the impression they considered him one of their own. It stood to reason then, that if there were a celebration going on outside he would likely be a part of it. Likewise, Nikki was probably being kept as a prisoner in one of the hotel's many rooms, but with hundreds to search through on multiple floors, the task seemed, at least, daunting, and at the very worst, impossible. 'Course, this was all conjecture, but there wasn't much else she had to go on.

Find Aiden, a little voice told her. *If anyone knows where his sister is being kept, it'll be him.*

The first few steps toward what was once the reception desk and the front entrance were agonizing. As she approached, the sound of grunting by the doorway made her pause. A man and woman in leather were entwined, kissing like two wild animals. The woman's hair was spiked into a Mohawk, and her eyes locked on Carole as she approached. Slowly, a growl began emanating from the back of her throat.

She thinks I'm trying to steal her man. That was the first thought that fired through her head. The clothes Carole wore were a little baggy, and maybe that gave it away she was a female and possible competition. With every step, the growling increased, but Carole didn't have a choice, the two of them were beside the exit, and that was exactly where she was headed.

Do something quick Carole, or this crazy bitch is gonna come after you.

She squished her face into a snarl and growled back. The man's face turned to see what was going on when the woman with the Mohawk grabbed his chin, kissing him long and hard.

That's it, Honey, you can have him. He's not my type anyway.

Heart hammering, Carole made it outside with a sigh of relief. To the left was a roaring bonfire and some type of fenced dome with a swarm of Wipers on top, cheering for whatever was going on inside. If it made these guys excited enough to cheer and whoop, she wasn't sure she wanted to know. But not all the Wipers were together. Pockets of others milled about, chanting and generally behaving wildly. It was like being at a frat party. Walk with authority, she told herself, or they'll smell you coming a mile away. That snarl was back on her face, and somehow it was working 'cause a Wiper moved out of her way in a hurry as she strode by. She was scanning left to right, looking for any sign of Aiden in the crowd, but with most of them focused on the action going on under the dome, it was hard to make out any faces. Then she saw Jeffereys, the bastard who had led the attack against the colony. Next to him was a man sitting on a throne made from what appeared to be human bones. He was Hispanic, and beside him was a woman wearing a collar. They were ringed by an entourage of bodyguards, one of them large and muscular, half of his left arm missing. On the edge of that group was a boy who looked positively minute compared to the hulking men around him. He was watching along with all the rest, but even from here she

31

could see his eyes were glazed over as though he were either incredibly tired, or had been drugged.

Getting near him wasn't as easy as it looked. The crowd was surging to get ever closer to the action below, and once she was nearly knocked clean off her feet. Then she saw what everyone was looking at, and the sight nearly sickened her. It was some kind of fight to the death. One man armed with a machete, a gaping wound in his belly, was attacking another wielding two axes. A half dozen bodies, many hacked to bits, lay at their feet. If the world had become hell on Earth, surely this was its epicentre. The only saving grace in the entire situation was the crowd's bloodlust, which kept their eyes focused squarely on the battle raging below and not on her.

After shoving her way through the crowd, she finally reached Aiden. Her plan was simple enough. She would draw his attention, stop him from hugging her or crying out, and then the two of them would make their way back inside, where she would ask him where Nikki was being kept.

Carole tugged at the sleeve of the leather jacket Aiden was wearing. When he didn't respond, she did it again, harder this time, and he finally glanced over at her before turning back as though she wasn't there.

"Aiden, it's me," she said, over the whoops and cheering.

Another look, this one confused.

"Honey, it's your mother, I'm here to take you home." She was pulling at his sleeve, coaxing him to move away from the others so they could make their way back to the hotel, but in one quick motion he wrenched his arm free.

This wasn't making any sense.

After The Shift, his memories had been largely intact. It was Nikki who had suffered nearly complete amnesia. Or could his strange behavior be influenced by whatever drug was surging through his system, making his eyes glaze over like some pothead at a Grateful Dead concert?

"Don't you remember me, Aiden?" She was trying to keep her voice down.

There seemed to be some inner struggle raging within him. "I'm not going with you," he finally said, turning back to the fight, and Carole fought with everything she had not to yank him off the stage.

Had he lost his young mind, or was he pulling the ultimate temper tantrum? "For God's sake why not?" she asked.

"You left me at the airport for dead. You abandoned Alice and me."

"No, Honey, that's not true, we looked for you, we searched, but it was chaotic."

"You always said you'd do anything to protect us, and you ran away the first chance you got. I saw them kill Alice, and I was sure I'd be next, but they didn't kill me. They made me one of their own, and now here you are showing up like all that's forgotten."

"These are bad people, Aiden. They're gonna hurt you."

"I'm one of them, if you haven't noticed already. Alvarez says I'm someone special. He calls me a prince."

"You *are* special, Honey. But look around you, these aren't people. They're animals and they're gonna make you do horrible things like … "

"Like running people over?"

"I did that to protect you."

"No, you did that to protect yourself." His tone was flat and matter-of-fact.

The searing pain of Aiden's words felt like a blade being thrust through her gut. She'd risked everything to keep her kids safe and make things right where circumstances hadn't allowed her to fulfill that obligation.

"I'm trying to save your life," she said, weakly, nearly defeated.

"Let me save yours first. Turn around and leave, just like you did before."

Tears of disbelief were forming in her eyes when a Wiper came tussling through the crowd toward Alvarez and whispered something into his ear. Carole shrank down so she wouldn't be noticed as Alvarez rose to his feet and tapped the edge of his cane against the platform. Slowly, the crowd grew silent, even the fighters in the pits stopped, looking up while blood ran down their bodies. Now all eyes were on Alvarez. He pointed his cane to the group now emerging from the hotel.

Carole struggled for a better view, and no sooner did she get it but the breath caught in her throat. A group of Wipers were coming this way, holding two men. Both had been beaten badly, but it was clear enough what was going on. Russell and Josh had been captured stealing food, and now surely they would be executed.

"Behold," Alvarez shouted. "The thieves among us. And what's the new penalty for stealing what is rightfully ours, my children?"

The crowd exploded in a chant of what sounded to Carole like '*Hit … hit … hit*,' and it was a full second later before she realized with a sense of growing horror that they weren't saying "hit" at all. They were saying pit.

Finn

Finn was approaching the trailer when he stopped to gaze up at the night's sky. It was packed with stars, and the enormity of the universe made him suddenly feel small and terribly insignificant. The strange lights, which had become a new feature of the heavens, weren't nearly as pronounced anymore. Not that they were gone completely. If one stared long enough, it was still possible to see ghostly waves lapping against an invisible shore line somewhere far above him.

Some things, however, felt far from insignificant. Like his ability to make his way from one end of the compound to the other without the help of those crutches. He'd been shot in the chest and side after all, not in the knees. But that gelatinous feeling, which had been a product of lying on his ass this last month, was now all but gone. And like those dimming lights up above, Finn's rage over what Bud did to him and Johnson had somehow faded: first to a thumping sense of anger and then to a burning curiosity. *Why?* That was the question his mind kept returning to. Finn studied the trailer before him. Bars secured each of the windows. A sign above the entrance explained why: *Jail*, it read, and Finn pulled open the door. He was going to talk to Bud.

Inside, a cult member stood at once. He wore a .45 1911 as well as a surprised look on his young face. It was Simon. In the corner, leaning against the wall, was an AK-47. Which made it the fifth type of rifle he'd seen so far. Once that initial burning shock of seeing armed cult members had worn off, the logical part of him had begun to scream. Each of these rifles required a different caliber of bullet. If this place ever came under serious attack, that tiny little detail could prove to be their undoing. It was far easier to replenish firing positions when all your shooters were using the same type of cartridge. No doubt, something he intended to mention to Emperor Larry, or whatever that slimy car salesman was calling himself these days.

The trailer was divided by a row of metal bars. With barely enough room to accommodate 20 people, so long as most of them were standing. Right now, only two were inside. The first was a scraggly-looking kid Finn knew vaguely as Romeo. The other was Bud, and he was leaning up against the bars with his eyes closed.

Simon saluted, just as Finn reached out to shake his hand.

"Glad to see you made a full recovery."

The suggestion made him laugh. "Not sure if I'd call it full just yet. Something I'm reminded of every time I lower myself onto the toilet."

Simon smiled and sat back down. "So, what can I do for you?"

Eyes closed or not, Bud wasn't sleeping, Finn knew that perfectly well. When your entire world was reduced to the back end of a camper trailer, you made it your business to know what was going on around you at all times, even when your eyes weren't quite open. Finn jerked a thumb in Bud's direction.

"I'm not sure, Finn, Larry said no one – "

"I'm not gonna do anything stupid. I just need to ask him a few questions. I'll speak to him through the bars."

"It's just that – "

Finn opened his coveralls, revealing the spot where the bullet from Bud's 9 mm tore through his chest and abdomen. "After what he did, I think I'm entitled to a few answers, don't you?"

A look of defeat crept over Simon's face. "OK, fine, but make it fast."

"You're a prince."

Simon removed a baton from his belt and rattled it against the bars until Bud's eyes opened. "Wakey, wakey, Bud. Got yourself a visitor."

An extra chair was by the desk, and Finn slid it over and settled into it.

Bud watched Finn wince as he sat. "I shoulda aimed for the head," he said. "But then I figured the blast would finish what I'd started."

"I guess that Dana's tougher than you thought she'd be."

"Girl's got a mean left hook." Bud's cold gray eyes rose until the two met. "Still chasing after those memories you're never gonna get back?"

"A man is his memories, Bud. Least I'm looking for mine. What's your excuse."

Bud ran a finger along the bars. "I'm sort of indisposed at the moment. But you didn't come here to gloat, did you?"

"No. I've been wracking my brain trying to figure out why Thomson put you up to this."

Bud laughed. "There is no Thomson, not anymore."

"He died during The Shift?"

"In a manner of speaking. His name is Alvarez now. He walks and talks like a man, but I can tell you he isn't human."

"Alvarez?"

"He can move from one body to another. Somewhere along the line, he stopped being Thomson when he found some poor schmuck named Alvarez."

"So, he's a ghost."

"Or a demon or something. They call it paranormal, but that's only 'cause we don't understand how it works. Could be it's as straight up as gravity or thermal frickin' dynamics."

"So what does he ... it want?" Finn asked.

"He wants the facilities destroyed and anyone connected to the project dead. He may have voodoo powers our brains can't grasp, but I've seen fear in his eyes."

"He's scared of us?"

"Not of you, but your story, where you came from. You know how all of this started."

"And maybe how to fix it."

"Ain't that easy, though. You ever operated a particle collider, Finn? Would you even know how to turn the fucking thing on?

Finn crossed his arms. "'Course not."

"But there's someone who will."

"What'd you mean, someone who will?"

"Alvarez wouldn't say more, just that someone would come along who would know, and if the colliders were destroyed, they'd never have a chance. Problem is, reversing something this big ain't like flipping a switch. It could make things worse."

"Or it might just set the world right again."

"Don't count on it."

Finn stood up.

"That's it, then?"

"Is what it?"

"I give you all this info, and you're just gonna walk. What about my family, man? I'm not an evil person."

Finn wanted to turn away, but somehow he knew Bud wasn't lying. "What did you remember after The Shift?" Finn asked him.

"Same as you. Pretty much nothing."

"So, why are you so sure this Alvarez guy's got your family? Hell, how do you even know you have a family in the first place?"

"First thing I saw when I came out was a briefcase on the desk. On the wall above it was a flatscreen monitor with a note taped to the edge that read, *Press Play*.' Which I did. Flashed a bunch of pictures of a woman and a child and told me exactly what to do. Then it said to look inside the briefcase, and that's when I saw the C4."

"Were you in any of the pictures?"

Bud's eyes dropped. "No, only they were."

"So, you took his word for it."

"'Course, I took his word for it. A man says he's holding your wife and kid, you don't play chicken with him."

"No, you ask for proof."

Bud's hand flew in the air. "What kinda proof? I'm standing there in a pair of boxer shorts. Feeling like I was soaking in formaldehyde for God knows how long. Some guy says do this or you're wife and kid are gonna die. Damn right I believed him."

"But you're not so sure anymore."

Bud took in a deep breath. "To be honest, not really, no."

"Then you're welcome."

"Welcome?" Bud spat. "For What?"

"For returning the favor. You no longer need to worry about saving a family you probably never had. But you will have to live with the knowledge that you took people's lives for nothing."

•••

Finn was pulling the trailer door closed when he saw the woman standing before him. Dark hair, shoulder length, pretty face. She looked thin, but then so did everyone nowadays.

"Nice to finally meet you," she said and extended her left hand, palm up. A movement Finn believed was an effort to shake his in greetings – strange as it was that she would have used her left instead of her right. But that wasn't it at all. She was showing him something on her wrist.

A tattoo just like his.

"Joanne Blackmore," she said. "Where can we talk?"

•••

A few minutes later, they were in the gymnasium. Not an ideal place, but it wasn't like the compound was crawling with private nooks where they could talk. Even here though, they would need to keep their voices down. Cult members were setting up the wooden stage and podium. Looked like Larry had something to say, and it wouldn't be long now before they found out what that was. Finn had been unconscious for more than a month, which meant Joanne knew Rainbowland ... or New Jamestown, better than he did.

"Lemme guess," Finn started. "You have questions."

Joanne nodded. "No one here will tell me anything. I remember waking up wet and disoriented and then being shoved into a car. Everything was so bright, my eyes stung with pain."

"They can't tell you more 'cause they don't know anything. I was once exactly where you are now. So sure that if only I knew what happened to me, why I woke up on the floor covered in goo, then everything else would fall into place. But here's the thing: Answers are real pricks 'cause they only ever lead to more questions."

"I don't need protection from the truth."

Finn wasn't convinced. The truth, this truth, wasn't an easy one to swallow. Joanne was looking up at him, her skin soft in the dim light, and the prospect of hurting her with what he was about to say made him sick. He took a deep breath. "You're a criminal, Joanne."

"Pardon me?"

Finn told her what Tevatron was up to and how Thomson had pushed the program too far. That destroying the world had been his aim all along.

"To end the world? But why?"

"If you had another hour, I'd be happy to explain it to you, at least the pieces I've managed to put together myself."

Joanne slid her back along the wall until her rear hit the gym floor. "And those other pieces? Where are they hiding?"

"Right now my best guess is Ely State Prison."

"What'll we find there?"

Finn sank down next to her. "The truth."

Larry

Putting the final touches on New Jamestown's new charter of laws was what Larry was supposed to be doing, not procrastinating by leafing through All Father's journal. His office was lit by a single energy saver bulb, the light a miracle made possible by the windmill mounted above the compound's roof. He could even hear it groaning as a gentle wind made the blades spin, recharging the battery bank down in the basement. It sounded like progress. Something All Father and the other culties knew little about before Larry showed up. But a morbid sense of voyeurism aside, there was a very practical reason Larry was going through All Father's journal. The old bastard had been the very one to help codify the original governing principals, archaic and impractical as they were in a world gone mad. Who better to help draft the language that would undo it all? If a fake dying wish from All Father had convinced this lot to embrace the militarism their continued existence depended on, then finishing off the remaining principals shouldn't be harder than just getting the words right. As much as Larry hated to admit it, these simple-minded cult members were an integral part of his labor force. If they thought for a moment Larry had been deceiving them, even for their own good, then who knew what could happen.

Larry was flipping a page in All Father's journal when something caught his eye. A passage where he discussed having a meeting with Carole and her daughter, Nikki. Carole was trying unsuccessfully to convince him that they needed to raid the airport in order to help find the son she'd left behind. He wrote how his heart felt heavy telling her no, that she'd become angry, but then something else had happened, and this was where Larry's interest was really piqued. AF writes:

"The child asked me a question that startled me to the very core. 'Your daughter, Abigail, when was she killed?' As a newcomer, there was no possible way she could have known about Abigail, let alone my deep-seated suspicions over the years that she'd been murdered. Surely, the stunned look on my face must have made them wonder if it was guilt or anger I was feeling. But nothing could be further from the truth. It was Abigail's prophecy that young Nikki's comment brought to mind. She had been able to look deep within me and see an old memory that even I had buried. Could she be the one?"

Larry paused there, not entirely sure what the old son of a bitch had been on about. Was All Father saying this Nikki girl, the one who had returned from the slavers thanks to Bud, possessed some hokey psychic powers? Pure foolishness.

Back in the day, Nutrilife had gone to all the New Age trade shows. You couldn't throw a rock without hitting a psychic in the head, all of whom specialized in regurgitating the same vague fluff in the hopes that some gullible boob would fill in the appropriate blanks.

But if this was all so much bullshit, then why was Larry now using the key he kept on a string around his neck to unlock his desk drawer? The one which contained Abigail's notebook with her controversial views on good and evil along with her many prophecies? Before, Larry hadn't bothered going over those for the simple fact that nailing All Father's ass to the wall had been accomplished rather easily. He didn't need to press further. Seeing the old man's diary entry, however, had made him feel it might be worth another look.

Several sections discussed an internal threat to the cult as well as an outside evil that was growing in power every day. At last, he came to The Shift and how Aletheia had instructed the cult members to immerse themselves in water troughs to shield against the reversal. It even predicted the time. July 4 at 6:07 p.m. EST. Wow, doesn't get much more specific than that. Not long after, it described two survivors who would "fit together like lock and key. Buried memories only she can see." It was a riddle. Larry hated riddles.

"Buried memories only she can see," he repeated. Is this what had made All Father's jaw drop?

Larry closed the notebook and tapped on his desk three times. Charlie, the cult member who guarded his office, entered and stood at attention.

"Bring Nikki to me."

"Right away," he said and disappeared.

•••

When the nock came a few minutes later, Larry told them to enter. He glanced up from what he was doing and was surprised to see Dana.

"Your guard wasn't there."

"I sent him to fetch someone. Something's wrong," he observed. "I see it all over your face. You're having a crisis of conscience, aren't you?"

She came in and sat down. "That's part of it, I guess."

"You're a member of the Coast Guard," he said. "I shouldn't have to tell you how the needs of the many outweigh the needs of the few. Besides, you're doing a kick-ass job, Dana. I know I don't tell you nearly

40

enough, but you are." Larry smiled, hoping he didn't look too much like a vacuum salesman.

"But that man with one arm I gave a strike to. It just seems these rules are getting – "

"Harsh, I know, and they're about to get harsher. The compound's dangerously low on food, exactly the time we have to pull together. If one individual doesn't carry his weight, it risks bringing us all down. No exceptions."

Dana paused, as though she were trying to decide whether to say something or not. "Romeo was caught shirking work detail again. This is his third strike, and I know you're well aware of what that means."

The annoyance that flashed across Larry's face couldn't have been there for more than a second, but he hoped Dana hadn't seen it. Romeo had picked the safe where they kept Abigail's disowned teachings. The very ammunition that won Larry that little power play with AF. The kid knew the risks, so why the fuck was it Larry's responsibility to drag his sorry ass out of the mud?

Dana was over by the door now. "We'll be banishing him in the morning with the standard rations. One bottle of water and three crackers."

Larry nodded absently.

"There was one thing Romeo said that you should know about. His exact words were "You tell Larry that if he doesn't want his dirty laundry laid out for everyone to see, then he better do something about this.""

Now Larry's face was really squished up, and there was no hiding it. If word got out that Larry had read through sacred scriptures he'd stolen from the cult safe and used those to blackmail All Father, it could unravel every ounce of trust he'd built up in the last two months. But would anyone believe a lazy-assed kid in the process of being ejected from New Jamestown? The key, Larry knew, was to take care of this quickly and quietly, so the kid wouldn't have an opportunity to get on a soap box and start spilling his putrid guts. More than that, he knew that anyone who ventured beyond the walls after dark and without a weapon wouldn't last long.

"Send him out tonight," Larry ordered her, right away sensing the hesitation in Dana's body language and pushing through it. "Romeo's lies are nothing more than a cancer that can't be allowed to spread."

"So, this whole business about cracking the basement safe and messing with the cult's sacred scriptures to get dirt on Peter. None of that's true, right?"

"Is that what that little prick's saying?" Larry spat, trying to sound indignant.

Dana nodded. She seemed to be waiting for his denial.

"Lies, all of it."

She grinned and said, "That's what I thought," her gaze holding on the faded booklet before him as she pulled the door closed.

Carole

It was quickly becoming clear that Russell and Josh were about to be marched underground and into the pits where they'd certainly be killed. One of the Wipers prodding them along was the woman from the lobby Carole had seen earlier, her hair shaved on the sides and spiked into a Mohawk.

Judging by Aiden's belligerence, Carole was growing more and more certain she wouldn't be able to convince him to leave with her. Nor did Aiden seem to have any clue where his sister, Nikki, was. Thus, Carole had a choice. She could either slip away while the Wipers around her were focused on Russell and Josh and the sick Roman-style gladiator match they would soon be thrown into, or she could do something else. Something crazy.

Carole took a deep breath, which quavered in her lungs with the rhythm of her pounding heart, and then rose to her feet. In a way, it was she who'd gotten them into trouble when she insisted coming up here in the first place. She knew the risks. Understood that they were high and was willing to pay the price.

"Take me instead," she shouted.

The Wipers turned, even Alvarez, still grinning at the parade of new victims. Carole glanced down at Aiden and saw his hand was on top of hers.

"What are you doing?" He only mouthed the words, but she got the message all the same.

"Trade me for them," she said.

Alvarez clapped his hands and then banged his cane. "This keeps getting better and better." Beside him, Anita was rocking back and forth as though she were getting ready to lunge. "Settle down, Darling, there'll be time for that later," Alvarez told her.

The Wipers escorting Russell and Josh had halted, waiting to hear what Alvarez had to say. He cleared his throat. "I'm a man of honor. A distinction I'm sure anyone here will attest to. Well, maybe only the few who speak English. Don Quixote was famous for bravely charging windmills he mistook for dragons. A foolish man, yes, but he had heart nonetheless, so I'll tell you what … " He peered down at Carole with ink-black eyes. "You do have a name, don't you?"

"Carole," she heard herself say from a million miles away as though she were speaking into a plastic tube.

"All right, Carole. I'll tell you what. You win in the pits against an opponent of my choosing, not only will I let you go free, but I'll even spare your friends."

"I have your word on that?"

Alvarez bellowed laughter. "What do you take me for, a common thug?"

Clearly, she didn't. Instead, she stuck out her hand so he could shake it. Alvarez stared at it with disdain, as though Carole were holding out the tail end of a stinky fish. "It's better for you that I don't." He tapped his index finger against the arm rest of his skull encrusted throne, and a thin trail of white smoke rose into the air. The look of fear on Carole's face was immediate and unmistakable. Alvarez looked like a man, but Carole was quite certain now there was nothing human about him.

•••

Within minutes, she'd been roughly ushered into the pit through the underground entrance. Above her, the crowd was rabid with anticipation, filling the air with chants and cackles in the strange broken English the Wipers spoke. Russell and Josh were positioned next to Alvarez. That's when Carole locked eyes with Aiden, perched forward in his chair. He'd felt so incredibly abandoned by her when she fled the airport. The boy's anger was understandable, but it was clear he didn't want his mother dead. An enormous Wiper with a single arm handed her a 3-foot two-by-four. Cut into the base was a crude handle, and it suddenly became clear this was a bizarre cross between a sword and a club.

Heart hammering wildly in her chest, her throat parched, Carole scanned her surroundings. The pit itself wasn't larger than a racquetball court. Set into the wall at either end were iron gates from which the fighters emerged. Carole was swinging her club like a baseball bat, trying to get used to the weight, the crowd above nearly deafening, when her opponent entered the arena. It was the woman with the Mohawk from the lobby, her face painted to look like a skull. She had a nearly identical weapon, which she appeared to wield with little effort. The muscles in her arms were taught. In the Old World, she might have been a Pilates instructor or a personal trainer. Here, she was a killer. Without warning, Mohawk charged at Carole with a terrifying cry, the two-by-four poised over her head. Carole didn't even know the fight had begun and quickly ducked out of the way. The two-by-four buried itself in the earth wall. Mohawk yanked it out and spun on her heels just as Carole reached the other end of the arena. Instinct had taken over, and it had mandated that staying as far away from this crazy bitch was the only chance she had. Mohawk tossed her weapon from hand to hand, spinning it around in a show of skill. Skill with any kind of weapon wasn't something Carole possessed. But what she lacked in skill, she made up for in determination. Another charge from Mohawk with an overhead blow, and Carole blocked it by raising her club. The vibration sent jolts of pain through her hands and nearly made her drop the weapon. Mohawk was winding up for another strike when Carole swung her club, connecting with the side of her opponent's head. Mohawk staggered back, blood running from her ear. She dabbed at it with the pads of her fingers, and when they came away red, her face contorted with rage. Carole took a deep breath.

Oh, shit, now she's really pissed.

A savage flurry of strikes followed from Mohawk. Carole was able to block two of them and dodge a third, but one blow struck her in the arm with the force of a truck. Clutching her two-by-four, she could already feel her arm starting to throb with pain. But to lose her weapon was to lose the fight, and to lose the fight was to lose her life as well as the lives of her friends. She ran to the far side of the arena to buy herself some time. Pulling in heavy gulps of air and never quite able to get enough. Hands reached through the fence to grab at her. She was in a nightmare, she decided. A nightmare like in those movies where if you died in your dream, you died in real life. Mohawk approached her slowly and with confidence as though she were stalking a wounded animal and didn't want the hunt to end too early.

Except, in reality, Carole was no animal, no one's victim, and the sadistic delight Mohawk took in maiming others was reason enough to knock her head in. Where before Carole had felt fear, now she could only feel white-hot rage. No way she was gonna let this savage beat her, no way in hell. Carole started to roar with anger, the veins in her neck bulging, her face turning red and contorting with the thirst for vengeance. The sight was having an effect on Mohawk. The tiniest hesitation in her step was now visible, like she'd backed a wild racoon into a corner and now that racoon was about to lash out. And that's exactly what Carole did. With the club leveled over her head, she came out shrieking madly as though she intended to flatten Mohawk's prickly hair and air condition her skull. When her opponent moved to parry, Carole changed her angle of attack and sent the two-by-four slamming into the side of her face. Mohawk's legs gave out and she dropped to the ground. Carole stood over her, ready to strike again if the woman dared to move, but she didn't. Despite the fact that her face bore a perfect

45

stamp mark from where the slab of wood connected with her cheek, Mohawk's chest was heaving up and down. Far from being stunned, the crowd erupted in cheers. They didn't care who won or lost. It was a good, entertaining show they were after, and apparently, Carole had given them the best one yet. Even Alvarez was clapping.

A second later, the metal gate nearest Carole swung open. That same muscular Wiper snatched the weapon from her hand, tossed it on the floor, and then brought her before Alvarez. The look on Josh's and Russell's faces wasn't nearly as ecstatic as she'd hoped it would be. Were they doubtful Alvarez would keep his word?

"A wonderful performance," Alvarez proclaimed gleefully. "But you and your two friends came into my home and tried to take what belonged to me." Carole was certain he was talking about her attempts to convince Aiden to leave, before she realized he was referring to the food stores the men had raided. "So, understand that it's purely from the kindness of my heart that I'm giving the three of you a 60-second head start."

Josh, Russell, and Carole all looked at one another, unsure before they broke into a full run, shoving their way through the crowd, fighting off hands that tried to hold them in place. Looming in the background was Alvarez' booming voice, and hearing it terrified them.

"Fifty … forty-nine … forty-eight … "

Larry

"Did you want something to eat?" Larry asked Nikki. "Silly question, 'course you're hungry." He went over to a cabinet where All Father once kept his incense. It was stacked now with his own private stash of premium canned goods. "You probably had beans for lunch."

"Wow," she said, looking over his shoulder. "That's a lot of food. Maybe about what we have left in the entire pantry downstairs."

"This isn't all for me," Larry lied.

Nikki nodded. "I figured that. Especially since there are so many folks who are practically starving."

"Uh huh." Larry was fiddling through a stack of canned fish, oblivious to the plight of others. That was his curse. "How does salmon sound?"

"Sure," she said. "Am I in trouble, Mr. Nowak?"

He laughed, nearly dropping the can opener. "Larry, Sweetie, call me Larry, and no, not at all. I've heard great things about you, and I wanted to see for myself."

"What sort of things?"

Larry scooped the contents of the can onto a plate and set it in front of her. It looked like cat food, might even taste like it, but the folks here were so hungry it could just as easily pass for a five-star meal. "Only that sometimes you see things that other people can't. What's that funny name they have for it, clairvoyance?"

She brought a fork full of salmon to her lips and paused before eating it. "Well, it's not really something I control. Happens all on its own. Sorta like breathing."

"Fascinating." He sat across from her and folded his hands under his chin. "Tell me. What sort of things do you see?"

"Flashes. Scenes. Most of the memories don't make much sense except to the person they belong to."

"So, you've had this your entire life then?"

"I don't know," Nikki said. "I don't remember anything from before, but my mom seemed to think this was something new."

"Carole mentioned you had a brother."

"Aiden," she blurted out before the pain settled into her eyes.

"Aiden, yes. And what about him? Was he also different after The Shift?"

"I don't think so."

47

"I'm gonna read something to you, Nikki, and I want you to tell me what you think it means." Larry flipped the notebook open to where he'd placed a bookmark. He read her the passage about the two survivors "'fitting together like lock and key. Buried memories only she can see.' That mean anything to you?"

Nikki's eyes were suddenly dilated, and she was looking at him strangely, her head tilted at an odd angle, the way pretentious people sometimes looked at paintings. She was either having a psychotic episode or a really intense daydream. And then, as quickly as it came, it was gone.

"What'd you say?" she asked.

"Never mind." He stood to see her out. She was in the act of rising from her seat when she stopped. "Your dad loved you, Larry. I know you don't think so, but he did. He just didn't know how to show it. I could see it in his eyes. How he looked at you when you were a baby."

She left after that, Larry thanking her, biting back the stunned expression hanging over his face like wet dough. He locked the door after that, to make sure he wouldn't be disturbed, and quietly wept.

Dana

"Why doesn't that chicken shit come and do it himself?" Romeo asked. Lou and Dana were there to escort the boy from the compound and leave him outside the gate. Simon was there along with Bud, who sat in the corner, smirking. "Larry doesn't like to get his hands dirty," Bud said. "Not if he can help it."

"Yeah, no shit." Romeo was pacing back and forth in the cell. "Did you tell him what I said, Dana?"

She nodded. "It's nothing personal, Romeo, we gave you chances to participate just like everyone else. There aren't enough resources to feed those who don't contribute."

The kid didn't have a snappy comeback for a very simple reason. Dana was right. He hadn't been pulling his weight. Instead, he'd been hiding under a cloak of perceived invisibility, certain Larry would shield him from the rules that the rest of the colony were bound by. And why? Because he claimed to have dirt on Larry. Dana wasn't under any illusion the man was a saint. An exalted ideal that was impossible to reach in a world desperate to tear itself apart.

Lou tossed a pair of handcuffs to Romeo. "Put these on."

The kid reached down slowly and picked them up. Bud was shaking his head. "That Larry sure is one helluva piece of work. You know, he stole my car on I-80 when I got out to help a family who was stranded. Pretty much left me for dead."

"I find that mighty hard to believe after what you did to Johnson and Finn," Lou snapped.

"Yeah, well we all have our reasons, don't we? It may be hard for you to understand, but that doesn't make what I'm saying any less true."

Dana rested her thumb on the grip of her SIG. "Only that you failed to mention any of this in the month you've been in custody."

"No one asked. Besides, who woulda believed me? I see what Larry's trying to do. Whisk this kid off in the middle of the night so he can't make a fuss. You're a smart woman, Dana. Doesn't that make you wonder just a bit?"

Outwardly, she was ignoring Bud's attempts to get in her head. She'd seen what Bud was capable of, and it didn't matter what his reasons were. A guy like that didn't have a shred of credibility in a world where your reputation was all anyone had left.

Lou finally opened the gate and approached Romeo. Beads of sweat were rolling down the kid's face. His cheeks flushed. "I know what happened to your wife," Romeo spat.

Lou stopped. "What horse manure are you shovelling now?"

"None. I'm being straight up. It wasn't an accident."

Even with his back turned, Dana could sense Lou's blood pressure rising. After examining the body, Dana's own finding's had been inconclusive, and so she hadn't seen any point in stirring the pot.

"Not an accident – " Lou stammered.

"He's trying to get to you, Lou," Dana shouted, although she knew her words probably weren't penetrating the sudden swirl of emotions clouding his mind.

"She didn't die in the river," Romeo said. "She died while being brainwashed. Larry let it out by accident one day. Said he and Timothy found her strapped to a chair in front of a projection screen with a metal contraption around her head to keep her watching."

Lou'd had enough, and he growled, grabbing Romeo by the collar and lifting him nearly a foot off the ground. Romeo's voice was reduced to a strained whimper, his feet kicking at dead air. "I'm telling you the truth."

"LOU!" Dana shouted. "Let him go," but the big man wasn't listening. She entered the cell and put her hands on him. "Lou, put the kid down, right now."

A sound from outside the cell of Simon scrambling for his rifle. That's when she noticed her gun was missing. She turned to see Bud holding it. The hammer was cocked. With a flick of his thumb, he snapped the safety back on and spun it so the handle was facing her. Dana grabbed it out of his hands and held it on him.

"Coulda killed all three of you if I'd wanted to, not to mention bubba over there," he said, pointing at Simon. "Woulda been free in less than 60 seconds."

"But you didn't," Dana said.

"No, ma'am, I didn't. Even though I suspect Larry will eventually come for me, too, the way he's come for the kid here. Only a question of time, really. But if I'm gonna be frank, there isn't much out there to run to. Certainly not Alvarez. Besides, I kinda like it here. Feel safe. Plus the sheriff's pretty hot." Bud winked at her, and that's when Dana holstered her pistol and headed for the door. A bag at her feet contained a handful of crackers and a bottle of water. She picked it up and said to Lou, "All right, it's time."

●●●

Dana, Lou, and Romeo were walking down the gravel path that led to the gate that spanned the bridge. Two wooden towers on either side were occupied by men with high-powered hunting rifles. In a third was a cult member with an AR-15.

Romeo's expulsion would mark the first person to ever be forcibly removed from New Jamestown. It was as simple as opening the gate and removing the cuffs.

"What if he's telling the truth?" Lou asked, not caring if Romeo heard or not.

She'd been thinking of that very thing since the kid began flapping his lips. Larry had already told Dana about Patty Mae's brainwashing, but what if there was more he was covering up? What if her death hadn't really been a horrible accident, but a murder? The stubborn streak she'd inherited from her father wanted the truth, no matter where it led. Even if that truth revealed Romeo's story to be utter bunk.

"We send him out now, and we may never know," Lou was saying.

"That's right," Romeo said, "There's more to tell, too, and you won't believe the half of it."

"Keep a lid on it," Dana snapped. She took a deep breath. "What are you proposing, Lou? That we defy Larry's orders."

"I'm proposing we get to the bottom of what's been going on. Sure, you're a young woman and to my knowledge ain't never been married, so it's maybe hard to fathom what it's like to be in my shoes. Losing someone you love deeply only to learn the details surrounding their death might be a big fat lie."

"Might," she said.

"But how we gonna know if we send him through that gate?"

Only one of the trailers that lined the gravel path wasn't being used. It had become a kind of storage shed when the main compound building was being erected and remained as such ever since. Dana pointed over to it.

"Today's your lucky day, Romeo."

The potential that the idea would blow up in her face was strong, the consequences of which would undoubtedly be bad. So, too, was the prospect of discovering a truth she wasn't entirely sure she wanted to hear, but one she couldn't stop herself from wanting to know.

PRIMAL SHIFT 7: SACRIFICE

Carole

They could hear the shrieks and the cries of the Wipers behind them as they raced up South Main Street. Without street lights, the roads were difficult to navigate. The moon looked down on them through thick cloud cover offering some much needed illumination. Carole, Russell, and Josh knew there would never have been time for all three of them to make it into the air duct in time. Besides, that would have given away their hideout and the nine others waiting underground for them to return. Surely, Holly had followed orders and clamped the vent shut when Russ and Josh were captured.

Shots rang out behind them. The Wipers had rounded the corner, and now they were firing. Sparks ricocheted off abandoned cars and the asphalt at their feet. They would go the long way around and hopefully lose the Wipers when they ducked into the 7-Eleven.

The group was just pulling even with 6th Street when they were bathed in the warm glow cast by a pair of headlights. A heavy truck was approaching. More gunfire zipped by as a Humvee skidded to a stop barely 10 feet away. The driver and passenger doors swung open, and two men in blue camo sprang out, aiming M-4 carbines at them.

"Don't shoot," Carole screamed. "We're not one of them."

The driver waved his rifle. "Hurry, get in. We only have two seats, so you better squeeze."

The driver then leaned over the hood and started firing back. A moment later, both men were inside. The driver hit the gas, and the vehicle charged through the intersection. Bullets dinged off the armor plating, and Russell leaned in toward Josh, who was sandwiched on a flat board between them. They were going really fast now, and Carole was happy to be escaping the Wipers. She was in the middle of thanking them for saving their lives when the front left tire of the Humvee clipped the low silhouette of an abandoned sports car. The truck suddenly jerked, skidding up on its side before impacting another vehicle. Josh was thrown immediately forward and into the windshield. Carole's face slammed against the driver's seat.

The engine was still rumbling when hands began pulling her from the wreck, asking if she was all right, sounding as though they were a million miles away. Then she saw the face of the soldier who'd saved her. Russell was there, too, but not the other two. From down the street, the Wipers must have seen what had happened and began heading their way, firing wildly.

"What about Josh?" she asked.

"Josh and Petty Officer Lewis are dead," the man said.

A name tag over the right breast pocket of his uniform read, *Callahan*.

"God bless the Army," Carole said.

Callahan hurriedly pulled a rucksack from the Humvee as well as his rifle. "Not Army, Lady. We're Navy. But I accept."

Russell put an arm around Carole while the soldier fired down the street to keep the Wipers at bay. A number of them were weaving between cars, some ducking for cover, slowly closing the distance. The horrible sounds they were making as they charged on made Carole think of the savages on remote islands in the pacific during the age of exploration.

"This way," Russell said, pointing frantically. "We can enter the 7-Eleven from the rear."

The soldier inserted a fresh magazine and pulled the charging handle. "What's in the 7-Eleven?"

"Our only shot at staying alive," came Russell's quick reply.

They made their way across 6th Street and ducked behind the row of businesses where the Victoria's Secret and convenience store were located. The goal was to get to the store before the Wipers could make it around the corner and see where they'd gone.

Callahan took position at the edge of the building, using the angle to cut the corner and keep the Wipers pinned down. They weren't well disciplined or particularly well trained given the erratic nature of their attacks, but even stray bullets could sometimes get lucky.

Russell and Carole reached the back door. It was a flat metallic job without a handle, but Russell had removed the locking latch long ago so he'd have an entrance in the case of an emergency. But without something to grasp, prying it open wasn't going to be easy, not in the dark.

"I left a chisel out here, and I can't find it," Russell shouted in a panic, and he dropped on all fours, rummaging through the high grass with his hands. Carole did the same, terrified that any second now the Wipers would have them surrounded.

Callahan turned back. "You two better hurry up."

There was a tactical flashlight on the edge of Callahan's rifle, and Russell yelled for him to toss it over. Callahan did, but the time it took to detach and throw it meant the Wipers had managed to close that much more ground.

Russell turned the light on, and a second later saw the chisel, wedged against the edge of the building. He picked it up, dug the tip between the door and the frame and worked to pry it open. Callahan was already falling back at a full run. Not because he saw them making progress, but because the Wipers were nearly on top of him.

Larry

"We owe a greater debt to the original Jamestown colony of 1607 than any of you can imagine," Larry said, gripping the edges of the podium with both hands. "More than just a namesake. The brave men and women who landed on the shores of the James River over 400 years ago were strangers in a strange land, surrounded by hostile Indians, struggling against disease, starvation, and other, unspeakable horrors. Today, we find ourselves facing similar threats. An evolving enemy bent on stealing our possessions, our freedom, our lives. In effect, destroying all we've managed to salvage from The Shift. This may feel like the same country you knew and loved, the one most of you grew up in, but like our ancestors of old, trust me when I tell you we are foreigners in a strange and terrifying land. That, dear people, is the reason I've brought you all here this morning. To discuss the coming changes."

The throng of colonists and cult members who filled the gymnasium shifted uncomfortably. Larry had worked hard this past month to soften the rougher parts of how he spoke. The use of profane language, the incessant use of sexual analogies, derogatory comments towards women: all things that weren't entirely gone, since they were part of the very fabric of his being. But Larry was a survivor, a man willing to do whatever it took to get his way and accomplish what he set his mind to. Some of the members of the colony were turned off by his crass manner, some, judging by the looks in their eyes at this very moment, surely despised him. He was OK with that. Because soon, they would come to recognize his true fucking genius and that without him, they would all be dead.

Early on, Timothy had given Larry a book about Julius Caesar called *The Transition from Roman Republic to Empire*. Caesar's adopted son, Octavian, started out as a candyass as well as a sadistic murderer, and yet within a short time he would become Caesar Augustus and lead Rome into its most glorious period. If a pimply 19-year-old, 2,000 years ago could pull it off, then you could bet your ass that Larry could, too.

"Here's my pledge to all of you. I submit that within a few weeks our food problems will feel like nothing more than a faint memory. I've commissioned that our foraging groups be doubled. In addition, as many are aware, canned goods throughout the city have been disappearing, and so I've decided to set aside a piece of land allocated for crops. Beets, cabbage, and carrots to start us off, with others to follow.

"Of course, all of this comes at a price. Some of you have taken advantage of the present situation and gotten a free ride. And I'm gonna tell you the buck stops here. Starting now, the three-strike system is abolished."

Thunderous applause erupted from the crowd. Even Finn, in a way, one of the newest members of New Jamestown was clapping madly until Joanne laid her hands over his. Larry wasn't done.

"In its place," he continued, "I've instituted the one-strike rule. Failure to pull your weight, failure to show up for a single work detail, will now result in a public whipping. A second offence will represent an immediate and irrevocable banishment from New Jamestown."

The audience was stunned. Perhaps the hardest hit was Dana since she would be the one dishing out these punishments. The need for order and obedience wasn't in question, but public whippings? What next? Hanging people from the walls? She glanced over and saw a similar disdain on Timothy's face. But not the other cult members. Sure, they weren't wearing those plastic flight attendant smiles like in the old days, but their new stoic paramilitary expressions were perhaps even more unsettling. If Dana thought Timothy was upset, she was about to really see the steam shoot out his ears.

"As such," Larry went on, "it's only fitting that the principles set forth by All Father also be updated." Larry pulled a sheet off a white board that stood directly behind him. On it in point form were New Jamestown's new principles:

The First Principle: Hurt no living thing by either action or omission without justification.

The Second Principle: Non-essential technology separates man from his creator and should be avoided at all costs.

The Third Principle: While all men and women are created equal, some are more equal than others.

The Fourth Principle: The consumption of drugs is forbidden and punishable by expulsion from New Jamestown. Alcohol should be consumed with moderation."

The Fifth Principle: From this point forward, Larry Nowak will remained head of New Jamestown indefinitely.

Larry hadn't even finished working through all of them when Timothy rose and stormed from the gymnasium. It hadn't been Larry's intention to start a war, but by putting down in writing what had always seemed obvious to him, he saw now that a conflict with Timothy was inevitable. And somewhere in the back of Larry's mind he realized he was about to feel what it must have been like for All Father.

Finn

It wasn't long after Larry finished the speech in which he effectively declared himself king of New Jamestown that Finn and Joanne left for Ely State Prison. They were suddenly very glad to be away, although the prospect of returning to the accusation they'd skipped a work detail left them feeling decidedly uneasy. Joanne was staring out the window, watching the sagebrush, as they made their way south along Nevada's Route 93A. A long two-lane highway that stretched into infinity. To Finn, it looked like they were in the middle of nowhere, but Lou's directions had been clear. West along I-80 and then south when they reached the 93. In the distance, were the peaks of the Goshute Mountains, just where Lou said they'd be. Ely State Prison and the answers both of them hoped to find there was still about two hours away. A gargantuan amount of time spent between two people who hardly knew a thing about their past. Didn't make for great conversation. Joanne's only existing memory was of that open field with tall grass, and it was with a certain amount of pain that Finn had explained its origin. A screen saver from Tevatron's main server. An image stuck in the minds of only God knew how many.

Securing supplies for the journey this trip wasn't nearly as simple as it had been the last time he'd come to Nevada. That had been before the threat of starvation had sent the colony down a slippery slope toward tyranny. Most of what they got came from Lou. Bottles of water, pumped up from the river, using the windmill and then filtered in a blue 50-gallon barrel. Tasted like horse piss, but he was told it was safe to drink. Food had been similarly scarce. Some smoked rabbit as well as a large hunk of mystery meat that Lou suggested Finn not ask about. The word going around camp was that wild dogs were being shot by the scavenging groups Larry sent out on a daily basis. Lou's final gift to Finn had been a scoped .30-06 hunting rifle along with a handful of bullets. Not enough for much of a gun battle. Although it was enough to defend themselves from anyone intending to do them harm. Perhaps the real purpose for the gun would be as a means to hunt for food once supplies began running thin.

Joanne was still staring out the window, lost in thought, the index finger of her left hand twisting her long dark hair into rings. She was a beautiful, dare he say, stunning woman, and back in New Jamestown Finn wasn't blind to how many of the men, married or not, gravitated towards her. For her part, Joanne seemed largely oblivious to their advances and innuendoes. Not that Finn thought she was playing dumb. Her strategy, if one could call it that, seemed to be refusing to read between the lines. If they wanted something, they sure as hell better have the balls to come right out and say it.

She glanced over and caught him staring. Finn snapped back to the road, feeling a blush rise in his cheeks.

A knowing little smile formed on her face.

"Penny for your thoughts," Finn offered.

"Is that all you think they're worth?"

He grinned and found removing it from his face was no easy task. This woman made him smile in a way no one had before. Dana was attractive, but far too idealistic and trusting. Before she disappeared, he'd often wondered if Carole had a thing for him. Nothing the woman had said. More just by the way her eyes seemed to follow him across the compound. But in each of those cases, that indescribable zing of electricity that sometimes passed between two people wasn't there.

"I'm worried about the kind of person I am," she said after a moment.

Finn saw she was serious. "You seem like a mighty fine person to me."

"Yeah, I do now, but what was I like before? We're not heading to the state governor's mansion to read a long list of the great things I did, Finn. We're heading to a state prison. What was I in there for? What did I do to get there?" She paused, and he could feel her looking at him. "What did you do?"

He didn't answer.

"You know, don't you?"

"I know what my file says I did. Although for the life of me I can't imagine ever having done something like that."

"It was murder, wasn't it?"

Finn nodded reluctantly. "First degree."

The deep breath Joanne took then made him wonder if she suddenly didn't feel safe.

"You don't seem like the dangerous type to me," she said studying him up and down.

He laughed. "Well, you never can tell, can you? It's always the quiet ones, isn't that what they say?"

"What makes us who we are Finn? You know, ever since I came out of that isolation chamber I've been asking myself that question, and I haven't come up with anything resembling a satisfying answer yet. Look at the Wipers. They lost every sense of what it meant to be human, and look what they've become. Animals."

"Yes, but not all of them," Finn said. "At least, not in the beginning." He was thinking of Betsey, the woman he'd met at the diner. "When all this started, I'd see Wipers running from danger, hiding, without a single sign of violence, but guess what, those were some of the first to die. Mother Nature's a cold lady indeed, let me tell you. Wasn't long before the peace lovers were weeded out by the strong. But you don't need a Wiper to see that. Just look what happened to Rainbowland."

"What's Rainbowland?"

"Exactly. That's what New Jamestown used to be called, but now it's gone extinct, thanks in large part to people like Larry and the Wipers. See, it was the protective bubble of law and order that gave peace lovers the luxury of nonviolence. And yet, once all of that broke down, it was only a question of time before the most aggressive began scaling a mountain of bones to reach the top of the food chain."

"So, you're saying they aren't evil," Joanne said, not entirely believing it.

"I'm not sure about good and evil. Everyone's fighting for themselves, that much I know. On some level, even the Wipers must think they're in the right. All I can say for sure is they're exactly what Mother Nature wanted. Just don't ask me why."

"And what about us?" she asked. "Where do we fit into this mess? Were you born a killer, or did life shape you into one?"

Finn didn't take his eyes off the road when he spoke. "Guess we're about to find out."

Carole

Carole held the empty plastic milk jug under the dingy pipe and turned the valve. A trickle of water came out, and she made sure to collect every precious drop. They were back in the boiler room, surrounded outside by Wipers trying desperately to find them. As they fled through the storage room of the 7-Eleven and the hole in the wall, Russell had reached back and pulled an empty coke machine to cover the entrance. After that, he had yanked the cable lowering the steel plate. The ruse wouldn't last forever, but hopefully it would buy them enough time to devise an escape plan. Staying here was no longer an option now that the Wipers knew of their presence. But the failure of their desperate mission to return with food, and for Carole, her children, had only highlighted the dire need to flee.

Tapping the water pipes to keep them hydrated was Russell's idea. This was, after all, a place he'd spent years of his life working. But even he knew the measure wasn't more than a temporary stopgap.

The water filling up the jug was brown with floating bits of rust. Carole sealed the valve shut and brought the water back to the group. She took a soft white T-shirt they'd snatched from Victoria's Secret, folded it once, and stretched it over a large white bucket. This would act as a filter to siphon out most of the larger impurities. When she finished, the first to drink were the youngest; Tamara, Jessica, and three other young girls. Then the adults.

"Here," she told Callahan after the kids were done. "For saving our lives."

"I'd like to think that anyone woulda done the same," Callahan said.

Russell disagreed. "Don't be so sure."

"If you're thinking about Wipers," Carole said, "they don't count. They're barely human anymore."

"Oh, they're human," Callahan said, passing the cup back to Carole. "Just the worst parts. I've got firsthand experience, trust me. For a while there, I didn't think our boat crew would make it out of San Diego alive. We piled everyone into Humvees and those old soft-top troop transports. We were looking for a sign of someone, anyone. Hell, we woulda been happy simply knowing what had happened. One part we were sure of, this hadn't been some kinda boom boom event."

"Boom boom?" Holly asked.

Callahan brought his hands up in the shape of a mushroom cloud.

"See, we didn't think there was anything wrong with people until our convoy was attacked. They used a road block to stop us and ambushed our guys from the surrounding buildings. Our own citizens firing on us with every kind of weapon you can imagine. Everything from arrows to AKs. Sure, we killed a lot of them, but what did it matter when they just kept coming? This one kid came charging out at us, firing an automatic rifle. I was in the back of one of those transport trucks, and the men inside were getting riddled to the point light was pouring in through the holes in the canvas roof. Anyway, I leveled my weapon hoping the kid would scatter back into the rubble, but instead the stupid punk pulls the trigger."

"So, you killed him," Carole said, unable to get the image of Aiden out of her head and the knowledge that soon that little boy would be him.

"I wish he didn't make me, I really do. We were fighting for our lives."

"That's the problem with Wipers," Russell cut in, taking another swig of water. "They don't give you the option of acting civilized."

Carole saw clearly enough that Callahan still didn't know what had happened to the world. So, she told him everything she knew about The Shift and the effect it'd had on the minds of nearly everyone on Earth.

"Hell, we thought we'd entered the damned *Twilight Zone*, but after hearing this I'm not sure what to think."

"Ideas like civilization, rule of law, and respect for your fellow man," Russell said before tilting the cup back for a another sip. "They're nothing but fancy ways of describing a world built on memories. The only reason we have 'em is because we spent so long killing and raping each other. But what happens when all that common sense, lessons built on eons of atrocities and ethnic cleansing, disappears overnight, eh?"

"Hell on Earth," Callahan replied.

Tamara was fiddling with a loose thread in her shirt. "Maybe the Wipers have to learn those lessons all over again," she observed.

Russell chuckled, and his frame, thick with tradesman's muscles, shook. "Not before they manage to kill everyone, including themselves, I'll bet."

"Maybe this isn't the kind of conversation children should be listening to," Carole interjected. "Besides, our focus should be on getting everyone here to safety."

Callahan nodded. "I think Carole's got a point."

Russell tossed the cup back into the bucket. "I'm all ears."

"There's a place I know that's a few miles north of the city," she said.

"Oh, not that again," Russell interjected. "For all we know, the Wipers have razed it to the ground."

It was becoming obvious to Carole there was something wrong with Russell. His attitude had become more and more negative since his capture by Alvarez. Was this his way of mourning the loss of Josh? Did he blame her for the death of his friend? Or did he feel that Callahans' presence was a threat to his authority? Then it struck her.

"You don't wanna leave here, do you?" she asked him, point blank.

He sat up immediately, as though she'd accused him of being the Grand Wizard of the KKK. "Sure, I don't wanna leave, but it's not like we have any goddamned choice, do we? That's what's boiling my blood the most, not to mention the fact that we have no clear idea if this Rainbowland place you keep talking about even exists anymore."

Callahan suddenly looked very worried. "Rainbowland? Sounds like one of those Facebook games. You remember, the one with the candy?"

Jessica nodded enthusiastically. "I used to love that."

"Look," Carole said. "I don't know for certain, but our options right now are pretty limited. Either way, we won't get far without some sort of transportation." She looked to Callahan.

"The Humvee was pretty banged up, but I can try it."

"What about you, Russell?"

He sighed. "I do remember seeing a truck one street over. I'm sure it still has lots of gas left since the back was open and the engine wasn't left running. Everyone should fit inside nicely."

"I gotta say, I'm still not sure about this Rainbowland place," Callahan said.

Carole tried to smile and found the act almost painful. "I'm sure you'll like it just fine, granted we make it out of here in one piece."

Jeffereys

Alvarez was in his suite when Jeffereys knocked on the door. Most of the Wipers were scrambling through the neighborhood, checking every building they could for signs of the escapees. They'd tracked the two thieves along with the military man who was with them to a convenience store nearby, but it was there that the trail had gone cold.

It was the middle of the day now, but inside Alvarez' room, the curtains were drawn shut, as was usual. A glow from dozens of candles gave the room a warm, almost holy glow. Anita was on her knees with the boss' pecker in her mouth.

Jeffereys coughed and then knocked on the door when it was clear they hadn't heard him. Alvarez turned and saw who it was, yanked his hips free from Anita's grasp, and closed the silk robe he was wearing. Anita glowered at him, and Jeffereys couldn't tell if she were angry they'd been interrupted or if she'd been turned on that he'd seen what they were up to.

Al was tightening the strings as he waved Jeffereys in. There was a tent in his robe, and Jeffereys suddenly felt even more uncomfortable.

"Don't mind us," Alvarez said. "Anita and I were just exercising. Isn't that right, Dear?"

Anita grinned and sauntered into the bathroom.

"Now, tell me you have some good news." Alvarez grabbed a violin case off his dresser and made his way over to the couch. He opened it slowly, waiting for Jeffereys' explanation.

Jeffereys swallowed hard. "We're still looking for them, but they can't have gone very far."

Alvarez crossed his legs and brought the violin up to his chin. "I see. So, you're telling me that three unarmed people managed to escape our entire force?"

Maybe it was the candles, or the strange melancholy song Al was playing on that fiddle, but Jeffereys was suddenly feeling very warm. "Not quite escape," he said, "but evade, temporarily."

The violin sagged in Al's hands. "Are you playing word games with me?"

"No games, no games. I'm telling you these people are slippery and might have been living right under our noses for a while, undetected."

"Yes," Al agreed. "They were coming for the food, weren't they? And how else would they know we had it unless they'd been watching."

"Exactly, which is why I think they must be nearby."

65

"Under our noses, you said."

Jeffereys nodded.

"What do we have in the floors beneath us?"

"We don't know," Jeffereys replied. "I mean, we've never been down there. The access door is sealed shut, and we haven't been able to open it."

One of Alvarez' eyebrows perked up. "They managed to sneak in somehow. Have a group check the ventilation system, in particular the grates. If any of them aren't screwed in firmly then you have your point of entry. Have another group get that door open. I want to know what's down there."

Alvarez stood up and ran a hand through his greasy hair.

"There's one other thing, and I think you're gonna like this."

"Uh, huh." Alvarez was checking his nails.

Jeffereys snapped his fingers, and two slavers entered, carrying an unconscious man in blue and gray fatigues. A name tag on his chest read, *Lewis*.

"This was one of the men helping the thieves. We found him in a Humvee. Another man in civilian clothes was beside him, dead."

"A Humvee, eh? Hmm … "

"I thought you might like that."

"And what about our friend here? Is he still alive?"

Jeffereys grabbed a chunk of Lewis' hair and lifted his head. "Barely."

"Well, see to it he gets better. Then you can torture him to find out where the other men in his unit are based and what kinds of weapons they have access to. If they're not willing to share, then we can't very well have them helping those hippies in Rainbowland."

Jeffereys snapped his fingers, and the slavers dragged Lewis' limp body away. "You should know that they've changed the name to New Jamestown," Jeffereys said, and hearing the news brought a grin to Alvarez' lips.

"That so? All the more reason we'll need to ensure they suffer the same fate as their namesake."

Finn

The Ely State Prison grounds were positively immense. A high fence topped with razor wire formed a perfect square around the prison grounds. At each corner, towers stood guard. Finn and Joanne were approaching a parking lot located just outside the perimeter fence when they saw that it was only half full. The hoods from many of the cars were propped up, probably the result of scavengers looking for batteries and other spare parts. A sight that made Finn more than a little anxious.

"You think people are living here?" Joanne asked.

"Not sure," he replied, still scanning. "If so, I hope they're friendly." They rolled up to the main gate, and that's when Finn heard the man's booming voice.

"Halt!"

He hit the brakes, and when the car skidded to a stop he saw a figure appear from the gate house, weapon drawn. It was an M-4 and the man was dressed in blue and gray fatigues. Another troop appeared and approached the car, holding a pistol in one hand and a Geiger counter in the other. He made his way around the entire vehicle, watching the needle on the device for any signs of radiation.

"They're clean," he told his partner before turning back to Finn. "This is a secure facility. Where have you come from?"

The troop had a strong New York accent.

"We didn't think you guys were still around," Finn said. "What's the Army doing headquartered in a prison?"

"We aren't Army, sir. We're U.S. navy, and you haven't answered my question."

Joanne leaned over. "We drove three hours from Utah. We're here to get information on two former prisoners."

The sailor tipped his cap at her. "I'm sorry for your trouble, but we aren't allowing ... " The walkie-talkie on the sailor's belt came to life, and the voice said, "Let them in."

"Yes, Sir," the sailor replied. He replaced the walkie on his belt and waved to the other man to open the gate. He leaned in the window and pointed straight ahead.

"Please make your way to the main complex."

Joanne thanked him, but Finn didn't move right away.

"Aren't you gonna go?" she asked.

Finn wasn't sure. When they first pulled up, a part of him had been relieved to see the military. Maybe it was the thought of voluntarily returning to a jail cell he'd escaped that was making him uneasy. Joanne urged him forward, and Finn shifted into drive and entered the prison courtyard. They parked where the sailor had indicated, and Finn reached into the duffel bag that was perched on the back seat and came out with a handful of .30-06 cartridges, stuffing them into his pockets. He then stepped out of the car and slung the rifle over his shoulder.

"Aren't you being a little paranoid?" she asked. "It's the Army."

"Navy," Finn snapped. "And I haven't heard of anyone dying from being over prepared."

Joanne shook her head teasingly as two new sailors approached them. Finn was just waiting for either man to attempt to confiscate his rifle or tell him he'd have to leave it in the car. Wouldn't have taken much more than that for him to get back behind the wheel and drive away, with or without the information he'd been searching for. But they didn't. Instead, the taller of the two, a man with the name Kulik and the letters *XO* embroidered on his uniform said, "Commander Zhou would like to see you."

When they entered the prison and found Zhou, he was seated in the visitors area, focused on fixing the misshapen brim of a cowboy hat. The room was filled with sailors and equipment, all seemingly centered around Zhou.

"A Texan shouldn't ever sit on his hat," he said without looking up. "Did you know that in some parts of the state it used to be punishable by up to 30 days in the county jail? Guess I'm in the right place." Zhou smiled as he stood, his teeth all white and perfectly straight. With nimble speed, he flung the hat aside and held out his hand. Finn took it. Afterward, Joanne did the same. There was a slight twang in the way the Asian man spoke. Sounded like a country boy or a cattle rustler. He wasn't very tall either. Maybe 5'4"or 5'5", slight build, his hair cropped short like the men around him.

"Commander Andrew Zhou," he told them, waiting for Finn and Joanne to introduce themselves, which they did. He flashed his infectious smile again. "I know that look in your eye. It's the one that says 'I wanted Commander John Smith or Captain Buck Rogers, but all I got was a Chinese guy from Texas.'" All three of them laughed, if a little uneasily. "My parents immigrated here from Hong Kong in the '60s. My real name is Li Yong, but my parents had this thing about fitting in, Texas being what it was in those days, so they changed it to Andrew, after the 17th president." The commander laced his fingers together and cracked his knuckles. "So, now that we've melted the ice a little, I need to get down to brass tacks with you folks. First, I need to know where you came from and how many survivors are currently at that location."

"I'd ask you the same thing," Finn replied. "In case you haven't noticed, there isn't any United States anymore. Fact, I'd be surprised if there were any countries still around."

"Well, we both want something. I think we can agree on that."

"That sounds about right."

"So, why don't I go first," Zhou said, sitting back down, "since we still have a ways to go before trusting one another. The men you see around you are the crew of the Navy sub *USS Alabama*. We were passing Cape Horn on July 4 when all communication went dead. Down about 500 feet beneath the ocean when it happened. We surfaced to re-establish contact. Trying to call home, just like E.T., but no one was picking up. The most likely scenario was an equipment malfunction, and so we headed back to Point Loma in San Diego, but it wasn't till we caught a glimpse of the shoreline through our periscope three weeks later that we knew we were in trouble. Buildings charred from fires that had been left to burn out of control and not a single sign of life. We also started picking up high levels of radiation. Wondered if the world had gone and nuked its ass back to the Stone Age while we were under the waves. At that point, we weren't sure. We moved up the coast and saw more of the same and so, running low on supplies, I turned us around and set course for Loma again. We left the ship in full hazmat gear, every man armed. Myself and 155 stepped off that ship. Now, we're barely half that, and I'm sure you know why."

"The Wipers."

"Wipers?" Zhou asked. "That what you call those sonsabitches?"

"Their ship was underwater when it happened," Joanne told Finn. "Must have shielded them from the effects of the reversal."

Zhou was staring at Joanne like she'd suddenly sprouted three heads.

"The Earth's magnetic field flipped," Finn explained. "Happens every so often in nature, but never all at once, not like this, and it did something to people's minds. Wiped them clean. Turned them into animals."

Zhou was nodding. "Wipers, I like that. How'd you know about the magnetic reversal?"

"Long story. The lights in the sky. They're mostly gone now, but that was our first clue. Some of us, like Joanne and me, were only partly affected. Which is why we're here, to put some of those pieces back together."

"I see, well, for your sake, I hope none of those pieces are west of here."

"Why do you say that?" Joanne asked him.

"Because every nuclear power plant in the country's in full meltdown right now. A big part of the reason we've been heading east. Based on the prevailing winds, there are only a few safe zones left in the country. One of those is Salt Lake City."

Finn was stunned. Pressed with the more immediate needs for survival on a daily basis, nuclear power plants spewing out deadly radiation hadn't been on his radar at all. Hell, it hadn't been on anyone's radar.

"I just sent a Humvee with two of my men up that way on a reconnaissance mission, and they haven't reported back in more than 24 hours. How familiar are you folks with the threat level in that area?"

Finn felt a sinking feeling in the pit of his stomach. If Zhou's men hadn't reported back yet, that meant they'd probably crossed paths with Alvarez.

Dana

"What are you doing?"

Dana turned, startled. It was her father, Richard, standing in the doorway. They were in the room Dana used as a coroner's office. Nurse Kim was helping her lay some clothes on the examining table.

"Give us a moment would you, Kim?" Dana asked.

Kim nodded and left.

The room itself wasn't much more than a cubby hole in the compound basement, but it was one that had seen quite a bit of usage. This was where Larry said he'd seen Lou's wife, Patty Mae, tied to a chair, being brainwashed. When Dana first found the body, it appeared to be a drowning, although the woman's lungs didn't have water in them. Larry had professed his innocence, and at the time she'd believed him. But after hearing Romeo's side of things, that perhaps Larry had been the one behind the brainwashing, well, she realized then that the investigation was going to be reopened.

Dana nudged the box containing the things found on Patty Mae's body.

"Lou's wife didn't accidently drown in the river," she said and paused. "Anyway, it's complicated."

"I'll bet it is. I've been talking to some of the fellas, and most of 'em aren't too happy with Larry declaring himself king."

"He's done a lot for this place, Dad. I'm scared to think what might have happened if All Father hadn't passed away."

Richard laughed sardonically. "I remember where Larry was when we were attacked by Jeffereys and his slavers. He was trying to hand them All Father to save his own skin. Don't think I didn't see it clear as day."

"Keep your voice down."

But this only made her father grow louder. "Keep my voice down? Is this where we're heading, Dana, Nazi Germany? Watch what you say, or the Gestapo's gonna knock down your door?."

"No, that's not what I'm saying. Larry's done a lot to keep us safe, and I wouldn't' want anyone to think I was talking behind his back."

"The only person I know who prevented Rainbowland or whatever the hell they're calling it these days from being burned to the ground was you, Dana."

"Oh, come on, Dad."

"No, I'm dead serious. You shot those bastards and stopped 'em from killing us all."

71

"I did what anyone else woulda done."

"Anyone but Larry," he shot back.

Maybe he had a point. Dana couldn't deny those thoughts hadn't crossed her mind. But did it matter if Larry did some underhanded things? Where would they be without him? More importantly, how many of these people were willing to make the cold, calculated decisions necessary to ensure the continued safety of the group?

"There's no need for New Jamestown to be a totalitarian regime led by a man who's shown he's only interested in saving his own skin. We haven't seen any new survivors show up for over a month. Besides, with less than 200 people living here, we could vote on important policies and projects, just like the Greeks did in the Agora thousands of years ago."

Great, now he was quoting the Discovery Channel. "Listen, Dad, I've got a lot of work to do." Dana paused. "Hey, shouldn't you be on work detail?"

"My back hurts."

The alarm on her face was immediate. "You heard Larry, you know what happens to those who don't carry their load. Do you wanna be banished?"

"I'm too old to be worked into the ground. If anyone asks, I'll say I was helping you."

He was walking a fine line that could get them both in trouble, but he could be such a stubborn bastard sometimes, her mother used to say he could argue with a wall and win.

"What are we looking for?" he asked, glancing over her shoulder.

"I'm not sure," she said, "But I'm hoping I'll know it when I see it."

She removed all that remained of Patty's Mae's possessions: A pair of white Reebok sneakers; jeans that were nearly shredded; a black T-shirt; three dollars in quarters; and the straightjacket they found by the river. "This is everything."

Her father looked down at the items. "Not much to go on."

"Besides a few superficial wounds, there wasn't anything I could see that woulda led to a cause of death."

"Given that neither of us are trained medical examiners," he said, picking up her black T-shirt and examining it, "I don't have much faith we'll find a whole lot."

"Hard to imagine anyone being able to throw a screaming, struggling woman into the river without being noticed." That's when Dana saw her father's nose tweak. "What is it?"

"I don't know." He held the shirt a few inches from his face. "I smell almonds."

"What?" She took Patty Mae's shirt and smelled it. "You're right."

And then suddenly, it clicked. Only one thing smelled like almonds and had the power to kill. Cyanide.

The odor of which only 50 percent of the population was able to detect.

She told her father, and almost at once he grabbed the shirt from his daughter's hands and tossed it back into the box as though it were covered with smallpox.

"Maybe we should leave this alone," he told her.

"Five minutes ago you were cursing Larry out, and now you're saying we should ignore a murder."

Richard grew quiet. Then: "Who here would have access to cyanide?"

"I'm not sure, but I need to talk to Timothy. He was All Father's number two. If anyone knows, it'll be him."

Larry

Walking among the workers, Larry could see the wall at the back of the compound was coming along nicely. Newly felled logs were being dragged toward the workspace by an old tractor they'd found in a nearby farm. A handful of cult members and citizens armed with rifles were spread out among the workers, keeping an eye out for Wipers. It wouldn't be long now before the entire enclosure was completely sealed and the few remaining guard towers were erected. A carpenter from South Dakota named Ralph Muir was the project foreman and the man tasked with ensuring Larry's vision for New Jamestown's defenses took shape. Once the wall was complete, the outer defenses would begin. A dry moat filled with sharpened stakes, the ground around the compound littered with mantraps. The trick, Larry had learned, wasn't to make the colony impregnable. It was to direct your enemy into predetermined kill zones. What looked like a way in, would only lead to death. A smaller gate at the back wall along with a dirt bridge over the moat would do just fine. Encouraging the Wipers to bunch up along a narrow causeway before filling them with lead.

Ralph was studying a plan laid out on a table. The sky overhead was filling with rainclouds, the wind picking up, and Ralph had to place rocks on each corner so the sheet wouldn't fly away.

"When will my wall be finished?" Larry asked impatiently, eyeing a worker sitting down and drinking a ladle of water, beads of sweat rolling down his face.

"I'll need at least a week."

"A week? I need this done in the next couple of days. We still haven't begun the outer defenses."

"Yes, I know." Ralph was speaking softly, but Larry could hear the man's temper beginning to rise. "They don't have enough energy, Larry, not without food."

"I'm working on that. I can't start planting crops till this wall is done, you get me? I plant it out there, and Wipers'll come in the night and snatch it."

"Yeah, I get you. But I've already got nearly 20 percent of my labor force on bed rest, suffering from exhaustion. It might help to inspire them if you … " Ralph stopped short.

"What?" Larry asked. "What would inspire them? Music? Is that what you were going to say, 'cause I can get some old speakers set up and send a scavenging party to find a stereo – "

"No, not music." Ralph was fixing one of the rocks back in place. "It might inspire the workers to dig down deep if you were out here working alongside them."

"Oh," Larry said. "That's a great idea, but my administrative duties are far too demanding. I just don't have the time."

Ralph nodded, like he knew Larry would have his reasons. Men like Larry weren't put on this Earth to toil around in the mud, and Ralph should know better than to even put him on the spot like that. "You have two days," he told his foreman. "See that it gets done."

Larry was about to head back to his office for a mojito and a bite to eat when he saw Timothy coming his way. The old codger didn't look happy.

This is all I need right now.

Larry put on his best PR smile.

"We need to talk," Timothy said.

"I know what you're going to say."

"Damn right you know. You broke your word, Larry. You said you'd step down when the colony was safe, and you lied."

"Is the colony safe yet, Timothy? I don't think so. The wall isn't finished. The rest of the guard towers need to be erected – "

Timothy's eyes dazzled with anger. "Don't play stupid with me, you know perfectly well what I'm talking about. All Father left me in charge, not you. You had a vision to get us back on track, and I let you realize that vision, but you've gone too far. Declaring yourself king, Larry. For God's sake, what the hell were you thinking?"

Larry cleared his throat and glanced around him. Ralph along with a handful of workers had stopped to stare. "Don't think for a second, Timothy, that I don't know why you put me in charge. I'm the kinda guy who gets things done. You're the kinda guy who leads from behind. I think you're really pissed off because deep down you know you need me, but I don't need you."

"In this new world, Larry, if a man doesn't have his word, what does he have?"

"I'm keeping people alive, that's what I'm doing."

Timothy was already walking away. "Are you Larry? Are you really, 'cause what I see is a bunch of people who are starving to death."

Larry watched his old ally storm off, a violent tangle of emotions boiling within him. The lack of security had been the key that had allowed Larry to wrest control of Rainbowland out from All Father's fingers, and now it seemed as though the lack of food might be what tore it from his own grasp. This was a serious problem. One he needed to fix soon 'cause if Timothy got his way, then Larry's days of living on easy street would soon be over.

Carole

Without a watch, Carole couldn't tell for sure how long Russell and Callahan had been gone. She only knew it was starting to feel like an eternity. They'd left to sneak out and find a car. A risky maneuver during the day, no doubt, but speeding through darkened streets at night with Wipers on your tail was far riskier. Those very thoughts were swirling through Carole's weary mind when she spotted Holly's 12-year-old daughter, Tamara, coming toward her with a face the color of starched linen. Even though she was at least four years younger than Nikki, Carole couldn't help but feel protective of the girl.

"What is it, Honey?" she asked.

"There's a man in the vent."

Carole's senses fired all at once. "A man in the – ?"

"Yes, I can hear him moving inside."

Carole snapped her fingers to get Holly's attention. "We have to leave, right away." She looked down at Tamara, whose eyes were starting to swell with frightened tears. "We're gonna be fine, Honey. You stay with your mother and help her get everything ready."

"What about you?" she asked.

"I'm just going to take a quick look is all, I'll be right back." Carole and Holly shared a furtive look, and the fear that passed between the two women was palpable. "I'll be right back."

The noises coming from the vents Tamara had mentioned could only mean one thing. The Wipers had found the loose grate in the hotel's lobby and were coming in after them. The smart thing to do was leave the boiler room altogether and head topside, except Carole had to make sure the folding ladder leading up to the vent wasn't there or the Wipers would be on them in a flash. The 20-foot drop from the hole in the vent might not kill them, but it sure as hell would break their legs.

Carole was turning the corner, walking on the balls of her feet to remain as silent as possible when a jolt of terror shot through every nerve ending in her body. A Wiper was climbing out of the vent, his feet perched on the top of the ladder. She could hear others behind him.

The choice was suddenly clear, turn and run or fight. The urge to run was almost blinding. An impulse that in her old life, as the wife and home maker, she might have given in to, but to run here and now meant the certain death of everyone in the boiler room. The Wiper's legs were on the second rung and struggling to find the third when she charged. She drew on the same inner strength she'd used to battle the Mohawked woman in the pits, growling like a wild animal. The Wiper on the ladder, head shaved except for a long pony tail of fire-red hair, had just enough time to utter what was probably a curse in mangled English before Carole slammed into the folding ladder, sending it toppling over. The Wiper landed with a crunch and howls of pain as he reached out with both hands to break his fall. Another Wiper stuck his head through the vent's opening and shrieked maniacally. That's when Carole took off running. It was only a matter of seconds before they'd find a way to get down.

She reached the others, and the look of panic on their faces was unmistakable. They'd heard the commotion and the screams and knew they would need to run for their lives.

"Everyone get top side," Carole shouted. They were little more than a group of women and children without a single firearm between them. Holly pulled the cable to raise the steel plate, and the children rushed through the hole. The last one to pass was Carole, and she caught the distinct sound of at least two Wipers jumping down to more screams of pain. Soon, the others would use the wounded to cushion their fall, and then there'd be no stopping them. Sliding through the hole, Carole pulled the cable and watched the metal plate fall into place with a loud clang, all the time wondering how long it would take them to figure out how to get it opened. The only other barrier was the one leading into the 7-Eleven, and Carole had to assume that location had already been compromised. That meant the safest way out was through the lingerie store's stockroom. She could only hope for all their sakes that Russell and Callahan would have the trucks ready.

"The records you're looking for are probably in the warden's office," Zhou said. "But you shouldn't be snooping around on your own without an armed escort." He pointed to a broad-shouldered black sailor standing next to him, an M-4 slung over his shoulder. "This is Foster, sonar operator extraordinaire and one of the worst Texas Hold'Em players in the fleet."

Foster cracked a toothy smile. "Still managed to bleed you once or twice, Sir."

"Hey, everyone gets lucky."

Finn was still stuck on something Zhou had said moments ago. "Armed escort. I thought you had this place locked down tight?"

"We do," Zhou told him. "Most of it, but you shoulda seen the state of things when we arrived. We figure that once the grid went dark and the power shut off for good, most of these cell doors opened automatically. What we saw when we arrived woulda turned your hair white. Thank God most of the damage had already been done. Men eating one another. The smell of dead bodies and human waste. Was like walking into an abandoned zoo where the animals were all mixed together and left to their own devices."

Finn wasn't all that surprised. He'd seen it before countless times. Without food, the Wipers inside had done what their brothers and sisters on the outside had done in order to survive, most of which was enough to turn the average man's stomach. He also empathized with the Commander's aims: to re-establish contact with what was left of the government. 'Course, Finn didn't have the heart to tell Zhou he was probably chasing a lost cause, that most of the people who made up the government were either dead or running through the streets, killing one another. Finn also hadn't come right out and told him they were once prisoners. He liked Zhou well enough, but didn't see the logic in tempting the commander with the idea of throwing them back behind bars.

"But some of the Wipers must have escaped because three of my men have gone missing, and all that was left were pools of blood. Musta searched this entire place, top to bottom, half a dozen times. Just keep an eye out. And if you see a piece of cheese on the ground, don't pick it up. It's probably a trap." Zhou was smiling, but Finn could see Joanne didn't share the commander's macabre sense of humor.

Finn and Joanne, along with their escort, Foster, left at once.

The warden's office was on the top floor of the prison, and that meant going through cell blocks D to A, in that order. But first, it meant going through the showers.

"I don't even wanna tell you what we found in here," Foster told them, his arms rippling with slabs of muscle. He was swinging his flashlight back and forth, each time illuminating tile walls caked with dark blood.

"Yes, better that you don't," Joanne said, feeling her gag reflex kick in.

"We already took the bodies out and burnt those. But you folks are better off plugging your noses."

Finn had no interest in taking in the gore. His light was aimed squarely ahead. Before they'd left, he'd duct taped the flashlight Zhou had given him to the barrel of his rifle. That way, he could keep both hands on his weapon at all times.

Positioned under one of the shower heads was a plastic bucket filled to the brim with yellow water. A single drop tumbled from the shower head and landed with a deafening echo.

"Thirsty, anyone?" Joanne offered with a wry grin.

Foster glared down at it, his weapon aimed at the object as though it might leap up and attack them. "That's not ours," he whispered. "We tapped an aquifer underneath the prison and been using that for drinking water."

"It sure as hell belongs to someone," Finn said. "And there isn't any blood in it so I can only assume it got here after all the carnage took place."

Wipers was the thought in everyone's head, although no one came right and said so. They didn't need to, Finn knew. They were sharing the prison. Zhou had said so himself. He'd even lost three men and conducted multiple searches. And that told Finn that, like most of the Wipers he'd come across, these guys were adapting to their environment.

When they finally cleared the showers, Joanne let out a deep sigh. Slowly, they padded their way up through cell blocks D, C, and B. No matter how many stairs they climbed, the horrible smells stayed with them the entire time, and even Finn found himself fighting for every breath. By the time they reached cell block A, they'd seen plenty of signs the area was well trodden. Inside one of the open cells was a set of towels, presumably taken from the showers. They'd been shaped into a kind of giant rat's nest. Even more surprising, the cell had paintings on the wall, albeit drawn in blood. Most of them were handprints, but others were so strange they likely made no sense to anyone other than their creator.

A series of open gates led from cell block A toward the prison's administrative wing. One door already ajar had a sign stencilled in bright red letters: *Only authorized personnel beyond this point. All others may be shot.*

Finn was about to walk through when Foster shouted for him to stop. Glancing down, Finn saw that his right foot was nudging the edge of a trip wire. Slowly, he backed away. Taking position beside the door frame, Foster used the butt of his rifle to trigger the trap. The sound of snapping metal was loud as a sledgehammer swung from the ceiling. Another step and it might have shattered his rib cage.

"Asymmetric warfare," Foster said with a smile. "That motherfucker woulda killed your ass dead."

Finn clapped him on the back. "Wouldn't be the first time."

They stepped past the sledge hammer dangling limply now in the doorway and entered the admin offices. Small rooms on either side furnished with desks and computers; exactly the sorts of things you'd expect to see among paper pushers.

And then there were the other things you didn't normally see. Bloody hand prints. Pools of dried bodily fluids where corpses had begun to break down. None of this was the sort of thing you ever got used to. At the end of the hall was an oak door with a brass name plate:

Gordon Sinclair.

And beneath that:

Warden

Joanne tapped the shiny name plate with her index finger. "Now there's one guy who seriously loved his job." She was about to push her way inside before Finn stopped her.

"Not yet. Not until we know what's in there."

"Yes," Foster said. "Or who."

Dana

The trailer was quiet when Dana entered. Mountains of canvas tent flaps and stacks of plastic chairs made it hard to see if Romeo were still here. There was no reason he shouldn't be. She'd left him cuffed to a seat at the back. The chances of him making a break for it were pretty much slim to none, especially since going beyond New Jamestown's walls meant almost certain death.

When she called his name, the answer that came from the back of the trailer wasn't at all what she'd been expecting.

Destruction is worldwide. Safety and a fresh start awaits you. Forty-one degrees, 14 minutes, 42 seconds north ... 111 degrees, 93 minutes, 0 seconds west.

She recognized it as the recording she'd heard over the short wave. The one that led her to the compound.

Drawing her SIG, Dana moved cautiously past piles of folded canvas to the source of the noise. That was when she found Romeo, sitting at the table, working an old style tape recorder.

"Whoa, down girl," he said, eyeing the gun in her hand. "It's just me."

She looked down at his wrists. "Where are your handcuffs?"

He pointed to the metal rail next to him where a single cuff was still attached. "It was chafing," he said, showing off the red ring around his wrist as if to prove his point. "'Sides, where am I gonna go?"

Dana tossed a handful of crackers and half can of tuna on the table. "I was on my way to speak with Timothy and thought I'd check in on you. I'm glad now that I did. You're one slippery fish, you know that?"

He didn't seem to be listening. "You should see all the shit they got in here." He played the tape again, and Dana shook her head.

"I've heard it before."

"Yeah, but did you ever ask yourself who made it?"

The voice on the recording sounded an awful lot like All Father, but the sound wasn't great, and every time she started to feel sure, an image of his son, Simon, would pop into her head. "It's hard to tell."

"Sure is," Romeo said. "'Cept, that isn't the half of it." He flipped the tape over and pressed play. The voice on this side was even harder to make out, but sounded similar.

"The reading Abigail has provided about the Chosen One's abilities is clear and unambiguous. A male and a female, one useless without the other. Drawing them here, that is the difficult part. Which is why I've made this tape to broadcast in all directions. Abigail had said they would be out there. Born anew from The Shift. And when they arrive, the next stage of our evolution will begin."

The tape clicked off and Romeo stared up at her. "Crazy shit, eh?"

"Is there more?" she asked.

"Nada. But that signal was what brought me here, too. Brought nearly everyone, I'd say. They're waiting for a couple of saviors to show up. Could be me, you know. Just saying."

Dana was deep in thought. "I doubt that very much."

Romeo flexed his biceps. "Check these guns out. They got golden child written all over 'em. But haters gonna hate, right?"

She wanted to laugh. Romeo was hamming it up, but all she could think about right now was Lou's wife, strapped to that chair. Was she being brainwashed, as Larry had assumed? Or were they looking for their savior? The voice on the other side of that tape was muffled, but could whoever had made it have also tortured and killed Patty Mae? And Abigail? Dana took the recorder from him. "You find anything else?" she asked.

"Think I've been sitting here meditating like one of those Rainbowites? 'Course, I have." He reached behind him and produced a role of 8mm film and held it up to the light. "Found this on an old projector trashed in the corner. Bunch of creepy psychedelic-type stuff. I mean really out there. Back before Larry decided he didn't need me no more, he mentioned finding Lou's wife watching some whacked-out homemade movie."

Dana took the film, too, and started to leave.

"Hey, what the hell am I supposed to do now?"

She was reaching for the door, getting ready to pick Timothy's brain. "Try meditating."

•••

Dana found Timothy on the compound roof, with a cult member making repairs to the wiring that led from the windmill to the battery bank downstairs. The charge on the batteries wasn't nearly as high as it normally was, and Timothy suspected rats had been gnawing at the wires.

Timothy wiped the sweat from his forehead with a rag, which he shoved into his back pocket. He didn't look at all happy, and Dana guessed it had everything to do with his angry altercation with Larry.

"I'm assuming you're not here to offer your help," he said.

Dana gritted her teeth at the biting comment. "I wish I could, but it's tough to maintain order in New Jamestown on a part-time basis."

"No doubt. Who would we have then to wield the whip Larry's too cowardly to use himself?"

"I need to ask you some things," she said, tiring of this little game.

"Certainly." Timothy nodded to the cult member. "Give us a moment, would you?" The man rose and went through the door that led from the roof back into the compound.

"So, you haven't come to commiserate about our new dictator then."

Chuckling, Dana shook her head that she hadn't. "I need to ask you about cyanide."

Timothy looked shocked. "Cyanide?

"Any idea who in the colony would have access to it?"

"Haven't the faintest. We have no use for it."

"Well, we think it may have been used to murder someone."

"You're kidding me." Genuine shock and concern filled his gaunt features. "Who?"

"Patty Mae."

"Lou's wife," Timothy said, and a look flashed across his face, but Dana wasn't sure what it meant.

"Her body, you'll remember, was found floating in the river."

"Oh her, yes," Timothy said. "A terrible thing. But I thought she drowned."

Dana watched as he went back to stripping the ends of the wires and attaching the two ends together. "It was made to look like she drowned. But maybe there's something else you can help me with." She removed the recorder from the pack she was wearing and played the tape. Timothy listened, his face a stoic mask.

"Any idea who's voice that could be?"

"I haven't the foggiest idea."

"There's something else on the tape, too. Something about broadcasting the signal to draw in people with special ... abilities. That mean anything to you?"

Timothy shook his head, although he didn't seem nearly as composed as a moment ago.

"I ask 'cause I'd be willing to bet whoever made this tape tortured and killed Patty Mae. Perhaps others as well."

The cult member came back just then.

"I wish I could help you more," Timothy said, "but as you can see, we're extremely busy."

"So, just for the record, did you ever have any contact with Patty Mae before her death?"

"Never saw the woman before."

84

"Thanks, Timothy," Dana said and left.

There wasn't any point asking him about the 8mm film Romeo had found. She'd approached him as an expert and perhaps a witness, but she couldn't understand why he'd fed her one baldfaced lie after another. She'd already learned from Larry, and then Romeo, that Timothy knew all about Patty Mae's brainwashing – or whatever her confinement had been about – and now here he was playing dumb. Maybe he wasn't a witness at all, Dana thought. Maybe he was a suspect.

Carole

All of them were huddled in the stockroom, waiting frantically for a sign from either Callahan or Russell. The peephole on the back door could swivel, but even so, all Carole could see was an empty alleyway. To make matters worse, the doors that led from the showroom were the swinging kind that didn't latch shut. Probably a great convenience for employees shuffling back and forth with racks of clothing, but right now it left them with no real way of holding the Wipers at bay once they managed to break through.

All that stood between them and death was the metal plate covering the hole in the wall, and that was being held in place by a single latch. Once they figured out the mechanism and stopped pounding on it as Carole could hear them doing now, their little group would be in dire straights indeed.

"What if they don't come?" Holly asked, her face a mask of fear. She was searching around for something she could use as a weapon, without having much luck.

"They'll come." Carole said. "In the meantime, we need to block these push doors with something. A length of industrial shelving hugged the wall next to the door. If they could slide it over, it might be enough to slow the Wipers down.

"Everyone, grab hold of it," Dana told them. They did as she said, some pushing, others pulling. It moved a foot before stopping.

"Come on, keep at it, Girls, don't give up."

Outside, the pounding had stopped, which meant the Wipers were likely trying something different. Time was running out. More heaving, and the giant shelf gave another foot. A handful more and it would be in place. The kids' faces were red, and Carole knew that if Russell and Callahan were here helping, it would already be done. A moment later, they'd managed to cover the first door flap when Carole heard the sound of sliding metal. The Wipers had found the latch and were raising the plate. They'd be here any minute.

"One last push, girls," Carole called out. "Dig deep." The veins in their foreheads were popping from the strain. Slowly, the shelf inched into place just as the Wipers pushed on the stockroom doors. They stopped with a bang and then another as the brutes tried to shove their way inside. No doubt, the Wipers were probably on the other side wondering what was blocking their way in. Carole rushed to the back door and put her eye to the peephole. Still no sign of the men.

"We might need to make a run for it," she told Holly, who didn't look happy at all with Carole's suggestion. Running outside with young children wasn't the smartest idea.

More banging, and now a Wiper had managed to squeeze his face in the crack. The little girls screamed. A steel rod used as a floor bolt to lock the back door rested in the corner. Something Holly must have missed in her search. Carole took it and thrust the end of the rod toward the man's face. At the last second, he moved away, and she pulled back. But this only made the girls scream louder, egging on the Wipers outside.

"We can't stay here," Holly cried, her daughter, Tamara, clutching her leg in terror. The two women exchanged a knowing glance that spoke of the untold horrors that awaited them outside. What was worse, dying in here like a cat stuck in a hole or taking your changes out there? Carole got Jessica's attention and then motioned toward the back door. The girl took a final look through the peephole before pressing the push bar. Suddenly, the room was flooded with light from outside, and one by one they all ran from the stockroom.

Almost at once, Carole caught the sound of automatic gunfire to the right of their location, which made going left, away from the fighting, a no-brainer. Carole, Holly, and Jessica all took one kid by the hand and led them through the alley toward East 400 Street. They were nearly there when a bizarre sight came lumbering around the corner. Carole blinked twice to make sure she wasn't dreaming. It was an ice cream truck, complete with a delicious- looking soft vanilla cone on the roof, and it was only then that she saw that it was Russell behind the wheel. He slammed the breaks and waved them over, like a getaway driver during a bank heist.

"We gotta go."

Carole went around back and opened the double doors. She was helping to load the children in when Russell called out. "Wipers straight ahead." They were coming out of the Victoria's Secret. Must have finally figured out they could pull the stockroom doors open and slide between the shelves.

Her pulse was pounding something fierce now as she helped to load all the kids onboard. She barely had time to climb on herself and shut the doors before Russell put the truck in reverse and floored it.

"Where's Callahan?" she called out, holding on to what she could.

"We got separated, and I haven't seen him since."

Suddenly, the sound of the gun battle made sense. Callahan was likely pinned down in the streets. "We can't just leave him." She was right, and Russell knew it. He cursed, almost in acquiescence, and slammed on the breaks. The Wipers were still chasing them fruitlessly down the alley when Russell popped it into drive, flicked on the ice cream jingle by hitting a switch on the dashboard, and punched the gas. A few of them managed to scatter out of the way before the truck came barreling through. But most weren't so lucky, and Holly clamped her hands over Tamara's ears so she wouldn't have to hear the sounds of their bodies being hit and then dragged under the tires.

Straight ahead was the spot where the Humvee had crashed last night, except the vehicle was no longer there. The sound of firing intensified as they drew near, and Russell said, "I should have my head examined for doing this." Spinning the wheel, he skidded the ice cream truck into the street. Up ahead, a group of Wipers was firing at an unknown target. A target that was probably Callahan.

The Wipers were weaving between the abandoned cars when they must have heard the ice cream truck barreling down on them, accompanied by a twisted child's song promising sweet goodness.

"Everyone, get down," Russell shouted.

Three raised their weapons to fire and nearly got a shot off before the truck slammed into them with a meaty crunch.
"Carole, be ready to open those back doors on my count."

The few remaining Wipers fired as they sped past. A handful of nickel sized holes appeared in a line across the back door. If Carole had still been standing she would have been dead. The truck lurched to a full stop, and Russell told her "Now!"

Carole swung open the doors, and there was Callahan, darting out from cover toward them. Just then, not 15 yards away, a Wiper took aim and fired. Carol shouted to warn him, but the bullet went wide. That was when she felt something strike her in the gut with the force of a hammer blow. Callahan spun when he saw what had happened and dropped the Wiper with two well-placed shots.

The next thing Carole knew she was on the floor of the truck, Holly holding her from behind, asking if she was hurt. Blood starting to ooze out between Carole's fingers.

Climbing on a second later, Callahan closed the doors and told Russell to go.

They sped away, hearing sounds of gunfire chasing them down the street.

The pain in Carole's belly was throbbing now, and Callahan opened a drawer filled with napkins and began applying pressure to the wound. Carole gritted her teeth and fought to stay awake.

You gave birth to two kids. This should be a cake walk.

The last thing she remembered was telling him the way to Rainbowland, her voice struggling to rise above a whisper, Callahan's young face hovering, reassuring her that everything would be just fine.

Finn

The Warden's office wasn't booby-trapped and showed no apparent signs of life. Signs of death, on the other hand, were in abundance. Perhaps the most disturbing thing wasn't the dried and splattered blood, nor the skeleton lying on the ground, wearing a dark-blue suit. Both of those Finn could live with. The strips torn off the leather couch, which sat beneath a wide bay window. Strips as though someone had been scratching at it and tearing at the stitching, that's what sent a chill rolling up his spine.

"He went crazy," Joanne said, her eyes jumping between the man and the leather couch.

"Not crazy," Finn replied. "He was trapped in his office after The Shift hit and slowly starved to death.

"So, he ate his sofa?" Foster asked, his face all squished up.

"Uh huh. Least he didn't try and eat himself."

Joanne around fruitlessly for something to cover him with. "Poor man."

On the warden's desk was a computer, and Finn knew he was going to have the same problem here he'd had at Tevatron's offices in Vegas. No power to turn it on.

Foster must have noticed Finn's disappointment. "Commander Zhou had the engineers rig up an old generator they found by the maintenance area. If you're willing to hump that computer all the way back, we may be able to get it powered up."

"Not a bad idea," Joanne said, and Finn was becoming more certain she was eager to simply get the hell out of here.

"We'll do that, but there's something else I'm looking for." Finn opened a filing cabinet by the desk and began leafing through folders. Certain kinds of sensitive documents don't normally get sent around via e-mail.

Joanne was right there beside him, peering over his shoulder, and something about the way she smelled made Finn's pulse begin to quicken. Didn't seem to matter that she was as dirty as the rest of them, somehow she managed to smell of vanilla.

Fighting to keep his mind focused, Finn was flipping past files with convict names and prisons when Joanne reached in and plucked a folder out. It was labelled: *The Florence McClure Women's Correctional Center in Las Vegas.*

"You recognize it?"

"No, but I also can't imagine the both of us would have been kept at the same prison."

"Good point." Finn finished that drawer and moved onto the next.

Foster was beginning to pace back and forth. "We really should hurry up. Staying in one place for more than a few minutes ain't a great idea."

"I think I got something here," Joanne said, holding up a sheet of paper. "It's a transfer order from Florence Mclure in Vegas to Tevatron's research facility in the desert."

Finn looked it over, running his finger down a list of women's names. "Maybe they're potential candidates, going for interviews."

"Looks like it," she said.

His finger stopped halfway down. Joanne Blackwood. "Getting hotter."

"Yes, you are," she said, and Finn felt the blush rise up his neck and into his face.

"Project Arrow," she said pointing to the letter head. "What's that?"

"Long story. I'll explain on the way home."

"You folks find what you were looking for?" Foster asked, throwing a quick glance into the hallway.

"Nearly," Finn told him, returning to the filing cabinet's middle drawer. He was almost at the end of the pile when he saw the folder he'd been expecting. This one also read Project Arrow. He laid it out on the desk and opened it up. The first page was a list a lot like the one Joanne had found, except this one had a list of men. Bud or Benjamin wasn't there. But Finn's name was, right at the top of the list. These were the male candidates remaining after the first round of cuts had been made. Also in the folder was a glossy Tevatron handout where they discussed the projects goals of treating PTSD and rehabilitating criminals. That part he'd already seen down in the underground lab, but the newspaper clipping he saw next was something entirely new. An exposé on public sector companies set up as covers for secret government black projects. The article talked about a whistleblower who leaked details of a secret project code named Arrow designed to test the effects of ultra high-powered magnets on human subjects. The goal was weaponization and mind control. They'd hidden funding for the project within the government's black budget and earmarked it for $10 billion a year.

"You reading this?" Finn asked.

Joanne took the clipping and was scanning through it when Finn noticed a tiny scrap of paper seesaw to the floor. He grabbed it and read it over twice, just to be sure his eyes weren't deceiving him.

Please ensure the following: Subject Francis Inn must never be informed his wife is a part of Project Arrow. Below that was his wife's name:
Joanne Blackwood.

Larry

The note on his desk was the first thing Larry noticed when he entered his office. Folded over twice in just the sort of style he remembered from his old school days as a teenager. The sweet smell of Gail Patterson, the dark-haired girl who sat next to him in 11th grade English class. She'd passed him a note. One Larry hoped contained passages professing her undying love for him. Instead, it read:

Can I copy your homework?

'Course, he'd let her, and it was after many other favors Larry had done for Gail that she started fucking Johnathan Baker, the school's track star.

See what happens to nice guys? You pussy shit! His father had shouted, berating him for over an hour.

Shaking off the memory, Larry closed his office door, went to his desk, and opened the note. He glared down at the words he saw written there with confusion and mounting horror.

"Did you know that Romeo is still in New Jamestown?"

The penmanship was extremely poor, as if someone were trying to mask their true identity. Larry let the note fall from his hands. He'd given Dana explicit instructions to banish Romeo from the compound as soon as possible. If this note were true, it meant she'd disobeyed a direct order. But why would she do that? Larry knew Romeo had incriminating information on him. That he'd asked the kid to crack the safe so he could steal the cult's scriptures. That'd he'd used what he found there to help take All Father down. Surely, she didn't think he'd killed the old man. Not that the thought hadn't crossed his mind. He remembered hearing the news, and being as shocked as everyone else. Well, maybe elated.

He would need to talk to Dana about Romeo and see if he could gauge from her reaction to his questions whether she was still trustworthy. Once that was settled, he would try and find out who had gotten in here and left this note. And why that dumbass Charlie hadn't stopped them.

But before any of that, Larry would attend to the rumbling in his belly. He stalked over to the cabinet trying to decide between chunky beef stew or canned salmon. When the door to his private stash swung open, all the blood suddenly drained from his face.

His food was gone

All of it. Every single last can, and now the feeling of hunger and confusion he'd been feeling over the strange note was being shoved aside by white-hot anger.

"CHARLIE!" he shouted to the guard outside. In came Charlie. And it was clear by the deep tremble in Larry's voice that something was terribly wrong. The concern showed on the young man's face as he entered. "What is it, Sir?"

"Who did you let in here while I was away?" Larry barked.

"No one. I mean, no one that I know of, Sir. But I'm only posted outside when you're present."

"Yeah, well now you're gonna stand there all fucking day long 'cause someone's been in here and gone through my things."

"Was something taken?"

"Yes, you moron. Something was taken. Just get back out there and do your goddamned job."

Charlie looked like a scolded puppy as he pulled the door closed behind him. And that got Larry wondering. Had leaving that note and snatching Larry's food been the intruder's only goal? A tangle of frantic thoughts was running through his head when his eyes settled over the locked drawer. The one in his desk where he kept All Father's diary and Abigail's channeled scriptures. He had to blink twice before his mind fully digested what he was seeing. The drawer wasn't fully closed. Larry wrenched it open and cursed as loudly as his lungs would allow. Just then the door swung open. Standing there slack jawed was another cult member.

"What is it now, goddammit?"

"We've got a problem."

Finn

They were halfway across cell block C when they heard the noise. Foster out front, Finn and Joanne close behind. All three of them turned at once. It sounded to Finn's ears as though someone was running a baton along the cell doors somewhere in D block above them.

Foster had his weapon at the ready, his finger not quite on the trigger, but resting alongside it. They stood there for a moment, frozen in place as the sound slowly drew closer.

"Think they know we're here?" Joanne asked, fear cloying her every pore.

Finn gave a short nod. "Maybe, but I'm not gonna stick around to find out."

Foster agreed, and all of them quickened their pace just a little more. Then the sound of clanging against cell doors intensified, as though they were also speeding, and now Finn was sure whoever that was knew where they were.

Every bone in his body begged for them to break into a dead run. He'd been cornered by Wipers before and knew perfectly well what they were capable of. Although a mad dash could easily turn an ordered retreat into a chaotic run for your life.

Unshouldering his .30-06 rifle, Finn used the bolt to load a round into the chamber. They were just coming to the end of cell block C and preparing to pass through the gated check point before descending into cell block B when Finn took a quick glance behind him. Three men in orange prison jumpsuits were standing at the end of the long hallway.

The animal-like way in which the men lurched toward them, each holding a curved piece of rebar, made it clear they weren't offering guided tours of the prison. No, these guys were Wipers, and Finn raised his rifle right as they broke into a run. He squeezed the trigger and the sound of the escaping round echoed violently. The Wipers dropped to the floor. One even dove into an empty cell, but either way it wouldn't have made a difference 'cause his shot went high. Finn turned to follow Foster and Joanne who were disappearing through the gateway on their way down the B block.

As he did so, a Wiper, rippling with muscle, who must have been lying in wait, came charging out from one of the cells, a crude homemade machete in hand. Finn swung the rifle around to fire, but the Wiper parried the blow, and the shot ricocheted off the wall. The rifle stock was just as good a weapon as any, and Finn buried it into the side of the

Wiper's face and then down on the hand holding the machete. The blade clanged to the ground.

In a few more seconds, the Wiper's buddies would catch up, and then Finn would be in real trouble. But the blow to the face hadn't knocked the Wiper out, and now the two of them were locked in hand-to-hand combat, Finn unable to use the rifle bolt to chamber another round. It was no better than a club, and this Wiper was holding onto it with everything he had. The wounds in his chest where Bud had shot him felt like hot daggers charring his insides. He wasn't in any state to go toe to toe with anyone, let alone with a prisoner who looked like he'd been preparing for a shot at Mr. Universe. It also didn't help that he had the warden's computer strapped to his back.

The right side of the Wiper's face was swollen and bleeding from where the stock of Finn's rifle had struck him, but the man was smiling, as though for him the pain was but an appetizer and Finn was the main course. That was when Finn caught a strange sight over the Wipers shoulder in the prison cell. Someone was emerging from under the lower bunk bed, as if crawling up from hell itself. An older man with a long white beard, and he, too, was dressed in orange, but his movements were slow and methodical, not crazed like the Wiper before him or the three others racing down the long C block hallway. The muscled Wiper had Finn pushed up against the wall, the length of his rifle at his neck, cutting off his air. He was going to choke Finn out. And the old guy with the beard, what would his role be in all this? Was he the one who liked to watch? Those were the jumbled thoughts coursing through Finn's oxygen-deprived brain when the old guy raised his hand. He was holding what looked like a hammer, but this one had a long curved spike at the end, and he swung it into the back of the Wiper's head. The sound was sharp and wet as Mr. Universe's knees buckled and his eyes rolled up in his skull before he collapsed onto the floor.

"Hurry," the old man said, pulling Finn into the cell and slamming the door right as the three Wipers arrived outside, out of breath and very pissed off. They were bashing the door with their weapons, hollering like mad, but even in his woozy state, Finn knew they weren't getting in.

The old man lifted the cot, revealing a hole just large enough for a man. It was dark down there, and Finn wasn't sure at all if he'd just been saved by one set of psychos to fall into the hands of another.

"If you wanna see your friends again, I suggest you climb in."

Larry

Following the cult member down the stairs, Larry wasn't sure how this shitpile of a day could get any worse. Dana, Lou, and Tanner were waiting for him in the compound's spacious kitchen. Directly behind them was an open pair of pantry doors. Standing there looking solemn was Dana, holding the Master padlock they used to keep it sealed at night.

"It's been cut," she said.

"How much did they take?" Larry asked, trying real hard to keep his cool.

Dana's answer was simple, but devastating. "Everything."

"Please tell me you know who did this, so we can string them up."

"We're working on it, Larry" Dana said. "But there's more. Whoever emptied the pantry also stole the seeds we were gonna plant along with the topsoil."

Larry couldn't believe what he was hearing. "I want you and every deputy you have to tear this place apart until you find the sonbitch who did this and recover what they stole."

Lou's eyes dropped to his feet. They were wet.

"What is it?"

"Well," Lou said. "I know you ain't gonna like this one bit, Mr. Larry, but we already found the seeds and the fertilizer. Least what I mean to say is we know what happened to 'em."

Dana was wringing her hands. "Someone dumped it into the river last night. Found the plastic bags washed up along the water's edge." She paused. "I just don't get who would wanna sabotage our food stocks, that's what we've been trying to figure out."

Larry didn't say a goddamned word. Not just yet, but he was pretty sure he knew who had done this.

A cult member raced in a moment later, panting for breath, and Larry hoped it wasn't more bad news.

"There's a group of people at the gates, and they're driving an ice cream truck."

Carole

A crowd had gathered around the ice cream truck as Russell pulled in. Callahan swung open the back doors and jumped down. Someone brought a stretcher from the medical tent, and Holly and Callahan helped get her onto it. Every breath Carole took was accompanied by stabbing pain. Breathing was one of those things you always took for granted, until bullets went and ripped your insides apart. Every searing breath she now took was a workout, as though she were trying to breathe in water. Carole heard a young girl cry out as her stretcher was lifted from the truck and she knew right away that it was Nikki. Her daughter appeared over her, fat tears streaming down her emaciated cheeks. Carole's heart surged at seeing her daughter, wondering on some perverse level whether she was hallucinating.

Everyone here looked so skinny. Even through the burning pain in Carole's abdomen, it was something she couldn't help but notice. She'd been gone so long from Rainbowland that the place she was seeing now – high walls and cult members armed to the teeth – might as well have been another camp altogether.

Looks more like a prison than a colony of survivors.

They brought her to the medical tent and transferred her to one of the cots. A nurse named Kim Grovesteader gave her a shot of morphine, and almost at once the pain faded from a shrill scream to a dull thud. Nikki remained by her side the entire time, holding her hand, even when the nurse told her it would be best if she gave her mother some room.

"I'm not going anywhere, Ma," Nikki told her, and Carole felt her heart nearly burst with joy. Others trickled into the tent. Lou, Dana, Tanner.

"Where's Finn?" Carole asked, her voice down to a whisper.

"Nevada," Dana replied, "but he'll be back soon."

"And Johnson?"

A question that made everyone look decidedly uneasy.

Dana put her hand over Nikki and Carole's. "You've been shot. Rest. There'll be plenty of time to fill you in on all the details later."

It was only after that the nurse was finally able to convince Nikki to wait outside. They needed to check Carole for other wounds and assess the severity of her situation. Carole watched her daughter rise and leave the medical tent, amazed and proud that in such a short time Nikki had blossomed from a troubled teenager and into a woman.

Nikki

It felt like an eternity before Kim finished with her mother. Nikki had waited right outside, pacing back and forth, the sky a beautiful pink and yellow with the setting sun. A sight she'd hoped was a positive omen. Ethan had stayed with her for a while, but the truth she hadn't been in the mood to talk or be comforted by anyone. All she wanted was to hear that her mother was going to be all right. Eventually, he seemed to get the message and left her alone. She'd helped to nurse Finn back to health during the month where he'd been in and out of consciousness, and she was prepared to nurse her mother for as long as it took.

Kim emerged from the medical tent and removed a pair of rubber gloves. Nikki tried desperately to search the expression on her face for a hopeful sign. "Will she be all right?"

"The bullet that hit your mother has caused a severe amount of damage."

"But will she be OK?"

"Her liver was hit, along with a kidney." Kim paused. "She's starting to show symptoms of septic shock. I'm not sure how to say this, Nikki, but it's only a question of time before she looses consciousness and passes away. I'm so sorry."

The words from that last part were coming in slow and distorted, as though nurse Kim had been shoved into slow motion. Her mother had been Nikki's reservoir of strength. There'd always been hope in Nikki's heart that she'd managed to find a place to hide after her truck was found abandoned by Finn and Lou near the hotel. Carole was waiting for a safe time to make the journey back, that was all, and in the end Nikki had been right. But this wasn't the way she'd hoped to see her again. "How long does she have?" Nikki asked, feeling the dread slithering up around her throat.

"An hour, maybe less."

A colossal weight came crashing down on Nikki's chest, making it hard to breathe, and Kim pulled her in close. "She wants to see you," the nurse said. "Your mother knows she doesn't have long. Go and spend the time you can together. It's a chance most of us here never got."

Nikki nodded, knowing Kim was right. Everyone in New Jamestown had lost someone during and after The Shift, and few if any got an opportunity to say goodbye. After taking a moment to wipe her eyes and collect herself, Nikki gave Kim a final hug and entered the medical tent. Carole's weary gaze traced her as she approached.

"Kim told you, didn't she?"

Nikki bit her lip. "You don't need to protect me anymore, Ma."

"I know that, Nikki." Carole smiled. "You're a woman now, you know that? But to me you'll always be my little girl."

Nikki knelt by her side, trying to keep from breaking down. Already, her mother's skin was turning yellow. Maybe in the Old World, before The Shift, a hospital existed where surgeons and organ transplants might have been there to save her life. Maybe if things were different something could be done to patch her mother up. But out here, in a wilderness of sorrow and pain, Nikki knew the recovery she hoped for was simply impossible.

"Listen," Carole whispered, struggling to breathe. "There are things I need to tell you. Important things."

Nikki leaned closer and caught her mom studying the deep groves in her daughter's cheeks.

"The Wipers have food. Lots of it. At the hotel. More than enough for everyone here."

"OK, Ma, I'll tell them." Nikki was holding her mother's hand now and the tears started to come and she couldn't hold them back anymore.

"And your brother," Carole said. "He's alive."

Nikki looked up, eyes wide and disbelieving. "Alive?"

"He's at the Grand America with a man named Alvarez. I tried to save him, but he wouldn't come. Promise me you'll bring your brother home, Nikki. Promise me you'll do that before they turn him into one of them."

Nodding, Nikki squeezed her mother's hand. The two of them hugged for what seemed like hours, Nikki refusing to let go until she realized she was the only one still holding on. She pulled away and looked at her mother's face and saw peace there for the first time since the plane crash. Carole was dead, and Nikki felt like a piece of her had died as well.

PRIMAL SHIFT 8: INVASION

Larry

Carole's body wouldn't be cremated. It was a decision Larry had made the minute news of her death had reached him. With hungry workers struggling to chop down trees in order to finish work on the enclosure, he couldn't very well divert them to gather wood for a funeral pyre. All Father's death, though not that long ago, was a different time, before Larry was in charge and back when food was almost plentiful. Besides, a grave site would give her daughter, Nikki, something to visit.

The act of sabotage and terrorism that resulted in the complete annihilation of New Jamestown's food supply already meant Larry would need to divert up to 70 percent of the colonists to hunting. Most of the farm houses in the area had been cleaned out long ago. Some of the property with livestock had proved to be the biggest missed opportunity. With no one to feed or give them water, most of the animals had died within the first two weeks. A time when Larry was little more than a city slicker still adjusting to the new reality he'd found himself in. Besides, canned food was plentiful and with a city full of unguarded kitchens, it was simply a question of backing a truck up to the front door and taking whatever was there.

Larry made his way downstairs and outside. A handful of cult members was getting ready to debrief the newcomers. To ensure they were trustworthy and prepared to work. If not, they could get back into their ice cream truck and fuck right off. He was no more than a foot from the door when Nikki appeared. There was something about the girl that gave him the heebie-jeebies. The way her crystal-blue eyes seemed to stare right through you. There were things she was capable of seeing that didn't make sense. A girl who had no memory of her own, but could see the buried memories of strangers. Somehow, she'd been able to see a time where Larry's father held him lovingly as a child, and he still wasn't sure if it had been a simple case of overactive imagination.

"There's something I need to talk to you about," she told him.

Larry rolled up his sleeves. "I'm on my way to an interroga … I mean, to a debriefing. It's gonna have to wait."

She was following him now, and he wished she wasn't a such a stubborn bitch like her mother.

"It's about the food," Nikki said.

Larry's ears perked up. "You saw who raided the colony's pantry?"

"No, it's not about that."

The disappointment in Larry's eyes was immediate. Having lost interest, he was about to turn around again.

"It's about the Wipers at The Grand America Hotel. They're sitting on a gigantic stash of food."

Larry stopped dead in his tracks, a single brow perked with interest. "Go on."

"They spent weeks stripping it from every part of the city. Kitchens, restaurants, schools. Anywhere with nonperishable goods became a target. That's why they haven't attacked. While we built walls, they built food reserves."

"Your mother told you this?"

"Some of it. The rest I got from talking to the people she arrived with."

Larry could sense she was holding something back. It almost sounded like she was trying to encourage him to launch an attack against the hotel. Nikki wasn't particularly known for her bloodlust, although the possibility of revenge was there since Wipers had just killed her mother. But there was something else going on, and Larry couldn't quite put his finger on it. The notion was a tempting one, no doubt about it, but first he'd need to know details about the hotel, it's layout, how many Wipers were there, and what kind of a person this Alvarez character was.

•••

The newcomers were being held in the sheriff's trailer. When Larry entered, only Lou, Tanner, and Ethan were there. Dana was off investigating who had robbed New Jamestown's food supplies.

Each of the adult newcomers stood and introduced themselves. The young children who'd arrived with them were being looked after by cult members.

A crusty dude who looked like he worked in a sewer was Russell. The man in blue and gray military fatigues was Callahan. Beside him was an attractive teenage girl named Jessica. Next to her was a thin and homely woman named Holly, and clinging to her arm was her daughter, Tamara.

"Good, now that we've gotten that out of the way," Larry said. "I'd like to know your intentions."

"Intentions?" Russell asked, as though Larry had broken into Latin.

"Yes, intentions. If you people are hoping to stay in New Jamestown …"

"New James … I thought this was Rainbowland," Callahan cut in.

"It was called Rainbowland, but it's since been improved and renamed."

Lou spoke up from the back. "We had a change in management you might say."

Larry looked at him and smiled weakly. "Thank you, Lou. I'll take it from here."

"Fine by me, Boss."

"Right now we're experiencing some shortages," Larry said, trying to crack his knuckles without having much luck.

"I noticed," Russell said matter-of-factly. "Most everyone here's little more than skin and bones. The Wipers got all the food now. Been hording it to themselves."

"That's the word on the street," Larry said. "But keeping New Jamestown strong and healthy will require each of you and your children to swear an oath to uphold our principles."

"I don't mind doing that," Russell said. "So long as they're fair."

"Oh, they're fair." Larry was looking at the soldier, certain he could be of use.

"I swore oath to the United States of America," Callahan said. "So, as soon as I can get my hands on a vehicle, I'll be heading back to my unit."

How naive, Larry thought. A real patriot. He wanted to tell this Callahan that the country he was sworn to protect didn't exist anymore, if he hadn't already noticed. There wasn't any point in burning that bridge just yet however.

"How many men in your unit are left?" Larry asked.

"I dunno," Callahan replied like an eager schoolboy. "Seventy. Maybe less."

"And what kind of weapons do you have?"

Callahan suddenly didn't look so interested in answering Larry's questions. "Look, Son, we're all on the same side here. There may be some room for cooperation is all I'm thinking."

For a moment, the soldier seemed to relax a bit. "We have enough to protect ourselves, but not any tanks or aircraft if that's what you're asking. We're submariners."

"*Das Boot*," Lou shot from the back. "Heck, I loved that movie."

Callahan gave him a thumbs-up, and smiles filled the room, Larry included. The wheels in his head were starting to turn, and already things were looking up.

Jeffereys

Ducking his head into Alvarez' suite, Jeffereys looked around and swore.

Where the hell was he?

Jeffereys had something to tell Alvarez. Something big. It had to do with Petty Officer Lewis and the ... conversation the two of them had. The kid held out longer than Jeffereys thought he would. Once the sailor was lucid enough to begin answering some questions, Jeffereys had gotten right to brass tacks. Who are you? Where is your base? How many of you are stationed there? What kind of weapons do you have? Standard questions really, but this was only round one, and Jeffereys wanted to give the kid a chance to open up without the use of force. The thought of torturing him had caused a flicker of hesitation in Jeffereys. Both of them were government employees after all, working for the man. Or at least they'd once worked for the man. The man was little more than a memory. Alvarez was the man now. Sure, in his former life, Jeffereys had been a meter maid, a person despised by the average Joe on the street because he did his job. So going in, he knew pulling out the sailor's fingernails and teeth would be tough, but uncovering the threat posed by him and his unit was far more important.

On a level that surprised even him, Jeffereys was happy he hadn't been forced to kill the kid. That he'd come to his senses after just a modicum of harm had managed to befallen him was good for everyone. Paper cuts along the webs of your fingers and under every nail was a start. Squeezing bottles of lemon juice into those really got him squirming. But the coup de grace was Lewis' pre-existing wound. A shattered right leg, broken when the Humvee he was riding in crashed and flipped on its side. The same Humvee that now belonged to them. In the end, getting Lewis to start talking, really talking, took little more than some added pressure to that broken leg. It was a gruesome business for sure, and Jeffereys didn't think of himself like one of these brutes Alvarez was having him train into an army. Sure, they could fire a weapon and drive trucks. Hell, they could even follow simple orders, but at the end of the day they were bloodthirsty savages. You could train a monkey to carry a glass, but that didn't suddenly make him a butler.

Before the world went crazy, those Wipers were neighbors who squabbled over high fences and county zoning laws. They relished seeing their enemies served with fines and warrants. Those same neighbors had developed new tastes. Being buried with paperwork no longer did it.

Now, they preferred to bury you up to the neck and whack the eyes out of your skull with a two-by-four.

No, Jeffereys and his men weren't like the others, not by a long shot, although he had to admit that when Lewis began squawking like a bird, giving up each of his delicious secrets, Jeffereys thought he was gonna blow a load in his pants. And he nearly did with the final bombshell Lewis laid on him. In fact, bombshell wasn't even the half of it.

That's why Jeffereys was stalking through the corridors of the Grand America, looking for Alvarez.

He finally found him standing in front of the hotel, looking up as though he were giving directions for a new sign that was being mounted. Next to him was Aiden, the child who had arrived with the brutes from the airport.

"A little higher," Alvarez said. "A touch to the left. Yes, that's it."

Jeffereys got outside and saw what they were doing. Dangling from the hotel's overhand was the body they'd recovered from the Humvee. Lewis said Josh was his name, and he'd been one of the survivors living directly under their noses. The same group that had snuck through the air vents and tried to steal their food. Now, his corpse was strung up with length of heavy ropes, perhaps as a warning to others.

"What do you think?" Alvarez asked.

Jeffereys blinked. "Seems like overkill – "

"Not you. I was talking to the boy."

Aiden squished up his face, as though trying to mask the horror of what he was seeing. "He's a thief, and he got exactly what thieves deserve."

Al laughed. "Quite right," and turned to Jeffereys. "So, was our friend willing to talk, or do I need to speak with him myself?"

"Took a bit of coaxing, but he spoke, and you won't believe the half of it."

"Really? Try me." All the humor had gone out of Alvarez' voice, and Jeffereys knew that fickle thing he called patience was running out.

"They aren't Army. They're part of a submarine crew. Couldn't reach their command structure over the radio and landed in San Diego some time after the shit hit the fan. The kid says they're about 70 strong with about 15 Humvees, well 14 now, and lots of small arms."

"Their location?"

"Ely State Prison in – "

"Nevada," Alvarez said flatly. "Yes, I know exactly where it is. The warden and I were on good terms. There was just enough in the budget we were getting from the military to keep this sad little man plied with

106

prostitutes and envelopes stuffed with cash. In return, he'd send me any prisoner I wanted and help dispose of the bodies when things went wrong. We went through so many in the beginning, you know, trying to calibrate the equipment. Cost of doing business, you might say." Alvarez looked up at Josh's body again. "Is that everything, or have you saved the best for last?"

Now it was Jeffereys' turn to gloat. "You know me too well."

"Do tell."

"The submarine crew is from the *USS Alabama*."

"Should that mean something to me?"

"I asked him the same thing. When he told me I nearly hit the roof. It's what they call a boomer. That submarine of theirs is carrying 24 nuclear missiles. All we gotta do is get our hands on the captain and a handful of his men. After that, we can rule the world supreme."

Jeffereys was dancing a little jig, the same sort of jig allied propagandists claimed Hitler had danced in June of 1940 upon hearing that France was ready to surrender. Either way, Alvarez was beaming with enthusiasm.

"We've got some planning to do," he said before leaving with the boy in tow.

Nikki

Only half of the colony showed up for Carole's burial, yet still Nikki was touched by their show of support. Nearly all of them brought their tools along. Saws, axes, shovels. The very instruments of their oppression. The moment she was done, they would be whisked back to work. Those not currently present were either out hunting game or manning the walls against the Wipers, who continued to observe from across the river. Nikki read a handful of passages from the Bible as they lowered her mother into the ground, her body wrapped in linen. The timber required to build the walls, towers, and outer defenses had meant putting a coffin together was impossible. That's what Larry had told her, and in her current state of mind there was no point in arguing. Nikki sprinkled a handful of dirt into the grave, still numb to the fact that the body lying there belonged to her mother. Hardest of all was knowing that she would never see her again.

After Nikki had finished, Tanner and Ethan, flanking her on either side, helped Nikki to her seat. One of the cult members rose to recite a few words from their own scripture. In keeping with their outward shift toward militarism, Nikki noticed they tended to now shy away from the more peace-loving sections. In a way, those parts had been destroyed along with All Father's body on the funeral pyre that day. The cult members spoke of eternal life and going to the great light, which sounded fine by her, but still made many of the other colonists decidedly uncomfortable. It was following this that Larry offered a few words, although they weren't at all what she had been expecting.

"As many of you know by now, there is a thief in our midst. First of all, I would like to assure each and every one of you that whoever is responsible will be caught and severely punished for this treasonous act."

Nikki could see Larry's gaze locked squarely on Timothy the entire time.

"A crime this serious can only be met with a single response. Death."

A cult member to Timothy's right shouted: "Brother Larry, it was your job to protect the colony, and you failed."

Another angry voice nearby spoke next. "How can you work us into the ground without food?"

Then someone else from the crowd: "What good are all these walls if we can't eat?"

Larry's hands flew up, palms out. "I've got half of you out hunting for food as we speak."

"And why aren't you out there with them?" a woman shouted. "We've never seen you lift a finger."

A large man wearing a cowboy hat and leaning on a pick ax was next: "There's a rumor going around you got your own stash of food. That true?"

Nikki saw Larry look directly at her, anger flashing in his eyes. She'd seen his private cupboard, although she hadn't said a word of it to anyone.

"That's a vicious lie, nothing more."

A middle-aged woman with short greasy hair this time. "Maybe we need to give someone else a shot."

"Make no mistake, people. I'll find out who stole our precious resources and set this right. All I'm asking is for a little more time."

There was a touch of fear in Larry's voice, a tiny quaver, as though he was starting to lose control and wasn't entirely sure how to get it back.

"A plan is currently in the works that will secure enough food for an entire year, maybe even longer."

"More useless promises," a man in a torn plaid shirt shouted.

That was enough for Larry, who turned and stormed off.

As far as Nikki was concerned, this was supposed to be a time to honor her mother's memory, not an opportunity for political grandstanding and uttering death threats. No doubt, stealing the food was a crime, but folks here were starving, and hunger had a funny way of bringing out the worst in people. She remembered Sprucewood Elementary where hunger had driven a group of Wiper children to cannibalism.

But even as Larry stormed away from the angry crowd, Nikki could see a single face among them was smiling. And she couldn't help but wonder what it was Timothy was so happy about.

Finn

"Herb," the older-looking man in the orange jumpsuit said, holding a weathered hand out to Finn. The parts of his face not covered in a frosty-white beard looked about as creased as the man's hands. Finn accepted the gesture and was about to introduce himself when the old man said, "You're Finn, I know."

Finn was checking his coveralls to see if his name had suddenly appeared over the breast pocket. It hadn't.

"I haven't survived this long on my good looks," Herb said, grinning like the Cheshire Cat.

They were in a hollow, somewhere between the walls in a tiny alcove Herb must have carved out for himself.

"The cell I pulled you into wasn't mine," he explained. "Belonged to a man named Jesus. I shit you not. Mexican fellow who was as quiet as a toothless woman and smiled about as much. Stayed away from most of the gangs. That's how it works in prison. A gang is a man's ticket to mutual protection. Watching each other's backs, you know."

"That isn't too different from how things are on the outside right now," Finn told him. He went to stand and felt a sharp pain in his side.

"You just relax a minute. That big guy might have broken a rib."

Finn explained to Herb how he'd been shot.

"Ah, that'll do it, too," he said, bursting into a phlegmy bout of laughter. "What was I talking about again?"

"Jesus."

"Yeah, that's right. 'Cept, he didn't pronounce it *Geezuz*. Way he said it sounded more like *Hay-zeus*."

Finn smiled, thankful for Herb's help and humor, but wishing he could get back to Foster and in particular Joanne. To make sure they were all right. He'd found information in the warden's office he hadn't expected. Finn had been searching for some more details on the crime he was accused of committing, and instead he discovered that Joanne was his wife. A pill he hadn't entirely managed to swallow just yet.

"Don't worry about your friends," Herb said, noting the concern clouding Finn's features. "They'll be just fine, and once you're able to get on your feet without feeling like you been shot all over again, then I'll do my best to get you back to them. Here," he said, handing Finn a cup of yellow water. The bucket at Herb's feet looked just like the one they'd seen in the showers. Finn was too thirsty by this point to be picky and drank it all down in one long pull. It tasted like rust.

110

"I know it looks like hell, but it sure beats the pants offa dehydration."

Finn handed back the cup and thanked him.

"Only thing Jesus wanted to do was bust outta Ely State, and he spent a long time chipping away at the wall under his bunk so he could do just that. Then one day, everybody loses their minds. I was in the showers at the time, saw guards and inmates rushing in together attacking people. Eight other men were with me. Three were killed outright. The rest of us escaped, but most of those were taken down over the next few days. And here I am, lone survivor. Maybe the last inmate from Ely State who didn't lose his mind." Herb looked long and hard at Finn. "You a religious man?"

The question threw him off balance for a moment. Wasn't a question he'd really given much thought to lately, not when you were focused on just staying alive. But more than that, he couldn't remember if at some point, before all of this, he had been.

"You don't need to answer that. Man's relationship with his maker is his own business. But I noticed something in people after the change happened. Was like a switch went off somewhere. The folks who had darkness in their hearts to start with, well that only got worse. Was like their inner demons, the real deep desires they kept tucked away so no one would see 'em. The change only seemed to magnify that."

"The evil became more evil."

"There you go. See, you went and said it in nothing but a handful of words. Some of the inmates who were half decent – and trust me when I say there weren't too many of those – well they were acting weird, too, but most of them were running away, trying to hide."

Herb's words were slowly sinking in. If there was truth to what he was saying, that the actions of those affected by The Shift wasn't entirely random, then what did it say about him and about Joanne?

"What's your story?" Finn asked. "What were you in for?"

Herb scooped up a cup full of yellow water and drank. "Lost my job in the fall of 1981 when the Reagan recession hit. Money stopped coming in, but the bills didn't, not that they ever do. What's a man supposed to say when he's got kids to put through college and a wife who's never needed to work her whole life? No one's there to catch you when you fall. We're all left to sink or swim by our own devices. It's the greatest thing about this country and also the worst. Anyway, the only ones still making money in all that mess were the banks, and so I went into a few and asked if they'd be willing to share. Took my pistol along, too, in case some of them refused."

"And did they ... refuse?"

"Those greedy bastards? 'Course they did. And when they finally caught up with me, the district attorney decided to make an example out of me so no one else suffering like we were would be tempted to follow in my footsteps." After a minute, Herb pointed the cup at Finn's chest. "How're those ribs doing?"

Finn tried to stand, and the pain this time wasn't nearly as bad. The difference must have been visible on his face because Herb said: "Few hours with Herb beats an army of doctors, doesn't it?"

Finn smiled and then broke into a laugh. "Now you're pushing it."

"A'right," Herb said, getting to his feet, lifting the hard drive and tying it to Finn's back. "Let's see if we can't get you to your people."

Dana

It took some time following Larry's well-meaning, but rather disappointing, speech, before any of the colonists agreed to return to work. Lou, Tanner, and Ethan were doing their part, attempting to reassure the masses that everything was being done to find food. But platitudes are cheap, and it was only when one of the hunting teams returned with two deer they'd killed, that the grumbling began to fade.

Since Dana had learned of the theft, questioning everyone in New Jamestown for leads had taken precedent. Always at the back of her mind was the niggling question of whether there were a connection between the stolen food and the murder of Lou's wife. Simon was next on her list of colonists to speak with, and when Dana found him heading back to the jail to watch over Bud, she asked if they could have a word. He agreed in the polite way he seemed to address everyone, and the two walked to the trailer that doubled as her office and New Jamestown's police station.

When they got inside, Dana removed her gun belt and set it in the desk drawer. Simon sat across from her. As she lowered herself into the chair, she studied him briefly for any signs of stress without detecting any.

"I think you know why I've asked you here," she said.

"Yes. I think it's horrible what's happened."

Dana paused, waiting for him to elaborate. Lots of horrible things had happened lately.

"Stealing from those who have so little is what I mean," he added.

He tripped over his words and for the first time seemed a touch nervous. Was the quiver in his voice simply the product of being questioned by an authority figure, or was there more to it than that?

"I didn't have anything to do with what happened, if that's what you're thinking. There are a few of us Rainbowites who still think doing harm to another is an absolute last resort."

"But you'd be willing to kill for the right reasons."

Simon nodded, reluctantly. "I wouldn't be guarding prisoners if I didn't, but the situation would have to leave me no other choice." He took in a deep breath. "Are you questioning my participation in the theft or my willingness to take a life?"

Dana glanced down at the names she'd already scratched off her list. "Maybe both. Where were you last night between 11 and 4 a.m.?"

113

"Sitting in the jailhouse, doing my job. I chatted with Bud briefly. Then he went to bed, and I read a book."

"Chatted?" Her eyebrow arched. "What about?"

Simon smiled. "Same thing he always talks about. You."

It suddenly felt 10 degrees warmer. A bead of sweat rolled down Dana's cheek.

Who's doing the sweating now?

"What book?" she asked changing the subject.

"Pardon me?"

"You said Bud was reading a book, which one?"

"Uh, *Animal Farm* by Orwell," he said.

"What about outside? Did you hear anything unusual?"

Simon shook his head. "Nothing out of the ordinary. If you're asking me if I know who did this or whether I've heard any names being tossed around, the answer is yes, and I won't lie, one of those names is yours, Sheriff."

Dana's head snapped up so fast it left a creak in her neck.

"Not that I put much weight in it," he amended rather quickly. "People are scared. And fear has a nasty habit of turning a bad situation downright dangerous. My father taught me that."

"You miss him terribly, don't you?"

"I think about him every day. About his final instructions to follow Brother Larry's every command. Rainbowland was his life, and he would have wanted it to live on after him." Simon began to stand up. "Was there anything else?"

"Just one thing." She produced the cassette recorder and hit the play button. Simon listened to the coordinates being read in that slightly distorted voice. Then she flipped the tape and played the other side. "You recognize the person in that recording?"

"To be quite honest, when you first started playing it, I heard my father's voice."

"That's what I thought, too."

"But then you played the other side, and I knew I was wrong. That sounded more like my uncle."

Dana swallowed hard. "Timothy?"

"Sure. He wasn't always in the cult, you know. Took a while for my dad to convince him to quit his job and join us."

"Really? What kinda work did he do?"

"Not sure, something in electronics, I believe. Worked for a big company that handled government contracts. I think it was called Tevatron."

114

Larry

About an hour later, Larry called the newcomers from the ice cream truck back to the police trailer for the second part of the debriefing. Larry's mood was decidedly glum when a knock came at the door. It was Dana and a cult member named Donavan

. The latter was well built for a former Rainbowite. His face chiseled with sharp features and eyes deep set and penetrating. He also was the first to become proficient with the most common rifle they'd found in the nearby farm houses, the AR-15, and for that reason, Larry had put him in charge of the colonial militia. A militia whose orders were simple: Keep the Wipers and any other aggressors outside the walls. And if there was one thing cult members did admirably, it was take orders. All they needed was continued assurances that this was how All Father had wanted things.

"You asked to see us?" Dana asked as she and Donavan entered.

"Yes, I was just getting to know our new guests."

Russell and the others nodded hello.

"It's come to my attention recently," Larry began, "that the group of sub-human savages holed up at the Grand America Hotel have taken every last bit of canned food in the city and are sitting on a massive stockpile. More than enough to sustain everyone in New Jamestown as we begin to make a difficult transition from eating out of cans to living off the land."

Russell agreed. "We watched for over a month as trucks came and went. A few at first and gradually more as Wipers were being taught how to drive and find weapons."

"We've noticed a change in the Wipers as well," Donavan added. "When they first attacked us, they used clubs and crude swords. Now, when they come in small groups, they shoot at the towers with rifles."

Callahan clapped his hands. "Good thing for us they couldn't hit the broad side of a barn."

"Not yet," Larry amended. "But like everything else, it's only a matter of time before that changes."

"I see where you're going with this," Dana said. "You wanna attack the Wipers and take their food? Sounds to me like an easy way of getting a lot of innocent people killed."

Now Lou chimed in from the rear. "Way I see it, we ain't got a ton of options. Sitting back and hoping for the best won't get us through the

115

winter. And I ain't saying this to save my own skin. Many of us have loved ones who are also starving."

"I'm sorry, but attacking the Wipers is plain suicide," Dana said, and suddenly the room exploded with arguments on both sides.

Larry called for silence. "No one's saying we're going to attack the Wipers. We're only talking. But I need to know from the people who've been there how feasible it would be before I make a decision." Larry looked at Russell, Holly, and Callahan. "This Alvarez character who leads them. What kind of person is he?"

Only Russell's face showed any real emotion. But the streak of fear visible beneath the man's hardened exterior spoke volumes.

"If I didn't think there was a bit of good in every man, I'd be tempted to say he was pure evil."

Russell described what he had seen the night they'd been captured, trying to steal some of the very food they were now discussing. How Alvarez had forced Carole into the arena and made her fight for their lives.

"And he kept his word?" Larry asked incredulously.

"Sure, he did," Russell replied. "But not out of the kindness of his heart. He ordered his men to hunt us down as we fled, hoping we'd lead him back to the others."

"So, he's smart and twisted," Dana added, her eyes narrowing as though she were fitting together two seemingly disparate pieces of a puzzle. "Charming combination. I just hope he isn't the same Alvarez I knew."

"History's full of twisted characters," Lou added.

Russell shook his head in despair. "It sure is. You find me somewhere with a touch of ethnic cleansing, and I'll show you an evil mind behind the whole thing."

"Anyone building up resources and training men on that scale," Callahan said, "has to be preparing for something big."

"Damn right," Lou shouted. "They attacked us once already, what's to say they aren't planning on finishing what they started?"

Larry was enjoying the pleasures of sitting back and allowing them to inch toward the solution all on their own. This Alvarez was apparently smart, but Larry was smarter.

"So, let's get down to brass tacks," Larry said, giving his knuckles a good crack and succeeding this time. "We need to know how many men he has, how they're armed, and what kind of defenses we're likely to encounter."

116

Callahan was the first to step up. "I'm a sailor, not a grunt, but I do know a thing or two about combat. From what I saw, Alvarez' men are using small arms. Handguns, shotguns, rifles. Stuff like that. Their tactical training was average to low. Very little discipline. Poor marksmanship. They sure do whoop and holler like Rebs in the Civil War, which can be intimidating, but it seems to me like this Alvarez is aiming to put as much lead on target as he can and hope he gets lucky. One thing I will give his men. They're bloodthirsty and above all, fearless."

"Fearless," Dana said, "because they're dumb as shit."

Callahan laughed. 'That may be true, but don't underestimate them."

"What about numbers?" Larry asked.

"A wild guess and that's all it is, would be a few hundred at any given time. Also keep in mind, Alvarez probably keeps a few men stationed on the hotel roof as lookouts. Not to mention any pickets he's got set up along the perimeter. Although judging from the few defensive positions I saw in the streets around the hotel, the guy's confident to the point of arrogant."

Larry took it all in and then turned to Donavan. "How many fighters can we assemble?"

He'd almost asked how many men, but quickly swapped it out for fighters. And it wasn't simply a question of playing the political correctness card. If they were going to do this, they'd need every man, woman, and child they could spare.

"New Jamestown has 192 individuals of fighting age. I used a cutoff age of 14. If we leave behind the minimum detachment to man the walls and operate the gate when we return, I figure we could muster 162. As well, at an average of four per vehicle, our convoy would stretch about 40 vehicles long."

"Alvarez' men on the roof will see us coming the minute we hit Main street," Dana said. "So you can forget the idea of a surprise attack."

Larry was studying the pattern in Callahan's camo jacket. "Sure would be nice to have some extra firepower on hand. What are the chances your Commander Zhou would join us?"

The touch of doubt on the young sailor's face made the answer perfectly clear. "Zhou's said his main goal is re-establishing contact with what's left of the government. If I had to guess, I'd say he'd probably see this as a territorial squabble and wouldn't wanna risk his men by getting involved."

"Typical foreign policy line you'd hear from the State Department," Lou spat.

But Larry was a salesman at heart and ready with a rebuttal to Callahan's objection. "If you and your fellow sailors plan on setting up shop anywhere nearby, then they'll have to deal with Alvarez and his army of Wipers sooner or later."

"Which is precisely why Petty Officer Lewis and I were sent here, to reconnoitre the area and report back as soon as possible. I'm sure they've already given us up for dead. I'd love to help you folks, really I would. I know this Alvarez guy needs to be taken down. I'm not making any promises, but who knows, maybe I can convince my CO."

"We'll be dead by then," Larry said. "We're Americans, and for all intents and purposes our compound is under siege. Just like they used to do in the Middle Ages. Roll up an army, surround the city, choke off its supplies, and wait till the people inside ran out of food. Was never long before the cats and dogs would go missing, then the horses and eventually the people. Soon, there wouldn't be any choice left but to swing open the gates and accept defeat. I know cannibalism's a nasty word, but that's where things are headed if we can't find a way clear of this mess."

"Pack up and come to us," Callahan said, and suddenly Larry could see the young man's age and idealism shine through.

"That's a sweet thought, really it is, but a couple hundred starving people is the last thing your commander needs showing up on his doorstep. If it were me, I'd turn them away. Besides, your base is in the middle of the desert. At least here we can plant crops ... " Larry stopped. Everyone was staring at him after that last bit. "Once we find the one responsible for sabotaging the colony, that is." To Donavan. "Send out a few scouts to map out the best avenue of approach and report back on any defenses we may have overlooked." Donavan saluted and left the trailer. "Can I count on the rest of you to help us?" Larry asked. He wasn't speaking to Dana or Lou.

"I'm not much of a people person," Russell offered with little apology. "When I agreed to come here, it was only so I could bring the women and children to safety. We ... I should say I, would never have left the boiler room if hunger hadn't forced us to take a foolish chance. I know Holly and Tamara want to stay. Won't be surprised if Jessica does, too, but I can take care of myself."

"Out there, all alone?" Larry asked. "Even if you manage to hide from the Wipers, it'll be lonely."

Russell chuckled. "Lonely's underrated. 'Sides, it never affected me all those years I worked those boilers. People rarely say what they mean or mean what they say anyhow, and I don't have much use for that."

"Fair enough," Larry admitted, wondering whether Russell's comment was meant as a personal jab. "We could certainly use someone with your skill set around here."

"I'm flattered," Russell said, "but I'll be leaving first thing in the morning."

There was a change on Larry's face, and Russell seemed to catch it right away. "I'm afraid I can't allow that."

"What'chu mean, can't allow that?"

Larry's eyes hardened. "It's quite simple. You've become privy to very sensitive information, Russell. The layout of our compound, the number of men and women defending it, but most important of all, our plan to raid the Wiper's base in the very near future. See, if this Alvarez ever got his hands on you, who knows what you'd tell him?"

"Not a damned word, I swear."

"No, you wouldn't intend to. I give you that. In fact, I'm sure you'd hold out for as long as you could. But there are ways to make men talk, let me assure you. Nasty ways I won't mention except to say that when they were done, you'd be admitting to wearing ladies panties if that's what you thought they wanted to hear. You catch my drift? What they're after is already in your head, and they can get to it. So, stay with us and enjoy your time in New Jamestown, and once we've conducted this ugly business and returned safely in trucks packed with food, then you'll be free to do as you please."

"So, we're prisoners, is what you're saying?" Russell asked angrily.

"Call it that if you want to, but I prefer to think of you as our guests. A guest who will be entitled to a fair share of whatever game those hunting in the forests behind the compound return with. Call it national security if it makes you feel any better."

'Course it didn't, and Larry could see that. But the truth was simple enough, and he felt he'd laid it out as clearly as he could. Russell could be a real asset to New Jamestown, so long as he continued to play nice. The man had information about the hotel's layout and where the food was stored as well as a skill set in short supply. If he was smart, he'd continue to cooperate.

●●●

After Larry thanked everyone, they stood and began shuffling out one at a time. All except Dana, who went to her chair and kicked her feet up on the desk.

"You know keeping them here against their will just means more work for Lou and me," she told Larry.

"Don't you think I know that? I wish there was another way. But what would you have me do? If the Wipers caught wind of this, it'd be bad for everyone. We don't have a plan B. And you saw those people at the funeral today."

"They're scared and hungry and being worked practically to death."

Larry put both hands on her desk. "Yes, I'm aware of that."

"He's doing to you what you did to All Father," Dana told him.

There was no need to explain who she was talking about. It was perfectly clear she was referring to Timothy. "Oh, believe me, this little movement he's started wouldn't have a leg to stand on if we weren't facing a food crisis." Larry paused and drew in a deep breath. "I hope you've got him in your crosshairs."

"He's definitely on my list of suspects," Dana said. "But without some reasonable proof, any drastic action against him could turn the entire colony against you."

"Sometimes if you know someone's guilty, you can always find the proof you need." Larry snapped off a single wink, and the look on his face made it perfectly clear what he was getting at.

"I won't plant evidence, Larry, if that's what you're saying. He may be your biggest opposition right now, but that doesn't prove he did this. But I promise you, I'll find whoever it was."

"I hope so."

"Since I have you here," Dana added. "There's something I wanted to ask you. What can you tell me about a company called Tevatron?"

"Tevatron?" Larry was drawing a blank.

"Bob, the man who was killed during the Wiper raid. He used to work for them."

The illuminating flash in Larry's brain just then had nothing to do with Bob. He remembered meeting up with Bud during their trek to Utah. Hadn't he mentioned something about Tevatron in those long hours the young man had spent talking?

"I've heard the name. Why do you want to know?" he asked.

"Just a lead I'm following." She glanced down, shuffling some papers on her desk.

"Well follow it quickly, Dana. The longer it takes to smoke this traitor out, the greater the chances we might all die." And with that, Larry turned, headed for the door, and paused with his hand on the knob. He was thinking of the note he found on his desk earlier. "I almost forgot to ask. How did everything go with Romeo?"

Dana swallowed hard. "Fine. I felt bad for the kid."

"Yes, but sadly it had to be done. I'm just so thankful that in these trying times we can trust one another."

"Me, too," she whispered back as Larry left, pulling the door closed behind him.

Finn

Finn's real purpose in coming to Ely State was to find details on what had landed Joanne and him in prison. He shifted the warden's computer tower now lashed to his back, trying to regain his balance. Herb had been leading him down a narrow passage between the walls when Finn had stopped to collect himself.

Discovering that Joanne was his wife had been the kind of curve ball that slides up and whacks you in the face before you know what's hit you. There was something incredibly surreal about finding out that a woman you barely knew had once been your wife.

And probably still was.

But beyond all that, the real question Finn was trying to answer in coming here was whether or not he was a murdering degenerate. It was downright impossible to reconcile the man he was now with who he might have been before The Shift. In a strange way, his conversation with Herb had helped square away at least some of his concerns. That the wicked were made even worse after the change was a step in the right direction, all of which could be undone if Finn were to discover he was really a serial killer or God knew what else.

Herb was staring at him now, ready to continue on. "You all right, friend?"

"Yeah," Finn said, wiping a thin layer of sweat from his forehead. "I'm fine."

"From here on out, we'll need to move quickly. We can't risk the kinda racket you folks kicked up on your way to the Warden's office. Oh, and keep your eyes peeled for booby traps. I've been finding more and more of 'em these last few weeks."

"I thought they were all yours."

Herb grinned, two teeth missing in the front, which made his mouth look like a row of piano keys. "Not me. The ones you call Wipers. And they're getting smarter." He lifted the homemade ice climber's ax he'd buried in that muscle-bound Wiper's head. "'Sides, Betty here and I don't need any of that Iraqi insurgent shit, not when we got each other."

"Touching. You're one of a kind, you know that, Herb?"

"That's the second time you've told me that, so I gather it must be true."

Finn paused, not able to recall making the comment before or even having it cross his mind. But there wasn't any sense pushing the point, and the two men set off again.

It wasn't long before the passage between the prison walls they were navigating through began to narrow considerably. Lengths of piping and electrical wires now long dead squeezed them even further. Fingers of light streamed in 10 yards ahead. Herb turned and touched his lips with his index finger.

"This is where some of them like to hang out," he whispered. His breath smelled of stale water and tuna fish. As both men cautiously approached, Finn could see that Herb was right. Two Wipers in blood-stained orange jumpsuits were sitting in a cell, speaking a language that sounded like gobbledygook. When the earthquakes hit right after The Shift, it must have weakened some of the walls. In this case, a small section of cinder blocks had toppled over into the cell, creating a window. Shuffling by at top speed would surely draw the Wiper's attention. 'Course, it didn't help one bit that this computer was strapped to Finn's back. The time for leaving it behind, however, had passed, and Finn knew the only way back would be to keep moving forward. The sounds of gravel and concrete crunching under their feet was ear shattering to Finn. Growing more certain with every step that at least one of the two Wipers would hear something.

For now, they were busy arguing. On the bed, a number of objects were laid out. A comb that, like them, was missing teeth, a knife made from a metal bracket, its tip filed into a lethal tip. The point was, most of this stuff was junk, but these two seemed to be yammering away like they were negotiating an OPEC deal. They're bartering, Finn saw and hoped their bickering would continue for as long as it took Herb and him to pass undetected. That very thought was going through Finn's head when the computer tower on his back knocked against the water pipe next to him. The sound it created was akin to an echoing boom. One that made Finn's heart momentarily stop in his chest.

The Wipers both looked up at once, and in a blur of movement, they were on their feet, coming for him, reaching into the hole in the wall.

Then one of the Wipers, his hands covered in bloody nicks and gashes, closed his vice-like grip around Finn's coveralls and began yanking him forcibly through the opening. The other Wiper was there beside him, closing in, eagerly. Finn felt his body slamming into the cinderblock wall that separated them. The rifle slung over Finn's back didn't make an ounce of difference in these tight quarters since getting it out and on target was impossible.

In another second or two, the other Wiper was gonna go for that knife lying on the bed and plunge it repeatedly into Finn's exposed belly while his buddy kept him held firmly in place.

Just ahead of him, Herb wore the sort of panicked look of someone powerless to intervene. Finn was pushing himself away from the wall so he could reach down and pry the Wiper's hands off him, when Herb tossed him the homemade ax.

Gripping it tightly, Finn swung down with biting force and sent the tip screaming into the Wiper's hand. He yelped with pain and tried to retract his hand, but the curved ax blade kept it firmly in place. Finn used both hands to free the ax, and the Wiper fell away, clutching a wound now spurting with blood. That's when his Wiper friend came forward with the knife in hand, just as Finn had predicted. But he and Herb were already beginning to move away. The Wiper stuck his head through the hole to reacquire them, and Finn stepped back and swung again, missing by inches as his target withdrew back into the jail cell, the tip of the ax chipping nothing more than a chunk of cinder block.

Finn and Herb didn't wait around to see what the Wipers would do next. Surely, they'd climb in after them and give chase. That was why they were determined to put as much distance between them as they could.

Soon, the narrow passage between walls opened into another cell. A set of stairs led down to B block, and the two men raced in that direction. Herb's goal of moving in utter silence had been dashed to pieces. Now, with Wipers likely alerted to their presence, the objective had changed from stealth to speed. Lumbering along with the battered computer tower strapped to his back, Finn now took advantage of the wider space they were in to unsling his rifle. He didn't have more than a half dozen rounds of 30.-06 in the pocket of his coveralls, but he was prepared to use the stock as a club if it came to that.

The two made quick progress through A block and into the showers. The tight corridors and blind corners made for an ideal location to be ambushed, which drove home the very unsettling point that they weren't out of the woods yet. Finn took the lead now, finger on the trigger.

He stopped to listen when he heard footsteps echoing up ahead. So did Herb.

"Sounds like a group of 'em," Herb whispered, tightening the grip on his hand ax.

They went around a corner where the change rooms let out to the shower stalls, and Finn's gut seized up the second he spotted the darkened figures. Then came the sound of weapons being charged and he knew immediately, if they were Wipers, the two of them would already be dead.

"Finn?" he heard a woman call out. They flashed a light in his face, and she squealed with joy. "Oh, thank God you're alive."

The two groups came together. Foster was there along with a handful of military men with rifles.

"A rescue party," Finn said. "I'm touched."

"We thought you were right behind us until we ran into another group of Wipers. We backtracked to get you, and that's when we found the dead prisoner. I was sure something terrible had happened."

"It would have," Finn said. "If Herb hadn't stuck his neck out to save me."

Herb grinned, and Joanne returned the gesture, despite the man's missing teeth and the mist of blood in his white beard.

"We should head back," Foster said. "It isn't safe here." The sailors turned to leave. Finn followed a few steps behind them before realizing that Herb wasn't coming. He stopped and turned around. "What's wrong?"

"Maybe I'm just an old bird who's gotten used to his own cage, but I can't come with you."

"But there's food and water and ... "

"And more danger outside these walls than there is inside 'em. Besides, I made you a promise, Francis, and I've fulfilled my end of the bargain."

Finn's jaw dropped open. "You know my name?"

"I was hoping you'd remember on your own, you see, but I guess those memories of yours really did get fried." Herb let out a burst of wet laughter that sounded like an old Buick turning over.

"We served time together, didn't we?"

"Bingo! You stood up for me once in the commons when a lowlife named Jeb Cain decided to use my head as a punching bag. See, Jeb led the white power boys, and if any of us Caucasians refused to join up, he and his friends would redecorate our faces. It was stupid what you did, Francis. Nearly got your ass killed trying to save a worthless old man, but I promised you some day I'd return the favor, and now I have." Herb began to turn and then paused. "Good luck out there, you're gonna need it."

And Finn watched numb with shock as Herb disappeared back into the shadows of Ely State Prison.

Larry

When he entered New Jamestown's jail, Simon rose at once, oozing the guilty look of a man who'd been caught sleeping on the job. A look that wasn't at all misplaced given he had been dozing off.

"I wasn't expecting you," Simon stammered. "Is there something I can do for you, Sir?"

Larry glanced over at Bud, who was sitting up straight now. The expression there wasn't all that different, except Bud wasn't worried about being caught snoozing. It was the threat of retribution from Larry that was undoubtedly on his mind.

"I need to speak with Bud," Larry said.

Simon nodded vigorously and began to sit down.

"Alone," Larry added.

"Sure thing." Simon shot out of his seat and was grasping the trailer handle when he said: "I'll be right outside if you need me."

The door closed, and now Larry and Bud were alone.

"I've held off coming to speak with you," Larry said.

Bud let his back rest against the wall. "I noticed. To what do I owe this pleasure?"

"You were working for this Alvarez character I keep hearing so much about."

Bud nodded. "I was."

"You also stole my C4, and if I hadn't sent Dana off to get it back from you, you woulda gotten away with a triple homicide – if you count Joanne Blackwood that is. Do you know how precious life's become since The Shift?"

"I was trying to save lives."

"'Course you were. For some reason, Dana saw fit not to execute you on the spot. She's young and naive. Frankly, I woulda blown your fucking head off."

"Compassion isn't your thing, Larry. I still remember how you drove off and left me to die along I-80."

"You broke rule numero one, Amigo. During an apocalypse, it's every man, woman, and child for themselves. You stepped out to save a bunch of retards who woulda only slowed us down. But I'm curious, what ever did end up happening to that cuddly little family you saved?"

Bud's eyes fell to his bedding, crumpled up around him. "They were killed the next day when we stopped in a small town to get supplies. I told them to stay in the car … "

"But they didn't listen," Larry said. "Now, why doesn't that surprise me? I think you'll agree, however, that two wrongs don't make a right."

Bud glanced over from the corner of his eyes. "What're you saying, we're even?"

"Well, not entirely. I left you on the side of the road. There's no denying that. For your part, you killed Johnson and tried to blow Finn to kingdom come, not to mention Joanne."

"Alvarez lied to me – "

"I'm sure he did," Larry cut him off. "That's what bad men do, Bud, they lie."

Bud was watching him, wondering perhaps what was coming next.

"How well do you know this Alvarez?" Larry asked.

"Well enough to know he isn't the sort to be fucked with. He's building an army of Wipers and training them how to fight. The Shift did most of the work for him. Weeding out the sick and the weak and the compassionate. The meanest of the mean, that's who survived, and those are the ones he's after."

"For what purpose?"

"It's simple. He wants to make the world his own personal hell."

"So far, he's doing a mighty good job."

"Just you wait. As soon as his men are capable, don't think for a second he won't come break down that gate and cart all of you off."

"Including you," Larry added.

"Don't I know it. But I won't go down without a fight, you can trust me on that."

"I like what I hear. How familiar are you with the hotel grounds?"

"Pretty familiar."

"Could you sketch them?"

"Why? Oh, you're not thinking of attacking Alvarez are you?"

The grin on Larry's face began to fade. "Why not?"

"He might look like a regular guy, but let me be the first to tell you that's exactly what he isn't."

Larry sat up straight. "You've been drinking the Kool Aid, haven't you?"

"I don't think he can be killed."

"Bullshit, Bud. If he breathes, he can be killed."

Bud was quiet. "Maybe you're right, but people are gonna die."

"This Alvarez has nabbed all the food within a 50-mile radius, maybe more, and he's got it stashed away for himself. I wanna set you free Bud, I really do. But there are two things I need from you. First, where do you think he's keeping that food?"

Leaning forward to grab the bars, Bud let out a great sigh. "I couldn't say for sure. I mean, I didn't see anything like that when I was there. The Wipers weren't capable of doing a whole lot more than grunting and cracking each other over the head."

"Then give me your best guess."

"Well, the hotel's a big place, so in a sense it could be anywhere, but knowing Alvarez, he'd want it somewhere close so he could keep an eye on it. My best guess would be the ballroom."

Larry knew perfectly well where the food was. Russell and the others had already told him that much, but what he really needed was to see if he could trust Bud. Now came another test. Larry went to Simon's desk and got a pen and paper. The top page was thick with Simon's doodles. Flipping it, Larry handed both to Bud. "Draw it for me."

And Bud did just that. Including the areas he could remember where ambushes had been set up along the road leading to the hotel. Afterward, he handed the drawings to Larry, who stood to leave. "You said there were two things you needed before you set me free," Bud said, trying to sound casual. "I did the first. Now what's the second?"

"When we go in," Larry told him. "I want you with us."

Bud's face went pale.

"Don't worry, you won't be armed. You'll be a kind of consultant. And if you live, then I'll set you free."

Dana

The object sitting on the police trailer stairs looked like a gift at first. But as Dana drew closer, she realized it wasn't a present at all. It was a large brown envelope. The kind you use to store important documents or to mail a favorite book to a friend. The tab was sealed shut, but it wasn't addressed to anyone. She entered the trailer, shaking the package. There was something small and hard in there. Lou was nearby, putting on his gun belt, getting ready to make the rounds to ensure everyone in New Jamestown was doing what they were supposed to. Mostly that meant working on finishing that wall, digging the mantraps Larry ordered placed around the perimeter, or off the colony grounds hunting game.

"What'chu got there?" Lou asked.

"Not sure," Dana told him. "Was on the stoop. You hear anyone knock on the door while I was away?"

"No, Ma'am."

She looked around for her other two deputies. "Where's Ethan and Tanner?"

"Tanner's out helping keep watch over the folks chopping the trees, and Ethan's gone out with the hunting party. Makes more sense given the food situation for him to be using his God-given talents with a rifle. I taught him myself from a young age."

"Makes sense," Dana mumbled in reply, still eyeing the envelope. She didn't like receiving mysterious packages. Especially not lately. The planned attack on Alvarez' stronghold, not to mention the ongoing murder investigation as well as the latest revelation that Timothy might have once worked for Tevatron, kept her nerves on edge.

It was only with the greatest difficulty that she'd convinced Lou to step aside and allow her to handle the investigation. Her argument that he was too emotionally involved to remain objective had proved very persuasive. And undeniable after he nearly strangled Romeo during the kid's supposed exile.

Dana tore the top of the envelope off and let the contents slide onto her desk. Out came a single cassette tape. The same type and brand she'd seen in the cassette recorder.

"So, what is it?" Lou asked, peering over.

"A tape," Dana replied.

"Haven't these people heard of CD players?"

The tape player was already on her desk. Out came the old cassette Romeo had found. In went this new one. Dana pressed play and listened as she heard a pair a voices begin speaking. But the volume was too low to make out any details. She turned it up, just as Lou began closing in to hear it himself. Both of them stared at the machine, confused at first as they tried to make sense of what they were hearing. Each one struggling to figure out why the two voices sounded so familiar.

"I been meaning to ask if you'd gotten any more information out of the kid?" a male voice asked.

"Matter a fact, I have," the female replied. *"He's already produced a few leads I'm following."*

"So whatcha think Larry would do if he ever found out Romeo was still here?"

Dana snapped the tape recorder off. She and Lou stared at each other, dumbfounded.

"That's you and me," Lou whispered, glancing around as though someone might be looking over his shoulder right now.

Dana's heart was hammering against her ribcage. "But how'd they manage to tape us?" She padded over to one of the windows and scanned the grounds outside. Most of the work being done was toward the rear of the fence line. Over by the main compound, a handful of workers were taking a break, chatting with one another.

"Someone musta bugged the trailer," Lou said in a low voice. "I can't think of another explanation that makes any sense."

Already, Dana was checking the light switch on the wall. "Pass me that screwdriver on my desk," she asked Lou, who tossed it to her and watched as she removed the face plate and found nothing out of the ordinary.

"Check those light fixtures," she told him. "It's got to be in here somewhere."

Off he went to the other end of the trailer.

"Too far," Dana shouted. "It's gotta be fairly close or it wouldn't have picked up our voices."

"Whatcha think this means?" he asked, no longer seeming sure where to keep his hands. "Could Larry be behind this?"

Dana thought back to the strange conversation between the two of them not long ago. Larry had asked if he could trust her. 'Course she'd said yes, and she'd meant it. Larry could trust her, but why pose the question unless he knew otherwise?

Lou asked again, about Larry being behind this, and Dana shrugged her shoulders. Quite frankly, she wasn't sure what the hell was going on. Someone was playing a dangerous game of chess, and she didn't want any of her people getting caught in the crossfire.

Both of them looked up at the air conditioning unit at the same time. It hadn't worked since she'd first set her office up in here. The broken unit itself was on the roof, but a latch on the ceiling opened up to expose the guts of the thing. When Dana turned the knob and lowered the door, a microphone dropped through the opening. Inside, a green light stared back at her from a battery-powered tape recorder. She removed it and put it on her desk.

"Someone wanted us to know we were being watched," Dana said.

"That much is clear, but who?"

"Whoever it is, they were telling us that they know we defied Larry's orders." Just as she said the words a sickening thought suddenly occurred to her. She turned to Lou.

"When's the last time you checked on Romeo?"

Finn

"Do you believe it?" Joanne asked.

They were in one of the prison's security hubs, Finn busy connecting the desktop he'd taken from the warden's office to a monitor and keyboard on the desk. The generators outside ran for an hour during the day and three hours when the sun went down. If they wanted to see what was on the warden's hard drive, they'd only have a limited window to get that done.

"You mean Herb's story that I saved his life?" Finn asked, fiddling with wires and trying not to curse.

Joanne blushed and waved the subject away with the flip of her wrist. "No, never mind, it's silly."

The brief look of confusion on Finn's face cleared. "Oh, you mean us."

"If we were, you know, married, like those papers said we were." Joanne paused. "I mean, wouldn't we have known … somehow?"

Finn thought back to the light and tingly feeling in his stomach the very first time he'd seen Joanne. He sensed she wanted him to say something romantic, like "I knew it the minute I laid eyes on you." And who knows, maybe that woulda been the truth, too, but for some reason Finn just couldn't bring himself to say the words. Did he feel like he'd known Joanne before? That was one explanation. She was a beautiful woman, no doubt about it, and he hadn't felt a woman's caress since he'd come to on that cold, hard floor covered in slime. She was still staring at him, looking more and more like she wished she'd never brought the subject up.

"Pass me that flathead screwdriver, would you?"

"Sure thing," she replied sharply. Finn felt her place it in the palm of his hand, and when he turned to thank her, she'd already left the room.

It took him another 10 minutes to get everything set. He turned on the computer and waited as it booted up.

After a moment, the words Ely State Prison flashed across the screen.

The warden's desktop was cluttered with folders, and it took Finn a few minutes to sort through them.

Pardons from the governor. Transfer orders. And then a folder off to the side with a single word: *Arrow*.

Finn clicked it. Inside were more folders. One of them bore his name, and that's where he went. Looked like the documents here were more of the same. Finn's vital stats. Time served. Conviction for murder in the first degree. Those words hung in his mind with deadly weight. At the bottom was a description of the crime. This was something new. He read it over and shook his head. He was involved in a bank robbery. He, Joanne, and a third person named Kevin Butler. He and Kevin led four tellers into the back while Joanne made the customers kiss the ground. According to the police report, when they refused to open the safe, Finn shot and killed them all. Four people dead all because of him. He felt the blood drain from his face, the palms of his hands grow sweaty.

Could this be true?

Then another file marked, *The Innocence Project*, about a group of law students who went over capital murder cases. A document recounted how during the trial, Kevin Butler had turned state's evidence and blamed the murders on Finn. But Kevin's psych evaluation had showed he suffered from psychotic episodes as well as schizophrenia. Not to mention that gun powder residue was found only on Kevin's hands, and the ballistics report showed the shots came from his gun. The Innocence Project members believed the D.A. was sure that a conviction against Kevin would mean he'd simply be shipped off to a mental ward, while Finn could be put to death. A move that would really jumpstart the D.A.'s career.

Apparently, Finn's true guilt or innocence took a back seat to some sleazy lawyer's political aspirations. Four people had been killed, and the community wanted blood, and this D.A. was gonna give it to them, one way or another.

Robbing that bank certainly wasn't the right thing to do, but the file did say he and Joanne were losing their house to foreclosure after Finn got canned from his job at the chemical plant in Henderson, a suburb of Las Vegas.

The blood was starting to return to Finn's cheeks. By the looks of it, he and Joanne were decent people, caught up in a desperate situation. They took matters into their own hands, and there wasn't any excuse for that, but knowing he wasn't the one who killed those people eased a weight that had been on his shoulders since accessing the Tevatron mainframe with Johnson.

Finn backed out and into a folder labelled *Expenses*. Here, a ledger with 4 million dollars deposited by Tevatron into offshore accounts owned by the warden.

The bastard had been paid one million for each of them and tried to whisk them away before the wheels of justice could get his murder convictions overturned. And who was going to stop him? The D.A. who

133

had recently become the state governor? The very man who stood the most to lose by the news of Finn's innocence?

Then another folder with a strange name caught his attention. *Limitless Energy*.

He clicked on it and hadn't gotten further than a paragraph in when he suddenly realized he may have just discovered the key to bringing everyone's lost memories back, including his own.

Dana

Dana and Lou rushed to the trailer where Romeo was being held. She grabbed for the keys in her pocket to unlock the door when she noticed it was slightly ajar. The only one with a pistol was Lou, and he drew it now. A terrible feeling was churning in the pit of Dana's belly. They entered the trailer and were greeted by stony silence.

"Romeo," she called out. But there was no answer. The air inside was warm and thick and smelled of meat stew.

They pushed ahead, past stacks of furniture and piles of canvas. At last, they found Romeo, seated at the back of the trailer, slumped against the wall. A thin trickle of blood ran down the side of his mouth. There was something else as well. A kind of frothy foam around his lips, as though he'd had a seizure. Dana laid her fingers along his carotid artery and felt for a pulse.

"Anything?" Lou asked, dread in his voice that the news was all bad. She shook her head.

On the table before Romeo was a bowl that explained the smell in the room: deer stew. The kid's right hand was even clutching a spoon. But the smell coming off Romeo that Dana picked up as she drew closer wasn't broth or even the sick sweet smell of death. Hell, rigor mortis hadn't even started to set in yet. That delicate smell wafting up from Romeo's lips, however, was the same one she'd come across when examining Patty Mae's things. The smell of almonds. Someone must have come in and offered Romeo a bowl of delicious-looking stew. The kind of offer a hungry young man just couldn't refuse. And there's no way he would have known the thing was laced with cyanide.

Lou pointed to his cheeks. They were flushed cherry pink, another telltale sign left by the poison. The foam and blood at his lips also seemed to indicate the seizure had forced his teeth to clench down on his tongue. She wasn't going to go fishing around in there just now, but Dana would be willing to bet he'd nearly bitten it off.

"Poor young fella," Lou said, reaching over and closing his eyes. "What was the point of killing him?"

Dana's mind was reeling. "To keep him quiet. Maybe to send us a warning at the same time."

That last thought seemed to give Lou pause.

"He's telling us to back off."

"Yeah, that may be it. Larry came into the trailer the other day and was asking a bunch of weird questions about whether or not he could trust me."

"And what'd you tell him?"

"That he could, of course. He didn't come right out and call me a liar, but I couldn't help but feel like he knew we'd gone against him somehow."

"So, you think he came and poisoned the boy?"

Dana was looking at Romeo's hand, clutching that spoon. "Larry doesn't like to get his hands dirty, but it's clear enough whoever was behind this was the same person who bugged the police trailer."

"They wanted us to find Romeo," Lou surmised. "Wanted us to be know they'd caught wind of what we were up to."

"I think so. Make us feel like our every move was being watched."

Lou looked over his shoulder, perhaps wondering the same thing Dana was at this very moment. Whether this trailer also had a secret tape recorder listening in on their conversation.

"There's one other thing to keep in mind," he said in a low voice. "This sick sonbitch may be trying to send us scurrying off in the wrong direction. Get us chasing Larry's tail so the real killer can have free rein to operate."

Lou did have a point. Larry had every reason in the world to be behind this, but she had to keep a clear head and not allow her mind to seize on the first possible suspect. There were nearly 200 people in New Jamestown, and theoretically, it could be any one of them. And the very thought gave Dana an idea.

"We gotta put the tape recorder back where it was. Pretend like we never found it."

"You sure about that?"

"Positive. Then you and I have a conversation where we say something crazy, the whole time making sure the recorder's picking it up."

"So, that whoever repeats it has to be the one who put the recorder there in the first place."

"Exactly."

"But what should we say?" Lou asked.

"That there's a serial killer in New Jamestown and that he murdered All Father."

"Whoa, murdered All Father?"

"Maybe not as far out as you'd think. But it isn't a theory I've ever heard anyone mention since we've been here."

"So, if rumors of a serial killer start floating around," Lou says. "All we gotta do is trace them back to the source, and we find our killer."

"Or killers."

"And what do we do with him?" Lou asked, motioning toward Romeo's body.

Dana sighed. "We're definitely up a tree if anyone else sees him. I mean, it'd be proof positive we defied Larry. I also figure whoever's responsible won't rat us out or they'd risk exposing themselves as the killer. One of us will have to load him into a car and bury him out there somewhere." She was pointing beyond the colony's walls as though it were on the other side of the planet.

They got busy wrapping Romeo in canvas. Then they dragged him to the front of the trailer, placing his remains behind a jumble of plastic chairs. It was a horrible thing to have to do, and Dana hated every minute of it. Fact, the act almost made her feel guilty, as though she was Romeo's killer, trying to hide the evidence of her crime. Here his body would stay until they could find a safe time to move him. The truth was, someone in New Jamestown was murdering people, and no one besides her and Lou seemed to know what was going on.

Once they felt Romeo's body was safely hidden, she and Lou returned to the police trailer and replaced the tape recorder up in the air conditioning unit, just as they had found it. But not before Dana scratched the edge of the tape with her pocket knife. After that they let it run in silence for a while and then slammed the trailer door as though they'd just returned from finding Romeo. It was all rather elaborate and to Dana's ear a little over the top, but a certain amount of continuity would be required if her plan had any chance of working. So, too, would their acting chops, and as she and Lou began that fake conversation in which they theorized that New Jamestown was beset by a serial killer, all she could do was hope it sounded natural enough.

The charade was just about over when the door to the trailer swung open and Tanner appeared, out of breath, but clearly with something to say.

"What's wrong now?" Dana asked.

"You better come. They just caught the food thief."

The news was surprising enough since whoever stole that food might also have been behind the murders. But it was something about the way Tanner refused to look her directly in the eye that worried her most of all.

Larry

Attacking the Wipers at the Grand America would, in a single stroke, solve three of Larry's biggest problems. First, it would help to weaken and perhaps remove the threat of hostile natives that were constantly scheming for a chance to destroy them. But more than that, it would end the food crisis and the major source of his political instability. A move that would undoubtedly castrate Timothy's plans of launching a coup d'état. Larry counted himself fortunate that All Father hadn't done the same to him. Had the old man allowed weapons in what was then Rainbowland and begun to erect proper defenses in earnest, Larry wouldn't have had a solid reason to oppose him. But Timothy's attempt to plunge the colony into further chaos by destroying the food supply and then organizing segments of the population against him had taught Larry an important lesson. Having faith in the loyalty of others is the quickest way of getting a knife stuck in your back. It didn't matter that the proof of Timothy's theft hadn't been found yet. In Larry's heart, he knew the sneaky bastard had done it, and soon enough the opportunity to strike back would present itself. The first step was knocking out the Wipers, and it was with that in mind that Larry left his office and headed down to the gymnasium where Donavan was waiting for him.

Larry arrived moments later and smiled when he saw the tables laid out with the weaponry they would use in the attack. Kel-Tec KSGs, a dozen AKs, and plenty of AR-15s.

One of the early scavenging parties had even found an old M60 and a box of belt-fed ammo to go with it. This they would mount on the lead vehicle. 'Course, there wasn't time or the resources to "up armor" any of the cars and trucks, so the convoy would need to rely on lightning speed.

Word about Larry's plans had spread through the colony like wildfire as soon as the meeting in the police trailer had concluded. As Larry had expected, the reaction had been mixed to say the least, but many here had already suffered at the hands of the Wipers in one way or another. Many even relished the chance to strike back. Without a doubt, gnawing hunger helped them arrive at that decision much more quickly. But even as nothing more than a distraction, the attack was sure to pay dividends. Dead New Jamestonians meant even less mouths to feed.

As part of the preparations, Larry recalled the hunting parties and put them back on finishing the remaining few feet of the palisade. A job he expected them to complete before sundown. After that, only the guard towers along the rear wall and the mantraps beyond it would be left. A thought that made Larry smile. If everything went to plan, they wouldn't need to hunt for deer meat again until at least the spring. Ever since his secret stash of premium food had been looted, like the rest of these poor slobs, Larry had been forced to eat whatever he could find. Sometimes, that meant eating dog. But soon, that would all be behind him.

Donavan had just finished ordering a group of cult members to see that the cars were gassed up and running smoothly when Larry called him over.

"I've been thinking about our strategy going in," Larry began, pulling a scrap of paper from his back pocket and flattening it out against one of the tables. "We'll approach from Main and State streets in two separate columns. That way, we won't be flanked by groups of Wipers that may be outside. At the first hint of our approach, I expect they'll start streaming out the front of that hotel like a swarm of ants, and that's where we'll cut them down."

Donavan approved, and Larry knew he would. That book Timothy had given Larry on the tactics of Julius Caesar had become something of a bible for him. It informed the way he ruled with an iron fist, the sorts of defenses and antipersonnel traps he would use to keep his enemies from overrunning New Jamestown. And it was also the philosophy upon which he based his attack strategy. But there was one more way in which this was true. The lesson Julius had picked up from Alexander the Great and which had been passed down to every great general since then: the idea of holding back a reserve force. A group you could call on in case things started to go cock-eyed.

Larry circled two groups of five cars. "Twenty fighters from each column will remain outside to guard the perimeter."

"Roger that."

Larry grinned. "We leave at the crack of dawn."

Donavan said he'd be ready.

"Oh, and there's one more thing," Larry added. "When we come back, I want you to keep an eye on Dana for me."

"The sheriff?"

Larry nodded. "I wanna know what she's up to."

"Not a problem."

There was a commotion at the gym entrance just then, and the two men turned to see what was going on. A mixed gang of regular colonists and culties tussled through the doorway, holding a man who'd clearly been beaten.

"We found the thief," one of them cried in triumph, and that's when Larry recognized who it was they were bringing before him, and suddenly all of his suspicions seemed perfectly justified. The thief was Dana's father.

Dana

At least 30 colonists were gathered in the gymnasium by the time Dana arrived. Seated on the floor before Larry was her father, Richard. The side of his face was bruised and swollen. Hostility and anger surged from the crowd. They were chanting things like "Hang him!" and "death penalty!" Dana and Lou pushed through the throngs of people till they reached her father. She bent down to see if he was all right.

A torrent of emotion hit Dana all at once. First, confusion over how he could possibly be guilty of such a thing and then just as quickly, anger at what these people had done to him.

"The hell is going on here?" she shouted. "Since when have we endorsed lynch mobs in New Jamestown?" She was looking directly at Larry as she spoke, and he didn't seem to like the insinuation.

One of the cult members in the crowd pointed at her father. "We found some of the missing food in the footlocker at the end of his bed."

"I didn't do it, Dana," her father said pleadingly. "I swear to God, I didn't do it." A thin line of blood ran from the corner of his eye where someone had punched him. The men and women surrounding them came closer, and Dana leaned over to protect him with her body.

"He deserves a fair trial," she said to Larry, who was looming over both of them. "We can't just run around executing people on a suspicion of guilt." She turned to the crowd. "If any of you were accused of this crime, wouldn't you want a chance to defend yourself?"

"I was digging in the ground to find worms yesterday," one woman said. "Do we want a society that protects criminals and punishes the innocent?"

The anger in the voices around her grew louder.

"What more do you need?" another man asked. "He had the food in his locker."

Dana's father was many things growing up. Often drunk and mostly lazy, but she'd never known him to be a thief. If anything, his honesty often baffled people. Once a clerk had mistakenly given him a 20 instead of a 10, and her father had given it back. As a child, she remembered the startled and almost derisive look the young cashier had given him. Like he was an idiot for being honest. Take the money and run, man. Those were the governing philosophies in the Old World before The Shift. The circumstances of the world often change, but rarely do the people locked within it. Once a thief, always a thief. If so, then shouldn't the opposite be true?

Larry did his best to quiet down the simmering anger. Dana was suddenly sure that if he told them to, the crowd would reach down and tear her father to shreds.

"What would this world be worth without the rule of law?" Larry asked. "Nothing, I say. None of you need look any further than the Wipers to see the results of their flagrant disregard for human life and decency. There is no room in New Jamestown for criminals. The theft of the colony's food supply has put all of our lives in grave danger. Mark my words, Richard will have a fair trial, that I can promise you. If he's found guilty, it's only fair that the punishment should fit the crime." Larry was looking over the crowd now, hushed in silence to hear him. "And let it be known that the consequence for such an act will be a swift and immediate execution."

The gymnasium exploded in a roar of enthusiasm, and Dana felt tears welling up behind her eyes. Everything in her heart said her father was innocent, that he'd even been framed. The thought of having to execute her own father was absolutely unbearable. As much as Dana believed in the rule of law and the need to uphold it, she knew she wasn't heartless enough to carry out her duty should it come to that.

She stood then and with Lou's help got her father to his feet and led him through the mob and toward the jail. In a strange way, it was the safest place for him. He'd be spared having to join the attack on the Wipers and certainly kept away from any nut job who felt the sudden urge to take the law into his own hands. He continued to plead his innocence as they led him away, but she couldn't help another thought circling through her head. Was a fair trial even possible in a small community that had already decided his guilt?

"What is it?" Joanne asked, responding to Finn's frantic summons. He could tell she was annoyed and not simply because he'd shouted for her come over. She'd stormed off in the first place because of the way he'd wiggled past answering her question about their relationship. But if what he was seeing in this file was to be believed, then there was a way to unlock the memories buried deep within them. Then they would know for sure. Know everything. Even the painful memories best left unexcavated.

"It appears that when The Shift occurred, it didn't wipe people's memories clean, not completely."

"That makes sense," Joanne replied. "Didn't you say you were starting to recall bits and pieces?"

The dream he'd had of Johnny tattooing those numbers into his wrist and of meeting Thomson. That was the memory she was referring to. 'Course, he hadn't given her details, anymore than to say fragments were starting to surface.

"Tevatron bribed the warden so they could use us as guinea pigs. Paid him millions of dollars." Finn explained about the robbery and how he'd been pinned with the murders during the heist. "Then I found this," he said, rolling his chair out of the way.

Joanne stepped closer to see what was on the screen. "It looks like research data on memory suppression."

"Apparently, Tevatron's got a facility somewhere emitting a low-frequency, low-intensity ultrasound pulse that's keeping people's lost memories from surfacing."

"To maintain the amnesia?"

"According to this, the tests to weaponize the mass amnesia wasn't holding for more than a few hours, so they started playing around with using low-frequency sounds to maintain the effects. They set up transducers designed to generate acoustic waves."

"But all the power's been shut off for weeks," Joanne said, curling strands of her dark hair with her fingers, a habit Finn had seen her do when she was thinking. "How could it still be running?"

"Good question. Even the solar plant at the Tevatron lab where I came to had gone offline after the quake."

"So, you think if we can shut that signal off somehow, then our memories might start to return?"

"Not just us," Finn said. "But the Wipers, too. And maybe following a guy like Alvarez won't make nearly as much sense once they remember they're really an accountant from Ohio who lost track of their family after The Shift."

"They'll stop being animals."

"Maybe not all, but most of them will. But there's a bigger problem. I've been over these files three times, and nothing here gives a hint of where this place might be. We can't flip the switch if we don't know where they've hidden it."

Larry

The next morning, 148 colonists shuffled into 37 cars. Except for colonist number 149, however, who was sitting in jail for theft. It seemed unlikely to Larry that a dumpy old man had been the one to actually commit the crime, but there was a power in making an example out of someone, anyone, that far exceeded the truth of who was really guilty.

Larry would ride in the lead truck with Donavan. A pickup they'd outfitted with the M60 manned by Callahan. It had taken some work, but in the end, Larry had managed to convince the young soldier that getting some retaliation on the Wipers for contributing to his friend's death would help to set things right. Once they were done, he could return to his people.

Cramped in the back seat were Bud and Russell. Both men had firsthand knowledge of the hotel's layout. He was relying on them to be his scouts in the same way that General Custer had relied on his Crow and Lakota trackers during the Indian Wars. Although Larry was quite certain this campaign would turn out far better for him than it did for Custer.

Lou's black battle wagon was second in line. Inside was his son, Ethan, along with Tanner and Nikki.

Remaining behind was a small contingent of men and women tasked with manning the walls and keeping things at home running smoothly. Among them was Dana. Larry's need for people with military experience was paramount for this operation, but given Dana's current state of mind after her father's arrest, he thought it best if she stayed behind to watch over things. The note on his desk insinuating that Romeo wasn't banished as he'd ordered was unsettling and had fed into his growing distrust of her.

A voice over the walkie-talkie called back that everyone was loaded in.

"All ready to go, Brother Larry," Donavan said. "Brother Larry?"

"Huh," Larry replied, deep in thought. "Hurry up then, we're already an hour late."

"One more thing, Sir. Once we open those gates, any Wiper spies hiding in the woods may give away our plans."

"No need to worry. I sent a special team out this morning to clear them out."

Donavan smiled, and Larry waved his hand outside the passenger window. Two men pulled open the main gate and saluted as the convoy rumbled past and over the bridge. The attack was under way.

•••

The streets of Salt Lake City were deserted. Of people that was. The rusting hulks of abandoned cars, on the other hand, were hardly in short supply. Many were lining the roads, their noses turned to look away like peasants before a passing king. That was how Larry felt at the head of the long column of cars.

An equal number was speeding parallel to him down State Street. He could see them now on his left, and if all went well they'd converge on the hotel and do the bloody business that needed to be done. It was clear driving through town that a path had been carved through cluttered intersections, likely by the Wipers as they cleaned the city out of every last morsel of food. The sights of weeds growing through gashes in the pavement and buildings with large cracks running up the sides, some crumbling in places, was rather shocking for Larry. Mostly since this was the first time he'd been beyond the compound walls in weeks, if at all. There'd never been a need to venture out into danger before. That was something the people below him did. Except riding at the head of a strike force was different. There was glory in that, and Larry was lapping up every bit of it. He was Julius, taming the wild Gauls.

Soon, the top of the Grand America came into view. Not nearly as white as when Larry first saw it driving in all those weeks ago, but certainly still an impressive sight.

"Two more streets then take a left," Bud said. The man was weaponless, of course. They needed manpower sure, but Larry was no fool. He reached down and felt for the Browning 9 mm at his side. Four magazines rested in the left pocket of the cargo pants he was wearing. The last time he'd used a pistol had been to kill three men during his life-and-death struggle to escape the hell hole that was New York City. Which was to say, firing a gun was nothing new to him. That wasn't what was worrying him, however. The silence in the streets was doing that just fine. A running gun battle to the hotel. That's what he'd expected, what Donavan and Callahan had suggested was the most likely scenario. They would race through the gauntlets and ambushes and storm the Grand America, the few cars in the rear forming a protective cordon around them. The truck window was open, a cool early morning wind splashing Larry's face and nothing but the sound of the engine.

"Here it is," Bud called out. The hotel took up an entire block, and tires screeched as the truck tore around the corner. They made another quick left and saw the overhang and the hotel's main entrance. Just beyond that was a grassy area and a large domed fence covering a pit in the ground. That must have been the arena, where Carole had fought to free Russell and the other guy – Josh? – the poor slob who hadn't made it.

Lou swore under his breath and pointed at the body dangling from the lip of the overhang.

Ahead of them, the second group of cars screeched up to the entrance, and men and women began pouring out, waiting for the assault to begin.

Larry popped the door and jumped out. Beside him, Callahan was scanning the rooftops with his M60, searching for Wipers.

The truth was, for all the war gaming he'd done in his head, Larry didn't have the foggiest idea in hell what he was doing. He'd expected ambushes along the way. None had come. Then he'd imagined the Wipers surging out at them from inside the hotel, the colonists riddling them with semi-automatic fire. But that hadn't happened either. Now a darker, more frightening prospect began to emerge. The very real possibility that they'd have to go in after them. A tangle of people with little combat experience pushing through a series of dark corridors. If the Wipers were waiting inside, then it would be Larry and his small army who were suddenly at a disadvantage.

Lou pulled the charging handle of his Hello Kitty AR-15 as he stopped next to Larry. He was trying not to look at the dead body. "Place is like a ghost town, and I don't like it one bit."

Neither did Larry. He turned to Donavan. "Half the group stays by the vehicles and guards the perimeter. The rest move in." And even as he sent the colonists forward, a single thought kept tugging an invisible string at the back of his mind: *Where the hell are the Wipers?*

Jeffereys

Peering through the scope of his Remington M-24SWS .308, Jeffereys was growing more confident that he and his men hadn't yet been spotted. They'd set out from the Grand America the night before, 450 strong, with the objective of assaulting Ely State Prison and capturing as many of the *Alabama's* crew members as they could. Above all else, their mission was to capture those capable of firing the nuclear warheads. No doubt, once they had these men, convincing them to cooperate with such a plan would be difficult, perhaps impossible, but Alvarez had assured Jeffereys that his powers of persuasion were not to be underestimated.

Driving through the desert on their way there, the long line of cars and trucks appeared to snake behind them for miles. Now, the bulk of Jeffereys' force was taking cover along the road, beyond the ridge line, awaiting his signal.

He steadied his breathing and levelled the scope's crosshairs so they rested over one of the two guards standing by the main gate. Like Petty Officer Lewis, the men were dressed in blue and gray camo. This one in particular was scratching his balls when Jeffereys pulled the trigger. The muzzle kicked up a spray of dust as the rifle let out a sound like the crack of a whip. A moment later, the sailor collapsed to the ground, a spray of blood fanning the wall behind him. Jeffereys worked the bolt and put his eye to the scope again to find the second sailor. He'd disappeared into the guard house, presumably taking cover and radioing for help.

Through the eyepiece, Jeffereys could see that the guard house had a large glass window facing out. Inside, a desk and a panel of electric switches on the wall beside it. And there poking above the table top was the crest of the second sailor's head. Jeffereys took careful aim, adjusting for wind speed, distance and gently squeezed the trigger. A hole in the glass appeared, obscuring his view of the target. But the blood now splashed against the back wall told him all he needed to know.

The shot from Jeffereys' rifle was the sound they'd been waiting for, and he watched as the main attack force came charging over the ridge at full speed, a cloud of dust rising behind the dozens of vehicles as they tore on. Their job was to ram the gates, assault the tower guards, and then swoop into the prison itself.

Lewis had made it perfectly clear they wouldn't be up against Navy Seals or Marines. Most of the men based at the prison were non-combat petty officers, engineers, sonar and fire control technicians. A prospect that gave Jeffereys full confidence that in a matter of minutes the battle would be over and that Commander Zhou and his remaining men would belong to them.

The fifth vehicle in the column racing for the prison was the same Humvee they'd captured in town. It peeled away from the others and headed across the open field and directly for Jeffereys. Sailors in the towers were already opening fire on the assault force. Rising to his feet, Jeffereys waved to the Humvee. One of the back doors swung open when it skidded next to him.

"So far, so good," Jeffereys said, handing his rifle to one of the slavers and crawling inside. A second later, they tore off to rejoin the attack.

Even bouncing over rough terrain, it was clear the first few vehicles had breached the prison's main gate. Cracks in the plan, however, were already starting to reveal themselves.

A large plume of black smoke billowed from one of the cars, likely engaged from a tower above. The problem was the road that led from the ridge ran along the perimeter fence and was vulnerable to enemy fire.

The other cars were moving to go around it, but it was gobbling up precious time, risking further fire from above.

Jeffereys got on the radio. "Go around the wreck, Goddammit." He shouted. This was a shock and awe campaign. There weren't any voters Alvarez needed to impress with low casualty rates. It was about getting the job done. High losses weren't an issue, but failure was. Jeffereys climbed through the hole in the Humvee's roof to man the .50-cal. He called for the truck to stop, and when it did, less than a hundred yards from the gate, he opened up on the nearest tower. He could see a sailor firing down on his troops with an automatic weapon. The truck rocked violently as his machine gun spit out bullets capable of chopping a man in half. Short bursts seemed to work best, and Jeffereys adjusted his fire as he watched puffs of concrete and glass explode around the shooter in the tower. At one point, the sailor took a direct hit to the chest and was flung back. Two more cars in their convoy were in flames as Jeffereys worked on the next tower. Once he knocked that one out, his men would no longer be running such a deadly gauntlet. But he needed to hurry, since the handful of trucks that had already breached the wall was now coming under heavy fire from inside the prison.

It took close to 50 rounds and several precious minutes before Jeffereys was able to silence the second tower with his .50-cal. Half a dozen of their own vehicles had either burst into flames or driven off the road, with most of the occupants dead or dying. A few spilled out unharmed and ran toward the objective.

Jeffereys ordered the driver forward, and the Humvee lumbered on, motoring past the gate where the sight made the blood in his veins boil. Most of the initial wave that had crested their attack lay dead in the morning sun. Enemy fire was landing all around, some of it hitting the Humvee from windows and doorways along the prison's ground level. But Jeffereys was thankful no one was shooting down on them from the rooftop. More and more vehicles streamed into the grounds behind him, engaging the remaining towers. Within another 10 minutes, the rest of Jeffereys' force had formed a semicircle around the prison, preparing to choke it off. According to Petty Officer Lewis, the submariners kept their own vehicles – mostly Humvees – inside an inner courtyard. Jeffereys' main concern was that they'd try to break out and escape. He needed to send a final group to capture those vehicles and close the noose. But first, he would try to appeal to their sense of self-preservation. Jeffereys retrieved the megaphone from inside his Humvee and rose back up through the gun turret.

"Commander Zhou," he said, as bullets whizzed by his head. "Your men are surrounded. If you surrender now, no one else will be harmed." Sporadic firing continued before Jeffereys repeated the message. A minute later, the firing had stopped altogether. It was starting to look like Alvarez might get his boomer after all.

Finn

At first, it sounded like the engine of a Humvee had backfired, but it didn't take more than a few seconds for Finn to realize they were under attack. Sailors streamed toward the open windows, firing at an enemy Finn couldn't see. Other men in blue and gray fatigues raced upstairs to the second story, presumably to gain the higher ground. Standing in the middle of the room was Commander Zhou, barking orders.

"Bring up the Javelins!"

That's when they heard the voice over the loudspeaker, telling them that if they surrendered, no one would be harmed. The man behind the voice sounded thin and weaselly.

"Hold your fire," Zhou called out.

"You're not thinking of surrendering, are you?" Finn asked in horror.

Zhou ignored Finn's question. "How long till that Javelin's in place?"

"Thirty seconds, Sir," came a sailor's reply.

"Regardless what's happened in the world," Zhou said. "We're still the United States Navy. They sent over their demands. I'm giving the man my answer." Zhou called out to the missile team. "Fire when ready."

Finn and Joanne raced to the set of double doors just in time to see the Javelin missile streak down from the second floor window and strike the front of the Humvee. The truck itself must have seen the attack right before because its tires kicked up clouds of white smoke as it tried to move out of the way. Wild .50-cal shots slammed into the building. They were aiming for the fire team.

A man in black leather, holding a megaphone, scrambled through the ceiling hatch and onto the pavement right as the impact flipped the back of the truck into the air. The explosion picked him up and tossed him several feet. Whether he was killed or not, Finn couldn't tell, although anyone left within the Humvee was surely dead.

The sailors inside the prison let out a cheer and gave each other high-fives.

"Suck on that, bitch!" one of them shouted.

Then came the sound of a car engine revving. Finn glanced back outside, and what he saw then made his heart lodge in his throat. One of the Wipers in a Camaro was coming right for them, aiming to use his car as a battering ram. Finn grabbed Joanne by the arm and pulled her out of the way just as the car burst through the set of double doors and directly into the prison's front lobby. The car came directly at Zhou, and the commander surely would have died if Foster hadn't tackled him to safety.

The Camaro and its driver continued at full speed until he crashed into the office, destroying everything inside, including the warden's computer.

But right now there wasn't time to worry about that. Wipers were streaming into the prison. An all-out gun battle was underway with sailors and Wipers falling all around them.

Finn picked up an M-4 from one of the dead. He had to get Joanne to safety before they were overrun.

That's when he saw Foster and Commander Zhou pinned down in a recessed doorway. He couldn't just leave them. There was an office right off the main entrance. Finn kicked the door in and shoved Joanne inside.

"Where are you going?"

"Hide in here. Don't move unless I come get you myself."

He slammed the door shut and raced for the Camaro. Peeling the man's head back, he saw that the driver inside was dead, but the engine was still running. Finn pulled the Wiper out, slid into the driver's seat, put the car into reverse and punched the gas. Tires screeched against the smooth concrete floor as the car shot backwards. Many of the Wipers were still moving through the narrow confines of the main entrance when they saw Finn coming. A few managed to get off a handful of shots, and Finn ducked under the seat for cover right as the car thudded into bodies and then the steel door frame.

More shots from Wipers outside, cutting through the Camaro's thin metal frame. Before him, the floor of the prison was littered with Wipers, dead and dying. Finn scrambled through the car's open window and ran for Zhou and Foster, already emerging from the doorway.

"You one crazy white boy!" Foster said as they took off to get Joanne and rally their men for a counterattack.

Larry

Unlike his idol, the great Julius Caesar, Larry Nowak wasn't the type to lead his men into battle in person. If the Wipers had charged out from the Grand America as they arrived, he'd have been the first to scurry behind the pickup and open fire, but rushing inside first? No, siree. That was a job for underlings. Donavan and Lou, in particular.

And on they went, drawing the rest of the armed colonists in with them. Bud was nearby, weaponless, but looking like he wanted nothing more than to join them. He was about to move in when Larry held him back. Bud turned. "You're not gonna let them go in alone, are you?"

There were others around in earshot. Colonists who'd stayed behind to guard the vehicles and whether he meant to or not, Bud's little question was threatening to make Larry look like a real pussy.

"Of course not," he barked in reply.

"I'll need a weapon."

"You'll do it Russian style and grab a gun from the first corpse you see."

Larry and Bud quick-timed it toward the front entrance and were just coming under the roundabout's overhang when gunfire erupted from inside. It was loud as hell. Much louder than Larry could have anticipated.

Had they caught them sleeping, Larry wondered pulling back the slide on his Browning 9 mm.

They reached the front entrance, and Larry dropped to one knee. "The ballroom, where is it?" he asked. This was the place Russell said Alvarez had stashed the food.

"Down that hall to the right."

A few colonists were hunkered behind them, presumably too afraid to enter what was sounding like a fierce firefight.

"We might have just whacked a hornet's nest," Bud said with an almost crazed look in his eyes. It looked like he wanted nothing more than to find a machine gun and mow down every Wiper he could find, Alvarez included.

Digging down deep, Larry rose to his feet and pushed his way inside. Even though it was early morning, the hotel's interior was filled with shadow and a rank sewery smell that nearly turned his stomach. This was hell on Earth, no doubt about it. Gun smoke clogged the hallway, adding to the illusion that the two men had stepped out of the real world and into Hades itself.

The ground floor opened into a three-way intersection. On the left was the check-in counter. Straight ahead a hallway which lead to a bank of elevators and perhaps a dinning room. To the right was another stretch of hallway and at the end, the ballroom and the stockpile of food they'd come here to claim in the first place. It wasn't any surprise then that most of the chaotic sounds of gunfire and the screams of the wounded were coming from that direction.

Wasn't long, however, before Larry saw the problem. Donavan hadn't sent anyone to secure the corridor that led to the elevators and dinning room. Instead, he and the group who'd followed him in had beelined it for the ballroom. As a result, he'd left his rear exposed to a counter attack. If the kid made it out, Larry would surely give him a truckload of shit for his oversight. Quickly, he waved two dozen colonists inside and ordered them to push on toward the dinning room and clear out any Wipers they found. The rest, he sent toward the ballroom where by the sounds of things, most of the reinforcements were needed.

In spite of his concerns of a counterattack, right now the dinning room was the safer of the two options. Which made going in that direction himself a no-brainer. He crossed the corridor at a full run, pulling a somewhat reluctant Bud behind him.

"Don't worry," he told him once they'd reached the other side. "You'll get your chance for revenge soon enough."

Bud didn't look all that convinced, but the truth was, Larry needed Bud for something else. "Where will we find this Alvarez?" he asked.

Dana

In less than an hour, Dana had managed to gnaw the nails on her right hand down to nubs. She was at the jail, talking to her father, but a part of her was right there with the dozens of men and women who'd driven off to raid the headquarters of a group that wanted nothing more than to smear them off the face of the Earth. There would be loss of life, that much was clear, but how many would survive, if any? That was the question causing her belly to work itself into a tight fist. She found her mind returning to Bud time and time again, and with each orbit, she pushed it away. The way he could have killed them all and escaped but instead chose to return her pistol and give her a wink.

Then Larry had gone and done something crazy. He'd set Bud free, and now she would need to get used to him as Bud, an active member of New Jamestown, rather than as Bud the convict. But none of that would mean a whole hell of a lot if he never returned.

"You're not listening, are you?" her father said accusingly. His shoulders were slumped, like a man who'd already given up.

"'Course I am."

"You ask me, attacking those savages is a damned stupid idea. If things go south over there, we won't make it through the winter."

He was talking as though that included him, somehow overlooking the death penalty he was facing. A penalty likely to be carried out as soon as Larry returned. And at whose hands? Certainly not her own. Surely, even Larry wasn't that cruel.

"You know I didn't do this," he said, his hands on the bars, and for a moment the sight made her think of Alvarez in the brig at Fort Baker, swearing on his life that he hadn't killed Keiths. Both claims she'd wanted to believe. And who wouldn't? As far as she was concerned, her dad was the only person left on Earth who hadn't lost his mind. Sometimes, the fear of loneliness can eclipse the fear of death. It was one of the ways the human mind managed to contort itself into all kinds of strange illogical shapes. She found her father's frightened face again, and the thought faded at once.

"No, I don't think you did it, but obviously someone wants us to think otherwise."

"I don't see who, I mean, I've been pulling my weight just like everyone else. I don't have a huge number of friends. But that shouldn't surprise anyone. There aren't a lot of people close to retirement around here."

Dana sighed deeply. She was studying the thinning lines under his eyes. "You know, in a weird way, the end of the world's been good for you, Pa. You kicked the booze and stopped watching CNN all day long."

He laughed and reached through the bars to touch her hand. "After we lost Gregory ... "

"We didn't lose him," Dana cut him off, hating when he tried to numb the reality of what happened. "Not the way people lose a sweater. He jumped off a bridge."

Her father's eyes fell, his face etched from years of pain. "Your mother left soon after that. Before long, there wasn't much to keep me going."

If his words had been a gleaming knife, they wouldn't have cut as deeply as they did now. "I was there, Dad, but that never seemed to be good enough for you. You were so busy focusing on what you didn't have that your eyes never saw the people right beside you. That's the real reason Mom left, not that you were ever one to deal with reality very well."

He didn't have an answer for that, and she was thankful he'd fought the urge to fill the air with lies and excuses. Flawed and damaged as he was, the man was her flesh and blood, a bond just as strong as it was frustrating.

"You need to stop talking like this. We're gonna get you out of here."

"Don't you see it, Dana, no one believes me. I've been framed, and I can't for the life of me figure out why."

Dana could think of a reason or two, and she was quite sure it might have something to do with her investigation. She could think of many people with the motive and opportunity. For Larry, it meant putting a face to the pantry thief and perhaps putting her loyalty to the ultimate test. For Simon, it could mean diverting suspicion away from him and perhaps avenging his father's death. For Timothy, it could be a ploy to create further chaos and instability in the colony in an effort to unseat Larry, with an added bonus of driving a wedge between the self-appointed king of New Jamestown and herself. And add to that a half dozen other suspects, all with a vested interest in destroying the status quo.

She pulled her hand from her father's and stood. "I won't let them get away with this, Dad. Something's rotten in New Jamestown, and framing you might have been a warning for me to back off."

He was staring up at her now, with a faraway look like he was retreating into his own little world. "I always thought one day I'd reach a certain age and be ready to die. You remember that Mrs. Sanders down the street. Eighty years old and shrivelled, begging for Jesus to take her. That's where I expected to find myself one day, wandering around, begging God to come down and take all my pain away. Maybe that's my destiny. Maybe it's everyone's destiny, but I'm not there yet, Dana. Not by a long shot."

Dana winked a tear away before telling her father she loved him. In spite of his imperfections, he was the only flesh and blood she had left in this shitty world, and she wasn't ready to let go of that.

A few seconds later, she crossed the dirt road and was in the sheriff's office. She flicked on the light, not able to entirely quiet the torrent of conflicting thoughts swirling around her. Thoughts of the attack were back again. About Lou, his son, Ethan, Nikki, Bud, and a score of others. Then she thought of Romeo. His body was still hidden in the trailer next to hers, and she would try and use the colony's near emptiness to remove any trace of him. It felt like an incredibly heartless thing to do, but so did taking a fall for refusing to send Romeo off to die. And with that, the tape recorder popped into her head. She reached up, unlatched the door that once led to an air conditioner and now housed the listening device. Taking it down and placing it on her desk, she could see right away that something was different. The mark she'd made on the tape with her pocket knife was gone. In fact, the tape itself was an entirely different brand, which could only mean one thing. Someone had been inside the trailer and taken the conversation she and Lou had planted. Now she could only hope that her plan might bear fruit before her father faced the gallows.

Nikki

The smoke-filled corridors of the Grand America Hotel reduced visibility to but a few feet. Nikki had been part of the group Larry had waved toward the elevators and dinning room.

The ear-shattering boom from guns firing behind them were starting to fray Nikki's nerves. Tanner and Ethan were right beside her, but the thought did little to calm her down. Nor was it able to diminish the feeling they'd entered some kind of twisted fun house. One many of them might never escape. She was clutching a pistol in her right hand, desperate not to let it fall from her grasp, but also careful to keep her finger away from the trigger.

The group Nikki was in inched forward through the haze. A blur of movement ahead made her body tense. Between the crackle of gun fire behind them, she could hear new, guttural voices shouting at one anther in broken English, and she knew right away they were Wipers. A handful of colonists in front opened fire, and that's when all hell broke loose. A bullet whizzed by her head and punched a perfectly round hole in the wall next to her. More bullets zipped by, and Nikki dove for cover, Tanner and Ethan pilling on top of her to block any incoming fire. People were shouting all around them. From out of the smoke, a figure in black leather charged, emptying an assault rifle into a cult member until his weapon clicked empty. He was reaching for a machete in his belt when Ethan dropped him with a single blast from his shotgun. The Wiper flew back against what might have once been an expensive painting, his chest peppered with buckshot. Another Wiper had knocked a colonist named Susan Miller to the floor and was in the process of strangling her when Nikki leveled her pistol. She was thinking of her mother and what Wipers had done to both of them in the airport.

She squeezed the trigger. Two shots rang out, hitting the Wiper both times in the chest, under the armpit. At once, his fingers relaxed on Susan's throat, and his eyes rolled up in their sockets. She rose to her feet, her hands shaking. The Wipers weren't coming anymore, and the lull gave them time to check on the wounded.

One colonist and one cult member were already dead with another five wounded. Given the racket going on near the ballroom, who knew how many more had been seriously hurt or killed.

Ethan came close to Nikki and asked if she was all right. She wasn't sure if he meant physically, but it hardly seemed to matter. The horror people were experiencing here would stay with them a long time.

Straight ahead was a series of high-end suites. Wipers could be behind each door, waiting to ambush them, a prospect that was absolutely nerve shattering. Nikki'd been trying to keep an eye out for Aiden the whole time, but in all the chaos she hadn't seen anyone matching his description. And given the carnage, she was beginning to think if he was still here he may have already been killed.

On her left, a group was entering the first suite when semi-automatic fire erupted from inside, riddling a middle-aged cult member caught in the open after kicking in the door. He crumpled to the ground as one of the colonists stuck his rifle around the corner and fired off a dozen shots. Another peeked around and then charged inside with his pistol. Two others joined him. More shots rang out, then a shout from inside: "Clear!"

Waiting in the back for everyone else to do the dangerous work was Larry, his own pistol drawn, the expression on his face beleaguered as though he'd been in the thick of things from the start.

When the next suite door was kicked open, Tanner, Ethan, and Nikki were the first ones in. She pulled the hammer back on her pistol, her heart like a caged animal inside her chest. This suite looked far more opulent than the others. On the right was a bathroom covered in marble. Tanner peered inside. It was lit by a flickering candle next to the sink. Not enough to read by, but more than enough to see the bathroom was empty. Across the narrow hall was a closet with two folding doors. Ethan was about to check it when they heard the noise. Sounded like someone puffing on a cigar around the corner.

All of them left what they were doing and headed in that direction. In the foyer was Alvarez, sitting in a plush, studded leather chair. He was kissing the end of the cigar in his mouth oblivious there was an attack on his headquarters or that his men were being decimated. But it was the figure standing obliquely behind him that caught Nikki's eye.

Dressed in dark leather, his hair showing the early stages of natural dreadlocks, was Aiden. Although his strange appearance wasn't the only thing different about him.

Ever since she could remember – which wasn't that long, mind you – there'd always been a twinkle in her brother's eyes. The kind she supposed was common to all little brothers who lived to tease their older sisters. But now that sparkle was gone, replaced by an almost soulless expression. Aiden stood there at Alvarez' elbow, glaring at them as though they were invaders instead of liberators. Nikki was about to call out his name when Alvarez blew out a thick cloud of cigar smoke and said, "Aren't family reunions touching?"

159

For a moment, Nikki was stunned speechless not only by Alvarez' cool manner, but also his knowledge that they were related. Was it the family resemblance or the eagerness on her face that had betrayed her?

Ethan was on her left, and he raised his shotgun against Alvarez at the exact moment the woman came bursting out of the closet, snarling like a wolverine as she jumped on his back. The shotgun in Ethan's hands went off with a loud boom. The shot went wide, creating a moonscape on the wall above Alvarez' head.

The woman sank her teeth into Ethan's neck and buried her nails into his face. Nikki tried to get her off, but Ethan was moving around too much, shrieking in pain. Tanner reached over to yank the crazy woman off when a shot came from Alvarez' direction. But it wasn't Al holding the gun, it was Aiden. Ethan fell to the floor, the woman still clinging to his limp body. Tanner pistol-whipped the back of the woman's head, knocking her out, then took aim at Aiden.

Nikki jabbed the pistol, and the shot went wide. She then ran to her brother, shielding him with her body.

"Don't kill him. Can't you see he's been brainwashed by this monster?"

Alvarez' eyebrows rose at the mention of the word monster. "Is that what you all think of me?"

That was when Lou, Larry, and Bud stormed in. His son lying on the ground, Lou's eyes went wide with shock and then rage.

The crazy woman from the closet was coming to. Lou must have assumed she was responsible, because he put the muzzle of his AR-15 to her head and pulled the trigger. A spray of blood hit Tanner in the face as her body fell, convulsing. This was the first time Alvarez betrayed the slightest hint of emotion.

Lou swung his rifle over with the intent of wasting Alvarez, Aiden, and maybe even her.

"Stand down, Lou," Larry shouted and when the big guy's rifle didn't budge, Larry barked at him like a drill sergeant. Lou blinked hard, as though he and the real world were slowly merging once again and then dropped to his son on the floor.

Alvarez tapped the ash off his cigar. "Larry," I presume. "I've heard so much about you." Then his eyes shifted to Bud, and a smile grew on his lips.

"I'm sure you have," Larry answered.

Donavan came in, followed by a group of colonists, their faces a macabre combination of dirt and spattered blood.

"Take Alvarez into custody," Larry told Donavan and his men. "I have a feeling he'll prove quite useful."

PRIMAL SHIFT 9: NEW WORLD ORDER

Finn

By the time Finn, Lou, and Foster reached Joanne hiding in the office, Wipers were once again pouring through the prison's front entrance. From the rooms and balcony that ran along the second floor, Zhou's men continued to fire down upon the invaders. Many of them had chewed through more than half of their ammunition. There was more in ammo boxes they'd brought with them from Point Loma. But what they lacked was the time it would take to feed those bullets into magazines.

Finn was quite certain Zhou never expected an assault from a force as large, determined, and organized as these Wipers. Small bands of raiders and scavengers were the fiercest opposition he'd faced since arriving at Ely State Prison. Not to mention the fact that they hadn't planned for stay for more than a couple weeks before moving on to Salt Lake City.

And that was precisely the city Alvarez' army of Wipers were from. Not a great way to promote SLC as a safe place to create a settlement.

Zhou was on the radio now, telling his men to fall back to the inner reception center. They'd set up a series of concentric defenses around the prison. The first was the outer perimeter fence and guard towers. Next, the main reception area and as a last resort, the inner reception area where back in the day prisoners were processed and shipped to their cells.

Sailors on the second level had to fight their way along a narrow walkway to reach that final defensive zone. But for those on the main floor – Finn, Joanne, Zhou, Foster, and the dozen sailors who'd joined them – the path to the inner sanctuary would mean heading through two long corridors.

Shots rang out behind them, and Finn turned in time to see they'd been spotted by incoming Wipers. He and the sailors nearby returned fire, in an attempt to buy time for the rest to escape. Foster stayed with Joanne and Commander Zhou.

One by one, the sailors peeled away to follow the main group. The idea wasn't only to kill the Wipers, but to keep them at bay. An improvised leap frog maneuver.

Charging at a full run, Finn caught up with the group of fourteen right as they rounded the first corner. Even before he arrived, he could hear shouting.

"Don't shoot him!" Joanne screamed.

That was when Finn saw what all the commotion was about. A man with a white beard wearing an orange jumpsuit had his hands propped in the air.

Even in the darkened hallway he could see it was Herb.

Zhou and his men had their weapons trained on him.

"He isn't a Wiper," Finn barked.

More shots from behind as one by one the sailors caught up.

"There's no time to talk, Herb," Finn told him. "We're heading to a better defensive position inside. This place is about to get overrun."

They were already moving past Herb when the old man spoke up. "You do that, and they'll have you right where they want you," he said.

Zhou stopped. "What are you saying?"

"I'm saying there's another way that leads underground," Herb told him. "Past the prison walls and out into the desert."

"But we'll maintain strength in numbers if we stay together," Zhou said. The shooting behind them was growing louder. There wasn't any time to talk it through.

"Wait a minute," Finn said. "Herb might have a point. If we sneak around the Wiper's flank, we may be able to pick them off from behind."

Zhou sighed and nodded. He was a man used to making split-second decisions, and Finn could see that now. "Old man, you better know what you're doing." Zhou held the walkie to his lips and spoke: "Lock down the inner keep, we're gonna try and flank these sonsabitches."

"Roger that," came the reply through a burst of static. "Locking the inner keep."

Herb led them down a side hallway that opened onto a door with a yellow sign that read *Braille Printing*.

"The escape tunnel's in here," Herb told them.

Finn tried the door and found it locked. Four sailors in the rear were firing at the oncoming Wipers. "You better hurry, Sir. We won't be able to hold them off for long."

Foster dug his shoulder into the door without much effect.

"Back away," Kulik, the sub's XO, called out as he came forward with a Benelli M3 shotgun. Everyone turned away as he fired once into the latch and another where the lock was located. He sunk the heel of his boot into it, sending the door swinging open.

"Always using your head, XO," Zhou told him.

Kulik smiled as they entered the room, slamming the door shut once everyone was inside.

Foster turned on the tactical flashlight at the end of his rifle. The expression on his face made it clear he didn't like this idea one bit. "The hell you bring us? Place is a damned death trap."

The room itself was no bigger than your average living room, but that was where the similarities ended. Long steel shelves stacked with paper lined the walls on either side.

Herb pointed at the giant machine nestled against the far wall. "This is the printing press where we made books for blind kids."

"That sure is touching," Foster said. "What we gonna do when the Wipers find us, hand em some pamphlets?"

"The escape tunnel," Herb said. "It's under the printing press."

Any minute now, the Wipers would clue into where they'd gone and start shooting through that door. Five sailors, plus Finn, grabbed hold of the printing press and began pulling it. Adrenaline born from the fear of being tortured and killed surged through their veins. The printing press glided away from the wall, and Finn realized the thing was on wheels. Foster shined his light on the floor where it used to sit and spotted a rectangular marking on the ground. A section of the stone had even been carved into a handle.

Herb was grinning like a gap toothed schoolboy. "What did I tell you?"

"For all we know," Foster said. "The old man's leadin' us into his torture chamber."

Finn pulled open the trapped door while the other men maneuvered the printing press against the door. If anything, the hope was it might buy them a little more time.

"Give me your light," Finn told Foster, which the sailor did with no small amount of reluctance. Joanne was by Finn's side. "You ready?" he asked her.

"Choosing between a dark hole and a bunch of Wipers isn't much of a choice," she said. "Let's go."

Five minutes later, they'd descended into a dirt tunnel beneath the prison. Finn was out front, followed by Joanne, Foster, Kulik, and Zhou. The last man was Herb, who dragged the stone slab over the entrance in the hopes that if the Wipers got into the room, they might not clue in to where everyone had gone.

Only a thin beam of light illuminated the dirt path before them. It was a tunnel dug by hand, likely using the very tools one might find in the Braille printing room. How long it had taken them, Finn didn't know. Nor how many prisoners had used it to escape.

A hundred yards of duck walking through the tunnel was starting to take its toll, Joanne holding onto his waist.

"We're almost there," he told her. But the cramped space wasn't the worst part. The lack of air was. Finn had begun to notice the problem shortly after leading the way inside, but with over a dozen people behind him – not to mention the Wipers in the hallways outside – it wasn't as easy as turning and heading out for a breath of fresh air. The only way out was to keep moving forward, and Finn struggled toward what he hoped was an exit. He was really starting to feel short of breath by the time he saw the ladder recessed into the dirt at the end of the tunnel.

The distance to the top wasn't more than 10 feet. Overhead was a large metal plate, one likely salvaged from the previous Braille printer. It didn't need to be all that large, just strong enough to keep the exit a secret. Finn used the palm of his hand to push it off the ground and out of the way. Warm sunlight hit his eyes, forcing him to blink away the jabbing pain. He set the metal plate off to the side and climbed out, immediately reaching down to help the others. As the sailors climbed free, they began setting up a perimeter. Their position was a good hundred yards past the road the Wipers had used on their approach to the prison.

Powdery sand and sagebrush lay at their feet. The hot Nevada sun beat down from above.

Near the prison entrance, a group of Wipers was still firing at a handful of sailors who hadn't retreated to the inner keep. The Humvee they'd hit with the Javelin earlier was upside down. A large plume of black smoke rising from the wreck. But there was no sign of the man with the megaphone, Finn noted.

Now that they were out, this was Commander Zhou's show. He divided everyone assembled into three groups of five. Once they made it through the gate, one group would cut right and the other left while Zhou, Kulik, Foster, Joanne, and Finn would engage the Wipers near the front door. Herb elected to stay behind. This wasn't his fight, but Finn was glad to have had his help all the same.

Zhou used hand signals to communicate with his men in the second-story windows. The last thing they needed was to be fired on by their own guys. Then they all dashed forward, taking cover behind the first vehicles they came to in the courtyard. As planned, one group fanned left and the other right. Finn peered over the hood. Directly ahead was a handful of Wipers exchanging fire with the sailors in the windows. Zhou's men were keeping them busy.

On the count of three, Finn and the others rose and began firing.

166

The Wipers were caught completely by surprise and were torn to pieces in seconds. Then, Zhou's men on the flanks engaged with a similar result. With fire raining down from behind and above, those poor bastards hardly stood a chance. Zhou rose, about to give the order to move in, when shots rang out from inside a nearby car. A Wiper hiding in a blue sedan was unloading on Zhou. Sparks ricocheted off the vehicle Zhou was using for cover. A shot spun the commander around and his hand sprung to the side of his head. Finn and the others zeroed in on the blue sedan and riddled it with bullets, killing the attacker.

Joanne rushed to Zhou's side. He was sitting on the pavement, his back against the tire rim, a hand pressed up against his head. Blood ran between his fingers.

"It's nothing," Zhou said.

Kulik was there in a flash, examining the wound.

"Grazed your skull, boss. You can thank your lucky stars these animal pricks don't maintain their weapons very well. He probably had you dead to rights, only he prolly never adjusted the sights on that AK of his."

"Hurry up," Zhou barked in his Texas drawl. "There isn't time to waste."

Kulik finished the bandage, and Zhou got on the walkie to the men in the inner keep.

"Bravo team, are you there?"

A few seconds later the reply came back. "We're here, over."

"Smith, get your men ready. In 30 seconds, I want you bursting outta there, hot. I have teams coming in the front and side entrances. We're gonna catch these bastards in a classic Heinz Guderian pincer movement."

"Roger that."

Cheers erupted over the walkie from the men inside.

A moment later, Finn, Zhou, and the others were rushing toward the front entrance, weapons at the ready. They arrived to find about a dozen Wipers in the outer reception area. Kulik rolled in a grenade and then ducked for cover. A cloud of smoke and fire shot past them, along with the sound of screams from the Wipers inside. That's when the door to the inner keep opened and Zhou's men came charging out along the second-story walkway. The sound of explosive gunfire was deafening. Within moments, this second group of Wipers was dead. More exchanges could be heard down the hallway as Zhou's men surprised more of the enemy.

Then came the sound of men outside, running for their lives. Car engines roaring to life and peeling tires. Finn and the others rushed outside to see streams of Wipers trying to flee. Some of them drove headlong through the perimeter fence since the inner courtyard was far too congested. In their desperation to escape, some had even leapt onto the hoods of moving cars and were holding on for dear life. Among them was the man in black who'd been wielding the megaphone. Finn took aim with his rifle and peeled off a handful of shots, knowing full well he was out of range.

They had the numbers, but what they'd lacked was the discipline. Some of the sailors continued to fire on the Wipers as they fled from the East side of the building. A couple of those fleeing drove Humvees, which could only mean that some of the Wipers had breached the area where Zhou kept their vehicles.

Finn went back inside and found Joanne standing in the middle of the reception center, surrounded by dead Wipers. She dropped her pistol and threw her arms around him, sobbing as though the barbarity of the experience was only now beginning to seep through.

"I'm just glad you weren't hurt," Finn said soothingly.

She squeezed him tighter.

"I guess this is where I'm supposed to say something insightful about good and evil and all that jazz."

"I'd prefer if you didn't say anything at all."

Finn thought that was just fine.

Dana

Dana pulled up to the trailer that contained Romeo's body and nudged the brakes of her pickup. The cars here in New Jamestown were all considered communal property, their keys left above the driver-side visor. It was a policy Larry had begun after taking over from All Father and one that made a lot of sense. One's definition of ownership tended to undergo a rather radical transformation once you were surrounded by a glut of stuff you'd never need.

She got out and scanned her watch, noticing it was approaching 10 in the morning. Larry and the others had been gone now since dawn without so much as a peep. Had they been overwhelmed by the Wipers and cut to pieces? Or were they in the process of loading the trucks with the food they so desperately needed? She hoped it was the latter and not simply because her stomach kept grumbling like a grumpy old man. Everyone who went on Larry's little expedition as well as those who'd stayed behind knew perfectly well the colony's survival depended on their succeeding.

But checking her watch hadn't only been a consequence of worrying about her friends. Dana knew that with nearly everyone gone, this might be the only opportunity she had to move Romeo's body. She reached the trailer where she and Lou had carefully wrapped and hidden his remains and opened the door. The very thought of what she was about to do had the undeniable effect of tying her stomach into knots. Inside the trailer, nothing seemed to be disturbed, but already, the air had become heavy with the smell of rotting food.

That isn't food, and you know it!

But the rank odor wasn't what was causing those knots, and Dana knew that as well. She'd been entrusted as sheriff of New Jamestown, and she couldn't help somehow feeling like an accessory to murder. Sure, she hadn't been the one to poison the stew and feed it to Romeo. If anything, she'd probably even managed to extend his life by a few days, for whatever that was worth, since the urgency with which Larry wanted him banished was tantamount to an execution anyway. But moving the body would ensure that whoever killed the kid would never be caught, and in that sense it made her an unwilling accomplice. Perhaps her desire to keep Romeo hidden, albeit fuelled by her attempt to save his life and more importantly, to find the identity of the person behind Patty Mae's murder, had in the end only managed to blind her. Moving the body had become more about covering her own mistakes, regardless of how well

169

intentioned. Wasn't there a saying about that somewhere? About the road to hell being paved with good intentions? She was starting to believe it now more than ever.

Dana's plan was simple enough. She'd pull the pickup next to the trailer, fill it with Romeo's body as well as some of the junk cluttering the place, and find a secluded spot to bury him with a shred of dignity. She only hoped the guard manning the gate wouldn't get too nosy. No doubt nighttime would have been ideal for all of this, but how could one explain a late night excursion in a world where the darkness contained real boogeymen?

Romeo's body was still wrapped in canvas and set behind a stack of plastic chairs. Another set of hands would've been ideal – Lou's in particular – but she knew she didn't have that luxury. Already, they'd waited too long. The smell was only getting worse. Before long, it wouldn't be the odor of rotting food assaulting her nose, but decomposing flesh.

Nearby was a stack of four bicycles with rusted frames and flat tires. She took one at a time and loaded them into the back of the pickup, along with some of the other junk she was sure no one in the colony would have an objection to throwing away. Finally, with a spot on the bed at the back cleared of stuff, it was time for Romeo. In life, he hadn't been a large kid by any means. Late teens, early 20s. And the very thought nearly brought tears to her eyes.

Dana grabbed handfuls of canvas and dragged him into the open, wondering how in death he'd become so heavy. From here, she eased him into a sitting position, at least as much as the fabric he was draped in would allow, and then jerked him onto her shoulder, just like she'd learned in Coast Guard basic training. The trick was getting him into the truck fast so it didn't look like she was moving anything other than a pile of weathered canvas.

Shifting the weight to one side, she nudged open the door and barely got down the three steps that led from the trailer when she saw Timothy. He was at the back of her pickup inspecting the items she'd placed there. As soon as he saw her struggling under the heavy load, he came to give her a hand.

"Here let me help you with that," he said, reaching to take hold of the end.

"I got it," Dana snapped.

Timothy recoiled and moved out of her way. She hadn't meant to get snippy, especially under the circumstances, but she couldn't risk him knowing what was inside. After lowering the pile into the back of the

170

truck and sliding it forward, Dana pushed the bikes over until they rested on top of Romeo's body.

But far from beating a hasty retreat, Timothy seemed to take sudden interest in what she was doing, scrutinizing the canvas.

"Might I ask what you're doing with all this?"

Dana swallowed hard and slammed the cargo door shut. "Dumping it. Keeping myself busy's prolly the only way to keep my mind off things." She was referring to the attack, and he seemed to understand.

"That looks like a perfectly good tent to me," he said, touching the flap with his index finger.

"Hard to see when it's in a bundle like that," she told him, heading for the cab. "But the inside's all torn up."

"I see." He was following her to the driver-side window as she climbed inside. He laid his forearms on the edge of the door. "It's a real shame about your father."

Dana started the truck and it growled to life. "You have no idea."

He glanced back at the stuff she'd piled in the back. "I'm sure he's swearing up and down he didn't do it." An empathetic look was on Timothy's thinning face.

Dana nodded. "What would you be saying?"

He smiled. "Probably the same. It's amazing though how little we sometimes know about the ones who are closest to us."

Was he trying to get to her? Retribution for inferring it was his voice on that tape recorder? Or maybe he'd caught wind of her interview with Simon. That All Father's son revealed Timothy had once worked for Tevatron. A topic she would need to discuss with him as soon as she was back.

"You aren't the only one who knows things, Dana. The dead have a way of demanding justice."

That one caught her cold, and for a second she wasn't sure if he knew what she was up to.

He wasn't done. "The world outside these walls may be dangerous, but sometimes the real danger is the one you can't see."

"What are you saying?"

"I think you already know, Sheriff. The string of mysterious deaths in what was once Rainbowland and is now, thanks to Larry, New Jamestown. Some of them appeared benign enough, but I'm sure with your keen eye you see otherwise. I've suspected for a long time there's a serial killer loose within these walls, and I need you to prepare for the very real possibility that your father might be behind these deaths."

Dana peeled away just then, and Timothy had to take a quick step back before his toes were crushed. It wasn't his rather empty insinuation that her father was a murder. She'd known him her entire life, and every part of her knew that was impossible. His real guilt was being a neglectful alcoholic.

She stopped before the gate, and a cult member came to her window. "You know we're on lockdown, Sheriff."

"I won't be long." She smiled at him and nodded to the SIG on the seat next to her. His main concern was for her safety more than anything, and she hoped the gun would convince him she would be just fine.

"Keep it between us then," he said and opened the gate.

Leaving the compound was something of a blur. Timothy's words still running loops inside her head. And not an ounce of it was on account of his suggestion that her father was a murderer. It was the biting realization that she suddenly knew who had planted that listening device, who had killed Romeo and possibly Patty Mae and perhaps a host of others. A list of the dead that may even include All Father and his daughter, Abigail. Timothy had given himself away in his attempt to cast a shadow of doubt over her father's innocence. Now, all she needed to do was prove it.

Larry

Driving up to the gates of New Jamestown, Larry couldn't help but feel euphoric. They'd taken the fight to an enemy who had invaded their land, kidnapped their people, and continued to harass them ever since. Not to mention an enemy who'd emptied the city of just about everything still edible; a strategy designed no doubt to starve them into submission while they prepared for a final assault.

Instead, here they were, returning in triumph, just as Roman Emperors had done nearly 2,000 years before. And like their Roman counterparts, their convoy was packed with booty. Nearly every last pallet of food from the ballroom had been loaded into vehicles and trucks.

In one of the hotel rooms they'd also found a handful of survivors from the Wiper's initial raid, the one where Larry himself had nearly lost his life. They'd been treated brutally by their captors, and any form of rehabilitation would take weeks or months.

The message, however, was loud and clear for any to hear. If you're taken, we'll come save you, eventually. Tied and gagged on the pickup's bed was Alvarez. He'd come along easily enough. Not that Larry was one bit surprised. All those stories the survivors told about this bad ass turning people to ash turned out to be the kind of hocus-pocus charlatans use to trick the weak minded. If anyone should know that, it should be Larry, charlatan supreme.

One thing was clear after attacking the compound. Most of the Wipers hadn't been there, which made taking Alvarez hostage, rather than killing him on the spot, all the more important. A move that would act as an insurance policy against any future attacks from the Wipers they'd missed.

The guards in the towers above New Jamestown's walls raised their weapons and cheered as the convoy rolled through the now-open gates. The children and elderly who'd stayed behind streamed out from the compound's main building as well as from Tent City, and Donavan honked the horn as they entered.

These jubilant smiles wouldn't last, however, and Larry knew that perfectly well. Sure, they'd accomplished a great deal today. But the raid itself hadn't been a bloodless affair. Surely nothing close to the antiseptic Desert Storm from 30 years before. More soldiers died of "natural causes" there than by bullets.

In Larry's war, 40 vehicles had left on the raid, and 40 came back, but the last three were filled with the bodies of the dead and many more of the wounded.

Among those who stayed behind was Timothy, trying his best to appear thrilled the attack had been a success, although it didn't take a genius to see the cocksucker was fuming on the inside. Prolly wished Larry hadn't made it back in one piece. Or that the food had been carted off by the Wipers, leaving them bloodied and empty-handed.

Donavan parked in the field next to Tent City, and Larry got out heading directly for Timothy.

"Congratulati – " Timothy began.

"Save it," Larry snapped, cutting in. "We're having a victory banquet tonight, and I want you to organize it."

The muscles in Timothy's face tensed like he'd just sucked on a lemon wedge.

"Also, organize a group to unload and stack this food in the gymnasium, would you? I'll see to it that a handful of guards accompanies you, so that no one's tempted to take anything that doesn't belong to them."

"How kind of you."

Donavan came to Larry as Timothy walked away. He and another cult member were holding Alvarez under each armpit. "What you wanna do with him?"

"We've got a rather comfy prison cell waiting for you," Larry told Alvarez with an acidic smirk.

"What about the dead and wounded?"

"Have your men start unloading them at once. And don't leave the dead out, or the dogs will squeeze through the palisade to get at them. They'll need to be buried."

"And the wounded?"

Larry had already lost interest. "I don't care, use your imagination. Commandeer extra tents if you need to. I'm sure we can shuffle people around to make room for everyone. Most of the poor slobs don't stand much chance of pulling through anyway. Look what happened to Carole."

Just then, Dana pulled up in a pickup and jumped out without stopping the engine. "Where's Lou and Bud?"

"Well, that's one way to greet your victorious leader," Larry replied. "Lou's with his son, who was wounded." Then Larry's expression shifted. "What do you care about Bud anyway?"

Dana suddenly seemed at a loss. "Uh, he was my prisoner."

"Well, not anymore. Now we have a new prisoner." And Larry pointed to the men leading Alvarez away, his arms tied behind his back. Her eyes transfixed on the man as he passed, and all the blood drained from her face.

"You know him?"

She nodded emphatically. "You should have killed him when you had the chance."

"And ruin a perfectly good insurance policy against the Wipers? Are you mad?"

"Having him here will only draw them closer."

"If it does, then we'll simply hang his head from the wall as a warning to all of them."

She was starting to ruin Larry's mojo. There was about a dozen other things he needed to take care of right now besides talking to her. Larry didn't get farther than a few feet when she called out to him.

"There's something very important I need to talk to you about."

Larry raised a hand, certain she was either about to try convincing him Alvarez being in New Jamestown was a bad idea or that her father somehow wasn't guilty of theft. Either way, it didn't matter. Sooner or later, both men would face justice for what they'd done, and there wasn't a thing Dana could do to stop him.

Nikki

Aiden sat across from Nikki, still clad in his black leather outfit. She'd ushered him into her the tent as soon as they'd returned, worried that Lou might try to seek vengeance for the bullet that nearly killed Ethan. His eyes were fixed on the cup of filtered water in her right hand.

"You thirsty?" she asked, holding it out to him.

He didn't make a sound at first, and Nikki was in the process of withdrawing the offer when Aiden snatched it from her hand and gulped it down.

"You're welcome," she grumbled.

He finished shaking the last drop into his mouth and let the cup fall to the floor.

"What is this place?" he asked her, glancing around at all the beds and the nooks crammed with people's meager possessions. For some that meant photo albums, family heirlooms, for others bundles of useless cash, most of it wrapped in withering plastic bags. It looked like a homeless shelter and must have seemed positively alien to her brother given where he'd just spent the last few months.

"You're in New Jamestown," she told him, scooping the cup off the floor.

He wiggled his torso to make the cot bounce, but there wasn't much give. "This your bed?"

"No, mine's up there," she pointed to the top bunk. "This one belonged to Mom."

Aiden grew quiet for a moment, as though he were contemplating whether or not to tell her something. "She came to the hotel, you know."

Nikki nodded, fighting back a stream of tears threatening to get through. "Russell told me."

Hearing it made Aiden's head tilt slightly. "I didn't know his name. Mom saved his life by going into the pit."

Nikki had seen the pit by the hotel as they pulled in. The grass around it was torn up, so that it looked like a patch of dried hellish mud, straight out of some freakish nightmare. "I'm not surprised she went in there. Mom was stubborn and brave."

"You keep talking about her in the past tense."

Her eyes suddenly couldn't meet his no matter how hard she tried. He still didn't know. Carole's duffel bag was still tucked under her cot. Inside were some of Aiden's clothes she'd brought from the house. Not much, but anything was better than the Wiper leathers he was wearing

176

now. "Here," she said, handing him jeans and a shirt. "After you get changed, we need to take a walk."

A few minutes later, they were leaving Tent City, past the three medical wards filled with patients – people she'd be helping to care for as soon as she was done with Aiden – through the parking lot, bustling with more people carting shopping bags stuffed with cans, and into the gymnasium. They approached the back gate, and she knew what she was about to do would need to be quick. There was so much work and not nearly enough hands to do it.

A narrow door had been cut into the rear wall, and she motioned to a guard who was manning it. He nodded and opened it for her.

"We won't be long," she told him.

"I need to follow you all the same, Nikki, least until we get those towers up back here."

That wouldn't be a problem, and Nikki told him so.

All three stepped out beyond the wall into what had once been a meadow behind New Jamestown. Following the logging and construction of the palisade it now looked more like the outdoor venue for a U2 concert. Deep muddy grooves were cut into the earth where the giant logs had been dragged and then raised into place. Mud seemed to be a consistent theme in her life these days.

About 20 yards away was a grave marker, and suddenly it all clicked into place for Aiden. His mother was dead, and Nikki could see he wanted to cry, maybe even ball his eyes out, but instead he simply bit his lower lip until a drop of blood rolled down his chin. He'd told Nikki the last he'd seen of his mother was her running away from the pit, a virtual army of Wipers after her. He must have known she probably wasn't going to make it, but it was hard to gather what thoughts settle in a child's mind who's been through hell. Maybe part of him wanted her to die.

Behind them, the man with the rifle kept a respectful distance, surveying what was left of the tree line.

The grave marker was simply two pieces of wood with Carole's name carved into the crossbeam.

"It was them, the Wipers, wasn't it?" he asked.

"They shot her. Russell and the others brought Mom here, but by then it was already too late. The bullet had destroyed her liver and one of her kidneys. She didn't have a chance."

Nikki went to put an arm around him, and Aiden pushed it off. "She tried to save me, and I wouldn't let her. I wouldn't 'cause I was pissed off you both left me at the airport to die."

"Aiden, we looked for you, I swear to God we did."

"Yeah, that's the same load of crap Ma tried to feed me."

"We saw that cart near the entrance and were sure you and Alice had made it out. When we realized you hadn't, Mom even convinced a group of men to go back and look for you." A memory of the airport flashed before Nikki's eyes, the man in the pilot's shirt, his sneering face as he prepared to rape her.

He was about to reply, but Nikki wasn't done. "You've always been a spoiled, self-centered brat," she barked.

"How would you know? You can't remember a thing before that plane crash."

"Maybe not, but I saw the way you were after, and all you ever cared about was yourself. Mom spent the last two months doing everything she could to make sure we were safe. The truth of the matter is she went back to that hotel looking for me," Nikki said. "Not that she didn't love you. It was that she'd lost the two people who meant the most to her and was determined to do whatever it took to get them back, even if it meant giving her life to do it."

Now, Aiden was crying. He fell into her arms, and she caught him, his body convulsing with violent sobs. And that's when something strange happened. That unusual ability Nikki had for seeing lost memories buried deep within a person's mind, memories covered by layers of time and traumatic injury. With Finn, she'd seen tiny snippets of past events he could no longer remember, but with Aiden things were different in a way she hadn't seen before. There were memories locked deep within his subconscious. More than she could count. And none of them belonged to him.

Finn

It wasn't long before the dirty work got underway. Burying the dead, caring for the wounded. There were almost no wounded Wipers, however, and Zhou expressed some concern that his men might be killing the survivors they came upon.

"It's not the right thing to do," Finn said. "But can you blame them?"

Zhou wasn't buying it. "Let me remind you, we still stand for law and order, a respect for human life."

Finn scanned the hole being dug in the chalky ground by the backhoe and the Wiper bodies stacked beside it like cordwood. It was hard to hear civilized talk in such an uncivilized world.

"What do you think they were after?" Finn asked. "Resources? Weapons?"

Zhou touched the bandage on his head and looked at the blood on his fingers. "A force that large and organized? This wasn't a simple raid. Those boys knew we were here. Had specific intel."

"Your men scouting Salt Lake City, do you think they were intercepted? How else would Alvarez know you were out here?"

"Alvarez?"

Finn explained who he was.

The look of concern on Zhou's face was suddenly magnified.

The change wasn't lost on Finn. "You know what they were after, don't you?"

"If he's as you describe, what else would a man like Alvarez want besides the launch codes to a nuclear submarine?"

Sailors wearing rags over their mouths began pushing dead Wipers into the pit.

"You can't stay here," Finn told him. "You've lost too many men. Come to New Jamestown. There's safety in numbers."

Finn told him where the colony was located and the safest way to get there. "Dividing our strength would be playing directly into Alvarez' hands. Don't think he won't try this again. Besides, you said yourself you were hoping to head east."

Finn could see Zhou was skeptical. "There's still a lot to do here before my men will be ready to make that kind of move."

"Just think what will happen if Alvarez' men return and finally get what they're after. Then no place would be safe."

Finn hoped his words were getting through to Zhou, but he wasn't sure if even common sense would be enough. Staying behind to help out wasn't an option either for Finn and Joanne. Discovering that Tevatron had a secret facility emitting some kind of memory-blocking pulse had changed things entirely. A new hope had emerged of freeing himself and the world from the hand keeping them in darkness. And if Finn was right, then maybe Zhou's naïve hope of re-establishing order and civilization actually stood a chance of becoming real.

Dana

Nurse Kim was tending to Ethan's gunshot wound when Dana entered one of the three medical tents. Lou was by his son's side, holding his hand. This wasn't the first time Ethan had been wounded. She still remembered vividly how the Wipers had nearly killed the boy as he'd tried to keep them from taking Nikki.

Tanner stood by the entrance, arms hanging limply, looking like a cross between a Terracotta soldier and someone suffering from PTSD.

"Callahan head back to Nevada already?" he asked.

"First thing this morning," she said, eyeing Lou with concern. "How's the big guy doing?"

Tanner glanced over at her and smiled weakly, a streak of soot down his face, his blonde hair uncharacteristically dishevelled. "'Bout as good as can be expected."

"What about you?" Dana asked. "Most everyone who's come back from the raid in one piece looks like they left a part of themselves back there."

Pulling in a deep breath, Tanner said, "When I went to the airport to help find Carole's son. That was bad. This was worse. The stench and the way they came out at us. Makes it hard to remember sometimes they're still human beings."

She nodded knowingly, but the truth was Dana hadn't been to either of those places. Sure, she'd experienced her own horrors after The Shift. Who hadn't? But she couldn't pretend to really understand what it was like.

With a few careful steps, Dana navigated between beds laid out with the wounded and settled down beside Lou. The big man's gaze was locked on his son, and for a moment she wasn't entirely sure if he knew she was still there.

Ethan was breathing steadily, in spite of the bandage covering his leg.

"One inch to the left and it woulda hit his femoral artery," Lou said without looking up at her. "You know how long it takes for a kid his size to bleed out from a major artery, Dana?"

"No, I don't, Lou."

"Less than three minutes. One inch and three minutes. That's how close he came."

"Will he walk again?"

"With time."

She rubbed the middle of his back, knowing the gesture wouldn't do much to take away the pain.

"I'm gonna kill him," Lou said, matter-of-factly.

"Who, Aiden?"

"If anything happens to Ethan, I'm gonna kill him with my bare hands."

"Lou, I know right now the rage is piling up inside you, but for everyone's sake I need you to keep your cool." He didn't answer her, and his silence worried Dana. "The kid was being brainwashed, Lou. Not like Patty Mae, but in a more subtle way."

Lou's head dropped at the mention of his wife, but it was too late to take it back. The normally sweet teddy bear of a man with a charming Southern drawl had been dealt a hand lousier than most. He'd been allowed to keep his family and had watched as, one by one, they were taken from him.

"I feel your pain," she said. "I'm just asking you to focus on Ethan right now. Trying to even things will only send you down a path there's no coming back from. Besides, Aiden's only a kid who's got a head spinning with crap."

Lou turned to her now for the first time. "Something tells me you didn't come here for the sole intention of talking me off a cliff."

"The lock pick we took off Romeo during his arrest," Dana said. "Where is it?"

He removed a key from a ring in his pocket and pressed it into her hand. "Top drawer of my desk. But I'm starting to feel like it may be my turn to talk you out of something stupid."

"You remember that tape we planted in the police trailer?"

Lou nodded, his mouth tweaked at a strange angle. "It's gone?"

"Not only gone, but it might have just led us to a prime suspect. I don't wanna say more before I know if I'm right."

"And what if you're wrong? If you're caught in a place you shouldn't be, then even I won't be able to save you."

"Right now, my father's being accused of something he didn't do, and if I don't get proof of who framed him, then Larry's gonna have him executed."

"Can you tell me who?"

"Not just yet," she told him, glancing around at a room brimming with half-conscious casualties. One of them was the newcomer she knew vaguely as Russell.

Dana stood and Lou took her arm. "Be safe," he told her.

●●●

The lock picking set was right where Lou said it would be, and Dana slipped it into her back pocket. She closed and relocked the drawer and was in the process of pulling open the trailer door to leave when she found Bud standing before her. He was smiling like the proverbial bird who swallowed the canary, the sun shining through a shock of wavy red hair.

"Why the look of disappointment?" Bud asked. "I thought you'd be happy to see I made it back in one piece."

Dana slammed the door and moved past him. "Not when others more deserving weren't as fortunate."

"You look like someone who could use a friend."

"Who, you?" she asked with disgust.

"Would that be so bad?"

"It might be for you when Finn gets back and sees you walking free."

"Me and Mr. Coveralls have started working through our differences. I was hoping you and I could do the same."

"Maybe some other time," Dana replied dismissively.

He paused and kicked at a loose stone. "I got all the time in the world."

"I'm sure you do."

She was walking away when he said, "You know how I can tell you like me?"

Dana stopped and turned, arms crossed over her chest. "How I like you? Really? Please enlighten me."

"It's a simple calculation, really. I take the great pains you go to, pretending to hate me, then minus the fact that you asked Larry whether I'd made it back or not, and the equals part, well you know all about that without me having to say a word."

"Who told you what I asked Larry?"

"New Jamestown's a small place, Dana. Could've been anyone." He was grinning now, and his cockiness made her all the more indignant.

"But don't worry," Bud said, moving away. "You're not really my type."

She was storming after him now. "Not your type? Is that so? I didn't know you had a type."

"I do, and it isn't you, but I'm flattered nonetheless."

"Was it because I beat your ass? 'Cause I'll do it again, if you think that'll settle things."

183

Bud laughed. "No, it's got more to do with your lousy ability to hide stuff."

"Excuse me?"

"Take the lock pick you got in your back pocket. The second you walked past me, I could tell what it was."

"I don't know what you're talking about. Besides, if I'm not your type, what are you doing looking as my rear end?"

Bud smiled. "We call them asses nowadays, not rear ends. You do raise a good point, though. Looks like we're even then. But don't worry, your secret's safe with me."

•••

Dana entered the compound through the basement, still fuming over her encounter with Bud. He had some special way of getting under her skin. First, when he took her SIG, then turned and handed it back to her with a wry smile. Now, with the lock pick. It was true, when she'd spoken to Larry she'd asked if Bud had made it back. But to jump from asking a simple question to "wanting" him was a real stretch, wasn't it? Besides, she didn't just dislike the man, she hated him. Sure, he wasn't horrible to look at, perhaps even handsome. And he certainly was sure of himself, a quality she'd been drawn to with Keiths and most of the other men in her life. In spite of everything she'd been through: dealing with Alvarez, fighting her way free of Jeffereys, and building a new life for herself here in New Jamestown. Could that hold men with an air of authority had on her still be so strong? Or were the tastes formed for the opposite sex in our youth, somehow fired by life's kiln into an immovable structure? She had every reason in the world to hate Bud's very guts, so why didn't she?

Dana was still busy shuffling those intrusive thoughts from her mind when she reached the stairs leading to the compound's main floor. In the distance, she caught the sounds of a bell ringing outside the gym doors. It was beckoning the people of New Jamestown to the banquet, and she knew the sound had the power to trigger a veritable stampede of starving folks.

In all her years, she never imagined that a plate of beans and canned ham could make her stomach grumble, but the proof was in the pudding. The battle to steel her mind against the temptation of filling her empty belly was a difficult one. But more was at stake than satisfying the needs of the body. Her father's life depended on her resolve and so, too, did the memory of those who hadn't been so fortunate.

A group of children ran through the common room, giggling and pulling at one another. She spied them from the top of the basement stairs, watching the way their clothes hung loose about their emaciated frames, the way their bones seemed to click together as they ran. The trick to keeping the food down would be to ensure they didn't eat too much or too fast.

After they had passed, Dana hurried through the commons and up the stairs that lead to the first floor. This was where Timothy's room was. She approached it, knowing the chances were good it was empty. Larry had commissioned his former comrade to help prepare the feast. A symbolic and rather passive-aggressive way of shoving the success of the raid and the food they'd secured directly down Timothy's throat. She'd learned from others who had overhead the exchange that the look of anger on Timothy's face had been more than apparent.

Dana arrived before the door to Timothy's room and reached for the lock-picking tools in her back pocket, pausing in the act. The smart thing would be to knock first, just in case Timothy was still in his room. Getting caught inside would be embarrassing, albeit explainable. A simple case of having entered the wrong room, she could say. But picking a lock, well that was another story altogether.

She rapped quickly at the door and waited. Outside came a second chime of the dinner bell. Then footsteps from down the hall. Someone a few doors over was walking around, maybe getting ready to head downstairs and join the others. If she was seen hovering in front of his room, word might spread to Timothy that the sheriff was snooping through his things. And that was a chance Dana couldn't take.

On her right was a broom closet no larger than a foot and a half deep and about as wide.

Hurrying over, she squeezed herself inside the cramped space at about the same time that the door down the hall swung open. She'd been fast, but not fast enough to close the door behind her.

But it was too late. If she pulled it shut now, then whoever was there would know for sure someone was inside, an explanation that would prove even more difficult.

From down the hall, two voices began to approach, a male and a female, both young. They sounded like cult members. Dana held her breath and prayed that nothing inside would shift or fall until they'd passed.

The voices and laughter died off as they drew nearer.
"That's weird," a male said.
"Come on," the female replied, annoyed. "I'm hungry."

"Looks like Brother Timothy's broken his own rule about keeping that closet door shut."

He was either going to open it and discover her or …

A firm push and a click as the latch snapped into place.

"Feel better now?" the girl asked and giggled. "Sometimes I swear you're more uptight than he is."

Dana listened as their voices trailed off. She waited another minute before coming out.

Reaching into her back pocket, she removed the torsion wrench and the half-diamond pick and slid them into the lock to Timothy's room. The trick was to apply pressure to the pick while it pushed at the pins until they rested on the sheer line. Each successful move was met with an almost imperceptible click. There were five pins in all. Dana moved the last one into place, the lock turned easily, and she let herself inside.

Larry

That euphoric feeling of triumph Larry had felt swelling within him on the way into New Jamestown still hadn't gone away. He watched the gymnasium fill as groups of hungry colonists streamed in.

The room was set with long, cafeteria-style tables arranged in a giant U. At the head was Larry, Donavan, and a handful of his most trusted lieutenants. Many of them former cult members. And the reason for that was simple. Regular colonists asked too many questions. Cult members did as they were told.

Timothy was perhaps the single exception to that rule. Putting him in charge of prepping the banquet had been designed to drive home a message:

Make sure you're on the right side of history.

There wasn't room in New Jamestown for naysayers and doubting Thomases. Another table was set up closer to the stacks of canned goods that now filled half the gym. There was Timothy, overseeing the selection and preparation of the food. For once, the sour expression on the man's face was absent. He no longer looked like he'd just taken a swig from a bottle of lemon juice. Perhaps the festive spirit was rubbing off on him.

But there was one thing missing, wasn't there?

One of the cult members was passing with a tray of food when Larry reached out and caught his arm. "I've got a bottle of Dom Pérignon up in my office, tucked away under my desk. Run up and grab it, would you."

"Sure thing," the cult member replied, handing his tray to a woman beside him.

The stream of cultists and colonists entering the gym had died to a trickle. The lack of echoing chatter wasn't surprising either. These people hadn't eaten a proper meal in weeks. Nevertheless, there was another thought on Larry's mind. As strained as their relationship had become over the last few weeks, he couldn't help but notice Dana's absence. Who could possibly pass up a celebratory meal at a time like this? And on the heels of that thought, came another, far darker question. Was Dana staying away to make a point, or was she up to no good?

Dana

Her heart doing a merry jig inside her chest, Dana knew she didn't have long. This wasn't how detectives searched for evidence in the old days, where a court order would buy them as much time as they required. No, this needed to be fast and dirty. A quick in and out. The only silver lining was that her hands weren't tied with concerns over what would or wouldn't be admissible in a court of law. This was far closer to frontier justice, although under the circumstances, how could it be otherwise?

Timothy's room was sparse and impeccably clean. A simple mattress lay on the floor. Next to that, a night table and against the far wall, a book case. She went to the closet and found a dresser surrounded by over a dozen blue pants and gray shirts, the cult's favorite getup. Timothy had continued wearing the former Rainbowland uniform even after Larry had changed it from the slacks and button down to military fatigues. The first sign the two men were not exactly on the same page.

Dana went in each of the drawers, flipped through all of Timothy's nearly identical outfits and even slid the dresser away from the closet wall. She'd figured the closet would be the best place to hide anything incriminating. She'd almost given up when a pair of work boots in the corner caught her eye. The sight of them was strange, especially given that Timothy wasn't one for manual labor. She picked them up to get a closer look, and that's when she noticed the spot on the floor where they'd been sitting. It was sprinkled with dried mud. She flipped Timothy's boots over, brought the sole to her nose and realized what she was smelling wasn't mud at all. This was top soil. The same top soil that had ended up in the river. They'd found a pile of it by the shore along with the bags it was packed in.

You sneaky son of a bitch!

Those were the words she kept whispering over and over. But the implications were greater than a few bags of soil. The person who did this had also emptied the food reserves, planting some of it in her father's footlocker.

But why frame her father?

He wanted to drive a wedge between you and Larry.

There was that little voice again, and now things were starting to fit into place, but dirt on a pair of boots wasn't murder. Dana would need more than that, and she was sure it had to be in here somewhere.

She went to the mattress and flipped it over, searching the floor underneath for any sign of a trap door or a loose plank of wood. Next, she turned to the night stand and pulled out the drawer entirely. Wedged underneath what looked like a handwritten prayer book, was Timothy's Tevatron ID tag. The picture on it was a younger version of the man she'd come to know. Below that was his title: *Electronics Supervisor*. Dana slipped the badge into her pocket and continued searching. She didn't have much longer before someone noticed she wasn't at the banquet and came looking for her.

A quick scan of the bookcase made it clear nothing was out of place. All the books were lined up spine to spine and organized by height and depth so there wasn't any room to hide items behind smaller books. Ancient Greek democracy, the fall of the Roman Empire. Most of these were about the classics, and many of them were large volumes. 'Course, Timothy might have hidden something inside by carving out the pages, but there just wasn't time to go through each and every book.

That's when the dresser in the closet caught her eye again. There hadn't been anything underneath it, but she hadn't thought to look behind the drawers. Out they came, one by one, remembering as a kid how knickknacks would sometimes fall to the bottom of her drawer and remain there for years. Her breathing quickened as she yanked out the bottom drawer. Even in the dim light she spotted something there. She reached in and was disappointed when all she came away with was a weathered old notebook.

Flipping quickly through the pages, she could see this was the closest thing the cult had to a bible. The words of their prophet, Abigail, as dictated by a spirit named Aletheia. The teachings were about love and peace and the kinda stuff that tends to get people killed, but here she was seeing something different. Something about a battle between good and evil and a pair of saviors who held the key to ushering in a new beginning. This wasn't at all what she'd heard All Father preaching about when he seemed to go on and on about love being the only good and evil being nothing more than an illusion.

She would take this notebook as well and was about to put the drawers back, somewhat disheartened, when something at the bottom of the dresser caught her eye, something she had overlooked. Dana reached in and found a small glass bottle. The inscription on the front made all the muscles in her face go slack.

Sodium Cyanide (granular).

Below that:

Tevatron Laboratories.

"I've got you now, you murdering prick." And that's when she saw that the bottle was empty and a darker realization struck her with blinding force. Timothy was going to poison the food. She had to get downstairs and warn them, but no sooner had she struggled to her feet than the room was rocked by an explosion the force of which flung her against the far wall. She opened her blurry eyes a moment later and saw that part of the ceiling was gone. Larry's office was right above her and she could look into it and she saw now that it was on fire. The explosion hadn't been in Timothy's room after all. Nor was it meant for her. That much was clear. There was little doubt that the real target of the attack was Larry. But whether or not he was still alive, she didn't know.

Larry

Timothy had just laid down Larry's food in front of him when the explosion went off. The gymnasium shook, but it was only when the lights went out that people's startled cries turned to panic.

We're under attack.

Those were Larry's first frantic thoughts.

They've brought heavy artillery, and this time we won't be able to stop them.

Terrified colonists fled out the push doors, filling the room with much needed light. Others followed. That's when Lou ran up to Larry and took him by the arm.

"Are you OK?"

"I'm fine," Larry replied. "Where's Donavan?"

"No idea, but we have to get you out of here."

They were leaving the gym and getting ready to cut through the main compound when Larry looked back and saw the strangest sight. One of the cult members, a young girl named Sister Margaret, had climbed into his chair and was gobbling up as much food as she could. A handful of others were doing the same to a half dozen abandoned plates, and for a moment they reminded Larry of wild animals, cramming their faces as if it were their last meal.

They went down into the basement and then out through the exit there, half expecting to find slavers swarming the compound. What Larry saw instead as he looked up, left him just as cold. The compound was on fire, and it looked like a chunk of the building had been bitten off by a giant. But what really sent the chills racing up his spine was the realization that the hole with the flames shooting out had once been his office.

With the power down, and the water pump offline, the bucket brigade once again flew into action. Donavan emerged a second later and took control, organizing the colonists into long lines that stretched to the river's edge. Others braved the flames to try smothering them with blankets soaked in river water. Some did their best to help douse the fire using the few extinguishers they'd collected from the surrounding houses.

It would be another 10 minutes before the flames were completely under control. The full implication of what had just happened, however, didn't begin to settle in until Larry saw Dana, limping out from the main compound. Her clothes were torn, and streaks of blood ran down her face. In her hand was a pillowcase, although it wasn't clear what was inside.

Lou ran to her, and she nearly collapsed into his arms.

"Timothy," she rasped.

Larry drew closer. "What about him?"

"Did you eat any of the food?" she asked them, fishing into the singed pillowcase and coming out with a bottle of Sodium Cyanide. "He meant to poison you."

This time, her eyes were fixed solely on Larry, and he felt the fingers of a cold, clammy hand seize his heart.

"The bomb waiting in your office was to make sure."

The blood drained from Larry's face.

"But there's more," Dana added. "Much more." And Larry listened as she struggled to explain what she had found in Timothy's room.

"But how did he get the C4 off the bridge?" Larry asked.

"I'm still working on that," Dana replied.

A woman's scream echoed just then from inside the compound. A second later, a cult member emerged with a girl in her arms. She'd been killed in the explosion. That was Larry's first thought, but soon it was clear he was wrong. The girl's skin wasn't cut or smeared with soot. No, this was Sister Margaret, the one he'd seen eating the food Timothy had personally laid out for him.

"Donavan," Larry barked. "Arrest Timothy at once and take all the food that was served and have it thrown out. There's no telling how much of it was poisoned."

Dana tried standing on her own before Lou helped her find a place to sit.

The initial streak of terror Larry had felt was beginning to fade. It its place now was searing-hot rage and the sudden thirst for revenge. This would be the first and last time anyone ever tried to fuck with Larry Nowak.

Finn

It was nearing dusk when Finn and Joanne spotted the gates of New Jamestown. From Ely State Prison, they'd opted to take Interstate 80, assuming the fleeing Wipers limping back to Salt Lake City would have instead opted for Route 50. Finn assumed his hunch was correct since they'd made it all the way back without any sign of them.

But now, approaching New Jamestown, Finn caught movement in the guard towers by the wall. The crack from a rifle broke the silence, the bullet bouncing off the dirt road less than a dozen feet before their car.

Finn slammed the breaks.

"Did they just shoot at us?" Joanne asked, the fear in her voice palpable. She hadn't been shy on the drive home about how much she'd been looking forward to leaving that stinky prison behind. Neither of them was expecting welcome home signs, but they certainly didn't think they'd be shot at.

Finn popped the driver-side door and stepped out to identify himself.

A call rang out from the tower to the people manning the gate, and slowly it began to open. No sooner were they inside than it was clear they'd arrived on the tail end of something bad. Colonist and cultists with rifles were rushing about. That's when Joanne pointed to the compound and the gaping hole in the second story.
"Oh my God, there's been a fire."

"Or a rocket attack," Finn amended. Once they parked, Finn went to find out what was going on. Simon was rushing past when Finn grabbed his arm.

"What happened?"
Simon told him about the attempt on Larry's life.
"Oh, crap. Is he all right?"
"Larry's fine," Simon said. "But I can't say the same for Timothy."
Simon tore free from Finn's grasp and broke into a run.
"Where's Dana?" he called after him, but didn't get an answer.

A moment later, Joanne was by his side, hand covering her mouth in disbelief. "This is horrible."

"The colony's seen its fair share of tragedy," Finn told her. "But never from the inside."

The two entered the main compound and found Dana on the top floor where Larry's office used to be. She and Donavan were peering in at the blackened, still-smouldering mess.

Dana saw Finn approach and came over, pulling them both into a hug.

"I heard someone tried to take Larry out," Finn told her. "I only hope no one was hurt."

Dana shook her head. "Two people were killed. One was a little girl."

Joanne gripped Finn's arm. "Oh, goodness."

"And now Larry's got himself barricaded in the basement surrounded by his trigger-happy goons."

"I believe it," Finn said. "They nearly turned our car into Swiss cheese as we pulled up."

"Everyone's seriously on edge right now. Might be best to go to the police trailer and lie low till everyone's nerves settle down. Itchy trigger fingers and paranoia don't make great bedfellows."

Dana's eyes traced over the cuts on Finn's face from when the Camaro's back window blew out. Or more accurately, when the Wipers attacking the prison's reception center tried to stop him from running them over.

"I never thought I'd say this, but Finn, you look like shit."

He smiled, believing her. "Listen, I know you're busy right now, but we need to talk."

Dana sighed. "Head to the police trailer and wait for me there."

•••

Finn and Joanne made their way out from the compound and across the dirt road that divided New Jamestown in two. Already, the number of people running around had diminished as armed cultists ordered people inside. They found Tanner standing guard by the trailer next to Dana's office. Directly across from them, two more guards stood by the door to the colony's prison.

Tanner waved at them and smiled.

"What are you doing?" Finn asked.

"Guarding a prisoner."

They were halfway in the police trailer when they stopped. "What prisoner?"

"Timothy."

"What the hell's going on here?" Joanne was the one to say it, but she practically took the words right out of Finn's mouth. They'd only been gone for a handful of days. How could everything have been turned on its head so quickly?

Inside, they found Lou, hunched over his desk.

Finn went to him right away. "Lou, you all right?"

Lou glanced up, in a daze, as though he wasn't sure who was speaking to him.

"Finn, you're OK." He snapped and grabbed him in a bear hug.

"I will be so long as you don't break my ribs."

Lou set him down and at once, the light seemed to fade from his eyes.

"Did you know the people killed in the explosion?" Joanne asked.

"Huh? Oh that, no ma'am. Well, that's not quite true. I did know Sister Margaret, sweet little thing. So much has happened since you two been gone." Lou took a deep breath and proceeded to fill them in on the sad news of Carole's death, the successful attack on the Wiper base at the Grand America, on finding Aiden, and how he'd shot Ethan. Then Lou told them how Alvarez was now their prisoner, and that it appeared Timothy was behind the attempt on Larry's life.

The news struck Finn like a blow to the gut. He fell hard into the chair behind him.

Foremost on his mind was the loss of Carole. Her abandoned car near the Grand America had left all of them with doubts that she was still alive, but hearing the news surprised and saddened him nevertheless.

Dana came in then, followed by Bud.

Finn stood at once and crossed over menacingly. "What's he doing here?"

Standing in his way, Dana put her arms up to block him. "It's all right, Finn. He's on our side now."

"Yeah, says who? Have you already forgotten what he did?"

Dana glanced over at Joanne. "Of course, we haven't, but Bud was being blackmailed."

Bud stuck his hand out. "No hard feelings?"

Finn smacked his hand away with a loud clack.

Dana looked around the room. "You all mind giving Finn and me a minute?"

Standing by Finn's side, Joanne squeezed his arm as if to say, "I'm staying right here beside you."

"It's OK," Finn told her. "Maybe I need a minute."

The others shuffled out, leaving Dana and Finn alone. The trailer grew quiet. Across the way, the sound of the windmill, damaged in the blast, but working again, squeaked along in a dull wind.

"You look like you've been through hell, Finn. Maybe you oughta rest a while."

"When we got to the prison, we found people there."

Dana walked around her desk, removed her gun belt, and sank into her chair. "That so."

"Not your run-of-the-mill survivors either. These guys were Navy men."

Her eyebrow rose.

"Thought that would get your attention." He knew she'd been Coast Guard. "Had been crewing a nuclear submarine in the Pacific when The Shift went down."

There was a pregnant pause.

"The USS *Alabama*," Dana said, almost to herself.

Now it was Finn's turn to be surprised. "How'd you know?"

She told him about Callahan.

"That makes sense. Commander Zhou mentioned he'd sent men to scout the Salt Lake City area and never heard back from them."

"Only one made it. The other joined the assault against the Grand America. So did Bud."

The thought of Bud made him think of Tevatron and the discovery he'd made on the warden's computer. The very reason he'd wanted to talk to her so badly. "There may be a way to fix this," he told her.

She glanced around the room, unsure what needed fixing first. "Can you be more specific?"

"Tevatron's got a secret facility emitting a low-frequency pulse that's keeping people's memories from coming back."

"How do you know this?"

"It's a long story. You're just gonna need to trust me. 'Course, there's a lot we still don't know. Like where it is and how it's being powered."

Dana scratched her head. "So, you think finding it and knocking it out would help?"

"Maybe not right away, but slowly, as Wipers start remembering they were once accountants from Topeka or the manager at Burger King, they may begin to rethink the rape and pillaging routine."

Dana smiled, then her eyes lit up. "Timothy worked for Tevatron."

The news made Finn shake his head in disbelief.

"I know, that was my reaction. Maybe he knows something about this facility."

Finn's eyes fell. He was still floored by how out of hand things had gotten since he'd been gone. "It's not easy to come back here and not know where you stand anymore. It's almost like I've woken up from another coma."

She winced and rubbed her hand along the desk. "You're not the only one. At some point, I'm gonna need to go next door and extract a confession from our friend Timothy. Find out why the crazy bastard thought it was a good idea to plant a bomb in Larry's office." Her gaze settled on Finn. "But playing catchup isn't why I wanted to speak with you." She reached into her pocket, pulled out a heavy set of keys, and unlocked the bottom drawer of her desk. Inside was a small steel briefcase. She removed it and set it down.

"This look familiar?"

Finn studied it. "Looks like the briefcase Bud brought to the Tevatron Lab when he tried to blow me sky high."

She tapped her finger on the metal case. The sound was hollow and menacing. "Looks the same, but it isn't. When Bud woke up at the lab in Long Island, a case filled with C4 and a DVD were waiting for him there. The DVD had instructions from a man named Thomson about destroying the lab in Nevada."

"OK," Finn said, utterly confused.

"I found this case at the lab in Nevada. It was in the room where we found Joanne's cryo chamber. I didn't say anything at the time and you were too out of it to notice. But on the DVD is a picture of you and instructions for Joanne to terminate your life."

"What are you saying here?" Finn demanded, feeling his voice rising a few notches higher. "That Thomson or Alvarez or whatever the hell he calls himself wanted Joanne to kill me?"

"Looks that way."

"And you let the two of us wander off into the desert together."

"Relax. Nothing woulda happened unless she'd come to on her own and watched the DVD. The message on there woulda been clear enough."

Dana opened the case, almost to show him she wasn't lying and then paused.

"What is it?" he asked.

She spun the case around. Some of the C4 and one of the detonators was missing. Now she knew what Timothy had used for the bomb.

Jeffereys

As he approached the Grand America Hotel, it was becoming clearer to Jeffereys with every step that something wasn't right. The quiet and stillness. That's what set off the first row of alarm bells in his head. The sun had set not long ago, and he listened for the common nightly sounds he'd become accustomed to. Brutes bickering in a strange guttural language he didn't quite understand, the ruckus from crowds that liked to gather around the pit and relish in watching a battle to the death, the random pop of gunfire and screams of agony. None of that was here. Only silence, and accompanying it was a cold and clammy hand of fear.

By the time Jeffereys reached the entrance, the feeling only grew stronger. Bodies lay scattered around the lobby. Half a dozen leading up toward Alvarez' suite and three or four times that many scattered like bread crumbs. All of them pointed toward the ballroom.

The attack on the prison had been a dismal failure. At least 40 percent of his army didn't make it home and hardly any of those who did were unscathed.

Some of them were running past Jeffereys now, into the ballroom. Others toward Alvarez' suite. But already he knew full well what they would find. More dead bodies.

When Jeffereys reached the ballroom and saw that most of the food they'd stockpiled was gone, he knew who was probably behind this. Certainly wasn't those submarine assholes. Those pricks were left licking their own wounds. Which only left one other group. Those annoying shit heads over at New Jamestown.

On more than one occasion Jeffereys had pleaded and begged Alvarez to hit them again.

"I have a plan," Alvarez had told him back then, "and it's going swimmingly."

Sure, it had taken time to train his men how to use weapons and drive cars. Then more time had been wasted hoarding all the food they could get their hands on. Jeffereys could understand how long-term strength depended on both of those things, but sitting back and hearing his spies report on the wall the colonists were building and the guns they were arming themselves with. He knew the dream of a lightning assault was gone the minute that group of pacifists had been outed. Knew they weren't going to be easy pickings. Not anymore. And that's when Alvarez had told him to relax, that he had a plan.

And what a plan that turned out to be.

Now the hotel was little more than a mausoleum. Those colonists hadn't managed to take all the food, which was some comfort. A single pallet remained, a few weeks' worth, month tops. Then they would be in the same predicament those hippies had been in.

But there was another problem. These wild men Alvarez had somehow been able to summon to the hotel were violent and unpredictable. If Al was dead – a conclusion that seemed to Jeffereys almost inevitable given the present situation – how would he be able to keep them from running wild? The big man had ruled them the way Kim Jong-Il once ruled North Korea. They revered him as a god, a deity who held in his very hands the power of life and death. And on more than one occasion, Jeffereys had witnessed the use of Alvarez' strange power. The display had been spectacular and disturbing, but the end result had been to keep the natives in check. It was a superstitious fear they had, and now that Bigdaddy was gone – might be gone – how long before they turned on him?

A well-muscled slaver named Tank approached, carrying a flashlight.

"Get that fucking light outta my face, will you?"

"Sorry, Sir."

"Did you find Alvarez?"

Tank's eyes fell to the grimy ballroom carpet at their feet. "Not yet. But we found Anita."

The muscle head didn't need to add that she was dead for Jeffereys to understand. He followed Tank back to Al's suite. Anita was up against the wall, her eyes open and staring. Someone had taken her out with a shotgun. The blood splatter on the wall told Jeffereys it was done at point blank range.

"She must have attacked one of them," Jeffereys said. "Hope she tore his balls off." A handful of slavers and other brutes was milling about, looking under the bed with flashlights, others were pulling back the shower curtain in the bathroom.

"You're not gonna find him. Al wouldn't have hid like a pussy."

Tank seemed to agree. "If they killed him, we haven't found his body yet."

"If they killed him … if they could kill him … they woulda hung his remains from the goddamned overhang as a warning to the rest of us. If he's not here, then those pricks are keeping him hostage." Jeffereys looked around. The others had stopped searching. "All of you, get the fuck out. I need a moment to think." One by one, the men started filing out of Al's suite. Jeffereys snapped his fingers, and Tank tossed him the light. "I want six men guarding what food we have left. No one goes near it unless I say. Got it?"

Tank nodded. "Got it, Boss."

The bed was unmade, and Jeffereys sat on the edge, wondering what to do next. Alvarez kept cigars in the nightstand beside his bed, and Jeffereys was sure puffin' on one of those beauts while sipping on a glass of brandy would do wonders for his stress levels right about now. Part of him was thankful Alvarez wasn't here when he returned from the botched attack on the prison. His orders were to return with as many members of the submarine crew as he could capture. And now that Alvarez was a prisoner himself, it removed the danger of being turned to dust for failing in his mission. Danger or not, Jeffereys also knew that he was Al's trusted right-hand man. It had taken a while for Jeffereys to submit to Alvarez' authority, since in the beginning, he and his men weren't exactly free to leave, but as the image of what Al was trying to create came into sharp focus, Jeffereys knew this was where he belonged.

He plucked one of the Nat Sherman cigars from the humidor in Al's drawer, and that's when Jeffereys spotted the envelope. He removed it casually, his eyes suddenly growing three times their normal size when he saw his name printed in red ink.

To Jeffereys

The urge to blink several times nearly overcame him, but when he looked again, his name was still there. Jeffereys clamped the cigar between his teeth and broke the seal. Inside was a piece of hotel stationary. He began to read.

Dear Jeffereys,

I hope this letter finds you well. If you are reading this, it can only mean that I've been taken by the enemy. No doubt, they intend to kill me. Perhaps they already have. Either way, I want you to know that everything is unfolding according to plan. Further instructions will arrive shortly.

Eternally,
Alvarez

At the top was a date, and this was what messed with Jeffereys' head the most. Alvarez had written it two months ago.

Dana

The silver briefcase with the C4 was still open when Tanner walked in. Dana snapped the case shut at once and slid it back into her desk drawer, where she locked it away.

"Am I interrupting something?" Tanner asked, his gaze fixed on the disturbed expression on Finn's face.

"Aren't you supposed to be guarding Timothy?" Dana asked him.

"I was until some of Larry's paramilitary guys came and took him away."

"What?" She shot up. "When was this?"

Tanner rubbed his hands together and then ran them through his short blonde hair. "I thought you knew."

"Where'd they take him?"

"The compound basement."

Dana sprung to her feet and headed for the door.

She could hear Tanner calling after her. "Did I do something wrong?"

She was the sheriff for God's sake, and Timothy was her prisoner. She'd pieced the clues together and set the trap that ultimately tripped him up. Those were the thoughts roaring through her head as she crossed the gravel road and yanked open the basement door.

Three cult members were in the hallway. No sooner had Dana come barrelling through the door than they had their rifles aimed at her head.

"Hold it right there," the first one barked.

Inside to her right came the sound of more guns being primed. Donavan emerged carrying a silver Colt 1911. The hammer was cocked.

Why did it seem like everyone was at each other's throats since Larry brought Alvarez back from his raid on the Grand America?

"Where is he?" She demanded.

"Who?"

"Larry, that's who. Where is he? I need to speak to him."

"He's not here," Donavan told her.

"Bullshit." She took a single step, and Donavan pointed the gun at her.

"The whole compound is on lockdown, Larry's orders."

"I'm the sheriff, dammit. Larry had no right to take my prisoner, no right. Larry, I know you're here. Come out and talk to me like a man."

A hand reached out from the room and lowered the cult member's rifles. Larry emerged a second later, a half step behind Donavan, looking like some Third World dictator. "Timothy tried to kill me tonight," Larry said in measured tones. "He isn't your prisoner, not anymore."

Dana could see he was trying very hard to control himself. Larry's left hand was tapping the side of his leg in an odd rhythm.

She pushed past both of them and into the room that contained the safe Romeo said he'd once picked. She'd expected to find Timothy huddled in a corner, but that wasn't so. Strapped to a chair in the middle of the room was Charlie, the young man who guarded Larry's office. He was surrounded by other cult members in military fatigues, his face showing signs of fresh bruises. They'd just started working him over.

"What the hell are you doing?"

"He left his post, which enabled Timothy to plant the bomb."

"So, you're torturing him?" Dana asked in disgust.

Larry laughed. "Don't be naïve. He was part of the plot."

"But how do you know that?"

"What do you mean how do I know that? It's obvious, Dana, and I'm not going to waste my time explaining to you the ways of the world."

"There was a reason All Father wanted an independent policing force."

"Yes, there was. He couldn't stand the thought of getting blood on his hands." Larry's own hand was still tapping his leg to some inaudible beat.

"He was trying to avoid lynch mobs like the one you've created here. You may be able to beat a confession out of some poor kid, but you'll lose the community's support if you try the same on Timothy. You gotta get it down voluntarily, and not on a scrap of paper written in blood." On a nearby desk was a pen and a stack of loose sheets. "Larry, I'm the one who brought you the evidence of Timothy's guilt. If it weren't for me, you'd be barking up the wrong tree, probably wondering who was out to get you. Give me a chance to get a proper confession from Timothy. That way, no one can accuse you of abusing your power."

Larry's hand was tapping faster now. "You've got 10 minutes."

•••

There was a certain amount of irony that Timothy was being held in the same room in which Lou's wife had been bound and tortured – and perhaps even killed. After that grisly spectacle, that very room had become the place Dana'd used to examine her body, the place where she discovered that cyanide had been the murder weapon.

Donavan unlocked the door and let Dana in.

The place was bare, except for a table and two chairs. In one of them sat Timothy. He watched her enter, with a touch of relief that she wasn't Larry or one of his cronies.

She settled into the chair facing him. "You know why I'm here."

Timothy was rubbing the thumb and index finger of his right hand together in slow circles.

"There's an old saying in the crime world, I once read. Serial killers aren't caught, they reveal themselves."

"Is that what you did, Timothy?" Dana asked. "Reveal yourself?"

He laughed. "You helped the process along, I won't take that away from you. But it was only a matter of time. That much was always clear. I thought I could control him, you know."

"Control him?"

"Larry. He was never really one of us, a pure Rainbowite. I was arrogant. I thought I could bend him to my will. That was my first mistake."

"No, that wasn't your first mistake," Dana disagreed. "Your first mistake was killing Abigail."

Timothy's shocked eyes rose to meet hers. The expression lasted only a moment before the veil descended again, closing her out, but it was more than enough to see she was right.

"You're dying to tell me why you did it, aren't you?"

Timothy stopped rubbing his fingers. "Larry found the holy transcripts of Abigail's channeling sessions. There is a passage within that reads: '*Your small, peaceful community will be led down a dangerous path by a corrupt leader. There is an enemy within what you have begun calling Rainbowland, a cancer that, if left untreated, will tear to shreds all that you have worked so hard to build.*' Larry was certain that corrupt leader was my brother, Peter."

"All Father."

"Yes, but Abigail wasn't talking about Peter. She was talking about me. The spirit she spoke to, Aletheia, knows a man's heart better than he knows it himself. Abigail told me herself Aletheia was becoming more vocal in her warnings about me. That the message needed to be recorded. The child was confused, and why wouldn't she be? I was like a father to her. And so there she was, our very own oracle, getting ready to name me as enemy number one and thereby guarantee my banishment from the very community I helped to build."

Dana drew in a deep breath. "But your real enemy was Aletheia."

"Abigail. Aletheia. By that point, the difference was purely academic."

"So, you poisoned her and threw the child's body into the river before she could attach your name to the prediction."

"I turned her into a God, is what I did."

"You murdered a little girl, Timothy, your own niece, so she wouldn't rat you out. She wasn't the only one, was she?"

That was when Timothy stopped talking.

Dana drummed her fingers on the table. "You're done, then? Should I send Larry's boys in to pull the rest out through your nostrils?" She was hoping he'd say no.

"What else do you need?"

"Everything, Timothy. I need to know about every goddamned person you hurt, and I want the truth."

The door opened just then, and Donovan stepped in the room. "All right, Dana."

Dana gripped the table. "That wasn't 10 minutes. I need more time." Her voice rose. "Go tell Larry I need more time."

Donavan flashed her an ugly look before slamming the door.

She sat back down. "You're life's hanging on by a thread right now, Timothy, and unless you give me everything, I won't be able to do anything to stop them."

The fear was starting to show in his face.

"Let's start with the radio transmissions. All Father said that wasn't him."

"If there's one thing you should know, it's that All Father didn't lie. I was the one who set up the short wave radio. The signal was meant to draw people to Rainbowland. See, your problem, Dana, is you don't know our divine scriptures. The two survivors they speak of, blessed by The Shift, one a key and the other a lock. Together, they possess the power to start a new age or destroy the world forever."

Dana paused, remembering the passage she'd read in Timothy's room.

"And Patty Mae's torture, where does that fit in?"

"What you call torture, I call identification. I was trying to find out if she was the one. She was only meant to be the first of many such examinations, but Larry managed to screw everything up and ... "

"You had no choice but to get rid of her."

Timothy cleared his throat. "Yes."

"Then you took care of All Father."

"A man with such a narrow, simplistic view of our teachings should not be leading the flock. Hurt no living being by act or omission. Quaint, isn't it? Then he struck out the passages in Abigail's work that contained references to evil. On that score, he believed Abigail must surely be wrong. Like the white robe he wore, my brother was convinced that evil was not a force in and of itself. There was only light or the absence of light. He thought if only his own light was bright enough it would clear away the shadow. Sounds sweet but maybe not when Wipers show up to rape and murder your people."

"If you wanted to rule this place so badly, why not take the reins yourself?"

Timothy laughed. "The real power always hides in the shadows. The same was true before The Shift as it is now."

"And stealing what remained of the colony's food supply and dumping that soil into the river was you exercising real power?"

Another laugh from Timothy, this one showing the signs that her point had hit home. "I actually took a page out of Larry's playbook for that one. He challenged All Father over the colony's vulnerability, and I was going to do the same. Implicating your father, Richard, was simply an innocent byproduct of pitting you and Larry against one another. There's nothing quite like dividing before you conquer."

"And I'll bet killing Romeo was just more of the same," she said with disgust. "You wanted us to think it was Larry."

Timothy was rubbing his fingers together again.

"I guess that brings us to the assassination."

"Hard as it may be to swallow, I didn't mean for anyone else to die."

"Coming from a man who's already killed four others, I find it incredibly hard ... "

Dana slid the paper and pen across to Timothy and told him to start writing it all down. He took the pen and no sooner had he started than Dana heard the sound of someone approaching outside. She sprang up and gripped the door knob, feeling it struggle in her hands as the person on the other end tried to get in.

"Hurry up, and don't forget the part about framing my father. The least you can do is save one innocent life."

Timothy looked up and continued writing.

From outside, Dana could hear Donavan telling her to open up. There was something she'd forgotten to ask. Her heart quickened, worried she wouldn't have enough time. She reached into her pocket and flung Timothy's Tevatron badge across the table. He stopped, studied it, and then looked up at her.

"Finn says Tevatron has a facility somewhere emitting a pulse that's keeping people from regaining their lost memories. You worked for those crooked sonsabitches. I need to know where it is."

"I haven't a clue. I was only a low-level electronics supervisor."

Donavan was pushing against the door now. "You've got less than a minute."

"I can tell you this: Whatever Finn says he found," Timothy said, "it shouldn't be running, not after all this time."

More pounding on the door, and now Dana had her whole weight pressed against it.

Then Timothy's eyes went wide. "I do remember rumors about a project designed to tap into ley lines."

"Ley what?"

"Power points," he said impatiently. The sound of Donavan pounding against the door was freaking him out. "They form a circular grid … like a wheel. The point where the spokes converge in the center is said to be a place of great power. Read the scriptures, it's all in there."

The door burst open just then, and Dana was sent reeling into the table. Donavan and a handful of cult members with guns came in and pulled her out of the room. Outside, Larry was waiting for her.

"He admitted to everything, including framing my father."

Larry's fingers were still tapping his leg, and the sight made Dana wonder about the man's state of mind. He nodded to the men holding Dana, and they began leading her to the exit.

"I got you all the evidence you needed," she called out after him. "But now you have to give him a fair trial."

Larry didn't answer her.

Nikki

A single lantern hung from a hook in the center of the tent, drawing deep lines across the faces of the people lying in bunks. Not far away, came the sound of weeping. The attack on Larry had left everyone feeling terrified and vulnerable. Aiden and Nikki were huddled together in her bunk, shivering in spite of the heat. The truth was, only she was shivering. Her brother didn't seem the least bit fazed, and Nikki wondered what horrors he must have seen to form such a hardened shell around his heart. He didn't really know who Larry was, of course, only that a bomb had gone off and a young girl had been poisoned. Enough to rattle even the hardened citizens of New Jamestown, but not Aiden.

She watched over his shoulder as he doodled in the palm of his hand with a pen.

"Whatchu drawing?" she asked, perhaps more interested in distracting herself from seeing Margaret's lifeless little face. They were on lockdown. Orders from Larry until he and his security guards got to the bottom of what had happened.

"Not sure," Aiden replied, closing the loop of a circle.

He was drawing a face, Nikki thought. Maybe her own.

Then her brother traced lines from the circle's outer edge toward the center. Now she knew she was wrong. Aiden wasn't drawing a face at all, he was drawing a bicycle wheel with spokes. The image took up his entire palm.

"You've only got one wheel, where you gonna put the rest of the bike?"

"It's not a bike," he said. "I've been seeing it in my head for a while."

Aiden's hand with the pen opened briefly, and Nikki saw an identical image there, too. She tugged at the sleeve of his shirt and saw others, all the same: large circles with spokes.

She reached out and ran her finger along the drawing on his arm and as she did a burst of light hit the back of her eyes. She'd sensed there was a veritable ocean of memories locked deep within her brother, and now she was seeing one of them, up close and personal. A man rushing through a door in the side of a tall mountain. The feeling was almost like she was in this man's body, distinctly aware of the way his trousers rubbed together against his thigh, the uncomfortable tightness of his shoes as he hurried along, the acute dissatisfaction he felt with the new paunch he'd found following the Christmas holidays.

Nikki glanced down and saw he was wearing a white lab coat. He was fast-walking down a long concrete corridor toward an underground railway. There were others on board, dressed just like him, and somehow she knew they were waiting. As soon as he was seated, the train sped away. Propped up on his forehead was a pair of protective goggles, and he lowered them as they began to pick up speed. The shrill sound as they raced through the narrow tunnel was painful, and the man fought the urge to plug his ears. After a few moments, the train pulled to a stop in front of a set of metal doors emblazoned with a biohazard decal. They disembarked and gathered around a robust man in a purple lab coat, holding a clipboard.

"Please use the protective eyewear we provided you and do not under any circumstances approach the glass shielding inside."

The man's pulse began to quicken. His mouth felt dry and sticky. But it wasn't from the danger inside that room, it was from what it represented. A new frontier of science.

The man in purple with the clipboard pulled the doors open, and everyone shuffled inside. A set of stairs on the right led to a room with computer monitors. But it was the sight before them that was truly impressive. Many of them stood, slack jawed, trying to put mental words to what they were seeing. A giant glass tube with a pulsing white light that stretched out into bright shards. It looked like a massive welders arc.

It looked like God.

Nikki felt Aiden's body tense. She was suddenly back in the tent, struggling to make sense of what she'd just seen. Then she understood the reason for her brother's tension. Lou was standing at the entrance. Aiden sat up at once, and Nikki stood up in case she needed to protect her brother.

Hands stuffed into his pockets, the big guy glanced from side to side as though he were fighting the voice of some inner demon.

"Ya'll go and blink your eyes for a second in this loony bin and everything goes to rat shit, don't it?" Lou offered with a half smile.

Nikki remained stone faced.

"I think enough folks have been hurt or killed already, Nikki. I'm sure we can agree on that."

"I think so, too."

"Not interested in adding to that list. That's why I'm here. I ain't got nothing against your brother other than he shot my son. Lucky for him he didn't finish what he started."

Nikki felt the tension in her belly settle ever so slightly. "How's Ethan?"

208

"Doing much better. Though I can't say the same for some of the others who got hit during the raid. Like that fella Russell who helped your ma escape. Got clipped with two shots from a .22. See, that's part of the reason I'm here. This place ain't big enough for two people to keep on being mad at one another. I don't forgive so easily. Got stubbornness in my blood. Ma used to say that I could argue with a fence post and win." Lou's belly rattled with laughter, and Nikki couldn't help but join him. Even the corners of Aiden's mouth rose.

"We're all on the same side now," Lou said and held a hand out to Aiden, who reluctantly took it. The two of them shook, and Nikki couldn't help thinking about the image on the palm of her brother's hand and the memory of a man she'd never seen before. A man who in all likelihood was probably dead.

Larry

First thing early the next morning, Larry and his security detail went to the guard tower that overlooked the main gate. It was chilly, and he breathed hot air into his cupped hands. Two of the now-paramilitary cult members were busy threading a rope through the guard post's timber frame, the end tied into a noose. Below that was a chair.

"Ring the bell," Larry yelled. "Wakey-wakey."

Donavan walked up the dirt road ringing the bell normally used to summon colonists to lunch and dinner. What better way to get people to come running than with the promise of food?

Slowly, puffy-eyed colonists and cultists started to emerge. It was well before breakfast, of course, but there was something Larry wanted them to see. Something that couldn't wait.

Soon, a crowd of well over 150 was standing before him in dreaded silence, all of them studying the noose as it swung back and forth in the soft breeze. Charlie, the guard who left his post outside Larry's office, was led out from the compound basement by two guards, his face bruised and swollen. Shortly after that came Timothy. He, too, had been beaten. Larry knew because he'd administered many of the licks himself. There'd been a rather unexpected satisfaction last night when he'd wrapped his hands around Timothy's neck and began to squeeze, watching as the life slowly drained from his body. Thankfully, Donavan had been there to talk some sense into him.

"If you kill him now, it'll ruin the spectacle tomorrow," Donavan had said. And how right he was.

Here they were now, Larry standing before the crowd, who could surely tell what was about to happen. Charlie was brought before them and forced to kneel down. Larry addressed those who had gathered.

"Charlie Smith, you are charged with one count of dereliction of duty and one count of high treason. How plead you?"

"Not guilty," came the shaky reply, although his lips were so swollen it was hard to be sure.

"This court finds you guilty as charged." Larry nodded at Donavan, who raised his pistol and fired point blank into the young man's skull. Charlie's legs buckled, and he collapsed, blood pooling around his body.

The crowd gasped.

Larry watched Charlie's right leg twitch and ordered Donavan to shoot him again. Catching sight of Dana in the audience, Larry could see she was upset, and the reason for her anger was perfectly clear. She'd asked for a trial and here he was, doing just like she said. If she dared open her mouth in protest before of all these people, her father would be next. That's how serious Larry was. He turned to Timothy.

"Timothy Wallace you are – "

"Just hurry up and get this mockery of a trial over with, would you?" Timothy shouted, his hands tied behind his back.

Larry looked at Donavan, who stood Timothy on the chair and placed the noose around his neck.

"Everything I did was for Rainbowland," Timothy shouted. "Can you say the same, Larry?"

Donavan kicked the chair, but it hardly budged. He shoved his heel against the edge twice more before it finally fell over. The rope went tight, and Timothy's face turned beet-red. The fall hadn't broken his neck as they thought it would. Perhaps the drop hadn't been far enough. Timothy's legs were kicking wildly, and a woman up front screamed before collapsing to the ground. It took nearly five minutes for Timothy to die, and by the time he did, his face was nearly unrecognizable.

Timothy's body swung back and forth, the rope creaking as Larry addressed the audience. "Make no mistake about it, things are about to change around here," he told them. "You break my laws, and this is what you'll get. Hanging from the end of a rope, or worse. Larry pointed to the former cult members dressed in army fatigues and carrying rifles. "We have the right to stop and search your possessions at any time. I've also instituted a 9 o'clock nightly curfew. Any colonist suspected of treason or terrorism will be detained. Any colonist found guilty will be put to death."

The murmurs from the crowd told Larry they'd got the message loud and clear. But just in case they forgot, he had one more reminder in store for them.

"Cut him down," Larry said, nodding to Timothy's corpse. "And hang his body from the bridge. I want anyone coming or going from New Jamestown to see what happens to traitors."

•••

Less than an hour later, Donavan entered the compound basement, which had become Larry's new office and stronghold. Larry was looking over inventory lists for the food they'd captured.

"What is it?" he barked.

Donavan stepped forward. "A report just came in from the spies you posted in the city."

211

Larry stopped what he was doing and looked up. "Talk to me."

"At least 2-300 Wipers have arrived at the hotel."

"Two to 300?"

Donavan swallowed hard. "Seems that way."

"Where the hell'd they go? The beach?"

"We don't know." Finn has suggested a large army of Wipers attacked Ely State Prison."

"Have you questioned Alvarez yet?"

"No, you said no one was to go near him until you gave the green light."

Larry nodded, tapping his leg. "A handful of stragglers, that's what I expected. Not 2-300. First things first, we need to find out what those Wipers wanted at the prison." He was pacing now, talking to himself. "Jesus, when they don't find Alvarez' body, they're gonna know he's still alive, and you know what they're gonna do."

"What?"

"They're gonna fucking come looking for him, whaddya think!"

Donavan bit his lip. "What do you suggest?"

"He's our insurance policy just like we planned, but we need a letter, written in his hand that tells these sonsabitches, if they dare attack, that their beloved leader is dead. We also need a carrot to go along with that stick. Say, a promise that after 90 days we'll let him go free."

"Release Alvarez?"

"'Course not, but it'll give us some breathing room till we get things inside New Jamestown back under control."

Donavan left quickly, and for a long time afterward, Larry continued to pace the floor of his new basement office.

That sonbitch Alvarez better cooperate. If he knows what's good for him.

Finn

Before today, no one had ever been executed in New Jamestown – or Rainbowland for that matter – and the shock of what many of them had just witnessed was still raw. After Larry dismissed the crowd, several had wandered aimlessly, like the victims from a multi-car pileup, staggering through open fields.

Outside the police trailer, Dana stood hugging her father. Finn knew the stress that she'd been under trying to prove he wasn't guilty. It didn't matter he'd been stuck in Nevada and hadn't seen it firsthand. The minute Finn rolled back into town, the deep lines below her eyes had said it all. But he was free and safe, at least for now.

"You seem different," Joanne said, walking beside him. They were heading back to Tent City, to see if they could help tend to the wounded. Maybe give Lou a chance to leave his son's bedside and stretch his legs.

"It's hard to watch a man killed before your eyes, no matter what he's done."

She kicked at the gravel. "That's not what I meant. You've been acting strange since yesterday, Finn. Distant. Is something the matter?"

Yeah, I'm trying to figure out if you were programmed to kill me.

'Course, he couldn't come right out and say such a thing. They were supposed to be married, a recent discovery, which in a strange way had been confirmed the moment he saw her. Doesn't matter what your mind forgets, it's all in the eyes, and you only need to look deeply enough to see if the connection goes back further than the last five minutes.

"Any new memories from before?" he asked, trying to skirt lightly around the real question on his mind.

"You mean before The Shift?"

"Yeah."

"I thought we'd been over this already," Joanne told him. "All I remember is the same thing as the others. The meadow with the tall grass."

"The background image to Tevatron's internal computer system."

"If you say so." She smiled, but Finn didn't smile back.

"There was a case," he started saying before he could stop himself. "With explosives and a DVD designed to blackmail you into killing me and destroying whatever was left of the Nevada lab."

"Pardon me?" She stopped and he stopped, too.

"Dana found it. Only told me about it yesterday."

"So, you've been going around thinking I might be trying to kill you? Is that it?"

"No," he said drawing the word out.

"Why didn't you say anything before?"

"I didn't know where to start. Oh, by the way … "

"Yeah, it's called being honest."

"Well, I don't believe it."

"Are you sure?"

Finn put his hands around her waist. "I know you couldn't live without me, even before I knew we were married."

She laughed and hit his chest. "Speak for yourself. Before you woke up from that coma, I was doing just fine." She started walking away.

"What do you mean, just fine?" he said, coming after her.

"Jealous much? You're not the only eligible bachelor in New Jamestown." She was swinging her backside now with mock sexiness.

Finn let out a bellow of laughter as he followed her to the medical tent, which was busy with visitors. Near the entrance was a woman he vaguely knew as Holly and her daughter, Tamara. They were holding the hand of a man named Russell, who'd been wounded during the attack on Alvarez' stronghold.

Ethan was at the other end. Finn and Joanne had expected to come relieve Lou for a few minutes, but that wasn't who they found by the boy's bed. It was Nikki and Aiden.

"If you only knew how much time we spent looking for you," Finn told Aiden. The kids got up at once, and Nikki threw her arms around him. Finn shook Aiden's hand.

"I'm so sorry about your mother," he told them.

Nikki and Aiden nodded without saying a word. What was one supposed to say to such a thing? A perfect example of how inadequate words were when stacked next to a human life.

"We were just visiting with Ethan," Nikki said. "He's asleep, but Lou say's he should be on his feet any time now."

Finn could sense there was something else she wanted to say. "Anything you wanna tell me, you can say in front of Joanne."

Nikki nodded before looking over at Aiden. "Show him."

Aiden glanced up at her and lifted his shirt. Drawn in black marker was the same wheel he'd sketched on his arms and hands.

"What are we looking at?" Joanne asked.

"Something very special," Nikki told them. "Maybe more special than ever before."

Finn folded his arms. "I don't understand."

"The first time I noticed was purely by accident," Nikki said. "I'd touched Aiden's shoulder and saw a flash of memory. Took a second before I realized it wasn't his."

Finn shook his head, trying to clear away the cobwebs. "Not his? Who'd it belong to?"

"Someone else."

"What are you saying, Nikki?" Joanne asked pointedly. "That Aiden has another person's memories buried in his mind?"

"Not someone's," she replied. "Everyone's."

Larry

Larry was in his new basement office, reading a letter, when Donavan came in.

"Alvarez isn't talking," his second in command told him.

He crumpled the paper in his hands. Another anonymous colonist was complaining to Larry that Timothy was executed without the benefit of a trial or community vote. If they didn't have the balls to say it to his goddamned face, then they should keep their mouths shut. That's what Larry thought. "Have you tried to persuade him?"

Donavan nodded that he had. "We've got his hands cuffed behind his back and his feet tied to the chair. Each of us even took turns smacking him around. All he did was laugh. Told us he would write anything we wanted, but not before talking to you."

"Me?"

"Says he wants to talk to our leader. Get some assurances."

"Did he say anything about why his men attacked the prison?" But before he replied, Larry could already tell Donvavan's answer was going to disappoint him.

"He wants you, Boss."

•••

It took all of five minutes for Larry to make his way from the compound basement to the trailer that was acting as Alvarez' prison cell. It was the same one where they'd kept Bud and later, Dana's father, Richard, but Al wasn't the sort of guy you let mix with impressionable minds. From everything Larry had heard, this prick made Hannibal Lecter look like Mr. Rogers. That was one of the reasons for all the restraints. But even the strongest-willed men only took so much. Sooner or later, they all cracked.

The trailer was hushed when Larry arrived, Donavan in tow. As expected, Alvarez was handcuffed and lashed to a chair. He couldn't reach out and take a swing or try kicking you in the nuts even if he tried. That worked just fine for Larry. And when all was said and done, wasn't that the true joy of torturing another fellow human being? The helplessness, the agonizing pain, and before long, the shouts for mercy?

Larry watched Alvarez' swollen eyes trace his movement into the trailer and across to a table where a variety of instruments sat waiting.

"You asked for me," Larry said without looking at Alvarez. He ran his hand over a row of scalpels, feeling goose bumps run up his arms from the cold steel. "Should we get started?"

"I wouldn't have asked for the boss if I weren't ready."

Larry's hand passed over several more lethal choices before settling on the pliers. People had an uncanny attachment to their teeth and fingernails. It was little wonder, then, how quickly they began to cooperate after a few were wrenched out. The trick was to inflict enough damage to get them singing the tune you were hoping to hear, without killing them in the process. Especially for Alvarez. But he looked like a strong, young Mexican-American. The kind that could take boatloads of punishment.

"So, Donavan here tells me you're looking for certain assurances," Larry said.

Alvarez nodded. "My men have probably already figured out where I am."

"I'm sure they have."

"You kill me, and these little toothpicks you call walls won't do a damned thing to save you."

There was a change in Larry's face when Al referred to his walls as toothpicks. A look very much like a man who'd been kicked in the nuts by a baby's shoe. The palisade was Larry's baby, and probably the very thing that had kept them from being overrun long ago. He wasn't going to let this gangbanging Spic take pot shots at his accomplishments.

In three strides, Larry was right there beside Alvarez, the right arm with the pliers coming down on his already bruised cheekbone. The strike made a clanking sound and opened up a deep gash under Al's left eye. Blood began running down from the cut Larry had just opened. "I'm sorry," Larry said. "You were saying something?"

Alvarez winced from the pain, trying to blink it away.

"You can't kill me, Larry, and you know it, so why don't you put the toys away and act like a man?"

Larry jammed the pliers into Alvarez' mouth, fishing around until he felt a molar clamped by the serrated jaws. His other hand was pushing against Al's face as he twisted and then wrenched the tooth free. A gout of blood filled Al's mouth, dribbling over his lip and down his chin. The Spic wasn't smiling, not anymore.

But it was clear the burst of dull pain was excruciating and it was only gonna get worse, that's the message Larry wanted to drive home.

"I'm not sure what you thought, but this isn't a negotiation," Larry told him. "You're gonna write a letter telling your slave trader friends you're all right. Then you're gonna sign it … they can read, I'm assuming?"

Alvarez spat blood on the floor next to him. "Jeffereys and his men can read just fine."

"Jeffereys," Larry said. "The same man who pulled a gun and waved it in my face?"

Alvarez smiled. "Yes, he said you shat your pants and couldn't wait to sell out that old bag, All Father."

Larry's face turned a deep shade of red. He glanced behind him toward the others present. All of them were staring at him now, but the only face he saw right then was Simon's – All Father's only son – and the expression on his young face was hard to read. It looked like he was trying to process two competing realities. The one where Larry was a good guy who saved them from certain death and another where he more closely resembled a weasel and a scumbag.

"You might not have killed the old man yourself," Alvarez went on, "but you sure as hell wanted him dead, didn't you?"

"Shut your lying mouth!" And this time Larry jabbed the pliers into Alvarez' windpipe causing Al's head to snap back and then forward. He started coughing and trying to catch his breath.

"That's it, Larry," Alvarez croaked. "Beat me just like your old man used to beat you every night."

That's when Larry saw red. Down went the pliers, skittering to the trailer floor. A split second later Larry's hands were wrapped around Al's throat, his thumbs pushing deep into Al's windpipe with uncontrolled rage. Alvarez squirmed under him, gasping for the very air Larry was denying him.

"How does it feel you son of a bitch?" Larry chanted. "Not so smart now, are you?"

A couple of the men watching moved to stop Larry, but by then, it didn't much matter. The deed was done. Larry stood, heaving, and turned on a pair of wobbly legs. His head was spinning, too. Behind him, Alvarez was dead. He wasn't sure how exactly he knew, but he did. It was then that Larry collapsed, suddenly aware that something was terribly wrong.

PRIMAL SHIFT 10: JUDGEMENT DAY

Dana

Dana had hoped that during Timothy's interrogation he might shed some light on the location of Tevatron's secret project, the pulse wave that was apparently being used to keep people's memories suppressed. If she'd only had enough time to question him properly, perhaps she might have teased a few additional morsels out of him. But Larry and his henchmen clearly had other plans. Timothy's last words had been to check Abigail's notebook, and that's exactly what she was doing now. Since finding it hidden in his room, Dana had held onto it as evidence, never entirely clear on how it would prove useful. But that was the funny thing about evidence. In the long run, sometimes the useless bits you collect become the most valuable.

Dana flipped through the frayed pages. To her eyes, many of the entries read like New Age mumbo jumbo. The kinda crystal-gazing stuff so popular throughout the '90s and relegated now to crackpot central.

It hadn't been longer than 10 minutes before she found the first hints of what she was after. An entry Abigail had recorded many years ago that spoke of sacred sites of tremendous power situated around the world. The Bermuda Triangle, the Pyramids of Giza, Machu Picchu in Peru, and many more. When certain key points were laid out on a map, a distinct shape began to emerge. That of a giant circle. Dana began etching it by hand on a piece of scrap paper.

She was just about done when the trailer door burst in. Dana looked up, startled. It was Lou.

"Larry just killed Alvarez."

•••

They headed first for the prison trailer where Alvarez was being held. But before she was even halfway across the gravel road that separated the two trailers, she caught the smell of something burning. Someone was having a late night barbecue. That was her first thought.

She and Lou arrived seconds later and found the jail empty. Even Simon, often on guard duty, was absent.

Next, they headed for the office Larry set up for himself in the compound basement. Dana pulled open the door and walked in to a cacophony of voices.

She turned the corner and found Larry, laid out on a sofa in his new office, a cult member in fatigues fanning him with a pillow. Another was

220

dabbing a wet cloth against a wound on his cheek. Others were standing around, bickering among themselves over what to do.

"What the hell happened?" Dana barked.

The men around Larry turned at once.

"I don't doubt for a second Alvarez deserved to die," she said. "But I thought this guy was supposed to be our bargaining chip?"

Larry sat up, and right away Dana saw there was something different about him. First of all, his hand wasn't trembling anymore, and there was a scar on his cheek, one that almost looked like a burn mark.

"He tried to attack me," Larry said. "I had no choice."

"Tried to attack you. Wasn't he was strapped to a chair?" This wasn't making any sense, and the strange look in Larry's eyes wasn't helping. "I'd like to examine the body," she told him flatly.

"I'm afraid that's quite impossible."

Quite impossible?

That wasn't the way Larry normally spoke, and something about that thought made goose flesh run up the length of her arms.

"I had Donavan take his body out behind the trailer and burn it."

"You what?"

"He was quite dead, I assure you."

"Yes, I'm sure you saw to that. And what now, Larry, when the Wipers come looking for revenge and we don't have Alvarez to keep them at bay?"

Larry smiled, and the burn mark along his face wrinkled. "Don't worry about the Wipers. I can handle them just fine."

"I don't know," Dana was frantically telling Finn less than 10 minutes later. "I think Larry's starting to lose his mind."

The fear and panic in her voice when she said they needed to speak was enough to let him know she was deadly serious.

"I still don't get how a man who's tied to a chair posed any threat." Finn said.

Dana was pacing back and forth. "He didn't. Look, Alvarez was a murdering bastard. I should know, but I thought we captured him for a reason."

"You think the assassination attempt rattled something loose inside Larry's head?"

"My dad used to watch those black and white World War II documentaries on the Discovery Channel when he wasn't plastered and glued to breaking news on CNN. I remember seeing one about how attempts on the lives of dictators always sent them into bouts of paranoia. Adolf Hitler, Saddam Hussein. He may be slick, but don't let Larry fool you, he's a dictator."

Finn couldn't agree more. Fact, he'd been waiting to hear those very words come out of Dana's mouth, but hearing them only made him all the more concerned. "The more reason you should be careful, Dana."

She stopped pacing and bit the end of her thumbnail. "It wouldn't be the first time someone was eavesdropping on the stuff I was saying."

Finn's eyebrows went up. Not entirely sure if she meant what she'd just said. Either way, it didn't matter.

"I'm not sure what's going on, but you saw how easily he executed Timothy, that poor guard, Charlie, and now Alvarez. No one's safe, Dana, especially if he finds you poking your nose in places he doesn't want you to."

She laughed. "Coming from the guy who's made it his business to poke his nose in dangerous places."

Finn was over by Dana's desk when he spotted the notebook. "What's this?"

"I spoke to Timothy about Tevatron before he was killed, and he told me to read through Abigail's channeling. So far, I'm not sure what to think."

Finn flipped through the pages when out popped the drawing Dana had made. He held the sheet up, staring at it in amazement. He was glaring at what looked like a wagon wheel with spokes that came together at a central point. This was the same picture Aiden had sketched all over his body. He looked at her, and the surprise on his face must have been apparent.

●●●

"We didn't know who else we could ask," Finn explained to Simon. He and Dana were standing at the door to the jailer's bedroom. Simon was wearing pajamas and looked like he'd been in the middle of a wild dream when they'd pounded on his door.

"Come in, come in," he said.

Dana closed the door behind them, and Finn handed Simon the piece of paper with the image of the wheel.

"Where did you get this?" He asked.

"It's a long story," Dana said. "Do you know what it is?"

"'Course, I know it. It's the planetary power grid. Ancient people sensed something of the power contained at certain spots and built important temples and structures to worship them. Aletheia spoke about these points often. Said at the center of the wheel was a source of unlimited free energy for anyone capable of tapping into it."

"Well, we think someone's already tapped in," Finn said. He pointed to where all the lines converged. "We need to know where it is."

Simon began rummaging through a box under his bed. "After my father died," Simon said and then stopped himself. "After Timothy murdered him, I should say, Larry's first order of business was to trash all my father's papers. Dumped them into a container to be burned. 'Course, what son wouldn't want to salvage at least a handful of mementos?"

Simon came out with a wrinkled map of North America, filled with lines drawn in red ink. "This map hung on his wall for years."

The deep-crimson lines came in from all sides, like the contrail from dozens of nuclear missile strikes, and each of them converged at a point north of here.

"Montana," Dana said in amazement.

Simon nodded and poked his finger at a spot on the map. "Chief Mountain, Montana, more specifically. That was where us Rainbowites – back when there was such a thing – set up camp every year to celebrate the summer solstice.

Larry

Larry was sure that voice he heard babbling inside his head, the one that sounded an awful lot like Alvarez, was the first sign of guilt over killing the man in cold blood. No doubt about it, that voice was pushing the buttons of a man who'd been through a lot lately. The attack on the compound, Timothy's attempts to raise a rebellion within New Jamestown, and then a failed assassination attempt. More than enough to rattle anyone, wasn't it? For Larry, wrapping his hands around Alvarez' neck and squeezing the life out of him had been the result of surrendering to an impulse he'd been powerless to resist. It wasn't going too far to say he'd almost felt himself a spectator in a hazy dream, a kind of marionette with strings that rose up through the jail cell walls and settled in the hands of some malevolent force.

And now that Larry thought about it, hadn't Alvarez' voice been whispering in his ear from the moment he began his interrogation? Soft and subtle. Then when the real man began to speak, Larry could hear two voices, as though he were standing in an echo chamber. Each voice was saying something different. Strapped to that chair, Alvarez' real voice had pecked at Larry's nerves with the sharpened precision of a bird's beak. But Alvarez' other voice, the one no one else could hear, was saying something completely different. It was egging him on.

Are you gonna let him talk to you like that?

That's it, Larry, show him who's boss. Show him who's the fucking boss around here!

He'd strangled Alvarez, in part, to silence the voices – both of them – but the act of killing the man had only made them grow louder. Now there was a veritable brouhaha going on within the narrow confines of Larry's skull.

It hadn't taken long for Larry to realize the continued presence of that voice wasn't a sign of insanity, nor was it guilt – a word that wasn't in Larry's everyday vocabulary. When bad shit happened to the people around him, it was usually because they either got stupid or tried to cross him, sometimes both.

Since the strangling, Alvarez' voice became loudest when the others around him were looking for direction. There was a kind of tug-of-war going on inside his head, and daresay his soul, a battle Larry feared he was losing.

Donavan entered the office. "It's done," he said. He was referring to Larry's request he bury Alvarez' remains.

Larry steepled his fingers. "Good."

"If I may," Donavan added. "There's one thing I don't quite understand."

Larry's eyebrow perked up. "Is there?" He could feel Alvarez pulling those invisible strings again. Tweaked eyebrows and steepled fingers wasn't Larry Nowak, and Donavan seemed to notice the change, although he certainly would never have guessed the reason for it.

"Why burn Alvarez' body, rather than hang him from the bridge as a warning, the way you did with Timothy?"

The question was a perfectly valid one, and up until that point, Larry hadn't given his order a second thought. Now that it was put before him, the answer suddenly became clear. He'd sooner hang himself from the bridge than desecrate Alvarez' body. The feeling had been strong, and in an eerie way that he didn't quite understand, the two men were now one.

"I didn't want to anger those pesky Wipers," Larry lied.

Donavan's eyes fell to his boots and the mud left there from the burial. "That makes sense."

"Of course, it does. Stick with me long enough, and you'll learn a thing or two about dealing with these savages."

Larry leaned back in his chair, and the loud squeak that escaped made his face scrunch up. "This chair, I hate it."

"It isn't comfortable?" Donavan asked. "I can have someone search each room in the compound for a better one. I'm sure someone would be willing to hand over whatever you'd like."

"No, I don't want a chair already flattened by someone else's ass. I want something larger and regal."

Donavan seemed to be repeating the words in his head, going through a mental rolodex for anything that might fit that description. "You mean like a throne."

The smile on Larry's face slowly took form. "Not like, Donavan. A throne exactly."

"We can do that."

"You never cease to amaze me, you know that? Oh, and one other thing."

Donavan nodded. "Name it, Boss."

"Unconditional loyalty is so very important to me. I'm sure you already know that. Soon, I'll be asking you to run an errand for me that will seem foolish, even dangerous, but I need to know you'll carry it out in complete secrecy, no questions asked."

"Will anyone get hurt?"

"They sure will."

Now it was Donavan's turn to smile. "I can't wait."

Nikki

She and Aiden were in the sheriff's trailer with Dana, Finn, and Joanne. They were discussing the conversation they'd had with Simon and the map he'd shown them with the ley lines.

"So, the cult has known about this place all along?" Aiden asked.

"Known its power," Finn told him, "which was why they made a pilgrimage to the spot every year, but if you're asking did they have any idea Tevatron had an underground laboratory in the area, I'd say no."

"What do we do now?" Nikki asked.

Dana opened the drawer to her desk and removed a silver briefcase. She opened it, revealing what looked like two slabs of Plasticine with a single timer.

Nikki's eyes went wide. "You wanna blow it up?"

"We believe shutting off that low-frequency pulse," Dana told her, "will allow people's memories to start rising to the surface again."

"A process that could take weeks," Finn added. "That is, if we can trust what was on the warden's hard drive."

A thought occurred to Nikki just then. "If Tevatron found a way to tap into this incredible power, isn't that something we could use? I can't imagine just blowing it to bits. I mean, think of how much good it could do. Free energy for everyone."

The others were quietly mulling over what she'd said. New Jamestown's windmill and the battery bank it recharged was enough to pump water up from the river as well as run most of their modest electrical needs, but they still needed to be careful. Imagine what the juice from the ley lines could do.

"She may have a point," Finn said.

Dana nodded, although it was clear she wasn't entirely convinced. "If there's a bright, blinking off switch, then great. Otherwise, I'm gonna make it a crater and free those Wipers once and for all."

Finn looked pensive, and Joanne put a hand on his shoulder. "What is it?"

He looked directly in her eyes, and even Nikki saw the fear he was trying to hide. "I'm scared things might not be as straightforward as we think they'll be."

"What do you mean?" Joanne asked.

"For one," Finn said, "I'm not so sure I want all those old memories back. Don't get me wrong, I've been digging through my past in search of the truth more than anyone, but mostly to make sure I wasn't the sort

of douche bag who deserved to have died during The Shift." He turned
to Aiden and Nikki and apologized for cursing. "I've started to find
peace with who I am now, but the old me, the one before the world went
insane. I don't know that man, and I'm not entirely sure I'll like him."

"I did," Joanne said. "Least, I must have."

A sad twinkle lit Finn's eyes. "What if gaining back what I lost means
losing everything and everyone I've met since The Shift? No one really
knows how it's gonna work. We might turn that pulse machine off and I
forget everything after July the Fourth. If I gotta choose between the
two, if those are my options, I'm not sure which one I'd take. You'd
asked me that question two months ago, and the answer would have
been simple, but so much has happened since then." He looked at Dana,
Nikki, and Aiden. "All of you would be strangers to me."

There was a knock at the door just then. Joanne was the closest and
she opened up. A cult member in army fatigues with a rifle straightened
his shoulders. "Larry would like to see Nikki and Aiden."

•••

Nikki and Aiden were led through the door and into the compound's
basement. Less than 10 feet down the hallway, two guards stood at
attention outside Larry's office.

The minute they walked in, Nikki could hear the eerie sound of
music. Sounded like someone was playing a stringed instrument and
quite well at that. It continued until the cult member led the two into the
office where they found Larry playing a beautiful antique instrument.

Larry glanced up at them. "They say that music sooths the mind and
boosts the I.Q." His gaze turned to Nikki. "Do you know what this is?"
he asked holding the instrument in the air.

"A fiddle," she replied, not entirely sure if this was a trick question.

He laughed. "A fiddle is something you don't mind spilling beer on.
This beautiful lady here is a violin."

"It's nice," Aiden said.

"Only six of these were ever made," Larry told them. "And this is the
sole survivor. There may be similar masterpieces housed in some dusty
museum somewhere, but with no one to take care of them, they'll slowly
begin to rot and die."

Nikki wasn't sure what Larry was talking about, but she knew it had
nothing to do with violins.

"Before The Shift, men like me only gazed upon art like this through
bulletproof glass. Back in those days, guns had the distinction of being
called the great equalizers. Didn't matter how big you were or what you

228

had in your pants so long as your aim was straight and true. I submit that The Shift is the real equalizer for a world that was so desperately out of balance. The old wicked ways have been torn to shreds, and now it's up to us to rebuild it."

"You make The Shift sound wonderful," Nikki said with disgust. "If it had never happened, my parents would both still be alive."

Larry made a series of quick, dismissive gestures with his hands. "One must break a few eggs to make an omelette, no? You know how that old chestnut goes, I'm sure. Shit has a habit of getting sloppy when you're changing the world."

Nikki felt the blood rising up her neck and into her face.

Larry didn't seem to notice, or care. He stood and laid the violin on his desk, circling around toward them. "Both of you kids have a gift." He stopped less than a foot away and laid a hand on each of their shoulders, his eyes, depthless sapphires that swayed back and forth in the dim light, seemed to stare right through them.

To Nikki, those eyes were far deeper than they'd been the time she and Larry had spoken in his office. Back then, she'd seen a father abusing a son for being weak. But now, much of that was buried over by something else, something darker.

The image she saw in Larry's eyes was a man in a purple robe sitting by an open window. Outside, an ancient city was engulfed in flames. The man had a laurel wreath on his head and a fiddle in his hands. But it was the smile on his lips that seemed the most out of place. He stuck the fiddle under his chin and began to play, humming along with a tune Nikki didn't know. She was seeing a memory from centuries ago, and that's when a name popped into her head.

"Who's Nero?" she asked him.

For a moment, Larry seemed startled. "A mad Roman emperor," he replied, almost instinctively.

"He also liked to play the violin," Nikki said, matter-of-factly.

"Yes, he did, and according to legend," Larry added, "he fiddled while Rome burned to the ground."

Except Nikki knew now that wasn't a myth at all. Nero really had celebrated the burning of the city he was sworn to protect, and whatever was in Larry was getting ready to do it again.

Finn

Early the next morning, Finn came awake when he heard the commotion from outside. Joanne was snuggled next to him in a cot barely large enough for one. A few of the other colonists were already up, along with about half the people who shared their tent.

"What's going on?" Joanne asked him with a hint of panic.

He kissed her forehead. "I thought you were asleep."

"These ears are dialed into danger."

He touched her cheek. "Wait here. I'll go find out."

Finn rolled out of bed and pulled on his coveralls and boots. The minute he got clear of Tent City, he spotted the source of the disturbance. One of the guards overlooking the front gate was shouting at someone on the other side. Had stragglers arrived, looking for a handout? There hadn't been many of those lately. Most everyone had either banded together and laid claim to a patch of land or died within the first few weeks of The Shift.

It was only when Finn reached the bridge and peered through the giant doors of the front gate that he saw who was on the other side.

"I know them," Finn shouted to the guard in the tower. "Open the gates and let them in."

Larry, Donavan, and a handful of armed cult members were heading their way. The guard turned to Larry who nodded and shouted, "Open the gate."

The latches, which dug into the ground, were raised, and the massive doors swung open.

In drove nearly a dozen Humvees. The one in front brandishing a .50-caliber machine gun manned by a sailor in blue and gray fatigues.

The lead Humvee came to a stop, and Commander Zhou got out, along with Callahan and Kulik, the Polish XO's shotgun slung over his shoulder.

Finn greeted them warmly. "Wasn't sure you were gonna make it." The sight of Zhou and his men was a reassuring one. Between Timothy's execution and Alvarez' murder at Larry's hands, things in New Jamestown had felt on the verge of spiralling out of control.

"Welcome to New Jamestown," Larry interjected. "You must be Commander Zhou."

Zhou held out his hand. "And you must be Larry."

"Indeed. But please forgive me if I don't shake, I'm afraid I might be coming down with something."

Behind them, the Humvees rumbled past on their way to the parking area by the rear wall.

"While he was our guest," Larry said. "Callahan has told us so much about you."

Zhou and Callahan exchanged a look. "Only good things, I hope," Zhou said.

"Always." The two men stood, smiling at one another.

"We don't intend to stay long," Zhou told Larry. "Our plan is to head east and attempt to link up with whatever might be left of the government."

"The government?" Larry asked. "That old thing. Don't you know it's long gone?"

"You know that for a fact?" Kulik said, shifting the shotgun onto his other shoulder.

Larry smiled with false modesty. "For a fact? No, but I arrived here from New York City, and I can tell you with some authority, there isn't much of anything left that way."

"Have you received any survivors from the Washington area?"

"We haven't," Larry conceded. "And surely that in and of itself can't be a good sign. The folks you see around you were brought here by a message broadcast over a shortwave radio. Other communities have surely sprung up since we arrived, but ... "

"But what?" Zhou asked.

Larry rolled his eyes in embarrassment. "Trust will always be an issue. Small groups of survivors spread out in a sea of Wipers. Sometimes, that brings out the worst in people, wouldn't you say?"

"What do you know of these Wipers?"

The grin on Larry's face was wide and almost menacing. "They shouldn't be a problem anymore."

Finn laid a hand on Zhou's shoulder. "There have been some developments lately you should know about."

"Oh, enough of that," Larry said. "There'll be plenty of time for serious talk. But first, let's welcome our guests properly. Surely, you and your men are hungry."

"Starving," Zhou replied, touching his belly unconsciously. "But I can't impose. I'll have my men form into groups and hunt for local game."

"Game-shmame," Larry sang. "Don't be silly. You're our guest. How many men are with you?"

"Our crew is down to 49 souls," Zhou said, and something about the way the commander said the word 'souls' made Larry's eyes sparkle.

231

"What an apt way of putting it. Well, tell your souls to meet us in the gymnasium. We're going to get you fed. New Jamestown is proud to host any member of the armed services."

Larry ushered Zhou away toward the compound then, and all the while Finn's gut kept telling him something wasn't right. Larry was never that nice unless he needed something or he was up to no good. Could he have plans on convincing Zhou's men to stay in New Jamestown? Bolster the colony's defenses with some extra muscle and fire power? Or could Larry have his conniving little sights set on something else entirely?

Jeffereys

In his note, Alvarez had said a message would arrive shortly, and as always, the creepy bastard was true to his word. Jeffereys was outside, overseeing the repair work on the cars and trucks that had managed to escape the Ely State Prison massacre, when a whistle came from the lookout on the Grand America's roof. One short blast, which meant whoever was heading their way was coming alone. It wasn't more than a minute or two later when a chocolate-brown Trans Am came screeching around the corner and into the hotel's roundabout.

The lone occupant emerged, dressed in full camo with a lock of short dark hair and nice features. The cleanliness of his skin told Jeffereys he was likely one of the ass jockeys who'd attacked the hotel while they were away. The one-armed Wiper by Jeffereys' side pulled a pistol from his pants waistband and would have taken a shot if Jeffereys hadn't put a hand on the barrel and told him to get rid of it. If this lone guy was looking for trouble, he woulda come out guns blazing. Jeffereys might not know him, but he was willing to bet this was Alvarez' messenger.

"That's close enough," Jeffereys told him. "State your name and your business."

"Name's Donavan. Got a package for Jeffereys."

Jeffereys smiled and pointed to the big guy next to him. "This here's Jeffereys. Slide it over."

Donavan did as he was told. Jeffereys took a step back while the one-armed Wiper knelt down and opened the bag. Packages had a nasty habit of going kaboom, and there was no way Jeffereys was going to take any unnecessary risks.

"Looks safe," the Wiper told him in broken English.

Donavan was already getting back into the Trans Am and looking mighty happy to be doing so. Jeffereys grabbed the package at about the same time as Donavan's car tires screeched away.

Inside he found a note and an Iridium satellite phone.

The note read:

Dear Jeffereys,

I'm a man of my word, not that you ever doubted that for a moment. I've changed my skin, so to speak. I guarantee the next time we meet you won't recognize me. But

233

*you were never fooled by appearances, were you? Prepare the men. Enclosed, you'll find
a radio. Keep it close and await my signal.*

Eternally,
Larry

Jeffereys looked down at the satellite phone, half expecting it to
crackle to life. He turned to the one-armed Wiper. "We've got work to
do."

Dana

"What do you mean it wasn't him?" Dana asked. She was standing over her desk, studying a road map, trying to plot the fastest route to the facility near Chief Mountain in Northern Montana.

"There's someone else in there with him," Nikki said. She sounded frightened. Aiden was close beside her, his blue eyes twinkling in the soft light.

Bud and Lou were at the back of the trailer, loading .45 slugs into a pair of Glocks.

Dana traced a line along US 287 North. "The trip to Montana will take us 10 hours," she told the two men. "Make sure we have extra gas cans and enough provisions in case we break down somewhere."

"Worst-case scenario: We call in AAA," Lou shot back, hardly able to get the words out before his belly started to gyrate.

Nikki wasn't amused. "Have you been listening to a word I said?"

Dana looked down at Nikki and the scowl across her face.

"You're right, Larry's been acting erratic, but couldn't stress be to blame for what you're saying?"

"To blame for what?" Bud asked, only now clueing in to the conversation.

Nikki explained, and at once Bud's face blanched.

"What is it?" Dana asked.

"The guy from Tevatron who blackmailed me, his name was Harry Thomson. When I arrived in Salt Lake City from New York, I met him again, only this time he wasn't Harry anymore. His name was Alvarez, and he'd gone from a pasty-white dude, to a short Hispanic-looking fella."

Dana glared at Bud, wondering if he'd lost his mind.

"Sounds crazy, I know, but I'm telling you the truth. Somehow" the guy's able to change bodies."

"Like one of those frickin' shape-shifters in that movie." Lou spat. "You 'member it? Oh, God the one with whatsherface ... "

"He can't morph his features," Bud said, ignoring Lou's pleas for help. "It's more like something inside him – "

"Jumps into someone else," Nikki said, finishing Bud's sentence.

"Yeah."

Dana let the highlighter fall from her hand. "So, you're saying whatever was in Harry Thomson went into Alvarez, and now it's in Larry?"

235

Bud and Nikki nodded at the same time. "Musta happened when Larry killed him," Bud said.

"You sure you aren't mistaken?" Dana asked, dreading the answer she knew was coming.

"I saw things," Nikki told her. "Old, horrible memories."

"Older than Larry?"

Nikki swallowed hard. "Ancient."

"*Night of the Mutants*," Lou said, crossing himself. "Thought that was gonna torture me all night."

"We need to leave," Dana said. "Straightaway."

•••

Twenty minutes later, Lou was out front with the battle wagon. Extra gas cans hung from the back. Inside was a range of small arms and enough food to last them a week. Dana, Nikki, Aiden, and Bud scrambled down from the trailer and got in.

Dana was putting on her seat belt when she paused. "What about Finn and Joanne? They're the ones who told us about this in the first place. If anyone should be going, it's them."

"Fine by me," Bud said. "But it's gonna get mighty cozy."

"We got some extra space up here," Dana told him patting the long bench-style seat in the front. "And we can sit someone in the very back."

All eyes turned to Aiden, who sighed. "I always get the short end of the stick."

"With age comes privilege," Nikki said, jumping out. "I'll go get Finn and Joanne."

She ran off while Lou killed the engine. There was no sense in wasting precious gas while the car idled.

They hadn't been waiting for longer than five minutes when Aiden tapped Dana on the shoulder. "I think someone's coming."

She glanced over, expecting to see Finn, Joanne, and Nikki, but instead she saw Larry and Donavan approaching along with a dozen armed men.

Larry drummed his fingernails on the passenger window. Dana rolled it down.

"Planning a sightseeing tour?" he asked.

"We're heading out on business," Dana told him with a dismissive tone.

"Oh, I see," Larry replied. "Business. Yes, of course, then I assume you've received permission to leave New Jamestown."

"Permission," Lou said, and it sounded like he chewed off the word before it fully left his mouth.

Larry leaned in. "Morning, Louis. We were having a nice meal with our new Navy friends when we heard a rumor citizens were planning an illegal excursion."

"We're free to come and go as we please," Dana told him. "I'm the appointed sheriff, don't forget."

"Were, Dana darling. You *were* the appointed sheriff, but not any longer." He reached in and tore the badge from her chest. "And nobody leaves New Jamestown without my say-so."

Larry turned to Donavan and the men behind him. "Confiscate their weapons, will you, and when you're done, see to it that our Navy friends are disarmed as well. If anyone resists, shoot them. We can't have hooligans running around endangering innocent lives, now can we?"

Larry

The number of firearms in New Jamestown was truly astounding, and it took the better part of the day to collect them all. The trick was to descend on each unsuspecting group of colonists with overwhelming force. A few of the more dim-witted folks had attempted to reach for hidden pistols and were cut down straightaway. Larry had made sure Donavan's orders were clear. One couldn't run a successful tyranny with an armed population running around. The arrival of Commander Zhou and his unsuspecting men had only been the icing on the proverbial cake and a sign that Larry's plan was coming together.

He was in the middle of relishing that very thought when Donavan entered his office and laid a box of spark plugs on his desk.

"The vehicles have all been disabled. Humvees don't use plugs so we boxed 'em in with the other cars."

"And the confiscated weapons?"

"Those are being stored across from the interrogation room."

Hearing that stirred something deep within Larry. An old memory that tasted about 100 years old. The image was faint, but clear enough. He'd been heading into that room to brandish his Rainbowite initiation robe. It was the day he was set to become one of them. The same day he'd discovered Patty Mae across the hall, strapped to that chair. He couldn't possibly have imagined then that Timothy had been the one behind it all, although at the time, finding the woman had helped to feed him the ammunition he would use to dethrone All Father.

Speaking of thrones, Larry was enjoying the polished oak seat Donavan had commissioned for him. It wasn't quite as nice as the throne made from human bones he'd enjoyed at the Grand America, but he couldn't have his taste for exotic furniture shocking the sensitive people of New Jamestown, not yet at least.

"Throw them in with the guns," Larry said about the spark plugs, waving a hand with disdain.

The sound of a struggle near the compound basement doors caught Larry's attention. Two men were struggling to enter. The guards at the door, trying to stop them.

"Let them in for goodness' sake," Larry called out.

The two men entered his office and stood before him. He vaguely knew one was named Hobbes and the other Singleton. Their clothes were torn and faces bloodied. It looked as though they'd been fighting.

"What seems to be the problem, gentlemen?"

Hobbes pointed at Singleton. "This bastard's a thief. He went into my footlocker and stole my 1933 Double Eagle gold coins."

Singleton was already shaking his head. "I paid you for 'em with six days of rations fair and frickin' square, and you shirked on the deal after you ate the food I gave you."

"Those cans were past the due date," Hobbes shot back as the two men began to bicker.

"Gentlemen," Larry said calmly without any success in stopping the squabble. The two men were still going at it. Larry slammed the desk with his fist. "Will you shut up? You're like a couple of kids arguing over a box of toys." Larry sat back in his throne and steepled his fingers together. "I know what we'll do. Donavan, go into the weapons cache and grab two machetes."

The blood in Hobbes' and Singleton's faces drained all at once. A minute later, Donavan returned with the blades.

"You're men, aren't you?" Larry shouted.

Both men nodded, fearfully.

"I thought you were. Then both of you will go outside and settle this as men."

Hobbes wiped the sweat from his brow. "You want us to kill each other?"

"Of course not. Chances are only one of you will die."

"He can have the damned gold coins," Singleton said, backing away.

Larry shook his head. "It's far too late for that now. You've already wasted enough of my time. We either bring you outside to settle this dispute with blood, or Donavan here shoots both of you dead where you stand."

The two men looked at each other.

"So, what'll it be?" Larry asked, picking dirt from his fingernails.

Donavan pulled a Glock out of his belt and aimed it at them.

"OK, we'll fight, we'll fight," Hobbes stammered.

Larry grinned. "See, I knew you'd come to your senses." He waved one of the guards over. "Take our two gladiators outside and then assemble the people of New Jamestown, will you?"

"Yes, Sir."

Then Larry turned to Donavan. "How many sick and wounded are we feeding these days?"

Donavan scratched the side of his head. "Oh, maybe 20. Most of those are from the attack on the hotel."

"Oh, yes, the valiant battle against Alvarez and the dozen Wipers who were protecting him."

The expression on Donavan's face registered confusion. He looked uncertain whether Larry was mocking the very people who had fought for them.

"We'll need to make room for our new Navy guests. See to it the sick and wounded are shot."

Donavan looked stunned. "Shot?"

"Yes, maybe you're right," Larry cut him off. "Bullets are so messy, aren't they? Best to use what's left of Timothy's cyanide. Good point. Oh and get me that satellite phone. I've got a call to make."

Donavan went to the other room and returned a moment later with the phone, looking decidedly uncertain.

Larry was thumbing the button as Donavan started to head outside. "And don't let those two idiots kill one another before I arrive. A little bloodshed is just what I need to cheer me up."

Joanne was playing with her long dark hair, staring off at nothing in particular. They'd just seen two colonists, Hobbes and Singleton, hack each other to pieces with machetes, cheered on from the sidelines by a rather maniacal-looking Larry.

"He wasn't always like this," Finn told Zhou, Callahan, and Kulik who were sitting nearby in the tent.

"That man's lost his shit," Foster said. "Gone medieval on our asses."

Zhou nodded. "You said there was an assassination attempt made against Larry?"

"Just the other day," Finn told him. "There's a fresh hole still in the compound to prove it. You think that has something to do with his paranoia?"

"It never helps. He certainly waited till our guard was down before he swept in and confiscated our weapons."

Kulik lifted the boot cuff of his blue and gray pants and revealed a Smith & Wesson Bodyguard .38. "But those sticky-fingered pricks didn't get my concealable."

"That isn't just paranoia," Joanne said, still staring off. "Foster is right. Larry's mental state is deteriorating, and fast. I mean, he made those two men butcher one another."

Finn didn't want to hear any more. He'd seen the carnage with his own eyes; Hobbes and Singleton swinging madly at one another, as if somehow they believed the loser would get a thumbs-down from the emperor and receive a summary execution.

"Is that what we've come to?" Finn finally asked. "Gladiatorial games designed to frighten and intimidate the rest of us? It certainly sounds like something Alvarez would do, but not Larry. The man was a weasel and a snake, but never a sadistic fiend." Finn turned to Zhou. "I made a terrible mistake telling you and your men to come here. I'll make it better, I swear."

Zhou looked like he was about to assuage Finn's guilt when Callahan spoke up.

"There's something I should tell you," he said, turning to his commander.

"Another confession?" Kulik spat. "What is this, a Roman Catholic pity party?"

Callahan ignored the comment. "When I arrived here with Carole and the others from the hotel boiler room, I told Larry who we were."

"Should it matter?" Joanne asked.

"A great deal," Zhou told her. "The nuclear arsenal onboard the *Alabama* is capable of destroying every major city on the continent."

"I knew Larry had something up his sleeve this morning," Finn admitted, "when I saw him pull his 'host of the year' performance. The man wouldn't butter a piece of bread unless he was sure to get half of it."

"Larry wanted Zhou here," Joanne said, her hand pausing for a moment.

Joanne's comment clearly worried Commander Zhou.

"I hate to be the one to say it," Finn told them. "But we need to head to San Diego and scuttle the *Alabama* before Larry or anyone else can get their hands on those nukes."

That's when the sound of desperate shouting outside drew their attention. It was coming from the medical tent next door.

•••

They arrived at the medical tent a second later to find Lou surrounded by Donavan and six of his men. Lou was demanding to know what business armed men had there.

"What's going on here?" Finn asked.

"None of your concern," Donavan barked back. "We need to make some room."

Lou's chest was heaving and his face flushed with anger. "Make some room. The hell's that supposed to mean?"

Finn could see Donavan was holding a tiny brown bottle in his hand, and he grabbed his wrist and held up the contents. Rifles from militia members snapped into Finn's face.

"Cyanide," Finn said, ignoring the rifles aimed at his temple. "You aren't here to move beds around, are you? Larry sent you here to kill the wounded."

"I've had enough of this," Donavan shouted. "You're all under arrest."

"Over my dead body," Lou growled and tackled two of the militia to the ground. One of their rifles went off and struck their own man in the knee. He fell, screaming. Now there were three men with rifles still standing, and one had the barrel pointed directly at Finn's chest. The man's eyes narrowed, and Finn knocked the barrel into the air and punched him square in the face. He moaned in surprise and pain before reeling backward onto his ass. Another rifle was swinging toward Finn, and just then when Kulik swung up with the Smith & Wesson .38 and put two rounds into the back of his head. Down went Donavan's man. If there was a point of no return, they'd just crossed it.

Donavan pushed through Callahan and Zhou and ran from the tent along with his two remaining men.

Lou was pummeling the cult members he'd tackled when Finn made him stop.

"Donavan's gonna be back any minute with plenty more weapons, and we don't have much to protect ourselves with. Get Ethan out of here while you still have a chance."

They removed the AR-15s and ammo mags from the militia. One of them was dead. The other three had only been knocked around.

"Tie them up and take them with us," Finn said. "They might come in handy."

"What about the rest of the wounded?" Joanne asked.

Zhou took Kulik's pistol and handed him one of the AR-15s. "The only way to help them is to stop Larry."

"I want my M-4 back," Foster whined.

"He's got a point," Kulik agreed. "We're too thin on firepower to do much good."

Finn headed for the tent flap. "We need to get back the weapons they took."

"They must be somewhere in the compound itself," Joanne said.

Zhou rubbed his chin. "If I were Larry, I'd have stashed those confiscated guns as close as possible."

The sound of militia shouting in the distance was growing louder.

"The compound basement," Finn said. "Makes sense."

Dana and Tanner came running into the medical tent just then. "I heard shots and saw Donavan running away." Her eyes found the dead cult member. "What the hell happened?"

Finn pulled the charging handle on the AR-15 he was holding. "I think we just started a civil war."

•••

That the sun was well on its way to setting was a blessing for Finn and the others. As soon as they left the medical tent, they caught sight of Donavan rallying the militia.

Finn leaned out and peered over at the guard towers by the front gate. "Interesting."

Joanne was right behind him. "What do you see?"

"The guards aren't facing out over the wall anymore. They're facing in. I noticed it yesterday, but it didn't fully register."

Joanne frowned. "Facing in, like ... "

"A prison. Yes." Finn turned to Zhou and the others. "Our best bet is to move through the parked cars out back and in through the gymnasium."

Zhou held up the .38. "I'll stay here with Callahan and Foster and keep them busy."

Finn, Joanne, and Kulik circled back into Tent City and made their way up toward the car park. Dana and Tanner were right behind them. Liberating the weapons and ammo Larry had taken would take plenty of hands.

Gunfire rattled off in the distance as they made their way between tents crowded with regular colonists hugging the floor with fear.

They reached the cars, ducking down behind them. Dana moved in beside Finn. "I won't be able to join you when you blow the source of that pulse into tiny bits," he told her as they caught their breath, the sound of guns and yelling rattling their nerves.

Dana looked surprised. "We could use you."

"Something more important's come up. Larry's got his sights set on snatching Commander Zhou's nuclear sub, and we gotta scuttle it before that can happen."

She understood, Finn could see that, but he could tell she was disappointed all the same.

"I don't think anyone's leaving," Tanner told them both.

"Why's that?" Finn asked, crouching to stay out of sight.

"Larry had Donavan remove the sparkplugs from all the vehicles."

Finn didn't bother asking about the Humvees 'cause he could see they were boxed in on every side by disabled cars and trucks.

"That's one more thing on our shopping list," Dana said, grimacing.

"Keep moving," Kulik shouted from the rear.

They made their way through the car park and around the back of the compound to the gym doors. Back by Tent City, Callahan and Zhou were firing sporadically, trying their best to present themselves as a larger force than they really were.

Finn, Dana, and Tanner were about to head inside when Kulik stopped them. "I've got an idea." He was looking back at the car park. The Humvees might not have sparkplugs, but Larry's men hadn't thought to remove the .50-cal from the mount on Zhou's lead vehicle.

"You'll be a sitting duck," Finn warned him.

The crazed glint in Kulik's eye erased the notion he could be reasoned with. He handed his AR-15 to Dana. "Don't worry about me. You just get our gear back."

Finn nodded and wished him good luck before the rest of them disappeared inside.

The gym was devoid of life, although it bore all the signs of a great party. Not long ago, Zhou's men were being treated like rock stars. Larry's strategy was certainly tried, tested, and true. Lull your victims into a false sense of security before you strike. It had been a rare bloodless move on Larry's part in what was quickly becoming a blood-soaked tyranny.

Up ahead, two armed cult members emerged from the basement. Finn and the others tried to crouch, but they were already spotted. The enemy's rifles rose up when Dana fired, dropping the first one. The echo of gunfire inside the gymnasium pierced Finn's ears. As though on auto pilot, he quickly drew the other in his sights and squeezed the trigger three times, sending the man spinning to the floor.

"There goes the element of surprise," Dana said, springing to her feet.

Finn caught the sound of a large-caliber rifle opening up outside and knew it was Kulik wreaking havoc with the .50-cal.

When they reached the two dead cultists, Finn snatched up their rifles, tossed one to Tanner, and slung the other over his back.

AR-15s at the ready, Finn, Dana, and Tanner made their way toward the stairway and into the basement.

Shots rang out from down the hallway, passing over their head. Finn ducked, and all three of them unloaded. The shooting stopped, but they could hear the distinct sound of someone moaning.

The basement had rooms on both sides of the hallway. They would have to check each and every one, Finn realized. If they were lucky, they'd find Larry hiding in a corner like the coward he was.

"That's the interrogation room," Dana said, pointing to the right. She nudged the door open and quickly closed it. "Empty."

Across from that was a room neither of them had been in. Finn grabbed the handle and found it locked. "Block your ears," he told them and aimed his rifle at the latch. He took three quick shots and then kicked the door. It swung open, revealing an assortment of handguns, shotguns, rifles, and piles of ammo.

"There's enough here to outfit an army," Finn said, jubilantly.

Dana was more surprised than elated. "No way all this came from the colonists and Zhou's men. They must have been stockpiling for a while."

"Quick, grab what you can," Finn told them. He wasn't more than five feet into the room when he spotted a box with an assortment of spark plugs. "These, too," he told Tanner, who swept in and plucked the box from his hands.

That's when the basement door from outside burst open, followed by the sound of men shouting. Finn and the others hadn't managed to gather more than a few M-4s and a handful of ammo mags.

Tanner peeked outside and turned back, looking white. "A ton of Larry's men just showed up. We better do something quick before they figure out we're in here."

"Don't panic," Dana said. She pulled out a crate under one of the tables and held up what looked like a green can of bug spray. "This a grenade?"

Finn took a look. "Yeah, but it lets off smoke, not shrapnel."

"Good enough," she said.

Already, footsteps and alarmed voices were heading their way. Dana pulled the pin. "Tanner," she called out. "Covering fire."

"Got it." Without even looking, he swung the barrel of his AR-15 into the corridor and let off every round he had in his magazine.

Dana was next and released the handle on the grenade before tossing it down the hall. Smoke filled the hallway, spilling into Larry's office and every other adjoining room. The cult members were coughing and sputtering as the three of them fled. First up the stairs and then out through the gymnasium.

Outside, Finn listened for a moment, finding the occasional clatter of gunfire, but not the .50-cal Kulik had been manning earlier. Coming around the corner, Finn's heart sank when he saw Zhou's Humvee on fire, along with the cars that surrounded it.

"Think he made it out?" Dana asked.

"It ain't looking good, although right now, I'm more worried that we didn't get nearly enough firepower."

They no sooner began hugging the wall by the car park than shots began landing all around them.

"They're sniping at us from the towers," Dana said, peering up. "Keep your heads down till we make it to Tent City. They may not be able to see us as easily there."

Then Finn spotted a handful of dark figures moving toward them, low to the ground. He raised his rifle and then let it relax when he saw

Zhou with a handful of others. Nearby were Callahan and Kulik, although the latter had a gash on the side of his head and blood running down his face.

Keeping low, Finn clapped Kulik on the shoulder. "You look the way I feel."

Kulik returned a sly smile. "Took a few of those worker bees out before they started lobbing in the heavy stuff."

Zhou didn't look nearly as jovial. "Did you get the weapons?"

"Only what you see," Finn told him. "The place was crawling with Larry's men."

"We need a lot more than that to make a difference, I'm afraid," Zhou said, handing them to Foster and the other men behind him. "Larry's militia's been cutting us to shreds out here. We're gonna need to break out of New Jamestown before he has a chance to regain control. But there's a problem."

"What's that?"

"I'm hearing word that Larry disabled all the vehicles."

Tanner produced the box of sparkplugs. "Ask and you shall receive."

"Cute," Zhou shot back, ruffling Tanner's blonde hair. "Now let's find an SUV big enough to blast through those front gates.

"I know just the one," Finn said, eyeing Larry's Escalade.

•••

The Escalade's nose facing away from the guard towers and the car's large profile meant re-installing the spark plugs hadn't taken more than a few minutes. Zhou, Callahan, Kulik, and Joanne snuck into the car one by one. Finn was about to go when he stopped and caught Dana, peering over at the towers. The shooting had died out a few minutes ago, and some of Larry's men were searching through the trailers. Another group was heading toward Tent City.

"Tell me you're still going to destroy that pulse wave," Finn said, with a pleading quality to his voice. He could already see Joanne waving him over. "I just hope Nikki or Aiden weren't hurt in all of this."

"Me, too," Dana said. "We'll escape as soon as we can. By the time you guys are done scuttling that sub, the first of those old memories should start trickling back."

A thought that for Finn wasn't entirely pleasant. "I'd be lying if I told you I wasn't worried destroying that place might bring back my old memories while erasing all the new ones I've made since The Shift."

247

Dana seemed to consider this, but there was something else on her mind, he could tell.

"I know what you're gonna say," he told her. "It's about coming back."

She nodded. "If Larry's still around, you won't be able to. Destroying that lab won't have an effect on the cult members since they were shielded from the effects of The Shift."

He hugged her goodbye and shook Tanner's hand, before he turned to get into the driver's seat.

"Be careful," Dana called out after him.

Finn laughed. "I'm still waiting for my shit luck to run out. Maybe today's that day."

He watched Dana and Tanner move away as he considered the best way to do this.

"Any suggestions?" he asked, the others crouched in the back.

"Ain't no one gonna open that gate but us," Kulik rightly observed.

"So, we ram it?" And as Finn said the words, Joanne began doing up her seat belt.

Zhou shrugged. "No other choice. Just remember, Finn, once you turn that engine on, you'll need to whip around and punch that gas pedal."

Finn paused with his hand on the ignition. It wasn't only that he was worried they were about to get shot from those towers or somehow go careening off the bridge. His real concern was how little they'd been able to prep for the long journey they were embarking on. Even in the old days, Salt Lake City to San Diego wasn't a short trip. They'd need to scrounge along the way and hope for the best.

"Everyone ready?" he called out. "Buckle up, kids, it's gonna be a bumpy ride."

Finn turned the ignition, and the engine roared to life. He slid the Escalade into reverse and hit the pedal. Tuffs of grass were tossed into the air as the car shot back. Finn then cut the wheel, and the Escalade whipped around. Like a well-practiced ballet, he threw the SUV into drive and sank his foot to the floorboard, pushing them back in their seats. Most of Larry's militia had already disappeared into Tent City. Finn could see the remaining guards in the towers, starting to react as they sped closer. The speedometer climbed past 60 as a militiaman on the ground sprang out of the way.

"Hold on!" Finn shouted.

The Escalade collided with the gate, doing 70, shots kicking up puffs of dirt all around them. The truck bounced and bucked before he realized they'd sliced right through it. So much for security. From there, they continued to pick up speed as bullets rang off the bridge's steel girder. It was acting as a kind of shield as they rocketed away. A few seconds later, the gunfire was behind them, and Finn was checking that Joanne and the others hadn't been hit.

"Now, let's hope we make it there before Larry figures out where we're headed and tries to cut us off," Zhou said.

The words were barely out of his mouth when Finn spotted something up ahead. He eased off the gas. Cars, dozens of them, three or four deep, blocking the road.

"Who are they?" Joanne asked.

"Wipers," Finn managed to say before bullets struck the hood. One went through the windshield and up through the roof. Finn tried to regain control and realized they'd shot the front left tire out. The Escalade swerved off the road and turned over twice in the ditch landing right side up. Blood was running down the side of Joanne's face where her head had struck the passenger window. The three in the back were in no better shape. White smoke rose up from the hood.

That's when the tap at the window came. Metal on glass.

Tink, tink, tink …

Jeffereys was knocking with the barrel of his Desert Eagle. Behind him was a bristling wall of guns, all aimed at them.

Larry

To say that Aiden and Nikki were the only things on Larry's mind right now wasn't too far from the truth. After his men had managed to quell the attempted revolt, he knew it was simply a question of time before they showed up. The only ones to breach the wall and escape had been driving an Escalade and he didn't think either of the children was on board.

Donavan and a handful of armed men were at Larry's side as they crossed the gravel road that cut the colony in two. They were heading for Tent City, the place he was sure they'd find the kids.

Dead bodies littered New Jamestown. Some of them were his men, but most were colonists caught out in the open when the bullets started to fly. They would need to be disposed of quickly, before the stink set in, although at this point it probably didn't matter, not with what Larry had in store.

He was quite certain getting his hands on that sub would help to solidify his power in the same way he was certain those two kids didn't realize the potential locked within them. One was useless without the other, but together, Larry could use the knowledge hidden in Aiden's mind to rebuild the world in whatever way he saw fit. Then, when he grew weary of making people suffer, he would end it all in a cataclysm of fire.

They were approaching Tent City when the satellite phone on Larry's belt buzzed.

"Alvarez, come in." The voice said. It was Jeffereys.

Larry snatched the phone with annoyance. "Alvarez is gone, you buffoon," he said, touching the scar on his cheek with the pads of his fingers. "If you received my letter then you should know that."

"My apologies, won't happen again, Boss. Listen, those birds of yours who flew the coop … "

"Yes, what about them?" Larry said impatiently. "Are they dead?"

"No, better than that. They're alive and kicking, and here's the best part. We got the captain of that sub and his XO."

"Excellent. Hold them till we get there."

Larry's first stop after speaking with Jeffereys was the medical tent. There were still a handful of patients lying there, many of whom were wounded during the attack on the Grand America and some of whom had been hit again in the present skirmish. He stopped before the bed of a man named Russell. The same one who'd helped Carole escape. After being wounded in the chest, nurse Kim had been forced to periodically remove fluid from his lungs. That made it hard for Russell to breathe and speak, but Larry was sure the man would be willing to share what he knew.

"I know this was where my men were attacked," Larry told him. "So, you must have seen it happen and heard what they said afterward."

Russell glared at him defiantly without saying a word.

Larry took in a deep breath. "I understand you worked the boiler room at the Grand America."

"I did," he wheezed, softening slightly. "Sixteen years I kept her running."

"Spent a lot of time by yourself down there, I take it."

Russell puffed up his chest. "Any company is bad company, as far as I'm concerned."

"And with all that time to think," Larry said, checking his fingernails. "At some point you must have asked yourself the big questions."

Russell stared up at him, blank faced.

"What happens when we die? You ever get to that one? It's pretty high up on the list, I would think. Far beyond, why am I stuck working this soul-numbing job, right?"

Russell almost smiled, but didn't. "I s'ppose."

"Here's my problem, Russell. Those people who killed my men, I need to know who they were and what they're up to, but more than that, I need your help to find two kids who are hiding from me. Aiden and Nikki. Guy like you laying around all day with nothing to do but listen to other people talk, you must have heard something?"

Russell started to shake his head.

"Think carefully, Russell. Think very carefully before you speak." Larry brought out a pistol from his jacket pocket. "Because if you can't give me what I need, then I'm gonna give you the answer to those big questions you always asked yourself."

"Even if I knew I wouldn't tell a grimy fuck like you," Russell said, grinning contentedly.

"That's too bad," Larry said before putting the pistol to his head and pulling the trigger. He turned to one of the militia. "Turn this place upside down if you need to, but I want those kids."

"Will do," the man said.

Larry motioned to Donavan. "Come, we've got a sub to catch."

A few minutes later, they'd left New Jamestown and were pulling up to the road block. Larry had ordered Jeffereys to assemble all the remaining Wipers and use them to block every major road in and out of

251

New Jamestown. He couldn't take the risk that either of those kids managed to escape the colony.

Finn, Joanne, and the three submariners were tied in the back of a suburban.

Jeffereys approached him, squinting, cautious. "Alvar – I mean, Larry?"

"Yes, it's me," Larry replied, climbing behind the wheel of the suburban. "Hold your men here and await further instructions. No one is to come or go. Understood?"

Jeffereys nodded.

Larry pulled out, and three cars filled with Wipers followed him. They were heading for San Diego and the *USS Alabama*. But more than that, they were heading toward a new world order. One that would begin with New Jamestown and the intercontinental ballistic missile that he would send to destroy it.

Dana

"Quiet down," Dana said. "Someone's coming."

Fear swept over Nikki's soft features. Aiden was huddled next to her, looking equally terrified. Only Bud was stoic, a Glock resting in his lap.

They were in the gymnasium, holed up inside a manmade cave carved from the pallets of canned goods. A feeling very much like hiding between the isles of a Costco store.

After Finn and company had blasted through the front gate, Dana had gone looking for the kids. She'd found them hiding under a bunk in one of tents, clinging to one another and trying to avoid the militia they knew was after them. If they wanted any hope of finding and destroying the lab with the low-frequency pulse generator suppressing people's memories, she would need Nikki and Aiden's help to do it. That Larry would want the kids for his own twisted purposes was an idea that had certainly occurred to her on more than one occasion, especially after reading through Abigail's notebook. The scriptures spoke of how they would usher in a New Age, presumably of peace and enlightenment, but Dana knew just as well that the children's powers could also resurrect all the doomsday weapons that had brought them down this path in the first place.

Since Dana and Bud had snuck them into the gymnasium, no fewer than a half dozen militia had come by to grab food. She'd expected that, no doubt, but she'd also figured this would be the last place they'd expect to find them.

Bursts of gunfire still echoed here and there. Enough to know they weren't gun battles at all, but executions. New Jamestown was quickly being transformed from a well-protected sanctuary into a concentration camp.

Eying the culties gathering food, Bud pulled the hammer back on his Glock. Dana laid a hand on the pistol.

"Only if they see us," she whispered.

The two cult members continued rummaging through cans, filling bags until they looked nearly ready to burst.

"And how long do you intend we stay here?" he asked.

It was a good point. "Until the sun goes down and we can make a break for it."

Nikki put her arm around Aiden and pulled him close to her.

"So, you've already got the C4 from your trailer?"

253

She didn't, and it must have showed on her face. Getting to the trailer without being seen would be tough. But without the explosives there might not be a way of destroying the signal. She looked up and saw the two cult members were gone. Now they would have to keep out of sight and wait for early dawn. After that, all of them would need as much courage as they could summon and a heavy dose of luck.

Larry

The sun hadn't come up yet when the convoy rolled through San Diego and reached Point Loma Naval Base. They'd driven through the night, stopping only occasionally to refuel. As per the instructions he'd given Jeffereys, a Plymouth van in the rear had been filled with gas cans, acting as a mobile Exxon station.

They were heading south on Catalina Road now, past check points devoid of any signs of life. Finn, Commander Zhou, and the other three were still tied, blindfolded, and gagged. They'd been thrown into the back like old luggage, and Donavan had stayed awake in the back seat all night, watching them for any signs of mischief.

"Wake Zhou up," Larry told Donavan.

Donavan reached over the back seat and shook the commander, removing his blindfold and gag.

"Where's the *Alabama*?" Larry asked without taking his eyes off the road.

Donavan's pistol was aimed at Zhou's forehead.

"Take a left on Rosecrants."

Larry did. On their right was a rolling hill covered with yellowing sagebrush. On their left, a concrete pier with the conning tower of a giant submarine peaking up above the waterline. Larry felt the edges of his mouth curl into a grin. Opening the window, he drew in a lungful of salty air.

"You recognize that smell, Donavan?"

Donavan tweaked his nose. "Salt water?"

Larry cackled laughter. "No, it's the smell of victory."

He turned the suburban onto the pier and drove up as far as it would go. "Hand me that satellite phone would you?"

Donavan did as he was told, and Larry held it to his mouth and depressed the button. "Jeffereys, come in," he said and felt a surge of impatience bubbling in his guts when there was no immediate reply. "Jeffereys, are you there?"

A crackle, then: "I'm here, Boss." He sounded like he'd been sleeping.

"We've reached the sub. It's time you took the men into New Jamestown and brought me Nikki and Aiden."

"Roger that. What about the others?"

"Ignore them, they'll all be dead soon enough."

Dana

Dana came awake with a start. She'd been having an awful dream about Jeffereys. He had her tied in that basement again, huddled with other women he'd kidnapped. The sound of his boots clanking down the old wooden stairs was the first sign of trouble, and she knew he was about to do horrible things to her. Jeffereys' rat face and slicked-back hair were barely coming into focus when Dana's eyes snapped open. Bud was beside her, sleeping soundly. She sat next to him, trying to catch her breath, unable to keep from admiring his rugged good looks. His strong, wiry body and manly jaw, along with that dollop of fire-red hair on his head. Reluctantly, she nudged him awake. His eyes opened, and he smiled when he saw her.

The sun wasn't up just yet, which meant this was the perfect opportunity to get what they needed before making a break for the lab they hoped would hold the answer to undoing the devastation caused by The Shift.

The gymnasium was deathly quiet as the four of them crept out from behind crates loaded with canned good and boxes of dried pasta. Slung over Bud's shoulder next to his rifle was a backpack he'd filled with the supplies they would need for the voyage ahead. Definitely one of the benefits of hiding inside the colony's food reserves.

Once outside, they made their way to Lou's battle wagon in the parking area. Dana handed him the spark plugs he would need.

"You'll need to make sure the gas tank is full." She began moving away.

"Where are you going?" he asked.

"You don't expect that pulse to go boom all by itself, do you?" she asked, with a wry smile.

"Just be careful," Bud told her.

As she crept into Tent City, Dana could see the guards in the towers, pacing back and forth. She clutched the AR-15 till her knuckles turned white, praying she wouldn't need to use it. The second danger she faced, heading to grab the C4 in the police trailer, was bumping into guards making the rounds. She would need to be quick and above all, quiet. Two things that didn't normally go hand in hand.

Weaving between the tents, Dana caught the frightened stare from more than one colonist, peering out at her from their bunks. Eventually, Larry's men had regained control and conducted a vicious bout of reprisal executions to solidify their hold on New Jamestown. Those

256

who'd survived were doing the best could to avoid bringing attention to themselves.

Soon, Dana came to the edge of Tent City and the row of trailers that lined the dirt road. She needed to run out in the open and make it inside what used to be her police headquarters without being seen. Her heart was hammering in her chest, forcing her to draw deeper and deeper breaths of air.

Get it together, Girl, you got one shot at this.

She took a final furtive glance before moving out. Her eyes focused solely on the trailer door. If she could just make it there, she'd be OK. A group of three men milling near the gate made her freeze with fear. Had they seen her? She stared for an agonizing moment, unable to confirm or deny the terror mounting within her. But their relaxed manner gave Dana the answer she was hoping for. She reached the trailer and was inside a second later, searching around in the dark to find her desk. Most of her stuff hadn't been touched after Larry stripped her and her deputies of their authority.

She fumbled the keys out of her pocket and used them to open the drawer. Inside was the silver case. All she needed to do now was get it back to Bud.

But what of the people you're leaving behind?

That little voice inside her head was at it again. Still, she knew exactly who it was referring to. Lou, Ethan, and Tanner, among many others. With the way things were going, New Jamestown was quickly becoming the New Auschwitz. There would be room to take them, that wasn't the problem, but it would mean finding them first.

Dana had no sooner nudged the trailer door open, the C4 briefcase in hand, when she heard gunfire. It was coming from the towers, and this time they weren't firing in at the people of New Jamestown. They were firing at something outside the walls. But what? The answer came a second later when a Jeep Cherokee came crashing through the colony's already damaged gate. Behind it, a long line of cars and trucks surged over the bridge, firing their guns as they came. Gripped in terror, Dana realized it could only mean on thing. The Wipers were finally here to finish them off.

Finn

Larry didn't waste any time taking his prisoners into the sub's missile control room. Wall-to-wall instrumentation along with consoles flickering to life. Wipers had AKs trained on Zhou, Kulik, and Callahan as they powered up the boat. Meanwhile, more Wipers outside detached the heavy cables that kept them moored to the dock. It was clear soon enough why Larry wanted Nikki and Aiden so badly. In the short term, with all of those memories locked deep within him, Aiden was the only one around who knew how to operate the sub. And if he could do that, then there was no telling what other uses his abilities could be put to.

Finn had hoped the tight quarters down here might present an opportunity to overpower one of Larry's men, but these Wipers were no longer the same mindless savages he's seen at the airport. They were trained and far more disciplined. And more immediately, they were glaring at Finn and Joanne as though they wanted nothing more than to cave their heads in with the butts of their rifles.

Donavan entered the missile room. "We're detached," he told Larry.

"Good. Now take these two up to the bridge,' Larry said pointing to Kulik and Callahan. "And have them blow the ballast tanks."

"Won't that make us sink?" Donavan asked.

Larry smiled. "A few dozen meters at most. But how else will we launch these missiles?"

Kulik threw Finn a look that bore the hallmarks of someone who was about to do something crazy, but trying anything now would only mean suicide.

Donavan and a handful of men led Kulik and Callahan out.

Now Finn, Joanne, and Zhou were alone with Larry and a half dozen Wipers.

"We already have the launch codes," Larry told them, "along with the keys from Zhou and Kulik required by the two-man rule. What we're really missing to get this party started is targeting."

He looked at Zhou. "And that's where you come in."

The commander shook his head. "That's the weapons officer's job."

Larry slammed the pistol he was holding across Zhou's face. "Well, now it's your job." He looked at Joanne. "Get her up."

A Wiper came and hooked an arm around Joanne. Finn grabbed hold of her.

"Leave her out of this," he told Larry. "You wanna use someone, use me."

258

Larry buried the pistol in his armpit and clapped. "Touching. Now make him go to sleep."

The Wiper let go of Joanne and brought his rifle down against the side of Finn's head. The sound of the impact rang in his ears as the room blurred and became wavy. A second blow, and all he could hear was Joanne as she begged. "I'll come, I'll come. Just leave him alone."

Finn's hand went to the side of his head, trying to regain himself. Joanne was placed before Larry, a Wiper holding her arms behind her back.

"Now, Commander Zhou, lock the first warhead onto New Jamestown."

"I will not," Zhou replied, defiantly.

Larry cracked Joanne in the face with the handle of his pistol. She let out a squeal of pain and turned her head. Finn rushed to his feet, but was thrown back by the Wipers standing over him.

"Let's try this again. Will you please target New Jamestown?"

Zhou paused before shaking his head.

Larry hit Joanne twice. She slumped forward, blood trickling from her mouth.

"You son of a bitch!" Finn cried. "I'm gonna kill you," he told Larry. "I swear to God … "

Larry laughed. "Oh, leave God out of this, will you?" He turned back to Zhou. "I won't ask you again."

"Please," Joanne said, her lips swollen and bloody.

Zhou looked on, and Larry wound up for another strike.

"OK, I'll do it." Zhou said at last.

Larry grinned, his teeth looking like tiny tombstones baked in the hot sun. "I knew you'd come around."

Dana

The cult members who, moments before, had been Dana's biggest threat, were now all that stood between her and the Wipers here to destroy New Jamestown. She fled from the police trailer toward the cover of Tent City, the briefcase containing the explosives tightly in hand. Dana glanced back once before she slipped behind the medical tent, and what she saw chilled the very blood in her veins. Dozens, maybe hundreds of Wipers charging across the bridge, shouting in their guttural language. She knew now what it must have felt like during the sack of Rome by the Visigoths.

Dana was bolting past the last few tents when a hand reached out and pulled her inside. She struggled for a moment before realizing it was Lou. Tanner was there with him, and both men were armed with rifles they'd apparently taken from the bodies of dead cult members during the uprising.

Ethan was on a cot nearby, his eyes closed, drawing in shallow breaths.

"Grab your son and bring him to the battle wagon," Dana shouted frantically.

"He ain't looking good," Lou said. "We can't move him."

"But you can't stay."

Lou shook his head. "I ain't movin' him, and that's all there is to it."

"You'll be killed," she pleaded.

"I've made up my mind. They'll get to Ethan over my dead body."

Dana looked over at Tanner, who grit his teeth.

"You, too?" she asked.

He nodded.

"Take my truck," Lou said. "Keys are above the visor. We'll hold 'em off as long as we can." He pulled the charging handle on his AR-15. "Go on and get before you lose your chance."

Dana hugged him and then Tanner.

"Soon as we destroy that pulse generator we're coming back for you."

Lou winked. "Don't hurry on our account."

Dana swung her own rifle around and with the briefcase in hand, headed out. She no sooner reached the car park than a shot rang out, ricocheting off the roof of a nearby car. Dana saw a man about 30 yards away, standing beside a vehicle, taking aim with an AK-47. Even in the early morning hours, she recognized it was Jeffereys. He fired another volley and with her heart racing, Dana hit the ground for cover. The AK's 7.62 round was a monster that could punch right through both ends of a car. Only the engine block gave her proper cover. She raised herself up onto one knee and took aim before squeezing the trigger. Her first shot passed over his shoulder. The second grazed the side of his head. Jeffereys dove behind a nearby tent.

The colony was in chaos. Wipers were swarming all over the place, firing their weapons at anything that moved. One group swung off the main body and entered the compound building. These Wipers were a far cry from the mindless killers who had attacked them two months before. Now they were trained and seemed to have arrived with a plan.

Jeffereys was still nowhere to be seen, so Dana broke into a run, reaching the battle wagon to find Bud, hanging out the driver-side door, picking off as many Wipers as he could.

Every dead Wiper was a good Wiper, but he risked drawing their attention. Dana hopped into the passenger seat and tucked the metal briefcase at her feet. Aiden and Nikki were hunkered down in the back.

"You kids OK?" she asked.

Aiden looked up at her. He was holding the .38 calibre Smith & Wesson Bodyguard she'd seen Zhou with before.

"Bud, if we don't leave now, we won't be leaving at all."

He stopped firing, handed her his rifle and jumped in. Dana flipped the visor, and down came the keys.

"Hope those spark plugs are in right," he mumbled.

Bud turned the key, and the engine sputtered but didn't start. He turned it again with a similar result. Glancing in the side mirror, Dana could see that a group of Wipers saw the back lights turn on.

"Keep trying," she shouted, opening the door to engage them. Short bursts seemed to work best, and she felt the AR-15 kick against her shoulder with each shot fired. She circled behind the adjacent car to draw their fire away from the battle wagon while Bud wrestled with getting it started. Dana managed to drop three of them when Bud got out of the car and opened the hood.

"You're kidding me," she called out.

He held her with a 'No, I'm dead serious' kinda look. "Keep it up, you're doing great."

If she wasn't busy fending off these Wipers, she'd have given him a piece of her mind. What she hadn't noticed was the Wiper creeping up in her blind spot behind the battle wagon. He charged in at her, emptying his pistol as he ran. Suddenly, the wagon's back door swung in the Wiper's face, stopping him dead. Then came the sound of three shots as the attacker crumpled to the ground. Dana ran back to the wagon and saw Aiden, sitting in the back with the pistol in his hand, Nikki beside him, plugging her ears.

Another bang, and this time it was Bud slamming the hood. He got in and turned the key. The engine purred and then roared to life.

"Used a little spit on the ends." Then came that wink again, totally oblivious that Aiden had just saved her life.

Dana leaned into the back seat and pushed the gun in Aiden's hand down. "Nice shooting. Now put that thing away and buckle up."

He smiled.

"Next stop, Montana," Bud yipped as he kicked the wagon into reverse, hit the gas, and then spun the wheel, until they were facing the front gate.

Sparks flew off the hood. Someone was shooting at them. Looking out Bud's window, Dana spotted Jeffereys firing from the parking lot, shouting at others to stop them from getting away. Had he seen Aiden in the back seat? Or was he simply trying to kill her once and for all?

Bud floored the accelerator, the battle wagon's engine growled. As they reached the trailers, Dana saw Jeffereys in the rearview, running toward the car he'd popped out of earlier. He was going to give chase.

"He's not giving up easy," Dana mumbled to herself, hoping they could outrun him.

Jeffereys

Dana and Bud were trying to whisk the kids away, and there was no way Jeffereys was gonna let that happen. It was following that first exchange of gunfire Jeffereys had with her, where he was forced to duck into what the colonists called Tent City, that he discovered what was happening. He'd found a woman named Holly and her daughter, Tamara, trying to hide under their beds. Jeffereys had asked them very nicely where Aiden and Nikki were, and it was only when he got forceful that the truth finally emerged. She'd told him Dana and Bud were taking them away in Lou's battle wagon. They were heading to Montana and a place called Chief Mountain.

That was when Jeffereys had popped back out of the tent and seen the kid gun down one of his men from the back seat. Soon after that, they had sped down the dirt road, knocking aside his troops like bowling pins as they fled.

No sooner had Jeffereys stopped firing than he jumped behind the wheel of a Trans Am and gave chase, stopping for only seconds to round up three other cars with men to join him. New Jamestown could go to hell for all he cared. It was the children that his boss, Larry, wanted, and he intended to do just that.

Rocketing over the bridge Jeffereys fingered the button on the Iridium satellite phone.

"Larry, come in. Over."

He dropped it in his lap and clamped both hands on the steering wheel in order to make a sharp right hand turn. Ahead of him were the distant tail lights from Dana's truck. The sun was also starting to come up, which would make it even easier to stay close and hopefully intercept them.

The satellite phone came to life. "Tell me you have them," Larry said sternly.

"They broke out of our noose, but we're on their tail. Don't worry, I think I know where they're headed."

"You better," came Larry's reply. "Your life depends on it."

Nikki

They'd been driving for hours when Chief Mountain in Montana finally came into view. It rose up from the desert like the remnants of an ancient stone wall weathered over the eons. The ground built slowly up around it, so that the 9,000-foot peak dominated the entire valley below. It was at the base of this mountain that Simon said the Rainbowites would gather during the summer solstice, but as Abigail's notebook showed them, it was the convergence of ley lines and not the mountain that made this place special. For Nikki, Bud, and everyone else suffering from continued memory loss, the secret facility hidden presumably beneath this slab of rock was the key to setting the world right again.

Dana glanced back from the front seat, scanning over Nikki's shoulder at the road behind them. "Do you think they're still following us?" she asked Bud, who was driving.

He glanced in the rearview mirror. "I think we lost them back near the state line."

Dana didn't seem convinced since there was another problem none of them had considered up until this point. Getting to Chief Mountain in Montana had always appeared to be the biggest challenge, but finding the entrance into the underground facility once they arrived might be something else entirely.

Nikki voiced her concerns to Dana, the whole while watching Chief Mountain draw closer and closer.

"You've seen Aiden's memories," Dana said. "Do you remember seeing any landmarks, leading into Tevatron's lab?"

Nikki shook her head. "I don't think so."

"Then take another look."

"It doesn't work that way, I already told you."

Dana drew in a deep breath. "Well, it's gonna have to. We're running low on options right now ... "

Dana's eyes were staring off at a point over Nikki's shoulder. She turned and saw a plume of dust rising about a mile behind them. Nikki turned. "Is that Jeffereys?" she whispered.

"You've got to hurry," Dana said, ignoring the question.

Aiden held out his hands, and Nikki took them. Right away, she was struck by an avalanche of memories flickering past her at lightning speed. So fast she felt as though she were flying through space. Faces, locations, a child blowing out candles on a cake, an old man staring listlessly out a bedroom window, a young couple stealing secret kisses during a family outing. Finding specific memories in all this mess was like spinning a globe and hoping when it stopped your finger landed on New York City. From somewhere far away, Nikki could hear Dana's voice urging her on.

Then Nikki thought of something she hadn't tried before. If she held the image of the man she'd seen in Aiden's head earlier, the one who entered the side of the mountain, maybe she could find him in all this mess and tease out more details.

A mass of flickering images, and soon a figure began to take shape before her. He was wearing a white lab coat, hurrying down a hallway. This was the right person, but she'd somehow skipped past the part when he arrived. The entrance to the facility was what she needed, not this. Clenching her brother's hands, she struggled to rewind the movie playing in her head, roll it backward to the part when he arrived. Suddenly, she saw the man's feet moving in reverse, slowly at first, then faster and faster. Soon, he was backing out a giant metal door into a valley at the base of the mountain. Behind her were two other peaks.

Her eyes snapped open as the battle wagon nearly swerved off the road. Nikki and Aiden were thrown from side to side.

The muffled sounds of shots from outside. Nikki was going to look when Dana pushed her head down. "Keep low, Jeffereys has caught up. They're trying to shoot our tires out."

Looking over the dashboard, Nikki saw Chief Mountain and the two smaller peaks nestled behind it.

"There's a valley on the other side," she said. "The entrance to the facility is there."

Bud was still swerving all over the road, his foot pushed all the way to the floorboard. "I don't know if we can outrun them," he said.

Dana unlocked her door and pulled the charging handle on her AR-15. With her free hand, she coiled the seat belt around her right arm.

"The hell you doing?" Bud shouted.

"Trying to save our asses. Now hold onto my belt."

Bud grabbed hold as Dana opened the door and leaned out, her rifle aiming at the half dozen cars giving chase behind them. She squeezed the trigger as Bud cut left, bringing them all within sight. The gun kicked in a hand already aching from trying to keep the sights leveled. Her other hand was wrapped in her seatbelt to ensure she didn't fall to her death. Dana squeezed off another six rounds. Most of them missed entirely, but one went through the windshield of a Dodge Caravan filled with Wipers, spooking the driver and sending the car skidding off the road and flipping upside down.

265

They were parallel to Chief Mountain now as Jeffereys' men began to return fire.

"Dana, get in here," Bud shouted at her.

Bullets shattered the window beside her, spraying glass into the side of her face. Dana continued firing until her magazine ran empty.

Swearing, Bud pulled her inside, blood running from the tiny cuts on her face. He struggled to drive with one hand, while wiping the shards out with the other.

Nikki glanced out the window and saw a narrow valley below them, filled with low brush. It seemed as though the road they were on descended gradually in that direction.

Then Jeffereys' car swung up on their right, and unloaded. The popping sound from their burst tire echoed loudly and all at once Bud lost control of the car.

"Hold on," he cried as the battle wagon cut left and smashed through the guard rail, rocking down the embankment like a kid on a runaway toboggan. Shrubs and brush smacked the windshield as they sped out of control.

Nikki was sure they were about to die, and she reached over and held her brother's hand. Then the truck hit a rock, causing it to flip, and Aiden's hand was torn away.

Dana

A thick cloud of smoke rose from the battle wagon's ruined engine. The truck had stopped, that was about all Dana could tell. She was dazed, her body aching all over. Beside her, Bud leaned against the steering wheel, blood dripping from his nose. His right eye was swollen shut.

In the back, things weren't any better. Nikki was rubbing the side of her head. But the seat next to her, where Aiden had been sitting seconds before, was now empty.

Dana peered through the cracked windshield and saw they were at the foot of the mountain. They had to get out of the battle wagon and find the entrance to the facility before Jeffereys and his Wiper friends showed up. She shook Bud, who leaned back and looked over at her with his one good eye.

"You get the licence plate on that guy?" he said touching his nose and staring down at his fingers covered in blood.

"No, but you'll have another chance when they get here." Dana turned to Nikki. "Can you walk?"

She glanced down at her legs. "I think so," she said, but it was clear that wasn't her main concern. Nikki stumbled out of the truck, calling Aiden's name.

Dana got out, too, her own legs feeling like she'd just taken a ride on the world's craziest roller coaster. She was scanning the area around the truck, looking for Aiden, when she saw the giant metal blast doors in the side of the mountain. They were open slightly, a white truck with a Tevatron decal on the side in the act of entering the facility; forever frozen like a seared clock after a blast. Clearly, The Shift had struck just as this poor guy was heading inside.

"Aiden?" she heard Nikki call out.

Dana was about to help in the search when she spotted someone near those blast doors. In three strides, she was back at the battered battle wagon, pulling out her AR-15 and the silver briefcase with the C4. Dana checked the magazine and turned to make sure they weren't about to be attacked by a hoard of Wipers streaming out from inside the complex. The tiny silhouette near the blast doors was still there, and it was waving at her. Although Dana's ears continued to ring from the blow she'd taken to the head during the crash, she could swear the figure was calling her name.

When the shape stepped into the light, she realized it was Aiden, waving them in.

Dana turned to tell Nikki and Bud when she saw a small dust cloud approaching.

Jeffereys and his men. They didn't have the balls to follow them down the steep embankment, but then again they didn't need to, 'cause here they were.

Dana raced to the truck and pulled open the driver-side door. Bud was looking for something to stem his bleeding nose. She swung the strap of his rifle over her shoulder and pulled him by the arm. "You're just gonna have to let it bleed for now," she told him, and the fear in her eyes must have driven the message home 'cause he stumbled out of the truck at once.

Together, they began heading for the blast doors. Nikki must have heard Aiden calling 'cause she was already there.

They slipped inside a moment later, and Dana was immediately shocked by the long concrete tunnel, just as Nikki had described, but more than that, she couldn't believe the lights were still working.

"We've found Shangri-La," Bud said.

Dana was still helping him along. "Yeah, too bad we have to blow it up."

The earthquake which followed The Shift had split the concrete in places. Weeds crawled up through cracks in the floor. They made it to an opening when Nikki said, "This was the underground train system I saw."

There wasn't any train though, and Dana glanced at Aiden, almost for confirmation, but the boy only shrugged. And why shouldn't he? All those memories buried inside of him were locked beyond his reach.

As they prepared to step onto the tracks, a deer jumped out and sprinted down the corridor, toward the blast doors. Dana clutched her heart. None of them had their weapons at the ready, and if that had been a Wiper, they might have been in real trouble. She unslung Bud's AR-15 and handed it to him, bringing her own around as well. They only had a half dozen mags left, so if Jeffereys was stupid enough to come in after them, then every shot would need to count.

Then came the clatter of gunfire echoing from the other end of the corridor. A moment later, Jeffereys' voice yelling "Hold your fire! Hold your fire!"

Dana turned and saw they'd slaughtered the deer that was bolting for the blast doors. A case of mistaken identity, but all the more reason why they didn't have a second to lose.

268

Larry

A loud hissing erupted as the sub's ballast tanks blew the last of the air out, allowing sea water to rush in. They were quickly losing buoyancy, and Larry felt the boat start to sink before it settled on the bottom of the shallow bay. They were only a few meters away from the pier where the *Alabama* had been docked. The distance wasn't big, but it would allow them to safely launch the sub's nuclear payload from underwater.

At gunpoint, Donavan had taken Kulik and Callahan to each station to ensure everything would go off without a hitch. The missiles themselves were still in good shape along with the fire control system used to open the hatches and boost them out of the water.

Zhou's cooperation inputting New Jamestown into the targeting system had been the final piece of the puzzle.

"Who thought preparing to fire a nuke would have been such a pain?" Larry commiserated. He was staring at Joanne, cradled in Finn's arms, her face buried into his shoulder. She hadn't been disfigured by the beating he gave her, not yet, but once New Jamestown and its occupants were reduced to a flaming pile of atomic waste, there'd be plenty of time to play.

"Any final words for your friends back home?" Larry asked.

Finn remained stoic, despite the trembling rage Larry could see building within him. "Have I mentioned how much I'm going to enjoy killing you?"

Larry grinned. "You have." And then slammed his fist down on the fire button.

All at once, the sub shook as the UGM-133 Trident II was ejected from the missile tube and cut through the water into the air. Once above the waterline, the engines ignited, lifting the giant destructive beast skyward.

A moment later, Donavan's voice crackled over the satellite phone. "Tracking confirmed. Missile launch successful."

Nikki

They stood before a pair of thick metal doors. A yellow biohazard symbol warning them of danger inside.

"This is it," Nikki said with confidence. These were the doors she'd seen back in New Jamestown after touching Aiden's arm.

Bud leaned in and kicked them open. "I'd prefer to take my chances with whatever biohazard's behind that door than stand here waiting for Jeffereys and his goons to show up."

Inside was the giant glass tube with the same pulsating white light Nikki'd seen before. Although witnessing it via the thin veil of someone else's memory was more like watching a movie than it was being there in person, the sight was still impressive.

Beside her, Dana, Bud, and Aiden stood hypnotized by the sight before them. It was almost mystical, drawing your eye no matter how much you tried to look away.

Dana was the first to move, stopping next to the glass tube before opening the briefcase. Nikki stepped toward the light. Reaching out a hand, she let her fingers touch the glass before the electrical charge made her yank them away. But that wasn't all she noticed. The glass tube with the light descended deep into the ground, farther than the eye could see.

Dana pushed the detonators into the plastic explosives and began setting the timer. Bud stayed near the door as look out.

"We don't really know what this'll do, do we?" Aiden asked pointing at the bomb.

"Finn said the pulse had to be stopped," Dana told him. "Cutting the power source is the quickest way to do that."

Aiden shook his head. "That's not what I mean. What if we blow this up, and all the memories we created after The Shift begin to fade?"

Dana stopped and peered up at Bud. The two exchanged a strange, almost sad glance before she went back to priming the C4. "I guess that's the risk we gotta take," she said. "Besides, the way Finn laid it out, it'll take days, if not weeks before that happens."

Nikki hadn't said a word, but she couldn't help feeling the bomb wasn't the answer. They would be destroying an incredible source of free energy. A tragedy in the highest degree, given the current state of the world. She remembered seeing the adjacent room filled with computer monitors. Maybe that was where the pulse was being controlled. If something had to be done, wouldn't starting there make more sense? Nikki was about to make that suggestion when Bud shouted a warning:

"Here they come." He slid behind the open door and out of sight, waving frantically at the others to hide as he set his rifle down and pulled out his Glock.

Jeffereys stepped into the room without seeing Bud and stopped, transfixed by the light. So were the Wipers behind him. There was an AK poised in Jeffereys' hand. With a savage blow, Bud used the butt of his pistol to chop at Jeffereys' wrist, sending the AK clattering to the floor. Next, he grabbed Jeffereys in a neck lock and put the barrel of his Glock to his temple. Now Jeffereys was looking back at the Wipers, their weapons pointed directly at both men.

"Tell them to move back, or I'll blow your head off."

Jeffereys waved his hands. "Do as he says. Do as he says."

Slowly, the Wipers backed away.

Dana called out to Nikki and Aiden. "Close those doors."

"You kill me," Jeffereys spat, "and you're all dead."

Bud stripped the pack off Jeffereys' back and tossed it to Dana. "Won't take those Wipers more than a few minutes to realize they don't need this grease ball and come charging in. Have a look in this backpack and see if there's anything useful."

Searching through it, Dana came out with the satellite phone. "This how you been keeping in touch with Larry," she asked, shoving it in his face.

Jeffereys' lips cracked into a sly smile. The same one he'd shown her back in San Francisco when he made her wear that pink dress. The night he'd tried to rape her.

Dana thumbed down the button and spoke. "If you can hear this, Larry, I want you to know your time running things is just about up."

There was silence for a moment before Larry's voice came on. "Is that so? That's interesting, because I'm sending a little surprise to your friends in New Jamestown."

Then came the sound of a struggle on the other end and another voice that sounded like Finn. "Dana, they've fired a nuke from the sub. It's gonna hit New Jamestown in eight min ... "

More shouting and then silence.

Dana looked over at Bud and then Nikki with shock and growing terror. Lou, Ethan, Tanner, and a host of others still in New Jamestown were about to be vaporised.

"I'm telling you, destroying the pulse isn't the answer," Nikki said, almost reluctantly. "There was something in my brother's memories I saw, something I didn't want to mention, but now I don't see any other way."

Dana took her by the shoulders. "What? What did you see?"

She pointed through another set of door to stairs that led to the control room. "We may be able to change the frequency so that it pushes all the old memories to the surface at once."

"If she's right," Bud said, tightening his grip on Jeffereys, "the shock of it should stun the Wipers long enough to let Finn and the others deactivate that nuke before it detonates."

"Wipers won't be the only ones who get stunned," Dana said, as they picked up the suite case with the C4. "If what you're saying is true, then anyone with suppressed memories will likely be knocked right off their feet."

The Wipers were heading back into the room with the shimmering light when Nikki and the others reached the control room. Computer readouts were on every wall, along with rows of servers blinking like a forest of Christmas trees. The image brought the edges of a faint memory into Nikki's mind. A tree with lights and presents underneath. Her father, Jim, was there wearing an old bathrobe along with her mother, Carole, sipping on a coffee. Nikki and Aiden were tearing at boxes covered in candy cane wrapping. It was her first memory, and the surge of emotion was both exhilarating and intensely painful. But that memory had far more dire implications. If that was how Nikki and others like her might feel with the return of a single memory, what would it be like when they all came charging back? That was why Nikki hadn't wanted to tell Dana about changing the frequency. Forcing all those memories to the surface wouldn't just hurt Aiden, it would kill him. It was the secret fear she'd harboured all along, always hoping she'd been wrong. But now she knew that wasn't the case. Stopping the Wipers and stopping Larry from laying waste to New Jamestown and countless other places would mean sacrificing Aiden, the only family she had left.

Just then, Jeffereys broke free and ran for the door. Bud managed to get off three rounds before Jeffereys disappeared.

"I'm sure I hit him," he said, about to give chase.

"Let him go," Dana said. "Just keep an eye on the door. He may be back with reinforcements any second."

Unable to keep it in any longer, Nikki told Dana about what this would do to Aiden. For his part, Aiden, swallowed hard as she got to the part where it might kill him.

"We don't have much time left," Dana said, then looked at Aiden. "What do you wanna do?"

Aiden nodded serenely, even though it was clear his heart was beating like mad. "If it'll stop Larry and save those people, then yes."

And with that, Nikki laid her hands on his cheeks and closed her eyes. She was searching through the ocean of memories within him, watching them whiz by like shooting stars. Then one came into focus. A technician sitting at a nearby console, tweaking a knob marked Acoustic Wave Modifier. She could see that turning it to the left lowered the ultrasound's intensity. Turning it to the right strengthened the signal.

The vision in Nikki's head faded, and she immediately walked to the far end of the console, flickering lights all around her, and pointed to the knob she'd seen in Aiden's memory. "This is it."

Dana studied it. "To the right?" she asked.

Fighting back the tears, Nikki nodded: "As far as it'll go."

Dana was reaching for it when an explosion blew open the doors to the control room, sending Bud flying backwards into a wall, knocking him unconscious. Rows of computer servers blocked them from the blast, but it was obvious Jeffereys and the Wipers meant business.

Unslinging her AR-15, Dana ducked behind one of the servers and opened fire, spraying bullets in their direction, blowing out computer screens and damaging the equipment as she unleashed hell.
"Nikki, turn the knob quick!" Dana said, glancing over her shoulder as she changed magazines.

Nikki's gaze bounced between the dial before her and Aiden on her right, his hands covering his ears and shielding his head from the bits of glass and plastic exploding around them. Almost in slow motion, she watched her hand reach out and crank it to the right. The last thing she saw was Aiden, screaming in pain before he sank to the floor.

Finn

Finn was down, nursing the crack to the skull he'd taken from Donavan after he'd tried to warn Dana about the missile launch. Larry was in the middle of telling them there was nothing they could do to stop the inevitable when an ear-shattering sound like the screeching of a train's wheels made Finn and nearly everyone else in the missile room clamp their hands over their ears. The pain was so unbelievable, Finn was seeing starbursts of color blooming before his eyes. Slowly, those colors morphed into the shape of a crib. He was crying for his mother, holding onto bars that would form a pattern in his life to come. Another flash, and now he was in a Wells Fargo. Heart hammering in his chest, he was with Joanne and that psycho, Kevin Butler, and they were shuffling tellers into the back room.

Money to pay the mortgage, that was the only thing on Finn's mind, but it was clear by the whacked-out look in Kevin's eyes that he was interested in something else. A middle-aged woman in a plaid skirt with a name tag that read *Doris* raised her hands and tried pleading with Kevin that none of them knew the combination to the vault. The one who did was the manager, Sam Hanover, and he was out to lunch. An answer Kevin didn't seem to like one bit and raised his pistol and blew each and every one of them away.

Another quick flash, and now Finn was standing before a judge, faced with the option of pleading guilty for murdering those four women, a penalty which meant he'd surely die in prison, or telling the truth and risking lethal injection. Finn could feel his lips mouthing the words: "Not guilty, Your Honor," when there was a final blinding light, and he was back on the sub.

The Wipers standing guard over them were now on the floor themselves, looking dazed and disoriented, as though trying to shake off a heavy night of drinking.

Only Zhou, Callahan, Kulik, and Donavan were still standing, which made sense since none of them had been affected by The Shift. Kulik leapt at Donavan and tackled him to the ground. The two wrestled briefly before the XO got him in a choke hold and put him to sleep. Meanwhile, Callahan and Zhou were busy disarming the Wipers who were still groggy. One of them had a .45 1911, which he stuffed in his belt.

Next to Finn, Joanne let out a moan as he scooped her into his arms. He didn't have the strength right now to help her stand since he wasn't sure he could do so himself.

Then Callahan called out from behind the control panel. "Aren't so tough without your henchmen around, are you?" he asked Larry, who was still on the ground.

"We've got to deactivate those warheads before the missile detonates," Zhou called out.

Finn shook, trying to knock the cobwebs out of his head. "What do you mean warheads? I thought there was only one missile?"

"There is," Zhou replied, his fingers dancing over the console. "But each Trident D5 carries up to eight independent warheads."

Just then, a horrible cry came from Callahan as he tried to get Larry to his feet. Larry had his hands clasped around Callahan's head, and smoke was rising up between Larry's fingers. He let go, and Callahan collapsed to the ground, his head continuing to smoulder. Kulik was swinging around an M-4 he'd taken off one of the Wipers when Larry charged past him and out of the missile room.

Finn struggled to his feet and rushed to Callahan's side. The smell of burning flesh made Finn's nose crinkle. Even as he approached, it was clear Callahan was dead.

"Ninety seconds before impact," Zhou howled. Sweat was pouring down his face as he called Kulik over to help him activate the self-destruct sequence on the Trident.

"Larry ain't going anywhere," Kulik said. "We're submerged."

Zhou shook his head. "Unless he's heading to the nuclear reactor. There's a chance he might be able to send it into meltdown."

Zhou and Kulik were punching buttons on the missile launch panel when Finn headed for the door.

"Finn, don't!" Joanne pleaded.

"I don't have a choice," was all he could say before he raced off to find Larry.

Dana

The Wipers that had come bursting in with Jeffereys were on the ground now, clutching their heads. So, too, were Aiden and Nikki. Glancing over by the far wall, Dana saw a crumpled form she knew was Bud. He'd been thrown back when the doors were blown open and as strong as her need was to see if he was all right, Dana couldn't take that chance until she knew where Jeffereys was.

With her finger on the trigger of her AR-15, she moved out from behind the row of computer servers to get a better grasp of the situation.

A dozen men in ratty leather outfits lay sprawled near the entrance. The Wipers had stopped screaming in pain, but they looked confused, as though stirring from a deep sleep into unfamiliar surroundings.

The first thing she did was to remove the magazines from their AKs as well as cycle out the remaining rounds from the chambers. Jeffereys was nowhere to be seen. She went so far as to check the room with the glowing lights, but didn't see a thing. Must have run off when he saw his men hit the ground, she figured. For a scumbag like Jeffereys, that wasn't surprising.

When she got back to the main control room, she found Nikki rising unsteadily to her feet, rubbing her head.

"Are you all right?" It was a dumb question, given she'd been on the ground not 60 seconds before, but what else could one say when years worth of memories were downloaded all at once?

Nikki was slow to respond, and Dana became worried.

Does she still remember who I am?

Nikki glared at Dana quizzically. "I think I'm OK."

"What's my name?" Dana asked.

A smile appeared on Nikki's face. "You're Dana Hatfield. How could I ever forget you?"

They dropped down to Aiden, who was lying on his back.

Nikki still seemed to be in a fog. "Oh, no. He's dead, isn't he?"

Pressing her fingers against his carotid artery, Dana felt for a pulse. "Not yet, but it's very faint."

Dana leaned Aiden forward and hoisted him over her shoulder. The pain in Nikki's face made her own heart break.

She then went over to Bud. His eyes opened as she approached. The poor guy'd been hit with a double whammy. Thrown against the wall and then slammed by the pulse. She helped him to his feet, and the four of them prepared to leave. The Wipers – a name which no longer seemed to

276

be relevant – were standing, many milling about aimlessly like patients in an asylum. Most likely, they would soon regain the full measure of their faculties, although it was anyone's guess what sort of people they would become. They were former accountants and doctors and grocery clerks turned murderers who would now need to carve out new identities.

Dana carried her rifle with one hand, the other steadying Aiden over her shoulder as they passed the Wipers and fled through the glowing chamber.

"You were right about not blowing this place up," Dana told Nikki. They were both looking at the light as they circled around to the underground railway.

The walk back to the cars outside would be a long one, but foremost on Dana's mind was New Jamestown and what, if anything, remained. She was in the middle of convincing herself that Finn and the others had managed to stop the catastrophe when the satellite phone crackled to life. "The nuke's been disarmed." The sound of Zhou's jubilant voice warmed Dana's heart. "I repeat, the nuke has been disarmed. A big hunk of metal's gonna fall out of the sky near New Jamestown, but that's about it."

Then she heard another voice, one that sent shivers up the back of her neck.

"Drop the rifle before I waste you all." Jeffereys had apparently been waiting by the tracks to ambush them. So much for her theory that he'd run away.

Dana set her rifle down.

"Kick it over." She did. "Good." Jeffereys picked it up and flung it away. Then he turned to Bud. "You, too, lover boy."

"It's over, Jeffereys," Bud told him. "Didn't you hear Zhou? The nuke's been disarmed. Your army is gone, and Larry is all you've got left."

"Shut your mouth," Jeffereys shouted as he took aim.

Dana stepped forward and kicked the rifle out of his hands, nearly falling over herself since an unconscious Aiden was still on her back.

Jeffereys scrambled to grab his AK when Dana shouted for them to re-enter the control room. As they hurried back inside, she kicked herself for having tossed away the Wipers' weapons and ammo.

Many of them were still shuffling around the control room when Dana and the others hurried through.

On the right near a row of hardhats hanging from hooks was a door marked *Power Plant Floor.*

"This way," she yelled. Jeffereys was probably right behind them, and she hadn't gone through all this to be shot right when the world finally had a shred of hope.

They burst through the door and came to two rows of massive metallic transformers, each bearing high-voltage stickers. Overhead a mishmash of wires connected each of the giant cylinders together. Dana hoped it would help them stay out of Jeffereys' line of fire, but it certainly wasn't somewhere they could hide forever.

They ducked behind one of the transformers, where Dana set Aiden on the floor. Nikki helped Bud sit.

"If your hands are wet, don't touch a damned thing or you're liable to get fried," Dana warned them.

"Wasn't intending to," Bud replied, holding out a pair of palms caked with dried blood. "Tell me you have a plan."

"I was kinda hoping you still had that Glock." she said, with a touch of desperation.

Bud shook his head. "When those doors blew, I barely kept my shirt on." And he was right, the fabric was shredded and soaked red.

Dana stood and peered around the corner as Bud said, "I hope you're not about to do something foolish."

She turned back and winked at him, just as he had done from his New Jamestown prison cell when he unholstered her SIG. "I got a mean right hook, don't you remember?"

Bud's fingers went to the edges of his cheekbone. "How can I forget?"

That's when she heard gunfire and saw a handful of the former Wipers gunned down as they ran into the plant. Jeffereys was a sadistic bastard all right, taking out his frustration by executing his own men now that they had become useless.

She couldn't stay here and risk Jeffereys finding Nikki and the others. She decided to take a chance and cross open ground in order to hide behind one of the other massive energy receptacles. The idea was to ambush Mr. Itchy Trigger Finger as he went by. Sounded reasonable enough when you're dealing with a gun-wielding sociopath.

Jeffereys was clomping down the metallic stairs, the sound a disturbing reminder of those basement stairs in San Francisco he'd come down when she was tied up and helpless. With fear rising up into her throat, Dana struggled to fight it. Taking a deep breath, she burst out and sprinted across open ground.

The rattle of gunfire was immediate and sprayed the ground around her. Dana slid behind one of the transformers as though she were coming into home plate.

"Think you can hide from me, you bitch?" Jeffereys screeched. He sounded drunk with bloodlust.

Dana circled around the outer edge of the transformer, moving closer to Jeffereys. If she could pop out where he wasn't expecting her, then she might be able to neutralize the advantage of his AK.

Crouching, she was waiting for him to pass when she spotted a sticker on the metal chamber which read *Energy Storage Unit*. These weren't transformers at all, they were giant batteries. Tevatron had cracked one of the holy grails of the energy industry, finding a way to bottle electricity that wasn't used immediately.

The clicking of Jeffereys' heels closing in snapped her back to reality. But the noise stopped just short of coming into view. He was standing beyond her line of sight, but what was he doing? Without a weapon of any kind, Dana knew she couldn't risk being seen first.

Then footsteps again, these ones faster. They were coming around from the other side. That's when she heard him rush up behind her. Dana sprang to her feet, but it was too late. Jeffereys was already there, pointing the AK right at her face, smiling as though he'd just taught her an important lesson: "Don't mess with the big boys."

His finger squeezed the trigger, and the AK clicked empty. Jeffereys' eyes grew wide. He'd emptied it killing those Wipers and shooting the ground at her feet as she'd sprinted from one storage unit to another.

Dana grabbed the barrel and rammed it up into his face, breaking his nose. Blood poured from his nostrils, but Jeffereys' shirt was already saturated. She remembered then Bud saying how he'd shot him as Jeffereys ran out. Dana went to hit him again, and this time Jeffereys blocked the blow and head butted her in the face. For a moment, her vision went black. Then another burst of pain as Jeffereys sent a crushing blow to the side of her head. Dana staggered, holding her arms up to ward off any further attacks. Her vision was coming back in bits and pieces, and when she saw Jeffereys coming in again, she ducked, then swung, but missed. A cut over her eye was blurring her vision even more. Jeffereys could tell and was laughing now, swinging furiously. He backed her into one of the storage units marked *Danger High Voltage*, intending to fry her to a crisp, when Dana spotted Nikki move up behind Jeffereys and swing a piece of pipe at his head. The force of the crack split his ear open. More blood, and now he was covered in it, but the blow only stunned him. Jeffereys spun to grab hold of Nikki, who screamed. That's when Dana snatched him by the collar of his leather vest and flung him toward the storage unit. He struck the metal surface, and his body began to convulse violently; the blood oozing out of him acting as a conductor. Dana and Nikki stepped back in horror as Jeffereys' body began to smoke and then disintegrate into ash.

Bud came limping around the corner, wincing with the pain of broken ribs and a wounded leg. All three of them looked on in amazement at the pile of soot that had once been a man.

"I've never seen anything like that," Dana said.

Nikki blinked the sight away. "I have. At the Grand America. Alvarez got real angry at a captive named Mary something, I never did get her last name. His touch turned her to ash."

"Maybe he figured out a way of tapping into this power source?" Bud asked.

Dana wasn't sure. But the question left her with another thought. What if The Shift had changed people in ways they were only beginning to understand?

Finn

The blazing-red battle stations light was flashing throughout the sub's narrow corridors as Finn hurried toward the reactor room. Although nearly twice as big as a 747, with every inch of space devoted to one purpose or another, it still managed to feel cramped and claustrophobic.

Finn checked the magazine on the AK-47 he'd snatched from one of the Wipers, saw it was full, and held it at the ready.

He entered the section housing the missile tubes that rose up from floor to ceiling, and ultimately, to hatches at the top of the sub. Nothing here was wasted. Sailor's bunks were nestled in and among the missiles, and Finn made sure to check as many as he could in case Larry was waiting to ambush him. The sickening sight of what he'd done to Callahan was playing over and over in Finn's mind. Larry's hands had been like lava and had made the sailor's skin turn to cinders.

Nearing the reactor room, his nose caught the smell of burnt flesh, a sure sign he was heading in the right direction.

Then came Zhou's voice over the loudspeaker. "Finn, he's breached the reactor room. You better get there quick."

Finn was at a full run now, his head still swimming from the onrush of memories he thought he'd never see again. Some of the more painful ones he could do without.

The sub's showers and medical room came next, and Finn was picking up speed, weaving past obstacles and through hatches as quickly as his legs could carry him. At last, he came to a door with the radiation symbol. Peering through the glass porthole, he caught sight of Larry, his hands flat on the control panel, smoke rising from his palms. He was trying to cause a meltdown within the reactor by frying the electrical equipment.

Finn tried the locking wheel, but it wouldn't budge. Larry must have welded it shut on the inside with those toasty fingers of his. Warning lights inside were flashing like crazy along with the faint sound of a voice warning of an impending meltdown. Larry knew it was over and was trying to take them all down with him.

Now Larry was coming closer, moving toward the door, sweat pouring down his face, the veins along his forehead bulging out. "It may surprise you, Finn, but there is no such thing as death. Nothing is lost, nothing is created, everything is transformed. A French chemist is supposed to have said that. I'll be back again, eventually. You and your friends on this sub, however. Well, this life is the only one you'll ever have. How does it feel knowing it's about to end?"

The flesh on Larry's face was starting to bubble. Finn dropped the AK, turned, and ran back to the missile room. He could only imagine radiation was already flooding past the protective doors and into the rest of the sub. They didn't have long before their skin began bubbling away as well.

When he arrived, Zhou and Kulik were helping Joanne to her feet and ushering confused Wipers into the corridor and up toward the front of the boat. Donavan was on his feet, too, gagged, his hands bound behind his back.

"I couldn't stop him," Finn said. "The nuclear reactor's going into full meltdown."

"But the sub's 30 meters underwater," Joanne said. "We're trapped."

"The escape trunk at the front of the sub has room for eight," Kulik said, pushing Donavan ahead of him. "Once we equalize the pressure, we can swim to the surface just like the Navy Seals do." Kulik winked at Finn. "Long as you can hold your breath."

Overhead, a female voice warned of a radiation leak.

"The Wipers," Joanne said. "We can't just leave them."

She was right. A couple were still on the floor in the missile room. "Go," Finn told them. "I'll catch up."

"The escape trunk is one floor up," Zhou told him. "We'll wait as long as we can."

The thought of going back to save the very people who had nearly killed those closest to him was a hard pill to swallow. But he knew leaving them down here to die was a decision that would haunt him for the rest of his life, a life that wouldn't last much longer if he didn't hurry.

Less than a minute later, Finn was back in the missile room. Two Wipers were on the floor near the entrance. One was unconscious, and the other was leaning against a bulkhead, rubbing his head like he'd taken a knock to the skull. Finn knew what he must be feeling, but it wasn't simply physical pain, it was severe disorientation.

Finn shook the man, who was already awake. "Can you walk?"

He glanced up at Finn as though he were a mirage.

Finn hauled him to his feet, then went to lift the other Wiper before realizing the second man was dead.

That female voice warning of a radiation leak came on again as Finn and the remaining Wiper went to leave the missile room.

Larry stepped into their way, grinning as he grabbed the Wiper by the neck. Smoke rose up from searing flesh. The man tried to scream, but couldn't make a sound. He collapsed and was dead before his body hit the floor.

"I was hoping I'd catch you before you left," Larry said, wiping his hands. Most of the skin on his arms and face had peeled off, exposing the tips of his cheekbones. His head was a grotesque dome, absent of hair or flesh. "You came to the reactor with the intention of killing me, and I wanted to give you a second chance."

Finn was backing away, searching around for a weapon.

"You don't need anything but your bare hands," Larry told him. "Convicted criminals in ancient Britain were strangled and thrown into the bogs. I've done such horrible things, Finn, and I want you to punish me."

The smell of sulphur was strong, and Finn's only thought was getting to the escape trunk before this sub became his tomb.

"Punish me, and I'll let you go," Larry said, his lips black and cracking.

Nikki had told them the evil inside Alvarez had somehow migrated into Larry, and now he could see Larry wanted it to live on in Finn.

Callahan's body was on the floor beside him. Tucked into the belt was that .45 1911 he'd taken off one of the Wipers.

"Attention," the computer's soft female voice warned. "Radiation levels critical."

"I told you before I was going to kill you," Finn said.

Larry was coming toward him, a twisted grin plastered all over his melting face.

"And I always keep my promises." Finn rolled and snatched the pistol from Callahan's waistband just as Larry sprang to wrap him in a fiery embrace.

Finn emptied all seven rounds, riddling Larry's head and face with quarter-sized holes.

Larry's eyes rolled up in their sockets as he sank to his knees and fell dead.

Finn sprinted for the escape trunk and found Joanne holding the door, her eyes tearing when she saw him approach. "I wasn't sure you were going to make it."

Zhou closed the hatch as Kulik opened the valve to equalize the pressure. Cold sea water rushed in, and Finn held Joanne tight.

"You smell like sulphur," she said.

"I know. There was something else I had to take care of."

When the escape hatch was nearly full, Zhou gave his final instructions. "Take a big breath and don't stop kicking till you break the surface."

Finn gave Joanne a final kiss. "See you topside."

Epilogue

New Jamestown

Barely a month later, a strange-looking monument stood in the center of New Jamestown. A concrete pillar on top of which sat a large and pointy – albeit dented – object. An inscription below it read:

Here lies the remains of the nuclear warhead sent to destroy us. Fired by the USS *Alabama and recovered from the Grand America Hotel, where it landed harmlessly.*

Larry's death proved nothing short of a rebirth for New Jamestown. So much had changed in the last four weeks. If All Father were alive, he would barely have recognized the place.

Dana Hatfield had been elected New Jamestown's first governor and undone all of the draconian laws and practices Larry had enacted.

In her place as sherrif, the colonists had voted for Lou with Ethan and Tanner as his acting deputies. Once his back healed, Bud became Dana's most trusted adviser, although in the eyes of many, sharing the same bed made that somewhat inevitable.

Shortly after, the cult was disbanded, along with the army fatigues Larry had made them wear.

Gone, too, was Tent City. Replaced now by rows of wooden dorms, each heated by its own wood-burning stove.

In time, Aiden, too, had recovered, along with his now encyclopaedic memory and a sudden knack for building technological gizmos. His latest project was a device designed to harness the awesome power they'd discovered up at Chief Mountain. A power that Alvarez, and later, Larry, had proven could be tapped by the human body itself.

Standing protectively by her brother's side was Nikki, every day becoming the kind of woman Carole would have been proud of.

While searching through what remained of Timothy's library, Dana had come across a book on ancient Greece and the evolution of the world's earliest democracy. After reading through it a number of times, she began to enact measures in New Jamestown that strove to emulate a purer form of government by the people, for the people.

But while much had changed for the better, there were still certain realities that would remain for the foreseeable future. The walls and guard towers Larry pushed so hard to have built stayed, along with the armed men who manned them. Needless to say, even after Larry and

Alvarez were long gone, the world would continue to be a dangerous place.

Less than a week after returning, Finn and Joanne would leave New Jamestown and set out with the aim of saving as many Wipers as they could. Reversing the pulse had left many of them disoriented and particularly vulnerable. A mission that also gave Finn an opportunity to reconcile his own new memories, many of which he preferred to leave forgotten. But there was a final element to Finn's journey, one he, Dana, and Joanne had talked about long into the night before they left. The possibility of finding other colonies out there, in all that darkness, just like their own. An idea that they all agreed was both exhilarating and terrifying.

From the author:

What drew me to telling this story? This is the sort of thing only writers are normally interested in, but I thought it might be interesting to offer some of my own thoughts and insights about *Primal Shift* and why I felt it was a story worth telling.

At its core, post-apocalyptic fiction is the study of thin lines. The thin line between order and chaos, between the human spirit (however you define it) and the bloodthirsty savage lurking within each of us.

With *Primal Shift*, I wanted to take these themes one step further by asking a simple question: How does memory shape who we are? If one were to sandblast our upbringing away like graffiti off a tenement wall, would most of us still choose to do the right thing? Simple to ask, but not an easy question to answer. As we learned during Hurricane Katrina, when times are desperate and people are hungry, they're capable of heinous acts of savagery. And yet, so, too, are they capable of unbelievable acts of selflessness and heroism. What is it within each of us that governs those responses?

These were some of the different sides of the human experience I wanted to examine in the novel. Many readers have written me letters describing how much they detested Larry, whom they viewed as a villain. But right up until the end of the story, I never viewed him as such. In fact, for me he represented the ultimate pragmatist. If he's evil, he's a necessary evil, and I really wanted to show both sides of that. For example, would Rainbowland have survived without a wall and some basic defenses?

Readers familiar with my work know I generally don't like spoon feeding the audience characters who fall into tidy little packages. The good guys often have tortured, sometimes questionable pasts. Likewise, the darker characters do things that make sense in a perverse sort of way. The goal is always to leave you feeling uncertain and asking yourself things like: "I grew to like Finn, but how do I feel after learning he might have murdered innocent people?" As I see it, it's my job to ask the tough moral or ethical questions, and yours to answer them for yourself.

Another theme I wanted to touch on in the novel was the use of force. Admittedly, a perfect society is one where murders and killings don't occur. A philosophy embodied by the members of Rainbowland. These were essentially Buddhist monks (of sorts) attempting to live in harmony with the world around them. Harm no living thing. That was their primary belief and yet, faced with a world that stretched these beliefs to the breaking point, they were forced to adapt or be destroyed. So, too, were the survivors who arrived expecting a safe haven from the barbarity around them, only to find they were more at risk than before.

As always, the primary goal of the story was to entertain, so if it helped you forget about the snow on the front stoop that needed shovelling or the lawn in desperate need of a trim, then I consider it a success. Perhaps the best way to guarantee seeing more stories is to spread the word by leaving a review.

Sincerely,
Griffin Hayes

WHAT'S NEXT?

Thank you for reading *Volume 2* of *Primal Shift*!
What did you think? If you enjoyed the story, please consider leaving a review!

Want more post-apocalyptic mayhem? Be sure to check out Hive: The Complete Collection.